FOR THE LOVE OF AN OLD HOUSE

RESTORATION & ROMANCE

HICKS • MACDONALD • CURTIS • ORCUTT

WATERBROOK
PRESS

RESTORATION AND ROMANCE
PUBLISHED BY WATERBROOK PRESS
2375 Telstar Drive, Suite 160
Colorado Springs, Colorado 80920
A division of Random House, Inc.

Scripture quotations are taken from the *King James Version*.

ISBN 1-57856-463-8

Library of Congress Cataloging-in-Publication Data
Restoration and romance / Hicks...[et al.].—1st ed.
 p. cm.
  Contents: The queen of the world and the handyman / Barbara Jean Hicks — Home for the heart / Shari MacDonald — Beside the still waters / Barbara Curtis — Don't look back / Jane Orcutt.
  ISBN 1-57856-463-8
  1. Love stories, American. 2. Dwellings—Conservation and restoration— Fiction. 3. Dwellings—Maintenance and repair—Fiction. I. Hicks, Barbara Jean.

PS648.L6 R475 2001
813'.60803543—dc21

2001035213

Printed in the United States of America
2001—First Edition

10 9 8 7 6 5 4 3 2 1

CONTENTS

THE QUEEN OF THE WORLD AND THE HANDYMAN

Barbara Jean Hicks

*To Lisa Tawn Bergren and Anne Christian Buchanan,
without whom Pilchuck would not exist.
Thanks for your guidance and your delight.*

CHAPTER ONE

By the time Chloe got wind of the matter, it was already too late.

She didn't know it was too late. Not until hours after she overheard the conversation in Bilbo's Bakery, where she'd stopped to pick up a half-dozen croissants for her grandmother on her way through town. A sort of atonement for having stayed away so long this time. Gran-Marie loved a good croissant, and Bilbo's did a decent job. Nothing like Boulangerie Paris in the city, but for a town the size of Pilchuck, Bilbo's was...well, *decent*.

Besides, it was located in one of those cavernous late nineteenth-century buildings that Chloe loved. On this particular midsummer day, the morning light poured through the tall, multipaned windows like melted butter, painting the rough brick walls and the wooden floor in soft, warm shades of russet and gold. Few things aged as gracefully, Chloe thought, as brick and wood.

As far as the overheard conversation, she couldn't have avoided eavesdropping if she'd tried to. It wasn't only that sound bounced off the high brick walls of the bakery like Ping-Pong balls. It was also that in a town like Pilchuck, everybody knew everybody else's business. And talked about it freely.

Chloe knew. She'd spent some time in Pilchuck, a good fifteen years ago now, living with Gran-Marie and Gran-Bert for her senior year of high school. She'd been back often enough, especially in the three years since Gran-Bert had died, to know that things hadn't changed much in the meantime.

At the moment in question, Chloe was standing at the counter, reaching into her handbag for her wallet. The door behind her opened and a woman's voice, high-pitched and vaguely familiar, floated over the spicy-sweet fragrance of cinnamon and brown sugar: "So. Guess who was back in the store for more supplies yesterday."

"Don't tell me." Another woman's voice, low and smug. "That fellow who's staying at Madam Marie's, am I right?"

"That fellow who's hiding out at Madam Marie's, is more like it."

Chloe cringed at the mispronunciation. "Madam" indeed! She could almost see Gran-Marie's pained expression, almost hear Gran-Marie's schoolteacher chant: "Repeat after me: *Momb-SEER. Mahd-moi-ZELL. Muh-DAHM.*"

Then suddenly the women's words registered. "Fellow"? "Hiding out" at Gran-Marie's? Ridiculous. The gossips in this town!

"Anything else I can get for you this morning?" the cashier prompted.

Chloe shook her head, frowning, and handed a twenty across the counter.

The smug voice, lowered to a conspiratorial murmur that nevertheless echoed in the room, intruded again. "Hiding out is right. Except for your place, the market, and the library, I don't think either one has set foot off the place in a month. Not even for fireworks on the Fourth!"

Chloe's frown deepened. *What on earth?*

"Oh, Madam's still been coming into town for church on Sundays," the first woman rejoined. "Alone, mind you. Looks to me like this fellow's not the churchgoing type."

"Surprise, surprise. So what did he lay down his cash for yesterday?"

"A whole long list of things. Wood putty, turpentine, sandpaper… I don't remember what-all."

Chloe held out her hand, trying to place the voices as the cashier counted back her change. Could one of them be Earlene? Earlene Boyd? That made sense. Earlene and her husband had owned the Coast-to-Coast Hardware on Main Street for years.

"Can't expect a body to remember much when a fellow looks like that," the second woman responded. She sucked in her breath. "*Ô la! la!*"

Ô la! la!? Chloe felt suddenly uneasy.

"'Ô la! la!' is right!" Earlene—Chloe was positive it was Earlene by this time—sounded almost gleeful. "I tell you, that man can come knockin' at my door any ol' time!"

"Looks to me as if you're not the first to say so." Woman number two, her voice again lowered provocatively: "Must be lonely in that big old house since Egbert passed."

Chloe stifled a gasp. The coins in her hand slipped through her fingers and clattered to the counter.

"Oh, True Marie!" Earlene tittered.

True Marie. Of course. Chloe felt the hackles rise on the back of her neck as Earlene went on: "You're not saying—oh, I'm sure not!"

How ironic, Chloe had told her grandmother on more than one occasion, that "truth" should be associated with someone so disdainful of the principle as was True Marie Weatherby—proprietress of the Belle o' the Ball Beauty Salon, consummate busybody, and Pilchuck's uncontested gossipmonger. And how unfortunate that Marie Antoinette Babineaux Delacroix Smith should have to share a name with such a woman!

"*Sans blague,*" Gran-Marie would say dryly. "No kidding!" That was all. Gran-Marie would never stoop to gossip herself.

"I mean, really, True!" Earlene's voice jerked Chloe back to the conversation. "The fellow's young enough to be Madam's son! *Grand*son, maybe."

"Exactly. And smart enough, I'll bet my bottom dollar, to figure out that Bertie left his grieving wife with more than just that tired old farmhouse," True Marie said.

Tired old farmhouse! The Smith-Irby homestead? Chloe was almost as outraged by the description as by the old gossip's insinuations about Gran-Marie.

"Mercy!" Earlene sounded both aghast and thrilled. "It does make sense, though, doesn't it? A rich old widow, a handsome fellow down on his luck. It wouldn't be the first time, would it?"

Chloe snatched her bag of croissants off the counter and turned abruptly, her face burning.

"Oh!" Earlene's hand flew to her ample bosom. True Marie simply stared.

They looked like a pair of mackerel, Chloe thought with disgust, their eyes rounded in surprise and their mouths forming perfect little o's. She lifted her chin and gave her long hair a peremptory toss. "I'll be sure to let my grandmother know how concerned you are— *ladies.*" Her voice dripped icicles.

She brushed past them, head high, and strode from the bakery, a gasp and an indignant "Well, I never!" trailing after her.

Forget it, she told herself as her car began to climb the hill out of town. *You've got little enough time off to let a couple of old gossips spoil the weekend.* She made the turn onto Ridge Road toward her grandmother's house, feeling her anger dissipate as she took in the view.

There was nothing quite like Tillicum County on a bright midsummer day, especially from the vantage point of Bramble Ridge. The green hills sloped gently toward the smoke blue San Juan Islands on the southern horizon and rolled away to the verdant Ruby River Valley to the east. Pilchuck, perched on the riverbank with Mount Balder looming over it like a sleepy, white-haired giant, was a fairy-tale village from here.

A herd of long-necked creatures grazing in a grassy field caught her eye. Alpaca, a more exotic form of livestock than the dairy cattle dotting the hillside on the opposite side of the road. The county was still essentially an agricultural center: several large dairy operations and a number of berry farms, with a few truck farms, an increasing number growing organic produce, thrown into the mix.

Chloe felt even better with her first glimpse of the Smith-Irby homestead high on the ridge, surrounded by tall oaks and maples almost as old as the house was.

It was a huge farmhouse, two stories, built in the 1890s in a combination of late Victorian styles—Stick, Eastlake, Queen Anne. Not as ornate as many of the West Coast Victorians built in the same period, but with enough bays, gables, and gingerbread to make it charming. It was painted modestly, in the colors Chloe remembered from her childhood: two soft, quiet shades of brown—mouse brown, she'd always thought of it—with vanilla trim and chocolate sashes.

Inside, the five-bedroom, two-bath house boasted five fireplaces and an intricately carved staircase with leaded glass windows on the landing—always one of Chloe's favorite places to curl up with a book, even now. The old house was much too large for one petite woman and one little dog, but Chloe could understand why Gran-Marie didn't want to leave it. Not only was it truly a grand house, inside and out; it was a repository of memories, an archive, a living, breathing monument to the history of a time, a place, a family.

For Gran-Marie, who had come to it late, it was a house of love. And for Chloe, who had come to it even later, it was a house of both love and healing.

She slowed the car to keep from plowing into the back of a tractor as it crawled up the hill. The problem was, she mused, there wasn't a Smith or an Irby left who cared about the house anymore; there was only Gran-Marie, not even related by blood to the Smiths or the Irbys, to carry on their legacy.

Chloe had thought seriously about moving her grandmother to Seattle, to an active adult community, or even a little house or condo of her own. Someplace Chloe could drop by every day, especially as her grandmother got older, just to check in with her. But the one time Chloe had broached the subject, on a purely theoretical level, Gran-Marie had gone practically apoplectic on her. The very idea of leaving felt disloyal, she'd said.

Even if she weren't attached to the house, her grandmother would never leave Pilchuck, Chloe told herself as she turned up the steep gravel driveway. For one, there was Saints and Sinners, the church she'd belonged to for nearly three decades. For another, there were Gran-Marie's monthly Ladies' Luncheons—*Les Déjeuners pour Les Femmes,* she called them—for the Ladies' Missionary Sewing Circle. Then there was her monthly breakfast at the Kitsch 'n' Caboodle Café with old friends from the local high school, where she'd taught French for twenty-odd years.

What Gran-Marie had in Pilchuck was more than Chloe had in Seattle. Except for Chloe's job, of course. A good job, with Jade,

Janus & McIntyre, one of Seattle's most prestigious architecture firms. Maybe the most prestigious.

At the moment, Chloe might not have much of a life outside her job. But when your life *was* your job, what did it matter? For a good job, especially early in one's career, one sometimes had to make sacrifices. She was only thirty-three. There was plenty of time in her future for all those things Gran-Marie had and she didn't.

All, that is, except for Gran-Marie herself.

She rounded the last curve of the driveway to the back of the house, where all thoughts suddenly deserted her. *What on earth?*

This wasn't Gran-Marie's yard. It was a construction zone. Piles of lumber, old and new, littered the grounds. A radial-arm saw mounted on a wheeled cart sat next to the driveway, an orange extension cord snaking down its side and around the corner of the house. Gran-Bert's old Ford pickup, which hadn't been out of the carriage house for years, was pulled up on the lawn close to the back porch. On the open tailgate sat a toolbox and a circular saw, the saw attached to a second long extension cord that trailed up the steps and through her grandmother's bedroom window.

And the back porch! Three of the posts, both stair railings, and several balusters had been replaced. It appeared, in fact, that half the steps and a number of porch floorboards had been replaced as well. The wood was primed but still unpainted.

Chloe frowned. She called her grandmother regularly, once a week at least. Gran-Marie hadn't said a word about having the porch repaired. Not that it was a bad idea; it was just a surprise, that's all. She'd have thought Gran-Marie might have consulted her.

She heard the pounding as soon as she turned off the engine to the car. *Bam-BAM! Bam-BAM!* Leaving her purse and the bag of croissants on the seat, she jumped out and followed the sound, wending her way through the maze of construction materials. She rounded the northwest corner of the house—and stopped short.

A man in paint-spattered jeans and a dusty T-shirt, a tool belt slung around his hips, stood several steps up on an aluminum extension ladder, banging rhythmically against the diagonal sheathing beneath an upstairs window. The siding below every single window had been ripped off.

"Excuse me!" She raised her voice in outrage. "What on *earth* is going on here?!"

◆　◆　◆

Nat Neville wiped the sweat from his brow with one forearm and peered down from the aluminum extension ladder propped against the house, trying to locate the source of the indignant question. The driver of the pearl-white Chrysler Sebring he'd seen whipping up the driveway, he assumed.

His eyes widened. *Whoa!*

He'd known some pretty women in his forty-three years, but the woman gazing up at him went far beyond pretty. Maybe even beyond beautiful. So far beyond, he was having a hard time focusing on her question, let alone coming up with an intelligent response.

If he'd taken the time to catalog her features, he might have found her lips a trifle full, her nose a bit too long, her dark brown eyes set just a tad too close. But taken together, set off by flawless, golden skin, she was extraordinary. Even the slight frown between her brows couldn't sully her beauty.

His fingers suddenly itched to untangle the mass of chestnut-colored hair that flowed around her shoulders, to smooth it away from her face and bury his hands in it. Did she wear it mussed on purpose, just to get that response from men?

"Well?" she demanded, tossing her head impatiently. Light rippled through her hair.

He frowned. "I'm sorry?"

"I said, what are you doing?"

His jaw tightened. Deliberately, he placed his hammer in its loop on his carpenter's belt. Deliberately, he stepped down the ladder, rung by rung, pivoting to face her when he reached the ground. Deliberately, he met her gaze—and felt a sense of satisfaction when she looked away first.

No one, but *no* one, spoke to him that way.

Only when her eyes returned to his face did he drop his gaze, still deliberate, to give her a leisurely once-over.

Leggy, he thought approvingly. Lean, but with curves in all the right places. Taller than he'd first thought, five feet nine or ten inches to his six feet even.

She wore a ribbed sweater, olive-green, and well-cut camel trousers. Tasteful. Expensive.

A princess, he thought derisively.

She tossed her head again. "This is ridiculous. I demand that you tell me what's going on."

Princess? Ha! he told himself. *Try queen.* And under the mistaken notion that he was her subject and ought to be groveling at her feet.

"Well?" she repeated imperiously, her frown deepening.

With deliberation once again, Nat placed a foot on the second rung of the ladder, then an elbow on his raised knee, and finally his chin on his knuckles. Again he met her gaze.

"Who's asking?"

CHAPTER TWO

Chloe Burnett was far from insensible to her effect on men. It was a burden she'd had to bear even before she started working around construction sites. She barely heard the hoots and wolf whistles anymore. These days when a guy in a hard hat with a tool belt slung around his hips leered at her, she gave him a frosty look and made sure to flaunt the rings on her left hand. A gold band and a good quality zircon that most men couldn't have distinguished from a diamond anyway.

She wore the rings "to keep the vampires at bay," she'd explained to Gran-Marie. "Sort of like garlic, only I don't have to go around smelling like an Italian restaurant."

Gran-Marie didn't approve. She'd told Chloe so. To her, wearing a wedding ring when you weren't married was tantamount to lying. "Besides," she'd say, "*les vampires* will not allow the wedding ring to get in the way. You will only keep *les chics types* away." Chloe didn't bother to tell her that all les chics types—the good guys—were already taken anyway.

The man she'd found banging on the side of Gran-Marie's house was clearly not a good guy. But he wasn't a vampire, either. Insolent, cocky, rude—yes. And wreaking who-knew-what kind of havoc on the historic farmhouse.

But predatory? Surprisingly, she didn't think so. Maybe he was just so practiced he had her fooled, but his cool assessment had more the feel of a scientist observing a specimen than a wolf salivating over its next meal.

The analogy was oddly comforting. "Chloe Burnett," she offered, her tone milder. She gestured toward the house. "I assume my grandmother knows what's going on out here?"

He ignored the question. "You're Madame Marie's granddaughter?"

Madame. He even nasalized the final em slightly. Chloe's opinion of the man went up a notch. Not that she was about to let him know. "Yes, I'm Madame Marie's granddaughter. Do you always answer questions with questions?"

His facial muscles relaxed a little. The sudden twitch that appeared at one side of his mouth might even have been the commencement of a smile. She wasn't sure, as it did nothing more than lift the corner of his mouth a fraction. Possibly a nervous tic.

"Not always." He finally abandoned the ridiculous chin-in-hand pose he'd assumed when he'd come down from the ladder. He wasn't more than two or three inches taller than she was. Still, considering her own height, that was taller than average.

He stretched his arms behind his back, straining his T-shirt across his well-toned chest and shoulder muscles. Was he trying to impress her? Like the construction workers who flexed their muscles when she walked by or the guys at the gym who sucked in their guts when she came around a corner? Or was he simply stretching?

Either way, she couldn't help but notice the way he was put together. Only in the same detached, professional way he'd taken note of her, she assured herself. A scientist observing a specimen. Or more correctly, an artist observing a model. As an architect, she was interested in physical structure. This particular man, for instance—

"You were saying?" he interrupted her musings, his voice a drawl. He crossed his arms over his chest, the gesture exaggerated, as if, of all things, he thought she was admiring the view on a *personal* level.

She jerked her eyes back to his: ice-blue, direct, and thick-lashed. Paul Newman eyes. Startling, especially in contrast to his sun-browned skin. A contrast she'd observed, in fact, the moment he'd first looked down at her from his ladder.

She gestured toward the back porch. "The house. What you're doing…" *You'd have to be half blind not to notice eyes like that,* she told herself. He was a little rough around the edges. His eyebrows were a bit unruly, and his hair, as dark as hair could be and still be considered blond, needed a trim. And he definitely needed a shave.

On the other hand, the stubble drew attention to his bones. He had good bones. No, *great* bones. As much as Chloe hated to admit it, if this was the guy Earlene and True Marie had gushed over, they'd really got it right: ô la! la! Unfortunately, he was just the kind to know it. Arrogant. Probably egotistical.

"Well?" she snapped.

He raised an eyebrow. "Well what?"

"My grandmother knows exactly what you're doing out here? This isn't just any old house, you know."

"No, it's not. And yes, she does."

Chloe pursed her lips in irritation. Getting information out of the guy was downright painful. "Well then, what *are* you doing?"

"At the moment, replacing the sheathing and panels below this window. Dry rot never sleeps."

"Dry rot!" The house was over a hundred years old, she reminded herself. A few spots of dry rot were more than likely. "You're a carpenter?"

He hesitated. "Let's call it all-around handyman."

"So you're not—"

"Did your grandmother know you were coming?" he interrupted.

"Of course she did. I told her I'd be here by noon."

"That's odd. She didn't say anything."

Chloe frowned. "Why would she?"

"Right." She couldn't read his tone any more than she could read his expression. Amused? Sardonic? "After all, I'm only the hired hand."

"Well yes." Chloe's frown deepened. She, on the other hand, was Madame Marie's granddaughter. Why hadn't Gran-Marie told her she was having work done on the house? "How long have you been working around the place anyhow?"

"A month or so. Since the middle of June."

A month or so! She'd talked to Gran-Marie at least once a week in the last month. Twice last week. And not a peep about repairs to the house. Or a handyman.

Not that she wasn't pleased the homestead was getting some attention. It hadn't had much since Gran-Bert had first taken ill. She'd noticed on her last few visits how shabby things had started to look. She'd even told her grandmother she wanted to come up and paint the kitchen when she could find the time.

But tearing off siding! And practically rebuilding the entire back porch! Why hadn't her grandmother said anything?

"Speaking of Gran-Marie…" Chloe looked around, noticing for the first time that her grandmother's classic 1970 Peugeot convertible was missing from the driveway. In fact, other than Gran-Bert's old pickup parked on the lawn and her own car, there wasn't another vehicle on the property. Wouldn't a handyman have a truck of his own?

The conversation she'd overheard in the bakery came back to her like a line from a bad movie: *Bet he's smart enough to figure out Bertie left his grieving wife with more than just an old farmhouse…*

Sudden, irrational panic swept through her. "What have you done with my grandmother?!"

"What have I *done* with her?"

Chloe's panic ebbed: No one could have faked the guy's shocked disbelief. Besides, she always got a little paranoid when she was overtired, and she'd been overtired for months. Years, it felt like.

"Good grief, woman," the handyman sputtered. "You act as if you think I've done your grandmother in! Do I really look like an ax murderer?"

She narrowed her eyes. Did he? What did an ax murderer look like anyhow?

Again, that twitch at the corner of his mouth. A tic or a smile?

"Never mind," he said. "Just so you know, your grandmother took Jean-Claude to the vet this morning. They should be home in—"

"The vet?" Once again Chloe's heart tripped over itself. The little Bichon Frise was the joy of Gran-Marie's life. If anything happened to him, she'd be heartbroken. "What's wrong with Jean-Claude?"

All at once the handyman *did* look like an ax murderer. Then again, a real ax murderer probably wouldn't feel the least bit guilty about his crime, let alone look it. This guy, on the other hand, looked as guilty as a kid caught stealing a candy bar from the corner store.

"What?" she demanded.

"Nothing serious. Anymore." He looked down, arms still crossed, and worried at a rock in the dirt with the toe of his shoe. He glanced at Chloe and then quickly away again. "He OD'd on Ding-Dongs a couple of days ago. But he's fine now. The vet just wanted to—"

"Ding-Dongs! You fed Jean-Claude Ding-Dongs? Don't you know chocolate is poison for dogs?"

"I didn't *feed* him Ding-Dongs. He got into my room and found my stash, okay?" The handyman looked even more guilty.

"A *stash* of Ding-Dongs? *Ding-Dongs?* I can't believe Gran-Marie would even allow the things in the house!"

"Good grief, they're not illegal drugs," he snapped. "We're talking about Ding-Dongs here!"

"Do you know what those things are made of?"

"If it's anything other than chocolate and marshmallow, I don't want to know."

Chloe didn't answer. Something he'd said niggled at her brain.

He kicked the rock he'd loosened across the lawn. "Jean-Claude's fine," he repeated. "They should be home any—"

"What do you mean, 'your room'?" she interrupted, the Ding-Dongs forgotten as the greater crisis loomed. "You mean you really are living with Gran-Marie?"

He looked suddenly wary. "Why?"

"Look, I'm getting tired of this runaround! Why can't you just give me a straight answer? Who are you, and what are you doing here?"

"I told you, I'm the hired hand." Exaggerated patience. "The name is Nat. Neville, if you have to know. As for living here, yeah. Madame Marie gets some help getting the house in order, I get room and board. A business arrangement, pure and simple."

"Since when do hired hands get room and board?"

"Look, it wasn't my idea. You have problems with the arrangement, talk to your grandmother. And if you're worried I'm taking advantage of her—don't. We have a written agreement. I insisted on it. Okay?"

Chloe's ire rose again. What right did he have to be annoyed? "What does it say, that she'll support you in perpetuity while you keep inventing things that need fixing around the place?"

The handyman snorted. "If you think I have to invent things that need fixing around this place, you're blind as a naked mole rat. We're not talking a few repairs here, Ms. Burnett. Like I said, we're talking dry rot. We're talking missing gingerbread outside and cracks in the plaster inside. We're talking new paint, inside and out. Refinishing the floors. Maybe adding a bath and remodeling the kitchen. In a word, we're talking renovation."

Renovation! Alarm bells went off in Chloe's head. Something wasn't right. Gran-Marie would never have started a project of this magnitude without consulting her.

Still the handyman wasn't finished. "We're talking upgrades to meet commercial codes, Ms. Burnett. Which, in case you didn't know, are a lot more stringent than residential codes."

"Of course I know! I'm an architect, for pity's sake!" Chloe stopped abruptly. "What are you talking about, 'commercial codes'?" She crossed her arms, unconsciously mimicking the man's pose, and glared at him suspiciously. "What's that got to do with anything?"

"You say you're an architect. You should know."

In response to Chloe's blank look, he jerked his thumb toward the house and said, his patience again exaggerated, "The bed-and-breakfast, Ms. Burnett. A lot of work to be done around here before your grandmother opens the doors."

"Bed-and-breakfast!"

A horn blasted. A lime green convertible barreled up the driveway, top down, and jerked to a stop inches behind Chloe's Sebring, scattering gravel. A small white dog leapt to its feet in the passenger seat, barking wildly.

Bed-and-breakfast?

Nat Neville reached Gran-Marie's door just before Chloe did. He opened it with a flourish. "*Voilà,* madame!"

Out stepped a tiny woman dressed in a swirling red knit jacket and a long purple skirt, Gran-Marie's trademark colors. Her close-cropped salt-and-pepper hair framed a face that might have belonged to a pixie. A beaming face. *"Merci, mon ami!* And I see you have met my granddaughter. A raving beauty, *non?"*

Nat raised his eyebrows and murmured dryly, "Raving." He lifted Gran-Marie's hand to his lips.

Jean-Claude barked sharply. Gran-Marie turned to accept Chloe's long, fierce hug and return it in kind. Her grandmother was so small, Chloe could almost tuck her under an arm.

Jean-Claude barked again.

"All better, little guy?" The handyman swept the squirming ball of white fluff up from the car seat and submitted to a torrent of doggy kisses.

Even then, even seeing Gran-Marie's easy familiarity and Jean-Claude's lavish affection toward a total stranger, even though she could feel the nerves at the base of her neck bunch up in protest—

Chloe wouldn't admit to herself that it was too late.

CHAPTER THREE

"Lunch in half an hour, Natty," Gran-Marie said, pronouncing the *t*'s precisely.

Chloe frowned. *Natty!*

"*C'est bon.*" Nat released Jean-Claude, who scuttled for the porch.

Chloe's frown deepened. *C'est bon?* The guy spoke French?

"Chloe, *ma chère.* You would like to freshen up and assist me in the kitchen?"

Sliding a hand to the back of her neck, beginning now to throb in the familiar rhythm of a tension headache, Chloe dug her fingers into the hollows on either side of her spinal column.

And she'd hoped this weekend was going to be relaxing. She really needed a break.

"Ma chère?" Gran-Marie repeated.

"Oh! Yes, of course."

It was that "Natty" business, she thought. For one thing, it sounded too much like Bertie, which was what her grandmother had always called Chloe's Gran-Bert. For another—what was Gran-Marie thinking, giving her handyman a pet name? Not to *mention* the use of Gran-Bert's pickup. And accommodations in her house!

Make that "bed-and-breakfast," she reminded herself, wincing. Clearly, Gran-Marie *wasn't* thinking.

"You are well, ma chère?" Her grandmother sounded concerned.

Chloe smoothed her brow and nodded. "Fine," she said, even

though by now her nerves were thrumming steadily. Any other answer and Gran-Marie would fuss. Why worry her?

"You looked for a moment as if you had swallowed a pickle," Gran-Marie said.

"I'll get my bags," Chloe mumbled, turning away. Gran-Marie didn't miss much.

"I'll do it," Nat jumped in.

"No!" And then, as if able to see her grandmother's raised eyebrows behind her: "No, thank you. I can manage."

Ten minutes later, her bags deposited in her room, the same sunny, gabled upstairs bedroom that had been her haven at seventeen, she fortified herself with ibuprofen and descended the stairs to the kitchen. It was time for a serious talk with her grandmother.

But where to begin? The bed-and-breakfast? The renovation? "Natty"? Jean-Claude overdosing on Ding-Dongs? Then she remembered the conversation in the bakery.

"Gran-Marie, we have many things to talk about. But first, about your hired hand living here."

Chloe grabbed an orange off the counter and sliced it into wedges with quick, decisive strokes. She glanced at her grandmother. "I think you should know that people are talking."

Gran-Marie waved a hand dismissively. "Bah. People will talk, ma chère, from here to eternity."

"Don't you care what people think?"

Gran-Marie drew her brows together. "I care for what is true."

"But it *isn't* true! What people are saying, I mean."

"Hello! Am I interrupting?" Nat said from behind them.

Yes, you're interrupting! Chloe wanted to scream.

"*Mais non,*" said Gran-Marie, once again beaming. "*Le déjeuner* is served."

❖   ❖   ❖

Quiche, croissants, and fancy-cut melon wouldn't have been Nat's first choice for lunch after a morning of physical labor. And Chloe Burnett, raving beauty or not, wouldn't have made his short list of dream luncheon dates. Short list? Ha! She wouldn't have made the top one hundred.

But Madame Marie was trying out bed-and-breakfast recipes, and whether Nat liked it or not, Chloe had every right to sit at her grandmother's table. There wasn't much he could do except try to be polite; he owed at least that much to Madame.

A month ago he'd run out of gas not a hundred feet from the gravel drive leading up to the farmhouse, on a country road in the middle of nowhere. At least it seemed that way at the time, though he'd later learned there were several farms nearby and he was only a few miles out of Pilchuck. Madame Marie had been more than generous since she'd found him at her door, weary and bleary-eyed, hoping for a gallon of gas to get him back on the road again.

She couldn't have helped but hear him coming. He'd stumbled over a loose step on the way up to the porch, sending an empty metal pail toppling down the stairs when he tried to catch himself. She'd opened the door before he had a chance to knock, her expression curious and concerned.

He felt so stupid, he remembered saying. Hadn't let the tank run dry in years. He was on his way to Heron Bay, no reason except that he'd seen the name on his map and been intrigued. Weren't herons the most improbable birds, he'd said, such a prehistoric design…

He'd been too exhausted even to realize he was rambling.

He still wasn't quite sure how he'd ended up sitting across the kitchen table from the petite, bright-eyed, and decidedly eccentric Marie Antoinette Babineaux Delacroix Smith. But after thirty hours on the road, snatching his sleep at rest stops in hourlong increments and picking at greasy french fries from an endless string of drive-through windows, he was too tired and too hungry to say no to a home-cooked meal. Especially pot roast with mashed potatoes and gravy.

As disreputable as he must have looked, he wasn't sure, either, why the tiny septuagenarian had invited him in to share her supper instead of slamming the door in his face and calling the cops to haul him away.

A good heart? Loneliness?

Maybe a little of both. Madame Marie, as she insisted he call her, had been widowed twice, and long before had lost her only daughter. Her granddaughter tried to visit every month or two, Madame Marie explained, but she was very busy.

Nat hadn't meant to fall asleep in his chair after supper that night. And when he woke up twelve hours later to the smell of bacon frying and found himself lying on a chintz-covered chaise longue with a soft afghan tucked around him and a fuzzy white creature asleep at his feet, he had no idea where he was or how he'd gotten there.

The cheery *"Bonjour, monsieur!"* and the beaming face in the doorway had brought it all back. "You slept well?"

"Thank you, yes."

In fact, he hadn't slept so well in months. He'd taken it as a sign. Of what, he wasn't certain; he wasn't accustomed to thinking in terms of signs.

To thank Madame Marie for her hospitality, Nat offered to repair the loose step he'd stumbled over the night before. Then he discovered a shaky handrail, a broken window latch, a leaky faucet in the bathroom…

By lunchtime, he was deep into the blackberry bushes that had nearly swallowed her back door. By dinnertime, he had a pile of weeds and brambles as tall as he was that needed burning.

And he felt good. Tired, but not the same deadening tired he'd felt yesterday. Or the last six months, for that matter. There was something about aching muscles that made a body feel alive.

It was over dinner, pork chops with curried apples and wild rice, "one of my Bertie's favorites," Madame Marie had told him, that she'd broached her bed-and-breakfast idea.

"The house, she needs some work before the guests could come. But maybe not so much," Madame had said. "A coat of paint, some small repairs. What do you think?"

She'd leaned forward expectantly, fingers steepled, dark eyes intent, and waited for his answer as if his opinion mattered, as if it carried weight. A sudden, unexpected rush of emotion he couldn't even identify left him unable to answer for a moment.

She waited.

"It's not my field," he finally got out.

"But what do you think?"

"I'd have to inspect the house more closely, Madame Marie."

"*Bon!* Perhaps in the morning."

Another rush of emotion, this time one Nat easily identified. Amusement, pure and simple. For a tiny woman, Madame Marie had enormous strength of will.

But he'd shaken his head. "I can't impose on your hospitality another night, Madame."

"Nonsense! After all the work you have done today? You cannot think you have imposed! Now, with just the glance-over—what do you think?"

"I've got to warn you, Madame," he'd answered reluctantly. "The rule of thumb when you're remodeling is to double the time and triple the cost you think it's going to take you."

But he'd told her what he thought. Outside, she needed to check for dry rot, maybe replace some siding and window sills. Do some structural work on the porch and around the doorways. Make a few repairs to the gingerbread trim. Possibly replace the gutters. She was lucky her husband had kept up with the roof, he said. It wouldn't need replacing for another ten or fifteen years.

Inside, he told her, he'd noticed cracks here and there in the plaster walls. The floors all needed refinishing. Depending on how much money she wanted to spend, to really work as a bed-and-breakfast the house should have another bath. And she might want to think about upgrading the kitchen. "Though I hate the idea of letting a contractor loose inside a great old house like this."

"*Oui?* Why do you say so?"

"I'd just be careful, that's all. It would be too easy to compromise the integrity of the original architecture. Old houses have character and histories. They need to be respected."

"*Mais oui.*"

"You wouldn't want to use vinyl siding, for instance."

Madame Marie looked horrified. "I should think not!"

"Another example. Bathroom fixtures. You said your husband had the plumbing and wiring upgraded in the seventies?"

She nodded. "He was working to woo me."

Nat suppressed a grin. Over lunch, Madame Marie had related with considerable relish the story of Egbert Irby Smith's five-year, mostly long-distance suit to win her hand. Having the old farmhouse replumbed and rewired sounded like just the thing a quiet, hard-working, fifty-year-old bachelor farmer would have done to woo a wife. Even an exotic, French-speaking wife ten years his junior.

"I'm surprised you didn't end up with an avocado bathtub."

Madame Marie's eyes danced. "Nearly. Harvest gold, she was called. But when Bertie saw my displeasure, he dug out the tub with the lion's claw that I wanted to keep—from *la décharge publique!*"

Nat took a stab at translation. He'd always been good with languages. "La décharge publique… The county dump, that would be?"

"Oui. And that was when I gave my hand to him." She sighed. "Twenty-five years we were married. He was a good man, my Bertie. Un chic type." She grinned impishly. "But after the bathtub, in matters of taste, he left the judgment to me."

Nat almost laughed. Maybe it was more appropriate to worry about letting Madame Marie loose on a contractor—pity the poor guy—than letting a contractor loose on the house.

He let himself get caught up in her excitement as they talked about where another bath might go, where she might find another claw-foot tub, how the kitchen might be reconfigured. He hadn't been so engaged in a conversation for months.

"You have done this work before, oui?" Madame Marie finally asked him.

"A little. Not for a long time."

"But you could?"

"Some of it. Most of it, probably." He saw exactly where she was headed. "But Madame Marie, I'm not looking for work."

Or was he?

"That is, I hadn't planned on sticking around."

"What had you planned?"

"Well…ah…" He drummed his fingers on the table and tried to think of something to say. The truth was, beyond sitting on a log to watch the sun set over Heron Bay, another ten miles down the road at most, he didn't have plans. Not for tomorrow, not for next week, not for next year.

"I'm taking some time off," he finally told her. "I haven't made specific plans."

She clapped her hands in delight. "Then you will work for me."

"Work isn't exactly what I had in mind."

"Oh, but a man needs to have work for the hands, Natty."

Natty. Was it the pet name that once again let loose a wave of emotion he could hardly contain? Or was it the simple truth of Madame Marie's observation? *A man needs work for the hands.*

She must have taken his silence as weakening. Maybe it was.

"Natty, I offer you work for the hands, food for the belly, and a place to lay your head at night. And I will pay you well on the top of it. What more could a man ask?"

He'd actually laughed. For the first time in months. A feeble laugh, admittedly. But it seemed a sign, in the same way his dreamless sleep the night before had seemed a sign.

"For a month, to start," Madame Marie coaxed. "Then we will see. *D'accord?*"

A month. Time he'd otherwise be… What? He didn't have a clue. *So why not?* In the absence of a good answer, he'd nodded in agreement. "D'accord."

And for the second night in a row he'd slept like a man with no cares.

Working around Madame Marie's house suited him well, he'd found. He could give himself wholly to it, lose himself in it. Forget himself. Forget everything.

Madame Marie's company suited him too. She seemed content to carry the conversation during their meals together, asking no questions, demanding nothing of him except his attention and his appreciation, which he was more than happy to give. Madame Marie talked. He listened. It was just the way he wanted things.

Madame Marie's granddaughter, on the other hand…

Already she'd asked too many questions. And she clearly wasn't going to stop now. "Where did you say you were from?" she asked as they sat down to lunch, pulling him from his musings.

Her tone was neutral, but she was only pretending to be polite, Nat could tell. Funny how two people could take such an instant dislike to each other. A good thing, too. The truth was, if he didn't find her high-handedness so offensive, he might have been attracted to Chloe. A complication he couldn't afford.

"I didn't," he answered bluntly.

"Let us begin with the blessing," Madame Marie soothed. She reached a fine-boned hand toward each of them and bowed her head.

Just as well, Nat told himself as she offered a simple grace, her fingers wrapped around his. Another minute and he might have said something regrettable. He didn't care in the slightest what Chloe thought, but offending Madame Marie was out of the question.

CHAPTER FOUR

When Nat Neville had said he was trading his carpentry skills for room and board, Chloe hadn't imagined he meant sitting down in the formal dining room as her grandmother's luncheon companion. A sandwich and a glass of lemonade on the back porch she could have understood. But this!

Gran-Marie's dining room table was draped in linen and set with her best china. The silver tea service that normally stood behind the glass doors of the mahogany china cabinet gleamed at Gran-Marie's elbow. A bright bouquet of zinnias and Shasta daisies arranged in a crystal vase graced the table's center.

How a perfect stranger had conned her grandmother into treating him like an honored guest in her home, Chloe didn't know and was afraid to guess. And how a common laborer could look as if he belonged at a table set for a formal tea was even more a mystery.

But somehow he did, even dressed in jeans and a T-shirt and in need of a shave and haircut. Gran-Bert, bless his farmer's soul, had been so ill at ease when the mysterious creature he'd married "pulled out the stops and put on the Ritz," as he called it, that Gran-Marie had nearly always reserved her "fancy" meals for her Ladies' Luncheons. For Gran-Bert, she'd made pot roast with mashed potatoes and gravy, served at the kitchen table on the chipped earthenware he'd eaten off all his bachelor-farmer days.

Yet here was Nat Neville, as red-blooded and male as anyone

Chloe had ever set eyes on, eating quiche and drinking tea out of a delicate china teacup like a blue blood.

Who did he think he was anyhow?

It rankled. It really rankled.

That, on top of her headache, on top of her worry that her beloved grandmother was going 'round the bend—if she hadn't done so already—had Chloe so agitated she could hardly think, let alone make polite conversation. But for Gran-Marie's sake, she tried.

"What brought you to Pilchuck?" she asked as they settled into lunch. A perfectly innocent question.

He shrugged. "I was on my way through."

She lifted a brow. "On your way through?"

"How goes *le hôpital,* ma chère?" Gran-Marie asked before Nat could respond.

Normally Chloe enjoyed telling her grandmother about the progress of the project she'd been managing the last three years, a phased hospital renovation. But at the moment she had other things on her mind.

"We're winding down." She returned her attention to Nat Neville. "On your way through to where?"

"Heron Bay."

"Oh? What's in Heron Bay?"

"And what will you do when le hôpital is finished?" Gran-Marie interrupted once again.

Chloe didn't want to talk about work. She needed a break from work. And she wanted to find out what Nat Neville was up to.

"I don't know for certain. I may be working out of the Vancouver office for a while. Nat, where was your last job?"

He hesitated, then mumbled, "California."

"Vancouver, British Columbia?" Gran-Marie persisted.

Chloe sighed. "Yes, Gran-Marie. Vancouver, British Columbia." She turned again to Nat. "So you're not licensed in Washington."

He bristled visibly. "I don't need a li—"

"They work you too hard at that Jade, Janus & Morgan," said Gran-Marie.

"Jade, Janus & McIntyre," Chloe corrected. "I'd check that out if

I were you, Mr. Neville. As I'm sure you know, there's the question of bond. Not to mention insurance. You've rehabbed period houses before, I presume?"

The set of his jaw made it clear that he didn't like her questions. Well, too bad. They were important questions. And it was a sure bet Gran-Marie hadn't asked them.

"Some." His tone was curt.

"I'd like to talk to someone who knows your work."

"Chloe!" Gran-Marie reprimanded. "Do you think that I would hire a man to renovate Bertie's house who did not respect its history and integrity?"

Chloe's growing frustration finally slipped over the edge. "All right then, you tell me, Gran-Marie! What did you ask him? What's his training? What's his approach to renovation? What does he know about Victorian architecture? What does he know about *this* house? All I'm asking for are his credentials!"

"Chloe!" Gran-Marie's eyes flashed.

"It's all right, Madame," Nat said, his voice low and his eyes fixed on Chloe's. "She's only trying to protect her interests."

"My grandmother's interests, thank you!" Chloe sputtered, outraged.

"She's right to ask questions," Nat went on, still looking at Chloe. "First, Ms. Burnett, my approach to renovation. In line with the secretary of the interior's *Standards for Rehabilitation,* my goal, and I quote, is 'to return a property to a state of utility, through repair or alteration, which makes possible an efficient contemporary use while preserving those portions and features of the property which are significant to its historic, architectural, and cultural values.'

"As to what I know about Victorian architecture, would you care to hear about Gothic, Stick, Queen Anne, or Craftsman? Shingle? Eastlake? Italianate? Greek Revival, perhaps?"

Nat paused for a long swig from his water glass. Chloe knew she should say something, but she was so dumbfounded by his recital she couldn't think what. She jumped when Nat thumped his glass on the table and continued.

"As to what I know about your grandmother's house, Ms. Burnett:

It's built entirely out of cedar from Innskeep Island in the San Juans. It rests on a granite foundation. In style it's a relatively modest member of the Stick-Eastlake-Queen Anne family with such typical embellishments as gable ornaments, gig-cut corner brackets on the bay window, and turned spindle work on the porch. It appears to be what was called at the time a 'pattern-book house,' designed by the Knoxville mail-order architect, George F. Barber. A fact that in no way detracts from its interest and historical importance," Nat finished, "as a fine example of Victorian farmhouse architecture."

Chloe knew her mouth was open in astonishment, but she couldn't seem to close it. Or say a word. What book had he got *that* out of?

"West Coast Victorians: A Pictorial Encyclopedia of Nineteenth Century Design," Gran-Marie furnished, as if she could read Chloe's mind. "The photograph looks to be taken after Bertie repainted the trim in '75. And I never knew she was pictured in such an encyclopedia! Nor in the *Pilchuck Post,* way back in '93. 1893, that is."

Nat leveled his blue eyes on Chloe. "The Pilchuck Public Library has impressive archives, Chloe. Here's a quote for you: 'Of all the fine residences recently built in Tillicum County, that of gentleman farmer Archibald Egbert Smith and his lovely bride, Lillian Rose Irby, is surely the finest.'"

Gran-Marie, beaming, touched Chloe lightly on the arm: "Of all the residences in Tillicum County, ours is the finest, my granddaughter! The journalist for the *Post* said she is a fitting residence for a man who… How does it go now, Natty?"

"For a man whose dairy herds made Tillicum County one of the premier agricultural centers in Washington state."

"Imagine!" Gran-Marie clasped her hands over her heart.

Nat pushed his chair away from the table. "Now, if you'll excuse me, I have work to do. Thank you for lunch, Madame. Delicious, as usual. I'll see you both for supper?"

"Lemon-pepper chicken and new potatoes," Gran-Marie said brightly.

Chloe, still speechless, merely nodded.

She didn't stay speechless for long. The minute she heard the back door slam the words rushed out: "All right, so the man knows his way around a library. Maybe he even has a photographic memory. So what? That doesn't make him the right man for this job, Gran-Marie. Did he talk about his training? Not one word!" She threw her napkin on the table. "Who on earth is he? Why is he here? And you, interrupting at every turn! What is it you're trying to hide from me?"

"Chloe Colette Burnett, what has gotten into you?" Gran-Marie asked, not even attempting to answer Chloe's questions. "You are rude to Natty, you spoil le déjeuner with your childish sniping, and now you grill your poor grand-mère like the policeman does the criminal!"

"I don't mean to be rude, Gran-Marie, but what can I think? When I walk into the town bakery and hear that a man is living with you—"

"So the gossips are busy." Gran-Marie frowned.

"When I find him here, acting as if he belongs—"

"You think so?" Gran-Marie brightened. "Bon! He is in need of a place to belong."

"When he tells me, as if I should already know, that you're opening a bed-and-breakfast—"

"She is the perfect house for the bed-and-breakfast, non?" Gran-Marie beamed.

"But why didn't you tell me, Gran-Marie? You've never said a word about wanting to open a bed-and-breakfast! Why haven't we talked this over?"

"I see I have caused you to suffer." Gran-Marie sounded distressed. "I am sorry, ma chère. I was not thinking." She took Chloe's hand in hers. "Perhaps I knew you would not approve, and so I have kept myself from telling you. But," she added, as if to reassure her granddaughter, "it is only a month since the bed-and-breakfast grew serious in my mind. And we are talking now, oui?"

"But only after you'd already decided!"

"Think of the house, ma chère," Gran-Marie insisted. "Is she perfect or is she not?"

Chloe swallowed. In fact, the Smith-Irby homestead was a beautiful specimen of late Victorian farmhouse architecture—as the author of *West Coast Victorians* had understood. Located on top of Bramble Ridge, with farmland all around it and a view of Mount

Balder when the clouds lifted, the house was just the kind of place, with a little work, that her city friends would flock to for a romantic weekend getaway.

"All right, maybe she is. But as for you, Gran-Marie…"

Gran-Marie lifted her chin. "As for me?"

"You're seventy years old, Gran-Marie! What are you thinking?"

"I am thinking," said her grandmother forcibly, "that seventy is too young to curl up the tail and die. I am thinking that this old house has as much of the life left in her as this old woman does, and we shall neither of us be put out to the pasture. I am thinking I still have work to do in this world, and Auberge de la Baie de la Ronce is it."

Auberge de la Baie de la Ronce. Brambleberry Inn. "Go with the English, Gran-Marie, or no one will know what—" Chloe stopped midsentence, catching herself. What was she saying?!

"Gran-Marie, please. I just don't think you understand," she tried again. "Running a bed-and-breakfast is like running a hotel. All by yourself! Concierge, clerk, caretaker, chambermaid, chef."

"So you think I should go with Brambleberry," Gran-Marie said thoughtfully. "Hmm. Brambleberry Inn…"

"I don't think you should go with anything!"

"It does not have the panache of Auberge de la Baie de la Ronce," Gran-Marie continued as if she hadn't heard. "But perhaps you are right. Not everyone had a Marie Antoinette Babineaux Delacroix Smith from whom to learn the language." She sighed. "The Americans, I fear, speak French like the Spanish cow."

Chloe stifled a snort. "Never mind that," she said severely. "Back to the start. Back to the so-called handyman. The one who drinks tea like an earl and memorizes pages out of encyclopedias. The one who has you wrapped around his little finger."

"Wrapped around his little finger?" Gran-Marie sounded indignant.

"Yes, wrapped around his little finger! It was him, wasn't it? He put this ridiculous bed-and-breakfast idea in your head."

"He did not. The idea, she is all mine. But the hard work belongs to Natty."

"Why? Why Nat Neville instead of someone you know? If you're set on renovating the house, why not hire a local contractor?"

"Whom do you mean? Bachelor & Sons, who will try to tell me I am in need of the dry wall over the lath and plaster and a pop-out garden window in my kitchen?"

Chloe shuddered. Her grandmother had a point. "So hire an architect to work with them."

"Non," Gran-Marie declared emphatically. "The bachelor and his sons are not for this job. For this job, I like Natty. And for an architect, I have you."

"I build hospitals, Gran-Marie. I haven't thought about houses since grad school."

"Maybe the time has come to think again." Gran-Marie folded her napkin carefully and laid it next to her empty plate. "You can always borrow the book from Natty."

"You can't learn architecture from a book, Gran-Marie! Any more than you could learn—I don't know—*brain* surgery. The point is, you don't even know who this Nat Neville character is. Where did he come from? What do you know about him?"

Gran-Marie raised her chin. "But I do know who he is. And I will tell you. He is a child of *le bon Dieu.*"

Chloe's heart sank. *Le bon Dieu.* The good Lord.

"Where did he come from?" Gran-Marie continued. "I will tell you. Le bon Dieu sent him to my door."

She might as well wave the white flag right now, Chloe thought with resignation. When Gran-Marie brought le bon Dieu into an argument, that was the end of the argument. Chloe knew.

"What do I know about him?" Gran-Marie went on. "This much, ma chère. Natty needs this old house as much as this old house needs him."

That was when Chloe realized that the bewildering late-life career her grandmother felt suddenly called to had nothing at all to do with a bed-and-breakfast and everything to do with Nat Neville.

And that was when she finally acknowledged that as far as talking sense into Gran-Marie, it was too late.

Now she was left to talking sense into Gran-Marie's handyman.

No sweat, she told herself. She had a pretty good idea what kind of language the man would understand.

CHAPTER FIVE

Nat could tell by the way she strode around the corner of the house, her chestnut-colored hair swishing around her shoulders, that he wasn't going to like what Chloe had to say.

She stopped below the ladder and planted her hands on her hips. "Make it quick," he growled. "I've got a lot to do."

"Oh, I'll make it quick, all right," Chloe retorted. "How much do you want, Neville, to make tracks out of here?"

He was so surprised that he lost the measured rhythm of his pounding, just missing a blow to his thumb. "I beg your pardon?"

"Spare me. How much is it going to set me back to send you on your way?"

Nat didn't move. His fingers clenched the hammer as he started counting silently, trying to smooth the ragged edges of his temper. He got all the way to fifteen before he felt safe enough to break the looming silence: "More than you could ever come up with, Ms. Burnett."

Like a good reason, he added to himself. Not to mention a smile and at least a modicum of courtesy—since she clearly didn't do respect.

Chloe's eyes narrowed. "Because you think you can get more out of my grandmother? Dream on, Neville. I'm not going to let that happen."

He snorted. "I told you we have a contract. You're welcome to look it over. Believe me, your grandmother's getting a bargain, Ms. Burnett. I'm here because she asked me to be. Period." He held a nail in place and swung.

"Right. Because all of a sudden, out of the blue, she decided to open a bed-and-breakfast." Chloe lifted her chin defiantly as Nat placed another nail and swung. *Bam-BAM!* "You know what's funny, Neville? I've never, ever heard Gran-Marie talk about opening a bed-and-breakfast. Not until you showed up on her doorstep looking for a job."

Again Nat's rhythm faltered. "Your point is?"

"My point is that she isn't doing this for herself. Don't you get it?" Chloe's voice rose. "My grandmother is seventy years old, for pity's sake. There's no way she can keep up with a bed-and-breakfast! The only reason she hired you to work on the house is because you needed a job and she felt sorry for you!"

Nat placed a nail and swung before answering, his voice low and dangerous: "You underestimate your grandmother, Ms. Burnett. And you underestimate me."

She snorted. "Because you can swing a hammer and you know a little theory about Victorian architecture? So maybe you do know your way around an old house. I don't know. What I do know is that this bed-and-breakfast idea is utter nonsense."

"Why?"

"*Why?* Didn't I just tell you that my grandmother is seventy years old? It's not as if she needs a career, Neville. She certainly doesn't need the money." Chloe narrowed her eyes. "But you already know that, don't you?"

Nat clenched his teeth and took out his fury on another handful of nails before he answered, his patience all but run out. "What is it with you and money? Believe me, *Ms.* Burnett, I don't need the money either. I'm not interested in anything you have to offer."

"So what are you saying, *Mr.* Neville? That you're renovating Gran-Marie's house out of the goodness of your heart? If you had any kind of feeling for my grandmother, you wouldn't let her do this!"

"And if *you* had any kind of feeling for your grandmother, you'd visit her more than five or six times a year!"

Chloe gasped. "Oh! You…you… Are you judging me?"

"I'm telling you that your grandmother's lonely. Take it however you will. And take it somewhere else. I've got work to do."

"This is just too rich. You take advantage of Gran-Marie's loneliness and then blame me!"

"If the shoe fits, wear it."

"Ooh!"

"Oh stop, Chloe. Your grandmother loves having company, and she thrives on 'doing' for people. You've implied it yourself. Why not a bed-and-breakfast? For pity's sake, let her be!"

Chloe tossed her head angrily. "You want me to let *you* be."

He stopped his banging and gazed down at her in disbelief. "Yes! I want you to let me be! What is it with you, woman?"

"What is it with *me*?"

"*Who made you queen of the world?*"

Again Chloe gasped, but Nat wasn't about to stop now. "Your grandmother's still a grownup, Chloe. Why don't we respect that? Leave the decision to her? If she wants me to leave, believe me, I'll leave. No protest, no argument. She says the word, I'm gone. I don't even care if she pays me for the work I've already done. But if she wants me to stay, I stay."

"You know as well as I do—"

"I'm not finished. You'd better start making your grandmother a priority, Chloe. Because loneliness and boredom are worse on a body, and believe me, *far* worse on a soul, than hard work ever was."

Their eyes locked for a long, silent moment. Neither of them blinked, neither of them wavered.

Then, without another word, Chloe whirled around and marched away, regal as a queen.

◆　◆　◆

The queen barely managed to make it around the corner out of Nat's view, however, before she burst into tears.

And she didn't make it past her grandmother at all. Gran-Marie came barreling out of the kitchen, Jean-Claude pattering behind her, at the sound of the front door clicking shut.

Judging by her grandmother's expression, Chloe knew that she must look a wreck. "Chloe! Ma chère! What is the matter?" Gran-Marie cried, opening her arms. "Come to your grand-mère, *mon enfant*."

Mon enfant. My child.

She felt like a child, all right, standing there in the hallway with Gran-Marie's arms wrapped around her, crying as if she'd lost her best friend. Sobbing! It was so unlike her. Cool, competent, strong, successful—those were the words for Chloe Burnett. She didn't snivel. She didn't whine. And she never cried.

Not since she was seventeen, when she'd cried enough tears to last the rest of her life.

Gran-Marie touched her arm. "It surely was not Natty who made you cry?" She looked so distressed that Chloe didn't have the heart to tell her that yes, in fact, it *was* "Natty" who'd made her cry. Besides, if she did, she'd have to explain that he'd made her cry only because he'd hit a nerve so raw that even a whisper across it would have made her wince in pain.

And Nat definitely had not whispered.

Shaking her head, she swiped a hand across her cheeks, not meeting her grandmother's eyes. "I'm sorry, Gran-Marie, I don't know what's wrong with me… Terrific headache… Things are just so *stressful.*"

"It is that Jade, Janus & Murphy," her grandmother said indignantly.

"McIntyre," Chloe corrected without thinking.

"Murphy, McIntyre, Morgan—who cares? To work you so hard is not right, ma chère! Le hôpital, he is sucking the life from you! You have no time for play, for friends, for anything! And what of *l'amour*? When will you have the time for love? I cannot believe this is the life for you."

"I think I'd better go lie down, Gran-Marie."

Again her grandmother's mood changed. "But of course, mon enfant. A cup of tea, perhaps, to take to your room?"

Gran-Marie's solicitude only brought a fresh spate of tears. How many times, right here in this house, had her grandmother brought a pot of tea to her room and sat next to her on the bed, rubbing a hand across her back, murmuring words of comfort and love, letting her cry?

Too many times to count.

And Chloe, as Gran-Marie's handyman-carpenter-champion had

so unkindly reminded her, couldn't be bothered to drive the hundred miles to visit her grandmother more than five or six times a year!

"I'm sorry, Gran-Marie. For being such a baby."

"Nonsense. Sometimes, ma chère, to cry is both necessary and essential. Go now. I will bring you tea."

Chloe slipped out of her sweater and trousers and donned an oversized sweatshirt and a pair of leggings. It wasn't as if she didn't want to see her grandmother more often, but at the end of the week, after working fifty or sixty hours and trying to keep up with even minimal household chores, she didn't have the energy left to get in her car for a trip to the grocery store, let alone to Pilchuck.

Flopping down on her back in the middle of the canopy bed, she wrapped her arms around an eyelet-trimmed pillow and stared up at the gossamer floral fabric stretched overhead. Mercifully, her tears had stopped. At least for now.

Her headache, on the other hand, was back with a vengeance. She took a deep breath and let it out slowly, willing herself to relax. If only…

If only what? If only her job didn't eat up her life the way it did? Why waste her time wishing things could be different when they couldn't be?

The fact was, landing an internship with JJ&M right out of grad school had been a lucky break, one she'd finessed into a staff position in the firm's hospital and clinic division after she'd earned her license. Sure, she'd had to make sacrifices over the last ten years. To be successful, you did. You couldn't stay ahead of the game without working ten-hour days and weekends; if you didn't get in there when there was work to be done, someone else did.

So, she admitted, life as a successful corporate architect did cut into your social life a little.

A little?

Okay. A lot. But she'd worked too hard to get where she was today to let it go because she felt a little lonely now and then. Her assignment three years ago as project manager for the Duwamish Hospital renovation had had nothing to do with lucky breaks and everything to do with commitment and discipline. She'd earned it. And she was proud of it. She wasn't afraid of hard work; at least Nat Neville couldn't find fault with her there.

Not that Nat Neville's opinion had anything to do with anything, she reminded herself. She'd been feeling guilty about neglecting Gran-Marie long before Nat had laid into her.

No, Nat Neville's opinion didn't matter a whit. But Gran-Marie's happiness did.

"Chloe?" Her grandmother's voice came through the open door.

She rolled to her side, still clutching the pillow, to see Gran-Marie in the doorway holding a tray with a violet-sprigged teapot and two matching teacups. Jean-Claude followed silently at her heels.

"Peppermint-chamomile. Good for reducing the stress, ma chère," her grandmother said. "May I share a cup with you?"

"Oh, Gran-Marie, please do." Chloe plumped her pillow against the headboard and pulled herself up to lean into it as her grandmother set the tea tray on the dressing table opposite the bed.

Jean-Claude whined, wiggled, and then made a running leap for the bed. Chloe helped the little dog up the last few inches, then sighed as he snuggled close, laying his head on her lap and whimpering soulfully. Maybe she should think about getting a dog.

Right. Like she was home enough to take care of a dog.

"Gran-Marie…" Burying her fingers in Jean-Claude's soft, dense fluff, Chloe took a deep breath before plunging on. "You know I love you, don't you?"

"But of course I do!" Gran-Marie, holding the teapot in one hand and a cup and saucer in the other, looked so startled that Chloe braced herself for a crash of broken china.

But her grandmother steadied herself and poured the tea without incident, handing the cup to Chloe when she was done. "Why do you ask such a thing, ma chère? Not, I hope, because we do not see eye to eye on everything."

Chloe shook her head. "No. I just want to be sure. You do know I'd visit more often if I could?"

"*Bien sûr.* It is understood," Gran-Marie answered as she filled the second teacup. "But," she added emphatically, "I still say to work you as hard as your company works you is wrong." She sat carefully on the edge of Chloe's bed, cup and saucer in hand. "Now. Drink your tea and promise you will not worry yourself over such things again."

Since the promise was one she couldn't make at the moment, Chloe settled for drinking her tea. It gave her a good excuse not to have to answer.

"Now," Gran-Marie said again. "So there is nothing between us but good feeling, Chloe, we must resolve our arguments. About the inn and also about Natty."

Chloe's heart plummeted, but she nodded. At the moment, resolving their arguments seemed as likely as either of them winning the *Reader's Digest* Ten Million Dollar Sweepstakes, but her grandmother was right.

"I couldn't change your mind if I tried to, Gran-Marie. And having inherited your gene for stubbornness, I doubt you're going to change mine, either."

"Then let us try for the compromise, ma chère."

"Compromise?" Chloe said skeptically.

Gran-Marie shrugged and smiled. *"C'est possible, mon enfant. C'est possible."*

Chapter Six

Chloe made up her mind to let Gran-Marie carry the conversation. For one thing, she didn't have it in her to spend any more of the weekend arguing. For another, she hadn't exactly given her grandmother a chance to have her say.

She could blame it on overwork, or concern for Gran-Marie's well-being, or even the feelings of guilt that Nat Neville had tapped into. She could even blame it on Earlene Boyd and True Marie Weatherby, the old biddies.

But the truth was, she'd acted with Gran-Marie exactly the way Nat had characterized her: as if she had a right to make her decisions for her. As if she *were* "queen of the world."

"First, ma chère…" Gran-Marie reached for her hand. "Let us ask le bon Dieu for guidance."

Chloe nodded and grasped her grandmother's outstretched hand, the skin cool and thin, the grip as strong and warm as its owner's presence and personality.

She wasn't surprised by Gran-Marie's wish to begin with prayer or by her simple and earnest request that God would lead them to understanding. Prayer was as natural to Gran-Marie as breathing.

Against God and Gran-Marie, Chloe had no defenses.

"So," her grandmother said, releasing Chloe's hand to lift her teacup for a sip of peppermint-chamomile.

"You first, Gran-Marie. I haven't listened well, and I'm sorry."

Gran-Marie looked pleased. "It is good, my granddaughter, that your heart is soft to the promptings of le bon Dieu."

Chloe shifted uncomfortably. It wasn't the way she would have described her heart, especially in the last few years. Gran-Marie wasn't the only one she'd been neglecting.

She pushed the thought aside. "Tell me about your idea for a bed-and-breakfast, Gran-Marie."

"She may be a foolish old woman's dream," her grandmother said. "But what is life without the dream? Le bon Dieu has blessed me with this house and all the beautiful things inside. Now I wish to share them."

"I understand. But do *you* understand why it is I'm concerned?"

"I have thought about the work she will take," Gran-Marie said. "I know I will enjoy the cooking and having guests at my table. But I admit, it is not so easy for me anymore, up and down those stairs to make the beds and clean the baths. So I have decided. I will hire a girl to help me. D'accord?"

Chloe brightened. Actually, hiring someone to help with the heavier work around the house was a good idea, bed-and-breakfast or not. Maybe someone who would be a good companion for Gran-Marie as well.

"You'll let me help you with the hiring?"

Gran-Marie hesitated, then nodded. "If it will help you to feel better."

Humor her, Chloe told herself. It was going to be months before the house was ready for guests anyhow. Anything might happen between now and then. "All right. I have to agree that this house is perfect for a bed-and-breakfast, Gran-Marie." She paused, not wanting to bring up "Natty" but knowing she had to. "Now, about Nat Neville doing the renovations. You're sure about him?"

Her grandmother sighed. "I know you are feeling protective, Chloe. But Natty is a good man, ma chère. A kind man."

Chloe raised an eyebrow. "Kind?"

"Yes, kind," Gran-Marie said firmly. "But there is something else about him…" She stared across the room, out the tall, lace-curtained window, as if she could see beyond the leafy branches, beyond the white puffs of cloud and the blue sky.

She turned her gaze back to Chloe. "I cannot put the finger on it, and you have not allowed yourself to see it, but there is a sadness about Natty. A brokenness."

"There is?" Chloe asked, surprised. She hadn't seen much but Nat's anger.

And he hasn't seen much but yours, an inner voice niggled. In fact, now that she thought about it, she was more than a little embarrassed by her behavior. Hadn't she set the tone between them from the very first words she'd spoken? And she'd accused *him* of arrogance!

Not that he hadn't behaved as badly as she had…

"He is a man in need of healing," Gran-Marie said. "A man in need of a *place* to heal. What better place than Pilchuck, my grand-daughter?" She touched Chloe lightly on the arm. "What better place," she added, her voice soft, "than this house which has been a place of healing in the past?"

Chloe couldn't have answered around the lump in her throat if she'd tried.

"Already I see le bon Dieu at work in him," her grandmother said. "The house, she is good for Natty."

Chloe nodded. *And you're even better for him, Gran-Marie. In the same way you were for me.* "And you believe he's good for the house as well."

"Oui. He has the necessary respect. If you have looked with close eyes at the back porch, you will know that he has the skill also."

Ashamed to say she hadn't bothered, Chloe nodded again. "And you're determined to let him stay here while he's working?"

Gran-Marie patted her arm. "You worry yourself too much over what the gossips say, ma chère. I care more for what le bon Dieu has to say. And le bon Dieu says Natty is his child and needs what my heart and this house have to give him."

Jean-Claude chose that moment to get up, make several turns, and settle once again, with a whimpering sigh, next to Chloe. She smoothed her hand down his back, remembering the day she'd brought the little Bichon Frise to Gran-Marie and told her he needed a home. Nat Neville wasn't the first stray her grandmother had taken in, and he surely would not be the last.

Halfway through her second cup of tea, Chloe realized her headache had disappeared, and she was listening more to the comforting cadence of her grandmother's voice than to her words. A distant buzz from somewhere outside the window, like bees in the lilac bushes, added to the sense of peace and tranquillity.

"Sleep, ma chère," Gran-Marie murmured, rising from the bed and taking Chloe's cup and saucer.

Chloe slid down the headboard and rolled over on her side, curling her knees and snuggling into the down comforter. "Mmm."

Jean-Claude, disturbed from his burrow, snorted in outrage and jumped to the floor.

"I love you, my granddaughter," Gran-Marie said softly. She placed a light, dry kiss on Chloe's forehead. "Perhaps when you wake, ma chère, you will apologize to Natty."

She picked up the tea tray and tiptoed across the room, Jean-Claude pattering behind her.

"Mmm." Chloe murmured again, wondering just before she drifted off to sleep if her grandmother was experimenting with posthypnotic suggestion.

◆ ◆ ◆

After his run-in with Chloe, Nat finished his work on the north side of the house with dispatch, a more productive use of his excess adrenaline, he decided, than the unintended tongue-lashing he'd given Madame Marie's granddaughter. He knew better than to let himself get all worked up. What on earth had he been thinking?

He opened the near door of the carriage house, which was large enough to have garaged three horse-drawn carts when it was first built and currently housed a well-appointed workshop and two cars.

One car, Nat amended as he rummaged around in a drawer for a tape measure. Madame Marie had left her Peugeot in the driveway after her trip to the vet this morning, and Nat's car stood alone against the far wall. He hadn't driven it since he'd added a gallon of gas to the tank and gotten it off the street and up the hill. For his present purposes, it was about as useful as a bicycle. A good thing Madame Marie had hung on to her husband's old Ford pickup. It was a real workhorse.

Tape measure in hand, Nat closed the door and walked back toward the house, where he had a pair of sawhorses set up near the open tailgate of the truck. He pulled a list of measurements from a pocket, calculations for a replacement sill on the front bay window, and then picked out a length of straight-grained cedar from the woodpile stacked against the house.

He was still surprised by his outburst toward Madame Marie's granddaughter. In the first place, he mused as he laid the cedar across the old sawhorses, it was going to take more than a tirade from a stranger to get Chloe to change her priorities. Why should she listen to him? She didn't even like him.

In the second place, how Chloe treated her grandmother really wasn't any of his business.

Except that in the month that he'd been here on the Smith-Irby homestead as both guest and employee, he'd come to feel that Madame Marie somehow *was* his business.

He stretched his tape measure along the length of the board and marked the wood with a pencil in several places, then picked up the small circular saw from the tailgate of the pickup, his temporary workbench.

Why did he feel so proprietary toward Madame Marie? Was it only because he had no one else in his life to think of as family? Because it had been so long since he'd felt as if he belonged anywhere outside the hospital?

He'd felt a certain sense of family there, he supposed. As much as he'd felt anywhere, at least since his parents had died. In fact, for the first six months after he'd left, he'd missed the place as though a part of himself was gone. He'd known who he was there, something he hadn't known outside its walls.

He positioned the blade to a penciled line, pressed the power switch on the saw, and began to push it through the wood, feeling the vibration in his arms and shoulders.

Funny how his perspective had changed so dramatically. Just in the four weeks since he'd stumbled up Madame Marie's steps to her front door, he'd started to know himself in a new and different way. Know himself, enjoy himself, appreciate parts of himself he hadn't explored in years.

He was also learning to appreciate small pleasures he'd forgotten over time. The smell of lilacs, the taste of a home-cooked meal, the feel of the sun on his back and the breeze on his face while he worked…

The blade hit air, and the scrap from the end of the board fell to the ground. Nat slid the wood across the sawhorses and repositioned the blade.

He was beginning to believe that he could build a new life for himself in a place like Pilchuck. He could brush up on old skills, as he was doing now, develop latent abilities, even discover new talents. For the first time in months, the world seemed rife with possibilities, and Nat felt young and strong and hopeful. It wasn't too late to re-invent himself.

As long as someone like Chloe Burnett didn't get in the way.

He buzzed through a third and fourth cut on the length of cedar before releasing the switch on the Skil-saw and setting the tool on the tailgate.

"Natty?"

Nat glanced up to the porch to find his employer with a tray in her hands and Jean-Claude at her feet, tail wagging.

"Bonjour, Madame."

"I am not so sure about this pie," she said without preamble. "You will stop the work for a minute or two and try her for me?"

Nat's mouth twitched. "It's a sacrifice, Madame, but for you, I'll make it."

He joined her on the wide back porch, solid under his feet where a month ago it had been sagging dangerously. Now, with a view of the creek and the gravel road winding alongside it toward the golden fields beyond, the porch was one of his favorite spots to relax.

Madame Marie set her tray on a wicker table between two match-ing wicker chairs. "The pie, she is French apple," she said. "But dif-ferent than I have tried before."

Nat took her elbow and helped her sit, then inhaled deeply as he took the other chair. His mouth watered. "Mmm. Just out of the oven?"

"Oui. The large one is for you, Natty."

Madame Marie's doubts about her new recipe were just an excuse for some midafternoon company, Nat decided after the first bite. There was nothing not to be sure of about the pie. Tart apples, sweet raisins, a dash of cinnamon and nutmeg, the unexpected crunch of walnuts, a smooth cream-cheese topping melting into the crevices. What was there not to like?

"You've got yourself a winner, Madame," he told her. Then, to be polite, he added, "What does your granddaughter think?"

Madame Marie shook her head. "She has not yet tried the pie." Worry lines appeared across her forehead. "I do not think my Chloe takes care of herself as she should."

"No?" Nat concentrated on his plate.

"This firm for whom she does her architecture. They give her too much of the work."

"Architects work long hours," he said. "Like doctors, lawyers, engineers. I'm sure she knew that going in." But maybe not how the job would consume her life, he admitted to himself, for the first time feeling a twinge of empathy for Chloe.

Madame Marie set her plate on the table between them. "Always she has the aching head. And now this crying! It is so unlike her, Natty."

"She's in there crying?" Nat was astonished. Chloe? The queen of the world? Maybe his words had hit their mark after all.

"Not now," Madame Marie said. "Now, she sleeps. But I worry for her, the way she cried! As if her heart were breaking. I have not seen her cry so hard since the year she was seventeen. When her *papa* and *maman*—my daughter, Colette—were killed in the auto accident."

Nat winced. He knew that kind of ache, though not at the tender age Chloe had felt it.

"And her questions!" Madame Marie said. "They make her grandmother also wish to cry."

"Questions?"

"Such as, 'You know that I love you, don't you, Gran-Marie?' As if she did not say so with every phone call. As if she did not bring me little gifts when she comes to see me. Freshly baked croissants, or *les chocolats,* or the Parisian magazines I cannot find in Pilchuck. As if she did not take the time to visit even when the work is piling high!"

"She just—all of a sudden burst into tears?"

"Oui. I heard her come into the front door and *poof!* She was crying the way she long ago cried for her papa and maman."

Perhaps he hadn't given Chloe credit, Nat thought. He surely had not been kind. The thought made him unexpectedly and inexplicably sad.

"It must have been hard, losing her parents when she was so young," he said. He remembered how difficult it had been for him when his own parents died, both unexpectedly, his father from a heart attack and his mother a few years later from a fast-growing cancer. And he, Nat, had been in his thirties at the time.

He turned his gaze on Madame Marie. "It must have been hard for you, Madame. Losing your child."

"Oui. But we had one another. Bertie and Chloe and I. And we had le bon Dieu." She straightened her shoulders. "Chloe and I still have each other and le bon Dieu. I must remember."

Nat set his fork across his empty plate, then cleared his throat. "Chloe came out to talk to me after lunch, Madame. I may have been…well, insensitive."

"If anyone has lacked the sensitivity, Natty, it is my granddaughter. She is a stubborn girl. Like her grandmother is a stubborn woman." Madame Marie met his gaze frankly. "But I have never seen her act the way she acts with you. I hope you will see that it is the strain of her work and her worries that make her seem rude, mon ami. In her heart, she is a good girl."

Nat was silent for a moment. Somewhere in his conversation with Madame Marie, his twinge of empathy for Chloe had blossomed into compassion. There were those who might consider that a miracle, he told himself, the corner of his mouth twitching in wry humor. Compassion had never been his strong suit.

"I'm sure she is a good girl," he said. "And lucky to have you, Madame."

"We both are blessed."

Did Chloe even understand how blessed? Nat wondered. An hour ago, he would have said no. Now, he was willing to let her surprise him.

CHAPTER SEVEN

By the time Nat figured out what Chloe was up to, it was already too late.

He didn't know it was too late. Not until hours after their trip into Pilchuck late that afternoon to pick up a tube of painter's caulk and a box of truffles.

"Gran-Marie loves a good truffle," Chloe informed him as she settled into the driver's seat of the Sebring and fastened her seat belt. She insisted on driving, and Nat, though he would have preferred to be behind the wheel himself, didn't object.

She pulled away from the house, giving the pile of lumber next to the driveway a wide berth. "The Sweet Shoppe makes their truffles fresh," she went on. "Nothing like the Belgian chocolates we get in the city, but for a town the size of Pilchuck, the Sweet Shoppe does a decent job."

Nat barely refrained from rolling his eyes. Nothing in Pilchuck measured up to what she could get in the city, he was certain.

"Of course I wouldn't expect a man who holds Ding-Dongs as the chocolate standard to know the difference."

His temperature rose for an instant, until he realized she was teasing.

That was his first surprise from Chloe. Teasing? He wouldn't have thought she had it in her.

"Excuse me?" he defended himself, pretending indignation. "For

your information, Ms. Burnett, I happen to be a man of discriminating tastes."

"Mm-hmm." She sounded skeptical.

"I am. Blindfold me, give me a Ding-Dong, a Twinkie, and a
truffle…" Nat paused for dramatic effect. "I'll choose the Ding-
Dong every time."

She threw him a quick, startled glance, as if she, too, was surprised. Then her mouth quirked in an impish grin that reminded
him suddenly of her grandmother. "Truly discriminating, Neville,"
she said dryly.

"All right, fancy-pants," he huffed. "Just how long has it been
since you had a Ding-Dong anyhow?"

"Please!" Chloe shuddered. "Trust me, Neville, one amaretto–
white chocolate cream truffle from the Sweet Shoppe and you'll
never eat a Ding-Dong again."

"One Ding-Dong for you, and vice versa," Nat shot back.

She laughed. That was Nat's second surprise—that a sound of
such utter and pure delight could come out of Chloe.

His third surprise came only a moment later:

"Listen, Nat, I'm sorry if I've seemed rude today," she said
so unexpectedly that he nearly choked on his astonishment. "I'm
probably overprotective of my grandmother. You've got to understand—Gran-Marie's all I've got. Despite what you think, I love her
dearly. Extravagantly. Fiercely."

Passionate words, Nat mused, recovering himself enough to nod.
Perhaps there was more to the snow queen than met the eye.

"And you, Mr. Neville," Chloe added, "have not gone out of
your way to calm my fears."

"About what?"

"About… Well, about anything."

Okay, Nat told himself, the apology *was* a little wishy-washy.
And she had her excuses lined up neatly in a row. She was even sug-
gesting that he bore some responsibility for her rudeness. Still, all in
all, even a weak apology from Chloe was a huge surprise.

"I forgive you. This time," he added, deciding that for the

moment teasing was his best line of defense. "What are you afraid of, by the way?"

She hesitated. "Let's just say you haven't given me any reason to trust you." Chloe slanted an unreadable look in his direction, then returned her eyes to the road. "I still don't know who you are. Why you're here. Why you've agreed to work on Gran-Marie's house for room and board and what amounts to pocket change."

"So you read our agreement."

"What there was to read. It wasn't exactly your standard contract."

Chloe slowed for a car pulling out of a gravel road ahead. They were nearly into town already; they'd passed the intersection where Viewmont Road became Main Street, and Nat could see a traffic signal ahead. One of four in Pilchuck. "The traffic is getting so out of hand," Madame Marie had bemoaned on their first trip into town together. He'd refrained from describing the freeways in L.A. or his recent bumper-to-bumper excursion north on Interstate 5 through Seattle.

"You're not going to tell me, are you?" Chloe broke into his thoughts.

"What? Why I'm doing the rehab, you mean?"

"That would be good for starters."

"I don't know that I can explain it, Chloe." He raked a hand absently through his hair. "I'm a give-me-all-the-facts-and-I'll-make-my-decision kind of guy. I don't take stock with 'signs.' I don't pay attention to my gut unless whatever it's telling me is backed up by solid evidence."

He hesitated, then blurted out before he could think better of it, "Do you believe in God?"

Again, she looked startled. "Yeah. Why?"

"I haven't thought much about God since I was a kid in Sunday school." He didn't know why he was telling her this, he felt foolish enough about it as it was. "But I think I'm here, in Pilchuck, at your grandmother's house, because I'm supposed to be. Because… Well, because God dropped me on your grandmother's doorstep, so to speak." There. He'd said it.

Chloe was silent for a long moment. Then Nat got his fourth surprise.

"Maybe you're right, Nat," she said quietly. And after another moment, "As my grandmother says, le bon Dieu works in mysterious ways."

She pulled into the parking lot of the Coast-to-Coast, found an empty stall, and turned off the engine before concluding, almost as if to herself: "Gran-Marie seems convinced. But then, that's Gran-Marie, isn't it? Once she's made up her mind, she's made up her mind for good. Still…"

Dropping her keys in her handbag, Chloe turned toward Nat and leaned against the door, her expression thoughtful. Her brown eyes searched his face, slowly, thoroughly, as if she were peeling back layers of skin, muscle, bone, brain tissue. As if by looking she could get to the core of him, understand him. Know him.

Ah, but her eyes were deep and lovely! A man could get lost in eyes like that.

Some other man, not Nat. Nat had too much sense to get lost in a pair of beautiful eyes.

Then, before he could gather his wits enough to look away, the sun dipped low and light streamed in at the window, making Chloe's chestnut hair a halo of fire, warming her skin to a burnished gold and her lips to the color of sweet red wine.

Nat held his breath. A fifth surprise, a sneak attack, astonishing and unsettling: He wanted to take Madame Marie's granddaughter in his arms and kiss her senseless.

Chloe's pupils widened. Nat thought for a moment that she too might be holding her breath. Then she dropped her gaze and reached for the door handle. "Let's walk down to the Sweet Shoppe first." Her voice betrayed nothing. "It doesn't stay open as late as the hardware store."

Nat slowly released his breath. So he wasn't immune to the queen of the world after all.

She, however, appeared to be immune to him.

He didn't know whether to feel annoyed or relieved.

• • •

Whew! That was scary, Chloe told herself as she locked the doors of the car from her key ring and joined Nat on the sidewalk, avoiding his eyes.

For a moment there she'd had a vision of herself in the handyman's arms. Scarier yet, she'd rather enjoyed the idea.

It didn't make sense. Then again, nothing about the day so far made sense. Especially since she'd awakened from her afternoon nap rested, refreshed, and headache-free, and she and Nat Neville had been getting along like nobody's business.

He had a sense of humor, for pity's sake! He'd certainly kept that under wraps earlier in the day.

Then there was his confession that he thought he'd landed in Pilchuck because God had dropped him on Gran-Marie's doorstep. That took guts. Most people Chloe ran across who believed in God seemed embarrassed to admit it, let alone admit to the possibility of divine intervention in their lives.

Nat had been self-conscious too, but he'd said it anyway. To a virtual stranger who'd already been antagonistic toward him. On the heels of Gran-Marie's claim that le bon Dieu had guided Nat to her door, she was having a hard time believing he was the threat she'd first imagined. Except to her grandmother's reputation in Pilchuck, of course—which was quite enough, thank you.

Still, the truth was, Nat intrigued her. She couldn't figure him out, pin him down, peg him. He was slippery. Contradictory. A fact that both pushed and pulled her. Who was he really, behind his well-toned muscles and his ice blue eyes and his stubbled jaw? Divine guidance aside, what exactly had brought him to Gran-Marie's door?

"Chloe," Nat intruded on her inner dialogue, "wasn't that the candy store we just walked by?"

She stopped, blinked, glanced at Nat and then at the window next to her. It was crowded with potted plants: trailing ivy, miniature roses, an angel-wing hibiscus with delicate pink blossoms turned toward the light. Buds 'n' Blossoms, a door beyond the Sweet Shoppe.

"Oh! Guess I wasn't paying attention."

"I'll say," Nat teased. "What are you thinking about so furiously?"

Her face grew warm. She wasn't about to tell him she'd been thinking about him. "Amaretto–white chocolate cream truffles," she said, heading for the chocolate store. "I'm buying you a single so we can settle this Ding-Dong thing right now."

"How can we settle the Ding-Dong thing without a Ding-Dong?" he protested, reaching to open the Sweet Shoppe door. "No way. I object. Unfair."

But he didn't protest a few minutes later when Chloe waved a truffle in front of his nose. Two bites and it was gone. "Now do you believe me?" she demanded.

His blue eyes gleamed. And for once, Chloe had no doubt at all that the twitch at the corner of his mouth was the first sign of a roguish grin. "I'm not saying," he said. "Not till you try a Ding-Dong."

She laughed. The teenager behind the counter shook his head, as if he couldn't believe how silly grownups acted sometimes. How long had it been, Chloe thought, since she'd acted just plain silly with a man? Or with anyone, for that matter?

Smiling at the clerk, she picked up her box of mixed truffles from the counter and followed Nat to the door, answering her own question on the way:

Too long. Far too long.

"He thought we were nuts," Nat said as the door closed behind him.

Chloe laughed again. "Little does the poor guy know." For pity's sake, she felt almost buoyant!

No doubt about it, she told herself as she fell into step with Nat. The man could be downright pleasant company when he wanted to be. And so could she.

She came back to earth with a thud the minute she walked past a sidewalk display of wheelbarrows and garden tools into the Coast-to-Coast and found Earlene Boyd behind the checkout counter.

Earlene barely glanced at Chloe, but when her gaze fell on Nat, it stopped, rested, turned speculative. *Click, whir, screak, clank, grind…*

Chloe could almost hear the woman's odious conjectures gather force and start to spin. *Must be lonely in that big old house since Egbert passed… A rich old widow, a handsome fellow down on his luck… It wouldn't be the first time, would it?*

It was a relief to escape down a narrow aisle behind Nat just to get out of Earlene's line of sight. Unfortunately, he knew right where he was going. Left at the rubber bins and garbage cans, right at the wire center between two rows of plumbing supplies, left at the key center, left again at metal molding and trim, and there was the shelf of sealants he was looking for.

The air in the store was stale and dusty, the narrow aisles with their crowded racks almost claustrophobic. But Chloe would gladly have wandered around for another half-hour, sneezing away, if she'd thought Earlene Boyd might disappear from the checkout counter in the meantime.

But Earlene disappearing was about as likely as Earlene admitting she was a gossipmonger, so Chloe followed Nat back through the hardware maze, resigned. Sure enough, there the old biddy was at the front of the store, her beady little eyes darting around until they came to rest on Nat, her gaze lingering as he and Chloe crossed the painted concrete floor to the checkout stand.

Nat seemed not to notice Earlene's critical appraisal, but Chloe was so agitated she nearly knocked over a pyramid of metal toolboxes on an end display. When Nat stepped up to the counter to pay for his purchase and Earlene actually lowered her head to gaze up at him through her eyelashes, Chloe couldn't stand it another minute.

She wasn't leaving this store till every detestable speculation spinning around in Earlene's brain was laid to rest. If Gran-Marie didn't care about her reputation, Chloe did.

She knew exactly how to bring the old biddy around, too. If, that is, Nat was quick-witted enough to catch on and follow her lead. Too bad she didn't have time to let him in on the specifics.

Quickly tugging her ring set from her left hand, Chloe deposited the gold band in her pocket and replaced the zircon on her ring finger. Then, fortifying herself with a deep breath, she stepped up to the counter, threw an arm around Nat's waist, and laid her head against his shoulder.

"Darling," she purred, "you're so good to me!"

CHAPTER EIGHT

This time, "surprise" didn't begin to describe Chloe's effect on Nat's nervous system. "Astonishment" wasn't even a strong enough word.

This time, Chloe shook Nat like a thunderclap. More. Like a 7.5 on the Richter scale.

There he was, standing at the checkout counter at the Coast-to-Coast ready to pay for his tube of painter's caulk, minding his own business, when *BAM!* There she was, hanging all over him, cooing like a dove.

"Chloe!"

"It's so sweet of you to be watching out for Gran-Marie, darling." Her voice dripped honey.

"Darling!" He stared at her in mystification. "What—?"

She jabbed him. Hard.

"Chloe!" he gasped, grabbing her hand reflexively. "What on—?"

"I don't know what I'd do without you, sweetheart," she broke in, at the same time digging her fingernails into the palm of his hand.

He wasn't an idiot. This time he kept his mouth shut.

"You've taken such a burden off my mind," purred Chloe, releasing his hand.

He rubbed dumbly at the five crescent-shaped imprints on his palm. Talk about a woman showing her claws! Those fingernails were dangerous weapons.

"Oh!" Chloe exclaimed.

Now what? Nat wondered, bracing himself.

"Hello, Earlene!" she said.

"Earlene?" Nat followed Chloe's gaze to the well-upholstered, fiftyish cashier standing behind the counter.

"Oh darling!" Chloe waved her free hand toward the woman. "You must've met Earlene Boyd by now. How many trips have you made to the hardware store in the last week alone?"

"A couple, I guess." He did recognize Earlene, though he hadn't known her name. She was hard to forget. Fat-cheeked, beady-eyed, and aquiver with nervous energy. She reminded him of a chipmunk.

"Earlene and her husband own the Coast-to-Coast, sweetheart. Earlene, I'd like you to meet Nat Neville. My fiancé."

"Your fiancé!" Nat and Earlene said in unison. Nat couldn't help snorting—which only got him another dig in the side.

"Chloe!" he gasped, his eyes watering.

"Darling, I know we agreed to keep it secret till we'd picked a date, but really, I just can't keep it to myself any longer. Especially…" Chloe paused and thrust her left arm over the counter, flopping her hand practically under Earlene's nose.

Nat stared. A good-sized diamond flashed from Chloe's ring finger. Had it been there all day long?

"Especially since you gave me the ring, my love," Chloe cooed, fluttering her eyelashes. She turned her attention back to the cashier. "I'm such a lucky woman, Earlene! To find someone so wonderful, who adores my grandmother as much as I do."

"Why, Chloe Burnett," Earlene gushed, lifting Chloe's hand to ogle the diamond. "Goodness, it's enormous!" She gave Nat an admiring glance before returning her gaze to the ring.

"You know how I worry about Gran-Marie being out there on the homestead all alone," Chloe said in a confidential tone. "Especially with the renovation and all. It's such a comfort to know Nat's keeping an eye on things, Earlene. Gran-Marie isn't as young as she used to be."

"Mercy, no!" Earlene said, dropping Chloe's hand.

Nat, for his part, was temporarily struck dumb. The surreal conversation, accompanied by the buzz of a key being cut in the back of the store and the soft whir of a ceiling fan, played like the rumble of snare drums on his nerves.

"Madam shouldn't be rattling around in that big old house by herself the way she's been since Egbert passed," Earlene went on. "And you so busy, Chloe—"

"Nat has a wonderful eye for Victorian details too," Chloe broke in. "And he's a marvel with a hammer and nails, Earlene. Why, even if we weren't engaged, there isn't another soul I'd trust for the renovation."

"Is that so?" Earlene sounded impressed. "So Madam's renovating, is she? And you engaged!" She clucked and shook a finger at Chloe. "Shame on you and Madam for holding out on us!"

"Cat's out of the bag now, though, isn't it? You're the first to know, Earlene."

"Really! I'm honored, my dear. And congratulations." She turned her bright, beady eyes on Nat. "You too, Mr. Neville."

Nat had no idea what Chloe was up to, but now that he'd had a few minutes to recover, he was beginning to see the humor in the situation. Not to mention the once-in-a-lifetime opportunity.

"Call me Nat." He reached across the counter to shake the cashier's hand, draping his free arm over Chloe's shoulder and pulling her close at the same time. "Pleased to meet you, Earlene. You will come to the wedding?"

"Oh, I wouldn't miss our Chloe's wedding. Not after all these years despairing she'd ever find herself a—"

"Nat," Chloe interrupted, her tone a trifle less honeyed, "we can't just stand here and talk poor Earlene's ear off when there's a whole long line of people waiting. Do you need some money, sweetheart?"

"No, I've got it." He slipped his arm from around her to reach for his wallet, glancing over her shoulder as he did. One scrawny old man in overalls stood nearby, chewing on a toothpick and holding a handful of screws. Behind him slouched a teenager with a shaved head and an earring, balancing a broom and a bucket. Hardly a whole long line.

So Chloe was tiring of the charade already, was she? Too bad, Nat told himself. He was just warming up.

"Earlene, you go ahead and take care of these gentlemen behind me while I dig around for some change."

"You take your time, Nat. And don't you worry about talking my ear off, Chloe. You know how I love to chat." She turned to the old man who was next in line. "Afternoon, Packard. You hear the news?"

"Couldna helped it, could I now?" His toothpick waggled as he spoke. "And here I figgered Chloe Burnett for one of them lifelong spinsters. Just goes to show, don't it?" He handed Earlene a dollar bill.

Nat felt Chloe's shoulder muscles bunch up beneath his arm as the old farmer held out his hand to Nat. "Packard Pruitt, Pruitt Berry Farms. Raspberries and cucumbers. This gal picked for me one summer."

"Did she now?" Nat gave the old man's hand a brief shake.

"Yep." The farmer held out his hand to the cashier for his change. "A priss, I told myself first time I seen 'er. Didn't expect 'er to last the week, but she stayed on all season long."

Nat's hand tightened around Chloe's shoulder. Good grief, the old guy talked about her as if she weren't even there. Or at least as if she didn't have feelings.

"This woman is full of surprises, Mr. Pruitt," he said curtly. "Don't sell her short."

Chloe, Earlene, and the farmer looked about as shocked at his words as he felt at having said them. Pruitt stomped out the door and Earlene recovered quickly, but Chloe was going to give herself away in about two seconds unless Nat did something drastic.

And he knew exactly what to do. Before he could think better of it, he swept Chloe into his arms, leaned over, and kissed her. On the lips. Soundly. Right there in the middle of the Coast-to-Coast, in front of Earlene Boyd, a kid with a shaved head and an earring, and a handful of other gawking strangers. As if kissing a beautiful woman in a hardware store was something he did every day.

And oh, what a kiss it was! His lips touched Chloe's, electrical impulses started leaping across synapses, and almost instantly pleasure exploded in his brain. No question Nat's dendrites and axons and neurotransmitters were doing their job.

What's more, she seemed to be enjoying herself as much as he was. For maybe ten seconds.

Then she pressed her lips together in an uncompromising line.

She didn't struggle against him, but Nat released her anyway. He'd never forced a kiss on anyone. He wasn't about to start now.

"Oh!" Now it was Chloe's turn for speechlessness. She couldn't seem to get out more than a sputter, and her face had darkened to a dull red. From embarrassment, or fury? Nat didn't have a clue.

"Sweetheart, I'm sorry, I couldn't help myself." Once again, gazing down at her adoringly, he pulled her to his side. "I'm just so happy you've decided to let the world know. We're getting married!" He turned his eyes back to the cashier, who was practically twitching with glee. "But I shouldn't have done that, Earlene, Chloe's shy about public displays of affection—you don't mind if I call you Earlene?"

"Oh no!" She handed change to the boy with the broom and bucket, barely glancing at him. "Earlene's just dandy."

"On the other hand, when you share a love like mine and Chloe's…" Nat gave Chloe's arm a quick squeeze. "Well, it's hard to keep a thing like that under wraps, Earlene. Know what I mean?"

"Nat! You…you…," Chloe sputtered again.

Nat grinned. He never would have believed it—Chloe, speechless! My, but he was enjoying this!

"Oh yes, I do know what you mean!" the cashier gushed, ignoring Chloe entirely. "All's fair, love conquers all and makes the world go 'round, et cetera, et cetera." She sighed. "And such a pleasure, Mr. Neville—Nat—to meet a man who's not afraid to show his feelings!"

Ha! If only a woman or two from his past could hear that, Nat thought. They'd never believe it.

He slid his hand up and down Chloe's arm, enjoying the feel of her warm skin through the silky sweater. He might as well enjoy it now. He had no idea what she was thinking, but her red-faced sputtering didn't bode well. He had an idea that once they walked out the door, she wasn't going to let him near her again. Ever. Even after he pointed out she'd started the whole thing.

"Darling," Chloe said, finding her voice at last, "don't you think we'd better be getting back?" She sounded a little shaky, but at least her flush had faded from a dull red to a rosy pink. "Gran-Marie's going to be waiting supper."

"We don't want to keep Madame waiting," he agreed, handing a bill across the counter.

"Well, congratulations again, you two," Earlene said, dropping Nat's change in his open palm without counting it. "You be sure and let me know when you've set the date, now."

"Oh, we will." Nat grinned.

"Right." Chloe nabbed the tube of caulk from the counter and put her arm through Nat's. "See you around, Earlene."

But the hardware clerk wasn't quite ready to let them go. "I only hope you know what a lucky girl you are, Chloe, finding a husband at your age," she said. "I read where it's more likely for a woman your age to be struck by lightning than—"

"Earlene," Nat interrupted, taking pity on Chloe at last, "I'm afraid you've made a mistake. I'm the one who's lucky." He turned his most adoring gaze on Madame Marie's granddaughter. "Look at her, will you! She's smart. She's beautiful." He lifted a strand of Chloe's hair to his nose and inhaled. Mmm… Gardenia?

"She smells like heaven," he added, trying not to wince as Chloe's nails dug into his arm. "And she's sweet-tempered as an angel, Earlene."

He met Chloe's eyes, which were flashing in a very un-angel-like way. Maybe he was laying it on a bit thick, but she'd started it. "We're both lucky, aren't we, my love?"

She closed her eyes, took a deep breath, and turned her attention resolutely back to Earlene. "Very lucky. Thank you so much for your good wishes."

She was clearly struggling to be polite to the woman, though for the life of him Nat didn't know why. The more important question was whether or not, once they got out of here, Chloe was going to work as hard to be polite to him. It was hard to imagine. But then Chloe had been surprising him all afternoon.

"Shall we go, sweetheart? We don't want to keep your grand-mother waiting."

Neither of them spoke again until they were back in the Sebring, doors closed, engine running, when Chloe said without looking at him, her tone subdued, "I don't know whether to thank you for playing along with me or be mad as hornets that you played along so well."

The choice was obvious to Nat, but he had enough sense not to say. "Care to elaborate on that?"

"Not at the moment."

And that, apparently, was that.

◆ ◆ ◆

Chloe made the trip back to Gran-Marie's house on automatic pilot, her mind occupied with other unsettling matters.

Like the shock of Nat's arm pulling her close, and the jolt of his steely words to old man Pruitt: *Don't sell Chloe short.*

Like the thunderclap of his kiss.

She gave her head a slight shake, as if she could rid herself of the images that way, untangle and make sense of the feelings. What on earth had she gotten herself into?

And now that she'd gotten herself into it, how was she going to get out?

That one was easy enough to answer. She was only in town another twenty-four hours. For twenty-four hours she could pretend anything. Including that she wasn't the least bit attracted to her grandmother's handyman. How hard could that be, when until the last hour or so she'd despised him?

She'd have to see him again, of course. No way was anyone reno-vating the Smith-Irby homestead without Chloe's input. Without, more specifically, Chloe's supervision. So maybe she hadn't worked on a residential project since her grad school days. That didn't mean she didn't have opinions. She did, after all, have an aptitude for aes-thetics. An educated awareness of space and form, color and light. A refined sense of rhythm and balance, proportion and symmetry.

In a word, Chloe had taste. A quality one could never count on in others.

Sure, Nat Neville had a way with a hammer and saw. But did he really have the "wonderful eye for Victorian details" she'd told

Earlene he had? Did he really understand what made this plane and that angle work? What made that plane and this angle *not* work? She wasn't about to find out after the fact.

She didn't know how she was going to fit in a trip to Pilchuck every week or two to keep tabs on the project, but she was sure she could figure something out. If she got the Vancouver assignment once the Duwamish Hospital renovation was done, for instance, she'd be less than fifty miles away. In the meantime, something would come up.

She took the turn onto Ridge Road with a heavy sigh. If all else failed, she'd just have to learn to get by with less sleep. The problem was, the less sleep she got, the harder it was going to be to stay on her toes around Gran-Marie's handyman. And after that kiss in the hardware store, staying on her toes around Gran-Marie's handyman was paramount.

CHAPTER NINE

Nat leaned back in the passenger seat, arms crossed, and stared out at the fields of grass and knee-high corn streaming by the window.

Funny how just a few hours ago he'd wanted nothing more than for Chloe to shut her mouth. At the moment, on the contrary, he would have paid a great deal more than the proverbial penny for her thoughts. What was going on inside that beautiful head?

He understood why she might be a little miffed with him for overplaying his part. The kiss in particular. The *warmth* of the kiss. She clearly hadn't expected he'd take the charade so far. He'd taken advantage of the situation, no question about it.

On the other hand, what red-blooded male wouldn't have?

Besides, he'd done her a favor by playing along. Especially since she hadn't bothered to give him a clue what their phony engagement was all about. *Especially* considering the claw marks and bruises she'd inflicted.

"All right, Chloe," he finally broke the silence as they approached her grandmother's house. "Enough's enough."

Chloe threw him a startled glance.

"I think I deserve to know what's going on. What was that all about back there?"

"Oh. That."

"Yeah. That."

She hesitated, as if she didn't know whether or not she could trust him with the answer. Nat clenched his jaw. What was it with her anyhow? You'd think he had claws and fangs.

"All right then." She turned off Ridge Road onto her grandmother's long, steep driveway. "It was about…" She hesitated. "I needed your help." Again she stopped, sighed, and then finished, "I was just trying to save my grandmother's reputation, Nat."

"Save your grandmother's reputation! What are you talking about?"

"Talk. That's exactly what I'm talking about." She glanced at him and then back to the gravel driveway. "There's been talk about you and Gran-Marie."

He jumped. "You're kidding!" Then he remembered the conversation he'd interrupted in the kitchen earlier in the day:

I think you should know, people are talking.

Bah. People will talk from here to eternity.

Don't you care what people think, Gran-Marie?

"What kind of talk?" he asked cautiously.

Chloe said nothing for a moment, then answered vaguely, "You know. Wealthy widow, con man…"

Nat let out a low whistle. No wonder she'd been so hostile toward him! "And Earlene Boyd must be one of the people talking," he mused aloud.

She nodded.

"Oh, Chloe. I'd never do anything to hurt your grandmother. Or you. I hope you know that."

She brought the car to a stop behind Madame Marie's lime green Peugeot and pulled the key from the ignition. "That's the thing, Nat. I don't know. All I have to go on is your word. And Gran-Marie's intuition."

"What about your own intuition?"

"I'd rather have facts."

Nat looked out the window, away from the house, toward the line of trees that marked the creek bed. Facts, he wasn't ready to give her. Facts, he still wasn't entirely ready to face himself.

He turned his eyes back toward Chloe and found her watching him. "Nat?"

"Trust me," he said.

For a long moment she searched his face. Then she sighed and reached for the door handle. Clearly it wasn't the answer she'd wanted.

He sat in the car for several minutes after Chloe got out, watched the late afternoon sun set her hair afire as she crossed the yard, noticed the gentle sway of her hips as she climbed the stairs to the back porch.

He saw her eyes as if they still gazed at him—those eyes a man could get lost in. He remembered the feel of her in his arms, and the first uncensored response of her lips to his kiss. He remembered as if he still held her.

Even then, even feeling the swift, sudden kick of desire and a soul-hunger so powerful it was almost painful, even though his longing threatened to sweep him out to sea in its tow—

Nat wouldn't admit to himself that it was too late.

◆   ◆   ◆

Trust him, Nat had entreated.

At this point, Chloe asked herself, what choice did she have? It was either trust him or move in with Gran-Marie for the duration. Something she couldn't possibly do.

The truth was, Gran-Marie had always been a good judge of character. Maybe Chloe didn't trust Nat, but she did trust Gran-Marie. If Gran-Marie trusted Nat, couldn't that be enough? At least to get through the rest of the weekend? They did need to reach some decisions about the house.

It would have to be enough, she decided. For the moment, she would put aside her questions and doubts and concentrate instead on plans for Gran-Marie's renovation. Renovation, after all, was something she knew. Something she could *do* something about.

"All right," she said as the three of them sat down to supper in the dining room, "we've got work to do. Let's talk exterior color schemes."

Gran-Marie looked pleased. "I have the idea or two."

"No drastic changes, I hope." Chloe speared a bite of new potato. "The neutrals you've stayed with all these years are so tasteful, Gran-Marie."

"Non," her grandmother said. "I am ready for the change. Brown is old. I want bright."

"Bright?"

Gran-Marie pierced a forkful of French-cut green beans. "Bright," she said firmly. "The pink of a flamingo, the yellow of a dandelion, and the blue of a peacock."

Chloe wondered if she looked as horrified as she felt. "You're kidding, I hope."

"Sans blague," said Gran-Marie, frowning. "About this house I do not kid."

"You know," Nat offered, his voice soothing, "if you wanted to paint the house in keeping with the style, I've been doing some research."

"Oui? Then you have seen the old houses dressed up like the rainbow." Her frown cleared. "Like the many-colored coat of Joseph."

"Like a circus carousel," Chloe grumbled. "Leave her with some dignity, Gran-Marie!"

Nat cleared his throat. "It's true, Madame, that the Victorians used many colors on their houses, perhaps five or six. To show off the gingerbread and the shaped shingle siding. The porch rails and balusters. The sashes. But to make all those colors work together, they had to mute them. 'Saddening' the colors, they called it."

Gran-Marie shook her head. "I will not have her sad."

The corner of Nat's mouth lifted. "Let's call it soft, then. Mixing a color with a little of its complement grays the tone. Makes it softer. If you want to be authentic, Madame, perhaps you and Chloe could choose a medley of five or six muted tones."

"Hmm." Chloe contemplated the slice of lemon-pepper chicken on the end of her fork. A palette of grayed tones was certainly preferable to flamingo pink, dandelion yellow, and peacock blue. "The idea has possibilities, Neville."

Gran-Marie clapped her hands, her face beaming. "We will get the paint chips soon and find the compromise, Natty."

After supper they retired to the parlor, where Gran-Marie dug out a pachisi board. Jean-Claude jumped up on the chaise longue where he could see the action and settled down on the afghan with his chin on his paws.

"Now," said Gran-Marie, "while we play our game, we will decide what to do with the floor in the vestibule."

"Ugh," said Chloe, rolling the dice. "I know the linoleum's right for the period, but that worn old stuff has got to go. How, is the question."

Nat picked up the dice as Chloe moved her marker around the board. "A heat plate and an old-fashioned wide-bladed scraper to start with. Maybe we can get it up without too much damage to the wood underneath."

"Then what?" asked Chloe.

"I say no more linoleum," Gran-Marie said.

"Perhaps a natural finish on the wood?" Chloe suggested.

"Maybe. Or we could paint it." Nat counted off spaces with his marker, claiming a spot from one of Chloe's playing pieces and knocking it back to the starting position. "The Victorians often painted their softwood floors," he added, as if he hadn't just done a very mean thing. "Spatter dash was a favorite finish."

"Spatter dash?" Gran-Marie picked up the dice and rolled them.

"Just like it sounds," Nat said. "Madame, you could knock Chloe's piece back home with that roll."

"I could knock you back home too, Natty. See there? But this time I will not." Gran-Marie moved a playing piece ahead without taking out either of her opponents. "I would like to hear more about this spatter dash."

"The earliest spatter-dash floors featured dark spots spattered on a gray background," he explained as the play continued.

Gran-Marie shook her head. "I am not so sure about gray on the floor. For the porch, yes. But in the vestibule?"

Nat leaned back in his chair. "You might like the effect of two or more light colors spattered on a darker background. One popular combination was red, white, and yellow on blue."

"Speaking of blue," said Chloe, "It's back to the beginning for you, Neville." She bumped one of his blue playing pieces off the board.

"I would like to see a picture or two," Gran-Marie said, then added smugly, "Oh, and so you know, *mes amis*—this game? He is mine."

"What?!" Chloe and Nat cried in unison. But there was no disputing it as Gran-Marie moved her last playing piece across the finish line.

Nat scooped up the markers and closed the board. "If you hadn't been so intent on knocking me off, she'd never have gotten away with it, Chloe."

"Me?! Knocking *you* off?!"

"Mes enfants! Does it not occur to you that Marie Antoinette Babineaux Delacroix Smith simply has the talent for pachisi?"

"Ha," said Chloe.

"It does occur," said Nat diplomatically.

"Merci, mon ami. Now," Gran-Marie said, "is my nose correct in telling me my granddaughter's bag holds truffles from the Sweet Shoppe?"

"Ha," Chloe repeated. "Do you really think you deserve a truffle after trouncing us so soundly?"

"We do have truffles," Nat said. "If Jean-Claude hasn't sniffed them out and devoured them."

Jean-Claude, hearing his name, looked up, yawned, and settled his head back on his paws. He clearly hadn't been caught up in the excitement of either the game or the conversation.

"I have hope that Jean-Claude's lesson has been learned." Gran-Marie pushed back her chair. "Chloe, ma chère, perhaps you will share your truffles if I can find some mint-flavored cocoa to go with them."

Nat built a fire in the parlor, just a small blaze, and the three of them ate truffles, drank hot cocoa, and tossed around ideas in its rosy glow. Chloe had to admit she was enjoying herself immensely. Thinking about design on the scale of a house was a refreshing change after three years of working on the hospital remodel.

"What do you think for the walls?" her grandmother asked between bites.

Chloe wrapped her fingers around her mug. "Painting would be easiest."

"But wallpaper is more in keeping with the times," Gran-Marie said.

"Stenciling had its heyday during the Victorian era," Nat volunteered. "The library has several books with instructions and period patterns. It doesn't look all that difficult."

Gran-Marie beamed. "C'est bon! We will check these books out, Natty."

At ten o'clock, they said good night and retired to their rooms. Chloe changed into an eyelet-trimmed nightgown and crawled into bed, but sleep was elusive. After all, she'd spent a good part of the afternoon sleeping.

So she tossed and turned and replayed the day. A day full of surprises. A day full of surprising *feelings*, not the least of which was her response when Nat Neville grabbed her in the Coast-to-Coast and kissed the living daylights out of her. Such hunger she'd felt. Such longing!

Maybe she'd been out of circulation too long. Maybe she should say yes to that nice Duwamish Hospital administrator who'd asked her out a couple of times. If she was going to complicate her life by getting involved with a man, a hospital administrator was certainly a better match for her than an itinerant handyman.

On the other hand, Nat wasn't your ordinary, run-of-the-mill itinerant handyman. What he was, she didn't know. But he wasn't that.

It didn't matter, she told herself firmly. Not as long as Gran-Marie was happy. And she was. Chloe hadn't seen her grandmother so carefree, so alive and engaged, since before Gran-Bert had first taken ill. Whatever else he was or wasn't, Nat was good for Gran-Marie.

She tried to remember what the hospital administrator looked like. Tall, slim, brown hair beginning to gray. Blue eyes or brown? She couldn't remember.

No matter. She knew she wasn't going to get involved with him. Or anyone. For one thing, she didn't have time. She'd never had time, as more than one man had told her.

Still…

That kiss had been awfully enticing.

She rolled from her back to her side, drawing her knees up, trying to get comfortable. She rolled from her side to her stomach, pulling the pillow over her head. Finally she rolled out of bed, threw her plush, apricot-colored robe over her nightgown, and crept down the stairs to the kitchen. There was one slice of Gran-Marie's French apple pie in the fridge.

But the light in the kitchen was already on, and Nat Neville, wearing a terry robe over a pair of cotton pajamas, was pulling the pie tin from the refrigerator.

"Wait just a minute," Chloe whispered indignantly. "That piece of pie has my name written on it."

"Oh?" Nat whispered back. "Then why was it calling *my* name loud enough that I could hear it all the way upstairs?"

Chloe closed the kitchen door behind her and said, her voice low, "You sure it wasn't a Ding-Dong calling?"

Nat shook his head. "We never stopped at the market. There isn't a Ding-Dong in the house." He grinned. "But if you promise to share one with me tomorrow, I'll share my pie with you tonight."

"It's *my* pie."

Nat pulled the pie tin closer. "Haven't you heard? Possession is nine-tenths of the law."

"Oh, all right then!" she grumped.

"Can't sleep?" he asked as they sat down at the kitchen table a minute later, each with a slim slice of pie and a glass of cold milk.

She shook her head. "I napped too long this afternoon. You?"

"Have trouble with insomnia. Though I have to say it's been better since I've been working for your grandmother. Oh, speaking of your grandmother—don't you think we'd better tell her we're engaged before she hears it from somebody else?"

"Very funny, Neville. But you're probably right. Knowing the Pilchuck pipeline, the news will be all over town by noon tomorrow. To tell the truth, I'm surprised nobody called tonight."

"Especially all those ladies who've spent years despairing you'd ever find someone," Nat teased.

"A gentleman wouldn't have brought that up," Chloe huffed. "Anyhow, yes. We'll tell Gran-Marie in the morning."

The kitchen door popped open. "Tell me what?" Gran-Marie asked, shuffling across to the sink in her paisley robe and her fluffy slippers.

Nat and Chloe looked at each other. The corner of Nat's mouth lifted. "I think you'd better tell her, Chloe. I'm the type who'd just blurt out that we're engaged."

Chapter Ten

"Engaged!" Gran-Marie whipped around so fast she wobbled. "You mean, engaged to be married?" She clapped her hands. "Le bon Dieu has answered my prayers!"

"Your prayers!" Chloe sat up straighter. "Gran-Marie, what are you talking about? Nat and I only met this morning!"

"Oui. It is a miracle! I thought from the way the two of you spit like cats at each other at lunch today that I would meet le bon Dieu in heaven before I saw you together."

"But—"

"I see now that the spitting was only to hide the sparks between you. But you cannot hide from l'amour, my dear children, can you? Not when le bon Dieu is the one to place the fire between you."

"But Gran-Marie—"

"You have made this old woman so happy, mes enfants!"

Chloe's heart sank. There were actually tears in her grandmother's eyes. "Gran-Marie… You've been praying that Nat and I would…marry?"

"Since the first night I met Natty, I knew he was the one for you, ma chère. Only I did not expect you to know it so soon as this evening. Our God, he is good, non?"

"Madame Marie," Nat said, "I'm afraid—*ow!*"

Chloe winced. "*Very* good, Gran-Marie." Maybe she shouldn't have kicked Nat's shin so hard; all she needed to complicate things any more was a broken toe.

Gran-Marie frowned in confusion. "What is this look on your face, my granddaughter? And, Natty, what is this 'ow'?"

"I was thinking how badly I treated Nat when I first met him," Chloe ad-libbed. "And how wrong I was." She threw him a pleading look. "Nat?"

"My leg," he said, still looking pained. "I've never felt anything like it."

"Not the sciatica?" Gran-Marie sounded alarmed. "Have you strained yourself with your hard working?"

"No, no, nothing as simple as that, I'm afraid."

"Maybe a pinch bug," Chloe suggested. "I hear they're bad this summer. Gran-Marie, would you like this last bite of pie?"

Gran-Marie shook her head. "*Non.* I only came in for a small glass of water. And because I heard voices," she added. "I wanted to see that my guests were well." She beamed. "I did not know how well! *Félicitations,* my dear children. We will have fresh strawberry crêpes in the morning to celebrate."

"What are you *thinking,* Chloe?!" Nat whispered fiercely when they heard the door to Gran-Marie's bedroom close.

"She was so happy," Chloe whispered back helplessly.

"And how do you think she's going to feel when she finds out we've lied to her?"

"Engagements don't always work out. Quick engagements, especially. We'll break up and she'll get over it. In the meantime, she'll be happy."

He looked at her as if she'd gone crazy.

"Why not, Nat?" Chloe chased a crumb around her empty plate. "Unless you've got a girlfriend stowed away somewhere?"

He shook his head. "I don't have a girlfriend, stowed away or otherwise. Which brings up that rock on your left hand." He lifted a quizzical brow.

"Cocktail ring. A zircon, not a diamond." He didn't need to know about the gold band she usually wore with it. She didn't think he'd approve any more than Gran-Marie did.

"And how long do you propose we carry on this charade with your grandmother?" Nat whispered.

She squeezed her eyes shut. If Gran-Marie found out the truth, she'd be so disappointed. And not just that her prayers hadn't been answered either. She'd be disappointed in Chloe.

What's more, she'd insist on telling Earlene Boyd the truth. Chloe shuddered to think what kind of rumors Earlene and True Marie might generate with *that* kind of material. They'd be practically apoplectic with glee.

"We'll have a fight tomorrow," she whispered back. "And break the engagement. But not until right before I'm ready to leave, okay? Let's not ruin the rest of the weekend."

Nat got up from his chair and carried his dirty dishes to the sink without answering. Turning around, he leaned against the counter, crossing his arms, and studied her for a moment. Then he sighed resignedly. "I must be as crazy as you are."

She let out her breath in a *whoosh*. "From the bottom of my heart, I thank you, Nat Neville. So what do you want to fight about?"

Nat shook his head. "I wouldn't worry about it," he said dryly. "I'm sure we'll think of something."

◆   ◆   ◆

Sunday morning and early afternoon passed so pleasantly, Chloe was actually disappointed she and Nat were going to have to spoil the day with a fight. Maybe it was sitting down to breakfast together. Sharing good food, which Gran-Marie had always maintained was a civilizing exercise. True, Gran-Marie's strawberry crêpes were a little hard to swallow, as she'd whipped them up especially to celebrate an engagement that wasn't going to last the day. Chloe didn't like lying to her grandmother, but she did enjoy the three of them getting on so well.

Perhaps it was going to church together that made them so amiable. Sharing a hymnal and a Bible, which was probably even more civilizing than sharing good food. True, the number of old acquaintances who came out of the woodwork to offer their congratulations was disconcerting, but Nat and Chloe both handled themselves, Chloe thought, with aplomb.

It was nice to be back in a church again. She hadn't attended many services in the last few years. God wouldn't begrudge her a little extra sleep on the day he'd purposely set aside for rest, she'd told herself. But the light radiating through the stained glass windows, the sound of voices raised in joyous song, the faint smell of lemon oil from the old wooden pews all conspired to remind her that spirits as well as bodies needed rest and regeneration. Pastor Bob's sermon on the seventh beatitude, too, was particularly apropos.

"Blessed are the peacemakers, for they will be called the children of God," he quoted from Matthew before he began his sermon. He talked about coming to peace with one's enemies as a process, one that required putting aside both one's weapons and one's armor. "Sheathing our swords is not enough. We must throw our swords down," he remonstrated, his face pink with fervor. "We must give up our shields. We must let fall the armor that keeps us from knowing each other and touching each other, mind to mind and heart to heart. To live the life God calls us to, we must be brave."

Both she and Nat had sheathed their swords since yesterday morning, Chloe mused. Perhaps even laid them down. As far as giving up shields and letting armor fall… At least she'd made an effort.

Nat, on the other hand, might as well be welded into his armor. It would take a blowtorch to get anywhere with the man. An amnesiac had more to say about his personal history than Nat did. And as far as expressing his feelings—

But then, he was a man.

Besides, she'd convinced herself it didn't matter who he was. Or what he was. He was in their lives, hers and Gran-Marie's, for a limited time. As long as it made her grandmother happy to have him around, Chloe wasn't going to complain. How could she? He'd done her a huge favor yesterday, and he was playing his part today like a regular Paul Newman.

After church they shared another civilizing meal, ham and sweet potatoes served up with an intriguing array of ideas for the kitchen remodel.

Then, while Nat took Gran-Bert's truck for a quick trip into town to Fairley's Pharmacy and Gran-Marie took Jean-Claude for a walk to get some exercise, Chloe discovered the Jaguar in the carriage house. And knew that she'd been duped. Not just by Nat either. Gran-Marie couldn't possibly be oblivious to a Jaguar in the carriage house.

She wasn't snooping. She'd had a thought that the carriage house might be converted into a lovely apartment. If Gran-Marie was going to hire a maid—or as Chloe was already thinking of her, a companion—wouldn't it be convenient to have her right there on the grounds?

Thoughts of apartments, maids, and companions fled, however, the moment she laid eyes on the Jaguar, a 1998 XKR forest green coupe with a buttery soft, beige leather interior and California plates with current tabs.

The doors and the glove box were unlocked, and Chloe discovered in short order that the car was registered to Nathaniel Carlton Neville at an address in Pacific Palisades. She got the distinct impression that Pacific Palisades was not a low-rent neighborhood.

She sank against the bucket seat, her mind racing. She'd suspected all along, of course, that Nat was hiding something. Nobody she'd ever met was as closemouthed as Gran-Marie's handyman. And no common laborer she'd ever run into could quote from the secretary of the interior's *Standards for Rehabilitation,* or speak even the limited French she'd heard Nat use with Gran-Marie, or drink tea out of a china teacup as if he'd been doing it all his life.

The question now was just how *much* he was hiding. Was he, as her grandmother seemed to believe, simply a broken man in search of healing? Or was he, as True Marie had suggested, a con man, the Jaguar charmed out of the last wealthy widow he'd taken advantage of? The idea made her blood boil.

Don't do this, she tried to calm herself. *You don't know. He could be anyone.* A dot-com millionaire, maybe, retired at thirty-five, renovating old houses as a hobby. A writer doing research. One of those guys in the federal witness protection program. That would explain a thing or two.

On the other hand, what if he was truly dangerous? On the lam from the police or a parole officer? A mental hospital, even? She blanched as sudden realization struck. In the end, there were only two choices. Either Nat Neville was something far different than he was pretending to be—or he wasn't Nat Neville.

What if he wasn't? What if the man who was calling himself Nat Neville had not only stolen a car, but stolen another man's identity?

Chloe thrust the registration back in the glove box and snapped it shut. *You're being paranoid*, she told herself. Still—

He was hiding *something*.

Why hadn't she acted on her intuition? Demanded that he either give her some answers or get off the property? She should have insisted that Gran-Marie let her handle the matter, le bon Dieu notwithstanding. She shouldn't have let Gran-Marie's vague assurances lull her into complacency!

Shivering, she jumped out of the Jaguar and slammed the door. Before she could take a step, she heard the growl of Gran-Bert's pickup. Gravel scattered in the driveway as Nat—or at least the man she knew as Nat—braked to a stop.

Chloe ducked instinctively. She was between the car and the wall, out of his line of sight but also unable to see anything. A door slammed. Footsteps retreated toward the house, hesitated, stopped. "Madame Marie?"

He'd noticed the open door to the carriage house, Chloe realized. The footsteps started in her direction, crunching across the gravel. Even as her brain told her that she was being ridiculous, Gran-Marie was right, the man was perfectly harmless—her heart slammed against her ribs.

"Madame Marie?" he called again. "Chloe?"

He couldn't have been more than a dozen feet and a few seconds away from discovering her when a flurry of sharp, excited barks pierced the quiet of the afternoon. The footsteps stopped again. "Jean-Claude! What is it, boy?"

The wild barking continued unabated. Chloe's heart leapt to her throat. Something was wrong. Jean-Claude never barked that way. And he was always with Gran-Marie.

She rose up enough to peer over the edge of the Jaguar's window.

The little white dog was doing a crazy dance, rushing toward Nat, leaping in the air and twisting around to race away again, then looping back to repeat the sequence, all the while barking insanely.

"Madame Marie!"

Jean-Claude raced away again. This time Nat dropped the bag he'd been carrying and tore after him.

At that moment, it no longer mattered to Chloe if he was Nat Neville or the devil himself. Leaping from her hiding place, she raced out of the carriage house and took off after him, her long legs stretched out in a dead run.

Something more than Nat's evasiveness was wrong.

Something had happened to Gran-Marie.

◆　◆　◆

"Madame Marie!"

Nat slid down the bank of the creek to where the tiny, gray-haired woman sat slumped against a boulder, one hand cupped against her forehead. Her face was ashen.

"Gran-Marie!" Chloe's voice came from behind him, a tumble of dirt and gravel heralding her descent of the slope. The Bichon Frise, meanwhile, paced back and forth in front of his mistress with an anguished whimper.

Nat snatched up Jean-Claude and thrust him, yelping, at Chloe. "Get back, give her room."

Then all his attention was focused on Gran-Marie. He knelt in front of her and gently lifted her hand away from her forehead. "What happened, Madame?"

"Silly… I bent to look at a flower, a pretty little thing…" She gestured vaguely. "And then my feet, they flew out from under me. *Poof*."

"You hit your head on the boulder?" She had a nasty contusion on the left side of her forehead, purple and swollen. His fingers probed her scalp for other injuries, found nothing.

"A little bump…"

"A little bump can be a bigger problem than you know, Madame."

He placed a hand on either side of her face and lifted gently. "Now look at me."

Good. Her pupils were equal, no dilation.

He moved his hands to her shoulders and down her arms, once again probing for injuries. "Do you know what time it is?"

"Afternoon. We had Sunday dinner… Three o'clock?"

Close enough. "Good." He checked her clavicle and moved down to her ribs. "What's the date, Madame?"

"July… Fifteen? Sixteen?"

"What year?" He quickly palpated her hips, thighs, knees, calves. She winced but didn't cry out when his fingers probed the inside of the left knee.

"The year, Madame," he pressed.

"Nineteen… 1996. No, '95."

Nat's heart jumped. "Do you know where you live?"

"1138 Ridge Road, Pilchuck, Washington."

"Good. And your name?"

"Marie Antoinette Babineaux Delacroix Smith," she rattled off. Then, as if confused: "But you know my name, Bertie."

His pulse quickening, Nat's eyes jumped once again to hers. Pupils still equal, no dilation.

"Who's president of the United States, Madame Marie?"

"That actor. Ronnie," she answered promptly. "I know you don't like him, Bertie, but…" She stopped, confusion clouding her features.

"Chloe!" he called over his shoulder. "Is your grandmother taking any medications?"

She hesitated. "I think so."

He frowned impatiently. "Well?"

"Something for her thyroid." She sounded frightened. "Is she all right, Nat?"

"I don't know. What else? Any over-the-counter meds? Aspirin?"

"Aspirin? Yeah, she's been taking aspirin for years, one a day. Something about her heart."

Madame Marie touched his arm. "Bertie?"

"Chloe!" Nat snapped. "Get an ambulance out here!"

"Wha—"

"Now!" Madame Marie's left pupil had suddenly dilated.

Subdural hematoma. He was almost certain. With an aspirin a day for the last three years, severe intracranial bleeding was almost a given.

Please, God.

He hadn't prayed for a long time. Not since he'd decided God wasn't listening. But he prayed now:

Let them get here in time.

CHAPTER ELEVEN

Chloe followed the ambulance all the way to the emergency room in Bellingrath, her foot to the floor, telling herself that if she saw flashing lights in her rearview mirror, she'd just have to pretend they weren't there.

But she covered the dozen miles without incident. In the hospital parking lot she whipped into an empty space, not noticing until she screeched to a halt that it was marked for handicapped use only. She hesitated a moment, then jumped out of the car. It couldn't be helped. All she could do was pray that nobody would need it in the next little while. She didn't have time to go looking for anything else.

By the time she barreled through the doors of the emergency unit, the EMTs were wheeling Gran-Marie across the lobby, feet flying. Nat was barking out orders as if he'd been running an ER for years: "Intubate! Start hyperventilating! Get me a nurse—twenty-five grams of Mannitol. Now!"

The rapid-fire words continued as Chloe stared, open-mouthed. "Who's in charge here? Get me the OR supervisor. Someone! I need a high-speed drill from ortho and a soft-tissue pack. Where can I scrub in?"

"What's going on here?" A large-boned woman wearing a white lab coat, her blond hair pulled back severely, had stepped through the swinging doors into the ER lobby. She stopped in front of Nat and crossed her arms. "And you would be?"

"Nathaniel Neville, M.D. Neurosurgery, UCLA Med Center."

Chloe gasped.

"Fine." The woman sounded unimpressed. "Carrie Evers, OR supervisor, St. Boniface Hospital, Bellingrath. Thank you for your assistance, Dr. Neville. We'll be happy to—"

"Look," Nat interrupted, "I'd love to chat, but I've got a subdural hematoma here. I need an OR ASAP."

"We're not set up for neurosurgery, Dr. Neville. We can have the patient in Seattle in forty-five minutes with air evac—"

"Forget it. I start surgery on this woman in the next ten minutes or she's dead."

Dead! Chloe's knees buckled. "No God, please God, not this, not Gran-Marie," she whispered, clutching at the back of a chair for support.

"I'm sorry, Doctor." The OR supervisor stood like a tank in front of Nat, arms crossed, daring him. "Without hospital privileges I can't allow—"

"Did you hear what I said? If you don't give me what I need, Nurse Evers, she's dead!"

A slight man dressed in scrubs pushed his way past the OR supervisor. Though small in stature, he carried himself with authority. "I'll take responsibility, Carrie."

"It isn't your responsibility to take."

Please God, Chloe prayed.

"I'm the ER supervisor. If a patient dies on my watch and I had a chance to save her, believe me, it's my responsibility."

"And if she dies despite the surgery?" Nurse Evers challenged.

"The doc knows what he's doing, Carrie. I took a CME class from him last year. Best stuff on neurosurgical emergencies I've ever had." The ER supervisor glanced at Nat, then at the EMTs working to keep Gran-Marie breathing. "Look. He does the surgery, the patient has a chance. He doesn't, she dies. Our choice."

No! Please God, no!

"I'm sorry. I still can't authorize the surgery."

"Then I will." He waved a dismissive hand and turned to Nat. "Tell me what you need, Doc."

"A room. An OR nurse. An orthopedic drill."

"I've got the drill and the soft-tissue pack, Doctor," a young woman wearing a nurse's uniform broke in. "And I'll show you where to scrub in."

Nat hesitated briefly, his eyes searching the room and stopping when they met Chloe's. His face was grim. "Pray, Chloe. I'll do everything I can, I promise. You pray." Then he disappeared through the swinging metal doors behind Gran-Marie's gurney.

Please God. Chloe sank into a chair and dropped her head in her hands. *She's all I've got. Please God. Don't let Gran-Marie die!* She prayed the same words over and over, like a mantra, until her heartbeat and her breathing slowed to something approaching normal.

She picked up a tattered copy of *People* magazine, leafed through it without taking notice of anything on its pages, closed it and picked up another. All she could see was Nat's grim face and Gran-Marie on the gurney. All she could think about was Nat in the OR with her grandmother. *Please God...*

For a single moment, when he'd thrust Jean-Claude in her arms and told her to get out of the way, anger had flared like a thunder-flash. Of all the arrogant, high-handed, dictatorial nerve!

Then he'd lifted her grandmother's hand from the ugly bruise on her forehead and started asking questions. In the space of a single instant her fears about who Nat was had melted away into nothing. Handyman, con man, thief—she didn't care. As long as he saved Gran-Marie, the man could be as dictatorial as Napoleon. He could be a handyman or a blue blood, a car thief or a collector, a con man or an upstanding citizen. He could even be an ax murderer. As long as he saved Gran-Marie.

O God, please...

For over three hours Chloe prowled the ER waiting room, unable to sit still longer than fifteen minutes at a time, afraid to leave even for a cup of coffee. *Please God,* she prayed. *Gran-Marie's all I've got. Gran-Marie's all that matters. Please God.*

She tried to distract herself by paying attention to her surroundings: the sharp, antiseptic, hospital smell, the traffic in and out of the emergency room, the quiet murmur and sharp commands of the hospital personnel, the sobs and moans of the frightened and the injured. At one point she even tried to analyze the architectural elements of the ER lobby, but the exercise didn't last long. What did any of it matter when her grandmother's life lay in the balance?

The only architectural feature she cared about in the entire hospital was one set of utilitarian swinging metal doors. She must have memorized every ding and scrape in the ugly things by the time Nat stepped through them, still wearing his scrubs and surgical cap, more than three hours after he and Gran-Marie had disappeared down the hallway. His face was gray with fatigue.

"Nat?" Chloe jumped up from her chair and hurried toward him, searching his face, anxiety tying her stomach into knots.

"She's going to be all right." He took her hands, squeezed them tightly. And sighed as if he'd been holding his breath for hours. "She's going to be all right, Chloe. We got it in time."

"Oh Nat. Thank God!" For the second time in two days, Chloe lost control of her emotions. This time, as the tears flowed down her cheeks, she felt no shame.

◆　◆　◆

Thank God, Nat silently agreed as he folded Madame Marie's weeping granddaughter in his arms. For so much more than Chloe even knew:

For strength, guidance, a steady hand. For ingenuity and illumination.

Most of all, for the chance to perform this one final, spectacular surgery to save the life of someone he loved.

Thank God, who had never stopped listening, Nat realized now—even when Nat had stopped talking.

He didn't know how long they stood there in the middle of the ER waiting room, he and Chloe, arms around each other, Chloe sobbing and Nat doing everything in his power not to join her. "It's over, Chloe," he murmured, stroking her hair, pulling her close, rocking her gently. "She's going to be fine, I promise you. Please don't cry, ma chère."

He knew it was no good telling a woman not to cry, but few things made him feel as helpless. A sagging porch, an engine that refused to start, a brain tumor—those were things he had a chance at fixing. But the things that made a woman cry? Even knowing that Chloe's tears were tears of joy, relief, and gratitude didn't diminish his sense of impotence.

What could he do except hold her? It didn't seem enough, but it was all he knew to do. He had no defenses against a woman's tears. That was the thing. In the face of a woman's tears he felt stripped down, helpless, vulnerable. Only a thin veneer of bravado away from his own tears, which he could not—must not, would not—allow himself to shed in front of Chloe.

He tightened his arms around her, suddenly needing her in a way he had not allowed himself in years to need another person. Words from this morning's sermon echoed in his mind: *We must throw down our shields; we must let fall the armor that prevents us from knowing each other and touching each other, mind to mind and heart to heart. To live the life God calls us to, we must be brave.*

"Chloe," he whispered against her hair. He lifted his head away from her cheek, met her eyes.

He held his breath. Her hair was tangled, her eyes red and swollen, her face streaked with mascara. She was the most beautiful woman he'd ever seen.

"You've got lipstick on your collar," she sniffled. "And mascara smeared all over your face."

She was also the most unexpected woman he'd ever known, Nat thought dryly. "Now that's the pot calling the kettle black," he teased.

She laughed—a thin, watery, but nevertheless joyous laugh that ended on a hiccup. "She's really going to be okay, Nat?"

"I promise."

She started to cry again. Throwing down her shield. Letting her armor fall.

That was when Nat realized that Chloe Burnett, ex-queen of the world, was the person he most wanted to be brave with. That was when he finally acknowledged that as far as his heart was concerned, it was too late.

CHAPTER TWELVE

As for Chloe, by the time she heard the whole story—Nat's story—it was already too late. She knew it the moment she heard the final word.

The first installment she'd already received, from Nat himself. His handling of Gran-Marie's accident, the way he'd taken charge in the ER lobby, his announcement to the OR supervisor that he was *Doctor* Nathaniel Neville.

Not just a doctor, she reminded herself, dabbing at the black streaks on her face in the rest room off the lobby. A neurosurgeon. A *neuro*surgeon!

She'd been right about Nat Neville from the very beginning. And she'd been dead wrong. She'd known all along there was more to the man than good looks and odd jobs, but not in her wildest imaginings had she ever guessed just how much more.

All the pieces that hadn't made sense since the first time she'd met him, from his impersonal inspection of her to the Jaguar in the carriage house, made sense now.

What didn't make sense was Nat the handyman. What didn't make sense was *why*. And it all made even less sense after she heard the second installment of the story.

She was sitting alone in the hospital cafeteria, where she'd agreed to wait for Nat while he showered and changed his clothes. When he'd told her he was always famished after a difficult procedure, her first thought had been to take him out somewhere extravagant, somewhere appropriate to the degree of her profound relief and heartfelt gratitude. But the only place in Tillicum County that fit the bill was twenty miles away. Gran-Marie should be waking from her general anesthesia within an hour or two, and Chloe wasn't going anywhere until she held her grandmother's hand and heard her say, "Bonjour, ma chère!" The Inn at Lummi-Ah-Moo would have to wait.

"So you got to see the doc in action, huh?" The question came from the table directly behind Chloe. A woman's voice, bright, cheerful.

"Did I ever!" a second woman answered. "The guy was just incredible! I mean, brain surgery with a high-speed orthopedic drill and a general surgery soft-tissue pack? I wouldn't have believed it if I hadn't seen it with my own eyes."

Chloe sat up straighter.

"Must have been a trip to be in the OR with him," the first woman said.

"You got that right. You know, I've worked with plenty of surgeons who think they're gods, or at least God's gift to the human race—"

"Haven't we all," the first voice broke in dryly.

Nurses, Chloe thought. Could they be talking about Nat and Gran-Marie?

"Well," the other nurse answered, "Dr. Neville just might qualify, the miracle he pulled off in there."

Chloe turned around as a pretty Asian-American in a nurse's uniform laughed and commented, "Just don't tell him that. He might believe it."

"Excuse me," Chloe said, "I couldn't help but overhear. It's my grandmother who had the brain surgery. One of you was the OR nurse for Dr. Neville?"

A pert redhead with her hands wrapped around a mug of steaming coffee nodded. "That would be me."

"I just wanted to say thank you." Tears stung Chloe's eyes once again.

"Don't thank me, honey. Thank Dr. Neville. Your grandmother's one lucky lady."

"Lucky" wasn't the word Chloe would have used, especially when she heard the rest of the nurse's story: Nat had performed his surgery on Gran-Marie in a hospital where he didn't have privileges, in a state where he wasn't licensed, and without the benefit of neurosurgical instruments. If he hadn't bullied his way past Nurse Evers, earned the support of the ER supervisor, improvised with what he could find— her grandmother would be dead.

That wasn't luck, Chloe told herself as the women picked up their empty trays and made their way through the maze of tables. The OR nurse had called it right the first time. It was a miracle.

Her heart made a funny little jump when she saw Nat push through the cafeteria doors a few minutes later. Freshly showered and back in his usual jeans and T-shirt, he looked like her grandmother's "Natty" again, not the exhausted, gray-faced surgeon who'd walked out of the OR less than an hour ago.

She hurried across the room, calling his name.

"Chloe. How are you doing?"

"I'm all right." She frowned. For someone who'd just pulled off the miraculous feat his nurse had described, Nat seemed remarkably low key. Shouldn't he be bouncing off the walls about now? Celebrating? Unless—

"Everything's still fine?" she asked anxiously.

He pulled a pair of trays off the stack and slid one her way, eyeing her warily at the same time. "You're not going to burst into tears if I tell you yes?"

He was teasing her. A good sign. "I think I'm about cried out."

His mouth quirked. "Then yes. Everything's still fine." He handed her a dinner plate and placed two on his own tray, side by side. "It's hard on me when you cry like that, Chloe."

"Hard on *you!*" She squinted her swollen, bloodshot eyes and covered her blotchy cheeks with her palms. "Look at this face, Dr. Neville. Does 'train wreck' come to mind?"

"You're exaggerating." His eyes danced. "A run-in with poison oak, maybe." He reached for the salad tongs and loaded one of his plates with greens. "And what's this 'Doctor' business, by the way?"

"You'd prefer 'Saint Natty,' maybe?" Chloe teased, placing a much smaller portion of greens on a salad plate. "It wouldn't be out of line, from what I hear." She added more soberly, "The hospital's buzzing about what you did for Gran-Marie, Nat. I don't know how I'll ever be able to thank you."

Again, that twitch at the corner of his mouth. "I've got an idea."

She flushed. "If you're insinuating—"

"Chloe, I'm shocked!" His blue eyes glinted. "I'm not insinuating anything. I thought perhaps, by way of thanking me, you might help me design a kitchen and a couple of bathrooms for your grand-mother's house."

"What?!" Chloe nearly lost a plum tomato in the canister of blue cheese dressing.

"I said—"

"I heard what you said, I just couldn't believe I heard it! In the first place, you're surely not going to keep up the handyman act! After this?" She waved her arm to indicate the hospital, Gran-Marie, the surgery.

"I have a contract with your grandmother, Chloe."

"You don't really think Gran-Marie should be thinking about a bed-and-breakfast now!"

"I understand it still may not have sunk in, but your grand-mother's going to be fine."

"But—"

"A little weak on her left side, maybe. I'll know better in a couple of days. But therapy should take care of that. Once she gets out of the hospital, there's no reason she has to cut back on her normal activi-ties."

"Normal, yes, but—"

"Is this the fight we're supposed to be having tonight?" Nat broke in as he ladled gravy over a healthy portion of turkey and mashed potatoes. "So we can break our supposed engagement?"

"No, it is not. This is serious, Nat."

"I know it's serious. Let your grandmother make up her own mind, Chloe. Don't take that away from her. Now are you going to have that last piece of lasagna, or is it mine?"

She sighed. "It's yours." She meant both the lasagna and the argument, and she knew he knew it. What else could she do? Hadn't she promised Gran-Marie that she wouldn't interfere with the bed-and-breakfast as long as they found someone to help her?

And didn't she owe Nat her grandmother's life?

"So you'll help me design the kitchen and baths?" He snagged the lasagna.

"Help? Dream on, Neville." She dished a serving of corn chowder into a bowl. "I'm the architect around here. If you're lucky, I might let *you* help *me*."

Nat grinned. "Fair enough. I certainly wouldn't let you loose on a brain."

"Very funny. And by the way, back to my grandmother." Chloe raised her chin defiantly, expecting him to object. "I'm moving in with her for a while."

Nat looked surprised, but he didn't object at all. "Great. I think you should. But what about your job?" He slid his tray toward the cashier.

"What do you mean, you think I should? I thought you said she was going to be fine."

"She is. But you know she'll love having you around. The job?"

Chloe pulled her wallet out of her purse. "Mine and his," she told the cashier, gesturing toward Nat. They made their way to a table in a quiet corner. "Like I said," she finally answered his question, "the project's winding down. My job captain can handle the walk-throughs with the contractors. And if I have to, I suppose I can make it to Seattle a couple of days a week."

"And after this project?"

She set her tray on the table. "Vacation, leave of absence, I don't know." She tossed her head impatiently. "You ask an awful lot of questions for a man who's dodged every single question I've asked in the last two days."

Nat took a seat across from her and reached a hand across the table. "I'd like to say grace. Do you mind?"

Another dodge, Chloe thought, but she took his hand and closed her eyes. Prayer was beginning to feel like a habit again. A good habit.

"So what's it all about, mystery man?" she challenged when he was done. "Are you going to tell me or not?"

It looked, at first, as if he wasn't. He lifted his hands, long fingers splayed, and stared at them. Studied them, as if his past and future were recorded in the lines and creases of his palms, as if the veins carried something more than blood. Sensitive fingers, Chloe noted, wondering why she hadn't noticed before. Delicate bones for a man.

"Nat?"

He dropped his hands and picked up his fork. "Not much of a mystery anymore, is it?"

"Why a UCLA Med Center neurosurgeon goes to work as a handyman for a little old lady in Pilchuck, Washington? Nah. No mystery."

"I told you. God dropped me on your grandmother's doorstep. I know it for certain now."

"You mean because you were here to save Gran-Marie's life?"

"No. Because she was here to give me back mine."

With that provocative statement, Nat began the final installment of the story, the part that filled in all the blanks and completed the puzzle for Chloe at last. It was a long and convoluted explanation, full of medical terms like "arrhythmia" and "premature ventricular contractions" and "fibrillation," but the upshot of it was that Gran-Marie had been right all along: Nat had come to Pilchuck to heal.

Not that his heart condition would ever be cured entirely, he said, but he was learning that he could manage it. This last month with her grandmother had helped him understand how. " 'Work for the hands, food for the belly, and a place to lay your head at night,' is the way Madame put it to me," he said.

He hesitated, and with his next sentence Chloe knew why. Some of that armor was falling away, and it couldn't have been easy. Not for a man as self-contained and sure of himself as Nat Neville was. "Important things," he said, "but not as important as your grandmother's companionship. Her acceptance. Working for her has given me the chance to explore my interests and abilities. Old and new."

In other words, Chloe thought, food, rest, and work for the soul as well as the body. A sudden sense of envy gripped her. Or maybe it was longing. For all those things that Nat was getting from Gran-Marie and she wasn't, simply because he was there and she wasn't. *But you're going to be,* she reminded herself. *At least for a little while.*

"Is renovating houses old or new?" she asked.

"Old and new. My father was a carpenter. I worked with him ten summers of my life between semesters. Renovating old Victorians in San Francisco. The city has a few," he teased.

"So you didn't learn everything you know out of books, after all," Chloe said. "I've been such a prig, Nat. How did you stand me?"

"I didn't. Not until your grandmother coaxed me into giving you a chance to surprise me."

"And have I?"

"Pleasantly." The corners of his mouth lifted. Both corners, Chloe noted, pleased.

"Not nearly as much as you've surprised me," she said. "Starting with those recitations from *Standards for Rehabilitation* and *West Coast Victorians* and the *Pilchuck Post.* A photographic memory, I presume?"

Nat nodded. "A boon in med school, believe me."

"Med school!" Chloe shook her head. "Talk about surprise, Nat! I'll never forget the way you took charge when we found Gran-Marie down by the creek this afternoon. Let alone in the ER when we got to the hospital. And especially in the OR—even though I only heard about it secondhand."

"Yes." Nat used his fork to move the food around on his plate without picking anything up. "The surgery…" He looked up. "I'm sorry it had to be your grandmother, Chloe. Sorry she had to go through the trauma of the accident, I mean, for me to get my life back. On the other hand, I think it had to be her. Someone I care about."

"Get your life back?" Chloe stopped with her soup spoon halfway to her mouth. It was the second time he'd used that phrase. "What do you mean, exactly?"

His expression told her he'd rather be talking about something else. Anything else. But he answered hesitantly, "I was…stuck. Back there at the point seven months ago when I walked out of surgery for the last time. Until today, that is. Feeling so angry and so lost I didn't know what to do.

"I'm not stuck anymore, Chloe. I got a chance to say good-bye. To let it go. Performing that surgery on your grandmother this afternoon was the highlight of my career. I could never top it. And I don't need to."

Understanding finally dawned. "You're not going back to surgery."

"No. I can't manage the PVCs if I stay in surgery. As long as I stay away from caffeine, stress, and excess adrenaline, the condition isn't life-threatening. Otherwise… Well, you get the picture. Stress and adrenaline is what neurosurgery's all about."

Chloe was silent for a moment, thinking about the things Nat hadn't said but she was certain were true. That his job had been everything to him. That in his mind, his job was his identity. That when his doctor had told him he needed to quit surgery if he wanted to live, leaving felt as much like a death sentence as staying did.

"I'm sorry, Nat. So what are you going to do now?"

"Finish the work on your grandmother's house and see what happens. I've got time. I don't need money. I might just decide I like living in Tillicum County."

"Gran-Marie would like that." Chloe pushed her plate away. "And speaking of Gran-Marie…"

Nat looked at his watch. "You're right, we should get back up to recovery. I imagine you'll want to be with her when she wakes."

"Don't you?"

"I most certainly do." He stacked their plates and stood, looking around for the busing station.

"Nat?"

"Hmm?"

"About that fight we're supposed to have?"

His head jerked around. "Yeah?"

She took a deep breath. "Do you think we could put it off for a few more weeks? Since Gran-Marie's in a sort of weakened condition?"

Nat's teeth flashed in the first full-fledged smile Chloe had seen from him. "I think that's an excellent idea…my love."

It was crazy, but that was the moment, not thirty-six hours from the time they'd met for the very first time, that Chloe knew it was too late for her heart. Nat Neville held it securely in his hands.

And if Gran-Marie's handyman thought they were only pretend-engaged, he had another think coming. Because the queen of the world was going to convince him otherwise.

After all, she had Gran-Marie's prayers and le bon Dieu on her side.

POSTSCRIPT

The wedding, dear reader, was a gala afternoon garden affair in mid-summer, a year to the day after Chloe had first found Nat driving nails in Gran-Marie's siding. Nine months after she'd cleaned out her desk at JJ&M to go into business with him as the Tillicum County Historic Design and Rehab Company. Six months after Nat had removed the zircon from her finger and replaced it with a half-carat princess-cut diamond.

Pastor Montgomery Bob of the Pilchuck Church of Saints and Sinners performed the ceremony on the front lawn of the old Smith-Irby homestead, which had found new life, in Madame Marie Antoinette Babineaux Delacroix Smith's capable hands, as the Brambleberry Bed-and-Breakfast Inn.

Earlene Boyd was heard to whisper to True Marie Weatherby at the reception, just moments before Nat and Chloe stuffed Ding-Dongs in each other's mouths—politely, graciously, with nary a crumb falling to Jean-Claude, who gamboled about their feet like a little white lamb—"I knew he was more than a handyman the first time I laid eyes on him."

To which the hairdresser was heard to gush in reply: "And I knew he was the perfect man for our dear Chloe. Isn't it just too romantic for words?"

MORE ABOUT PILCHUCK

Want to keep up with life in Pilchuck? Read **PILCHUCKLES**! Published periodically both online at www.barbarajeanhicks.com and as a free e-mail newsletter, Pilchuckles features articles "written" by the eccentric characters of Pilchuck, Washington, depicted in the romantic comedies of Barbara Jean Hicks. The e-zine is edited by Barbara's alter ego, Pilchuck's own Bobbi Jo Wicks.

Back issues are available at www.barbarajeanhicks.com; follow the link to the Pilchuckles site. To receive the newsletter at your e-mail address, send an e-mail to bjhicks@ix.netcom.com with the subject head "Pilchuckles Subscribe."

ACKNOWLEDGMENTS

Special thanks to Bill Hicks, brother, carpenter, and contractor *extra-ordinaire;* to architects Keith Howell (Keith Howell Design, Seattle) and Sue Lang (Clark/Kjos Architects, Seattle); and to Allen R. Wyler, M.D., Medical Director, Neuroscience Services (Swedish Medical Center/First Hill, Seattle). Thanks also to Celeste, Eric, Helen, Kevin, and Pam for your support and invaluable input.

You rock!

HOME FOR THE HEART

Shari MacDonald

*To my ya-yas, Valerie Master and Angie Conibear-Sander,
from Princess Aspartame. (That's uh-SPAR-tuh-may, to you.)
Sing it, girls!*

CHAPTER ONE

Flynn stretched one bony, sun-browned arm behind her neck and scratched at a swollen mosquito bite on her left shoulder blade, fighting to keep her balance on her bike's banana seat. Despite the generally lazy feeling that saturated the day, she was in a decided rush. Thankfully, it was a short ride from her grandparents' house to her destination, Kenilworth House. But then, every place in Snow Hill was a short ride from every other place. That was just one of the things that made it a thirteen-year-old city girl's summer paradise.

Flynn pedaled hard, her dark braids catching the air. Summer had arrived at last at Maryland's Eastern Shore, and she wasn't about to waste a single precious moment of it. Far too soon the store windows would be filled with back-to-school signs, and she and her brother, James, would be sent packing: back to their quarreling parents and the noise and dirt of the city. But for now, there was only Snow Hill, the prettiest little town in New England, or anywhere else as far as she was concerned. And the people she loved were there: Gran and Gramps; their oldest and dearest friend, Virginia Kenilworth ("Virgie" to Flynn and her family); and, more often than not, the dreamiest boy on the planet—Virgie's grandson, Charlie.

Flynn pedaled faster at the thought of the teenager, her feet following the lead of her heart. At sixteen years old, a whole three years older than she, Charlie was everything Flynn figured a boy should be. Tall and slim but quite strong. Thick, dark hair that held just the tiniest bit of a wave. Gray eyes the exact color of mist, which sometimes gave her the eerily pleasant feeling that they were pulling her into their depths.

The sun beat down on her shoulders, bathing Flynn in warmth and comfort. It was almost like being in the presence of an old friend.

She leaned into the corner of Churchill and Market, knowing that she'd have to hurry if she was going to catch Charlie at home before he made plans for the day. There was a distinct possibility that he had already made his way down to the river's edge. Almost daily, he took advantage of the good fishing in the black waters of the Pocomoke, which conveniently ran through his grandmother's backyard. Flynn knew that if he was already out on his battered old canoe, angling for largemouth bass or bluegill, it would be next to impossible to lure him back to shore.

As she pedaled, Flynn kept her eyes on the road. So focused was she on keeping her balance on the turn, she nearly ran straight into the figure that suddenly appeared before her.

"Whoa, there, squirt!" The older boy laughed and stepped out of her path just in time.

"Charlie!" Flynn slammed back on her pedals and took a gulp of air.

"You almost flattened me." His expression was stern.

Flynn stared at him, her eyes widening. "I'm sorry," she said, truly repentant. She couldn't stand the thought of Charlie being angry with her, and it wasn't just because she wanted him to take her to the beach.

"All right then." He flashed her a bright smile. "All's forgiven. Where are you off to in such a hurry?" Charlie began walking down the street in the opposite direction from where Flynn had been headed.

"To your house," she said breathlessly.

"Really?" Charlie considered this. "To what do Grandmother and I owe the honor?"

"I want to go to the beach," she said bluntly. "And you're going to take me. No one else will."

"I see." The corners of Charlie's mouth turned downward, and he placed one hand on his chin. "When you put it like that, I don't see how a guy could possibly refuse."

"Oh, *Charlie!*" Flynn giggled.

He stopped dead in his tracks, a stricken look on his face. "Unless, of course, he'd already made other plans."

"Aw, Charlie, do you mean it?" Flynn swallowed hard. He was probably going somewhere with that horrible Jennifer who had been hanging out with him and his friends lately. There was something seriously wrong, Flynn felt, with a girl who was all big hair and red lips. She doubted Jennifer even knew how to fish.

"Well, as a matter of fact, I was on my way to ask a certain young lady if she would join me…"

Flynn's face fell.

"…for a canoe ride!" Charlie laughed as Flynn shrieked and grabbed his hand.

"You mean *me,* Charlie, don't you?" she cried. "Say you do!"

"Well, of course. You know you're my best girl." He reached out and tweaked her nose. "But I don't see any reason why we shouldn't go to the beach instead of taking a canoe ride."

"Yeeesss!" Flynn flung one hand triumphantly in the air.

"Come on, brat," he chuckled. "Let's go ask your grandparents' permission."

"Oh, they already said it was okay, Charlie." Flynn grabbed his hand and began to tug. "Let's go get your car."

"All right, all right," he agreed. "But let's at least check in at your house before we go. I want to know what time they expect you back."

Flynn rolled her eyes. "Oh, all *right.* Honestly, Charlie, sometimes you are such a *grownup!*"

Charlie gave one unruly braid a tug. "Yeah, well," he said. There was sadness in his voice that Flynn did not understand. He didn't much sound like he enjoyed being an adult, she thought. "I'm afraid none of us can stay a kid forever."

◆   ◆   ◆

Flynn worked her way down the seashore, dragging her clamming rake behind her, listening carefully for the sound of the tines scraping against a shell. Whenever she heard a scratching noise, she dug through the mud, shook it loose, and caught the clam in her rake's basket, throwing back all those clams that were less than one inch in diameter.

With each new discovery, she let out a loud *whoop* and signaled wildly to Charlie, who was reclining in a sand chair about fifty yards away, reading *Beowulf* for a summer literature course. Each time, he smiled broadly and waved her on, urging her to get the full bushel Assateague State Park allowed each visitor to collect in a day.

They had been there for less than two hours when she saw Gran and Gramps approach. She recognized their matching round figures from a couple of hundred yards away. It would have been hard to miss them, huffing and puffing their way across the sand. A split second later, she realized that the thin figure several feet behind them, moving more slowly and accompanied by one of the pastors of their church, was Virgie.

Flynn wasn't surprised to see Virgie in the company of the youth pastor. She knew Virgie to be a godly woman, and it was during one of her regular visits to Kenilworth House for afternoon tea that Flynn herself had made the decision to follow Christ. Virgie had been helping her to learn about the Bible, and about God, ever since.

No, Flynn didn't think it odd that Virgie was with Pastor Kurt. What she couldn't figure out was, why had this odd group followed Charlie and her to the shore?

For one crazy moment, Flynn thought that she must have done something terribly wrong and that they were coming to punish her. But that didn't make any sense. She couldn't remember doing anything that would incur her grandparents', or anyone else's, wrath.

Caught up in his book, Charlie didn't notice Flynn's Gran and Gramps until they were nearly at her side. Then he climbed awkwardly to his feet, looking startled and concerned.

Instinctively, Flynn started toward him. But before she could take more than two steps, her grandfather had placed a firm grip on her arm.

"Wait here, child," he said softly.

"But Charlie—," she began.

"Charlie is going home with Virgie, dear." Gramps rested one gnarled hand on the crown of Flynn's head.

"But why? We just got here!" Flynn tried to wrest her arm away, but Gramps's grip was like a vise.

"I'm afraid Virgie has some bad news for Charlie," Gran said in a low voice, as Gramps started to lead her away. "He needs to be with family now."

Frantically, she twisted in his grip, seeking out Charlie. The pastor had put one arm around the boy's shoulders, and Virgie was shaking as she spoke to him.

Flynn froze.

At first Gramps pulled impatiently at her arm. Then, seeing the stricken look on her face, he stopped and knelt beside her.

"Sweetie," he said, "there's been a terrible accident. Virgie just got the call. You know that Charlie's parents, as well as his aunt and cousins, were traveling to China, where his uncle was working this summer?"

Flynn nodded mutely. She remembered that Charlie had been disappointed not to be going with his family. But he had agreed to stay home, take a summer class, and look after Virgie.

Gramps gave Gran a troubled look. She nodded for him to continue.

"I suppose it's best if we tell you. You're going to find out anyway. The plane went down, sweetheart. It doesn't happen very often, but planes do crash, you know. Charlie's entire family was lost. He and Virgie have only each other now."

Flynn's heart ached for Charlie. She wanted to run to her friend, but what could she say that could possibly make a difference? It had to be a mistake. People didn't die just like that, did they?

"Come on with us." Gramps urged her onward. "That's a good girl. Leave Charlie with Virgie for now. There will be plenty of time to talk to him later."

As they made their retreat, Flynn helplessly watching the scene unfold behind them while being dragged away, she couldn't shake the horrible feeling that things would never be the same for Charlie and her again.

CHAPTER TWO

Fifteen Years Later

"Oh, don't be such a stick-in-the-mud, Romy." Flynn Kelley abandoned her packing efforts long enough to cast a pleading glance at her closest friend. "Come to Snow Hill with me this weekend!"

Romy Vandenberg stretched lazily from her position on Flynn's bed and wiggled her bare toes, her lacquered nails winking at her expensive footwear, banished to a corner of Flynn's bedroom in the brownstone the two women shared.

"Blah-*blah*, blah-*blah*, blah-*blah*. Snow Hill *this*, Snow Hill *that*." Romy opened and closed her thumb and forefinger in imitation of a jabbering mouth. "You've been yammering on about this obscure little *hamlet*—"

"It's a village, Shakespeare."

"—this obscure little *village* for as long as I've known you. That's what? Three years now."

"Two and a half," Flynn corrected her, turning back to her half-filled Louis Vuitton case. "It only *feels* like three."

"Ah. Good. Insult me." Romy nodded. "*That'll* motivate me."

"Poor baby. So maligned." Flynn pitched a rolled-up sports-sock ball over her shoulder, narrowly missing her roommate's head of tousled red hair. "Some producer you are. You'd think you'd show some interest in the location." To Flynn's surprise, Romy had approved Kenilworth House as a project for their cable television program *Home for the Heart,* based solely on the photos Flynn had submitted several months earlier. She was eager to be assured that her friend and producer did not regret her decision. "Believe me, it's worth the trip. Snow Hill has a historic district that's to die for."

As the host of *Home for the Heart,* a popular historic-home-renovation program, Flynn had earned an extensive and devoted fan base. One that embraced both men and women, yuppies and blue-collar workers. Romy's talents had played no small part in her considerable success. "History like you wouldn't believe," Flynn continued to gush. "Charm galore. Seriously, you'll *love* it."

Romy rolled lazily onto her stomach. "Honey, I've already agreed to let you take this little on-air jaunt down memory lane, so you can stop with the hard sell. If you love it, I'll love it. I trust your judgment. For the most part."

"Gee, thanks."

"Seriously. I don't need to experience this little slice of Americana firsthand to know it'll be great television. Anyway, you go up there every month. That should be enough torture for both of us.

"Once again, thanks for your enthusiastic show of support," Flynn grumbled.

Romy gave a deep sigh and sat up on the bed.

"Tell me again why I'm supposed to care about this place so much?"

"Because *I* care about it, and you're my best friend." Flynn abandoned her task and dropped to the opposite corner of the bed, her curls tickling her cheeks. Though there was a seven-year difference in their ages—Flynn was a mature twenty-eight, Romy a playful thirty-five—the two women considered themselves peers and had developed a spirited, sisterly relationship during the time they had worked and lived together.

"It's just got so many great memories for me. All the times when Gramps took James and me canoeing, and Gran made snicker-doodles and lemonade."

"And Opie would drop by to see if you wanted to go visit his pa and Barney down at the station."

"Har, har." Flynn's dark eyes narrowed to slits. "Perhaps you'd prefer to have a host for the program who wasn't so all-American? Maybe the girl-next-door angle isn't working anymore?"

"Okay, okay. I'm sorry." Romy threw up her hands. "*Do* go on."

"Never mind. It doesn't matter. Really." Flynn stood and scooped up a handful of delicates from the top drawer of her polished Queen Anne bureau. "You don't have to come, Ms. Party Pooper. I'll get you out to Snow Hill soon enough." Flynn couldn't help but grin. She'd long dreamed of getting her hands on Kenilworth House. Romy was being particularly flexible, penciling the historic landmark into the schedule before the project was even approved by the state.

More than fifteen years earlier, Kenilworth House had been added to the list of more than one hundred certified historic homes in Snow Hill's historic district. This meant a landmark review would have to be completed before any renovations were begun. Flynn had been working on the process for months, hoping that they'd be able to tackle the project for the upcoming television season, and it was beginning to look as if she just might get her wish. She'd heard in the last week from one of her sources that the approval of her designs was imminent. With any luck, the historic landmark review committee would finalize their approval in the next couple of months, and her team could get started on the upgrades to the estate.

"You're welcome to stay there anytime, you know," Flynn told Romy. "Virgie always tells me that she has extra room, if I ever want to bring a friend."

"Yeah, well she should start charging you rent. You're there often enough," Romy said. "You practically live there half the time."

"Yeah." Flynn slipped a pair of canvas tennis shoes into one zippered pocket of her bag. "Maybe one of these days I'll live there for real." She mumbled the last sentence under her breath.

"What? What does that mean?" Romy demanded, jerking up to sit ramrod straight. "What are you talking about? Do you know something you're not telling me? Oh my word! Are you planning to quit and move off to the middle of nowhere? And just when the ratings hit their highest point yet! You can't *do* this to me, Flynn! Think of my career! Think of the crew!"

"Cool your jets, Rom." Flynn lowered the top of her suitcase and mashed it down with one fist, gauging how much room she had left in the small bag. "I have no immediate plans."

"So, what's up then?"

Flynn tried to find the right words to explain. Her work was fulfilling. She was passionate about it, even. Still, she couldn't help but dream of a day when she wouldn't be bouncing from city to city, when she'd have an actual, real-life home complete with gardens and children and—God willing—the love of her life.

Romy fluffed one of Flynn's goose-down pillows and dropped it behind her back, against the antique Shaker headboard. "Ye-es?"

"I hate to say anything. It's terribly tacky."

"Spill it," Romy demanded.

"Oh, all *right*." Flynn chewed on her lip. "The thing is, Virgie has hinted to me, on more than one occasion, that she'd like me to live at Kenilworth House one day. That is, after she's gone. I've offered to buy it from her—goodness knows I should be able to afford it by now—and to let her keep living there for the rest of her life. Take care of her, sort of, even though I wouldn't actually be living there yet. But she's stubborn, you know." She threw Romy a speaking glance. "Like some other people I know."

"Do tell." Romy batted her tawny lashes.

"Anyway, she's mentioned—several times in the last few months, in fact—that she won't live forever and that she'd love to see me living there after she's gone."

"You're kidding! I smell an inheritance coming!" Romy arched her graceful brows.

"Don't be crude, Romy."

"Crude, schmood. What did you say?"

"What do you think I said?" Flynn crossed to her wardrobe and pulled a holey gray sweatshirt from the top shelf. "I told her that as far as I was concerned, Kenilworth House would be empty without her, and I refused to talk about a day when she wouldn't be living there."

"Oh, Flynn." Romy flopped back against the stack of pillows. "Where did I go wrong?"

"What are you talking about? I care about Virgie, not her house!"

"Sweetie, you can deny it all you want, but we both know you're interested in both. Now, don't get your feathers in a bunch. Clearly, you're far more interested in the woman than the property, but one doesn't necessarily exclude the other. What? Don't look at me like that. I'm only being practical. Maybe she had something she was trying to tell you." A light filled her eyes, turning them a lighter shade of hazel. "Maybe she's going to leave the house to you in her will!"

"What?" Flynn spun on her. "You're kidding, right?"

"You mean the thought seriously hadn't occurred to you?"

"I just thought she meant I could buy it from her." Flynn felt her cheeks flush. "Or maybe she was just, you know, trying to be sweet. That she meant it as a compliment or something. Or maybe she was *baiting* me. She's not above trying to get a rise out of someone. I've seen her do it a hundred times before. Anyway, I honestly didn't try very hard to figure out what she meant. It didn't seem that important."

"Hmm. Could be an inheritance," Romy insisted. "Although, there's that rotten grandson of hers to contend with. What was his name again?"

"Charlie the Horrible," Flynn said, sounding grim.

Romy shook her head sadly. "Parents can be so cruel."

"Ha-ha. Sarcasm doesn't become you." Flynn made a face. "It's not his *real* name, sap. It's sort of my pet name for him. His real name is Charles Kenilworth. Don't pretend you don't remember."

"Ooh. A *pet* name you say?" Romy drew up her knees and draped her arms around them. "Sounds yummy."

Flynn scrunched up her face. "Stop it. I've told you before, there is nothing *yummy* about Charles Kenilworth. Unless you have a taste for rat stew. He's a rodent, pure and simple."

"Now, don't beat around the bush, Flynn. Tell me what you really think."

"Honey, you *don't* want to get me started." Flynn rifled through her T-shirts, selecting one white and one navy.

"Maybe I do. I mean, I know you consider him Enemy Number One. But was what he did really *that* bad? I still don't quite get it."

Flynn tossed in the shirts, slammed her suitcase shut, and gave the zipper a violent yank. "Please. What *didn't* he do?"

"If you prefer."

"Seriously?" Flynn felt herself becoming increasingly agitated. She couldn't remember the last time she'd discussed the subject. She hadn't felt comfortable talking about Charlie to anyone since his parents had died.

"Seriously." Romy leaned back against Flynn's headboard, tucked her legs under the weathered quilt, and settled back against the shams. "Tell me a story, Ma."

"There's no story," Flynn insisted. "I'll admit, Charlie *was*, as you imply, a very attractive boy. And, yes, I may have had just the teensiest crush on him." Flynn tried her best to sound detached, but from the look on Romy's face, she could tell she was failing. "There's no accounting for taste at that age," she sniffed.

"Details," Romy demanded.

"We've covered this before," Flynn began, but the look Romy gave her stopped her in midprotest. "Oh, all right. He was handsome, I guess. I mean, he was no Johnny Depp or Matt Dillon."

"Sweetie, you're dating yourself."

"Well, regardless. He was a looker, I'll give him that. And sweet. At least at first. Even though I was a good bit younger, he always took the time to hang around with me. Not many teenage boys could be bothered to do that."

"Uh-huh."

Flynn looked up to find Romy smirking.

"Now, don't give me that look," Flynn warned. "It wasn't like that. At least, not at the end. You know the summer I turned thirteen," she said unevenly, "Charlie's parents were killed in a plane crash." She began to pick nervously at the loose threads of her favorite quilt.

Romy grew serious. "I remember. How horrible!"

"I know." Flynn stared down at her hands, noticed what she was doing, and hastily dropped the fabric between her fingers. "After that, Charlie changed. He wasn't the same boy anymore." She drew a steadying breath. "Virgie took her son's death awfully hard. But she had Charlie to take care of, and she had to keep going."

"That poor boy."

Flynn shifted nervously on her upended suitcase. "Well, yes. It was terrible for him. But there's no excuse for what he put Virgie, and everybody else, through afterward." She sucked in her breath.

"He was just a hurting teenager, though, wasn't he?"

Flynn shook her head. "Virgie tried to love Charlie through the tragedy; she really did. Everyone did. But he wouldn't have any of it. He was angry, rebellious, and defiant. Virgie was devastated. She needed Charlie's love as much as he needed hers, even if he wasn't willing to accept that love. But he wouldn't take it. Or give it."

Romy leaned forward and rested her arms on her knees, giving Flynn a thoughtful look. "You make this whole thing sound personal."

"It *is* personal. Charlie hurt Virgie an awful lot, and I love her. She's like a second grandmother to me. And since my own grandparents died—what is it now, eight years ago?—she's meant more to me than ever. I can't stand to see her hurt!"

"It sounds like he hurt you, too."

"Well, he did, if you must know. Is that what you've been doing—trying to get me to admit it?" Flynn knew that she sounded like a pouting child, but she couldn't help herself. "After he went off the deep end, everything changed. Gran told me I couldn't go see Virgie anymore. She didn't really explain; I didn't understand what was going on. Years later Gran explained that she, Gramps, and Virgie had been worried about what kind of influence Charlie would be on me. He'd gotten so wild. And they didn't trust the new friends he started hanging out with. He was a teenager, running with a rough crowd. As rough as a crowd gets in Snow Hill, I guess."

"So help me, I'm picturing the Sharks and the Jets."

Flynn gave her a halfhearted smile. "No one explained why I couldn't go see Virgie, so I took matters into my own hands. I decided to go over and visit Virgie. I've told you this before, haven't I? Well, anyway, on the way I passed a group of guys smoking behind the guesthouse. One of them saw me and grabbed me by the arm. They started to argue real loudly about what they should do with me so I wouldn't rat on them. Charlie came back just then and yelled at them, and they scattered. But he wouldn't talk to me about what happened. He just walked away." Flynn struggled to maintain her composure. There was no point in losing herself in her feelings for a boy who had forgotten her long ago. A boy who no longer existed.

"Virgie saw me crying and made me explain what had happened. The next day Gran and Gramps sent me back home to D.C. I didn't get to go back to Snow Hill until after Charlie was long gone. That was three full, long years later. Gran and Gramps came out to see us a few times in the meantime, but it wasn't the same." She spun on her heel. "I needed Snow Hill. I needed the people I loved: Gran and Gramps, Virgie. I wrote Charlie a letter, asking him to talk to Virgie and my grandparents about letting me visit Snow Hill again. But he sent the letter back. Unopened."

"And you still haven't forgiven him." It wasn't a question.

"Don't be silly. I've forgiven him." Flynn shifted uncomfortably, turning away from Romy's compassionate gaze. She knew what was expected of her. "I just haven't *forgotten*."

"Right." Romy's nod was unconvincing. "I guess that's your business." She shrugged.

Flynn turned back to the window, seeking out the city lights. "You don't think I'm being, you know, harsh?"

"Of course I think you're being harsh." Romy said. "But," she added brightly, "I love you anyway." She paused. "You about done there?" she said at last, jerking her chin toward the suitcase.

Flynn stared blankly at the bag. Her mind was spinning. She had no idea what she'd just packed. "I guess."

"Then let's blow this Popsicle stand. We both need a distraction. If I'm not mistaken, we have just enough time to get something sinfully fattening for dessert before hitting a movie. And if you're *reeeeeally* nice to me, I may just pack a bag tonight and come with you tomorrow, after all."

Flynn's spirits lifted the slightest bit.

"Perfect!" she said. "Remind me to pick up something sweet for Virgie. I'm worried about her. She's looked a little peaked the last couple times I've been to see her. I think she's worried about Charlie."

"You're kidding. Still?"

"Oh, about a year ago he ended up with custody of a daughter he

fathered back during his rebel years. The girl is giving *him* grief now."
The irony pleased Flynn, though she didn't dare admit it aloud.

Romy leveled a curious look at her. "How come you're privy to
all these private family details, anyway?"

Flynn shrugged. "Charlie lives in Philadelphia now, but Virgie
tries to keep in touch with him. For some reason, she likes to tell me
about him." She rolled her eyes. "Goodness knows why."

"I suppose she has her reasons."

"Mmm."

"Like maybe she wants you to know that he's not as bad as you
think, Flynnie." Romy scooped up her black, square-toed boots from
the corner and jammed first one foot, then the other into their gap-
ing mouths. "I mean, it sounds as if he's turned out to be a decent
enough guy. He's raising his daughter, after all. That's a good sign,
right?"

"Maybe. And I wish him all the luck in the world, as long as he
stays in Philadelphia, where he belongs." Flynn grabbed her handbag
off the top of her vanity. "Now, come on. Let's go."

She was slipping her leather jacket over one shoulder when the
phone rang.

"I'll get it," she called to Romy, who was heading to her room to
claim her own coat. "I'm right behind you." Flynn grabbed the
portable receiver. "Hello?" she said in clipped tones, eyes flickering to
her watch. They'd have to hurry if they were going to catch an early
show.

"Hello, Flynn?" a stiff voice said as she shoved her right fist
through one armhole.

"Yes?" Something in the man's tone made Flynn stop dead in her
tracks.

"This is Charles Kenilworth." A sense of foreboding overwhelmed Flynn. She could think of only one reason for him to call her.

"I'm sorry to bother you at home, but—"

"Virgie," Flynn almost whispered. "Has something happened? Is
she all right?"

"No, I'm afraid she's not," Charlie said, but his voice betrayed no
emotion. "She's very sick. I understand you were planning on com-

ing to see her this weekend. But Grandmother is asking to see you now. I think it's important that you come tonight. For her sake."

Flynn already had her packed bag in hand. Panic at the news of Virgie's condition battled with petty feelings of irritation. *What's that supposed to mean? 'For her sake'? As if I wouldn't want to see her simply because I love her?*

"Don't you worry, Charles." She forced out the words evenly. "I'm on my way."

CHAPTER THREE

Flynn sped down Market Street toward Kenilworth House, shifting shakily and blinking back the tears that, to her frustration, would not stop rising to her eyes. Although Romy had offered to drive, Flynn had insisted upon manning the wheel for the three-hour journey to the historic beachfront community on Maryland's Eastern Shore, grasping at the one thing she felt she could still control in her suddenly topsy-turvy world.

"Everything's going to be okay," Romy murmured for perhaps the hundredth time.

Flynn refused to be soothed. "You don't know that, Romy," she snapped. "Virgie's an old woman. Anything could happen."

"That's true," Romy agreed. "But God's in control, right? That's what you've always said, anyway."

"I know, I know," Flynn said miserably. *So, if you're in control, God, don't let anything happen to her, okay? You gave me Virgie as an anchor in this world, and I'm not ready to let go of her yet.* "I just can't bear the thought that I might lose her."

"Sweetie." Romy patted Flynn's free hand, her fingers warm and strong around Flynn's cold, shaky ones. "Virgie's no spring chicken, you know," she said gently. "You're going to lose her one of these days."

"I realize that." Flynn sounded nearly as testy as she felt. "But 'one of these days' doesn't have to be today, now does it?"

"Well, not necessarily," Romy said. "She's not in the hospital, so maybe it's not as bad as you think. Still, it might be a good idea for you to prepare yourself for the worst, just in case."

An uncomfortable silence fell over them as Flynn withdrew her hand and made the final turn down the driveway to Kenilworth House. With one fluid motion, she downshifted her cherry red Miata, cranked the key counterclockwise, and grabbed for the door. Before Romy could say another word, Flynn was out of the car and hurrying toward the grand entrance.

The house was painfully short on modern conveniences, one of the primary reasons Virgie had agreed to let Flynn update it, but long on beauty. With its forest-colored shutters, contrasting against the milky exterior, and its intricately worked gingerbread trim, the classic Victorian looked like one of the expensive miniatures available at upscale hobby shops. Only the general shabbiness of the house, which had received only the barest of maintenance attention since the mid-1800s, kept it from being the perfect model of Gothic Victorian architecture.

God, please don't take Virgie now, Flynn prayed silently as she surveyed the shabbiness. *Not when I'm so close to restoring her home to its glory and to making changes that will make her life so much easier in so many ways.* But Flynn knew it was a lie, and she realized that God knew it too; she wanted Virgie to stay alive for no one's sake but her own.

Without even stopping to knock, she threw open the front door and sprinted up the stairway toward Virgie's bedroom, calling out a halfhearted greeting as she ran. Though the older woman's energy and strength had waned in recent years, she'd rebuffed Flynn's recent suggestions that she move her bedroom down to the main floor, preferring her cozy suite on the second story with its view of the dark, swirling Pocomoke River and the surrounding thick cypress.

On clear days in Snow Hill, Virgie generally left her windows open wide well into the evening, the better to catch the occasional whiff of salt air from the Atlantic, ten miles to the east. As she stepped through the heavy oak door, Flynn noticed that tonight all three windows were tightly secured, leaving the room stuffy and uncomfortable, not at all the way Virgie customarily kept it.

Fighting the urge to throw open the windows, Flynn paused and took quick stock of her surroundings. Her attention was immediately caught by the room's central piece of furniture, the ancient canopy bed that had been in the Kenilworth family for generations, and, more important, the woman who occupied it.

Throughout Flynn's life Virgie had been round and healthy. In another person who lacked Virgie's inherent dignity, such a build most certainly would have been considered "dumpy." In Virgie's case it simply gave her the appearance of additional character. Now Flynn barely recognized her friend. She was startled to see how Virgie's health had deteriorated in the four short weeks since she'd last visited her; it seemed impossible that someone could lose as much weight as Virgie had in such a brief time. A month ago Virgie had appeared remarkably, and oddly, slender. Tonight she looked pitifully withered. Her cheeks were drawn, her once-pudgy fingers knobby against the faded quilt draped across her shrunken frame. Worst of all were Virgie's eyes. Usually clear, they were now dull as she stared into the distance at something only she could see.

A couple totally unfamiliar to Flynn stood at Virgie's side. The woman was young, twenty-five years old at the most, and her fine, fair hair just hit her slender shoulders. Flynn watched as she first adjusted Virgie's head on the pillow, then held a blue plastic cup with a straw in it in the air in front of Virgie's mouth and urged her to drink.

The man stood close by, carefully watching and tacitly approving each act of kindness. He appeared to be several years older than his golden companion, perhaps thirty years old. His face was somehow childlike, yet at the same time worn; still youthful, but with the first few wrinkles spreading out like tiny *W*'s from the corner of his deep-set gray eyes. His hair, too, was like a child's: dark and thick and tousled, in desperate need of combing. Yet his height and bearing clearly communicated that he was indeed a mature man; his shoulders were broad, and he had to hunch over slightly to catch every syllable the woman beside him was uttering.

The man turned and saw Flynn standing in the doorway. In a

moment, recognition registered on his face, even as Flynn made a conscious effort to appear impassive.

"Flynn," he said coolly, the childlike openness and the look of compassion he'd held for Virgie draining from his sculpted features. "Thank you for coming." As when he had spoken to her on the phone, he kept his voice low and void of emotion. Virgie did not stir.

Flynn moved forward, but the man took several long, quick steps, meeting her at the door before she could ease into the room. Laying one hand on her arm, he steered her into the wide, dark-paneled hallway, pulling the heavy door shut behind him with a solid click.

"Charles." She gave him a severe nod, holding her arm stiffly in his grip. "Thank you for calling me."

"Grandmother insisted." The way he said the words left no doubt in Flynn's mind that he would not have called her if Virgie hadn't been coherent enough to demand it.

"I'm glad she did." Flynn carefully extracted her arm from his presumptuous hold. "Please tell me what happened." A second door slammed shut somewhere in the distance, and it registered that Romy was probably bringing in their overnight bags.

"Apparently Grandmother has been sick for some time." Charlie spoke slowly and laboriously, as if doing so were somehow a burden.

"Sick? In what way?"

"It's cancer."

Flynn closed her eyes and imagined herself back at her apartment, being teased by Romy, unaware of the news that lay just ahead. If only she could go back in time several hours, several days. How good and simple and peaceful everything had been just hours earlier. Why had she not appreciated it?

"It doesn't look good," Charlie added unnecessarily. Averting her eyes to avoid his gaze, Flynn looked down at the floor and noted, to her surprise, that in his haste to get to Kenilworth House, he had pulled onto his feet two different colored socks: one charcoal, one a deep blue. This evidence of Charlie's humanness at first startled Flynn, then irritated her. She had no desire to feel pity for this man. He was no friend to her.

"Why isn't she in the hospital, for heaven's sake?" she snapped. "I don't know what you're thinking, Charles, but Virgie needs medical treatment. If you're such a doting grandson, then why aren't you and your girlfriend, or whatever she is, taking decent care of her?"

Charlie arched one thick, dark eyebrow at Flynn.

"Why aren't you doing more than feeding her chicken soup?" Flynn sputtered lamely.

"You must understand, my grandmother is very ill." His voice was stiff.

"Well, *obviously.*" Flynn glared at him, her anger rising. "Which is why I insist that she go to a hospital at once! There must be something they can do. Clearly, she needs to see her doctor."

Charlie dragged one hand across his stubbled chin. "I assure you, she has already seen her doctor. Many times since the beginning of the year, I've just learned. Grandmother called me this morning, and I flew down immediately. I've been piecing together what's happening ever since. Apparently she's known about her illness for months, but she's chosen to keep it from everyone until now. The very end."

Flynn realized that he was probably just repeating what the doctors had told him, but she glared at him as if he were responsible for the prophecy.

"I suggested she go back to the hospital tonight, but she refuses. Perhaps you'll have better luck, since the two of you are obviously so close. What's the phrase? *Thick as thieves?*" His dislike of Flynn was nearly palpable, though for the life of her, she could think of no reason for it. After all, she was the one with reason to dislike *him.*

"Months?" Flynn stared at him. "But she never said anything to me!"

"So you're not as close as all that? Imagine my surprise." Charlie did not even attempt to hide his disdain.

Flynn felt her cheeks burn. "Oh, and I suppose she told *you?*"

Charlie looked at her sharply. "If you were really so close with my grandmother, you'd realize that she does things in her own way, in her own time."

"And this is her way and time? Telling us that she's sick only after she's...she's—"

"On her deathbed?" Charlie said harshly. Flynn cringed. "Apparently it is."

She shook her head. "I don't believe it. This can't be happening."

"I assure you, it is." Charlie turned back toward Virgie's door. "She specifically asked to see you tonight. I realize it's late, but if you would be so kind as to speak with Grandmother for a few moments, I would be grateful."

Flynn stared at him, weighing the cost of telling him what he could do with his gratitude.

"I'm here, Charles," she said, carefully measuring out each word, "because I love Virgie very much. I am not, despite what you have deluded yourself into thinking, here as any favor to *you*. I assure you, you couldn't keep me away from Virgie when she's hurting if you tried."

The look he gave her made it perfectly clear that he *would* very much like to try. However, apparently thinking better of it, he simply gave another crisp nod and led the way back to the room. Flynn carefully stayed several steps away, determined not to let him seize her by the arm again.

Upon entering the suite, she quickly noticed another figure she'd missed the first time around. A slim young girl with dark hair and even darker eyes stood just beyond the bed, her back against the wall. Nervously, she watched as the blonde, who Flynn now realized with chagrin was a nurse of some sort, took Virgie's vital signs. The activity had apparently roused the older woman, because when Flynn entered this time, Virgie noticed her immediately.

"Ah, there's my other girl," she said in a creaky voice, apparently making an indirect reference to the adolescent beside her. "Come here. Sit beside me."

Flynn obeyed, carefully perching at Virgie's side.

"Well, what do you think, my dear?" Virginia said weakly. "How do I look?"

"Frankly, Virgie," Flynn said truthfully, "you look like death warmed over."

Charlie cleared his throat. Casting a quick look in his direction, Flynn saw a man who looked as if he wished desperately he could interrupt but didn't quite dare.

Virginia smiled weakly. "Honest to a fault," she said. "That's just one of the reasons I keep you around."

"Yes, well, I'm afraid *you* haven't been too honest with *me*, dear." Flynn squeezed Virgie's hand lightly. Beneath her fingers, Virgie's skin was cool and loose, the bones of her hand more prominent than ever. "How long have you been sick?"

Virgie's dull eyes suddenly flashed. "Long enough to have thought through exactly how I wanted to spend my last days." There was finality to her tone.

"You could have told someone," Flynn suggested in a quiet voice.

"And have you and Charlie moping about, getting all sentimental and macabre on me? No, thank you." The old glint was back in Virgie's eyes. "Although it might not have been such a bad idea after all, having the two of you here together. But there's time enough for that later."

Flynn stared at her. Virgie really *was* far-gone. The woman wasn't even coherent. She threw a glance at Charlie, who appeared equally disturbed by Virgie's statement.

"Well, dear, we wouldn't have had to be as morose as all that," Flynn said brightly. "Maybe we would have just liked to be here, to give you the support you needed while you were sick."

"You've already given me everything I've needed," Virgie insisted. "And now, I'm going to return the favor."

"Sorry?"

Virgie's fingers pressed lightly against Flynn's. "The time has come to tell you something important. I've been considering this matter for years. I want you to do something for me, dear." She peered over Flynn's shoulder. "You, too, Charlie."

Charlie stepped forward obediently. "Anything you say, Grandmother." He laid one hand on her bony shoulder.

"I want you two to go to my roll-top desk in the library. In the top left cubbyhole, there's an envelope with papers in it. Go down and read them, then come back up here to see me."

Charlie shook his head. "Is this about business, Grandmother?" he asked. "Because if it is, I'm sure it can wait. It's much more impor-tant that you—"

"Don't you argue with me, Charles Simon Kenilworth!" Virgie barked.

"Yes ma'am." Charlie caught Flynn's eye and jerked his head in the direction of the hallway. Perturbed at being thus summoned, Flynn got up to follow him.

"We'll be right back." She planted a quick kiss on Virgie's well-creased brow, then reluctantly turned away. "What's this all about?" she hissed as she followed Charlie to the door.

"You think I know? I thought you were the one privy to all Grandmother's ridiculous plans." He stepped out of the room and started down the hallway without waiting to see if she followed.

"Her *what?*" Flynn hurried after him. "I suppose you are referring to the renovations?"

"If that's what you call this plan of yours to tear up my Grandmother's house for the benefit of an audience whose taste in programming could reasonably be questioned, then, yes. I'm referring to your 'renovations.'"

"I—," Flynn sputtered. "You—"

Charlie continued to stalk away. "I really don't think this is the time to discuss your plans for my family home. Or your motivation in implementing them. If you don't mind, I'd like to get this little errand over with and get back to Grandmother."

How very devoted of you, Flynn thought acidly, but her concern for Virgie was stronger than her irritation, and she determined to bide her time. Charlie Kenilworth was right about one thing at least: There would be a better time to talk about her work at Kenilworth House.

She kept her eyes trained on Charlie's back as he stormed toward the library. It was odd to see him playing the devoted grandson after all these years. She knew that Virgie still loved Charlie dearly; Virgie had always spoken highly of him, even during his most rebellious years. But she had told Flynn too of the heartbreak she experienced in not being closer to her grandson. Though Virgie had forgiven him for his youthful transgressions, he had never been able to fully accept that forgiveness, and their relationship had been strained ever since.

So what was his angle? Flynn had a hard time believing he was there solely out of concern for his grandmother. Obviously, his nose was out of joint about the plans to feature the house on *Home for the Heart.* Well, that was just too bad. She and Virgie had an agreement. It was none of his business, anyway. It wasn't as though it was *his* house!

By the time she got into the library, Charlie was already rifling through the desk. Roughly, he pushed one stack of papers aside in order to access the shelf Virgie had specified.

"That's it. There." Flynn pointed at a large manila envelope.

Charlie cast her a withering glance. "*Thank* you."

"You're *wel*come."

He jammed back the tiny metal brackets holding down the envelope's flap and pulled out a thick stack of papers.

"What is it?" She peered over his shoulder without actually touching him.

"It's the last will and testament of Virginia Grace Kenilworth." His voice was grim. "This can't be good," he muttered.

While Charlie scanned the papers, Flynn's mind raced, spinning wildly back to Romy's earlier prediction. Surely Virgie couldn't have left *her* the house? Regardless of her plans to restore it? If that were true, Charlie would certainly—and, even she had to admit, quite understandably—go ballistic.

She stepped back involuntarily, watching as Charlie's face reddened.

"What does it say?" she almost whispered.

He threw down the papers and scowled at her. "Please. You expect me to believe you really don't know?"

"I don't 'expect' anything when it comes to you, Charles," she said, hearing the tiredness in her voice. "But I assure you, I *really* don't." Her eyes flickered in the direction of the papers. "What is it?"

"Here." He thrust them at her. "Read for yourself. I'm not an attorney, but I believe I have a fair understanding of the language. It appears you and I will be *partners* after my grandmother's death."

"Excuse me?" Flynn looked at his offering as though it might somehow poison her. "What sort of partners?"

"Co-owners, if you will." Charlie's lips formed a grim line. "Of Kenilworth House."

Flynn lowered herself into Virgie's desk chair, her fingers grasping the reassuringly solid wooden armrests.

"Congratulations, Flynn," Charlie spoke in a low, angry voice that Flynn heard as if from a distance. "It appears you've gotten exactly what you've wanted all these years. But I think it's only fair to warn you that, as my grandmother's closest remaining blood relative, I intend to fight you every step of the way!"

Chapter Four

"You think I planned to inherit Kenilworth House? Is that it?" Flynn looked up at Charlie, resenting his six-inch advantage in height.

"I don't think it," Charlie said evenly. "I *know* it."

Flynn took a deep, calming breath and leveled her gaze at him, feeling her strength return. Whereas the news of Virgie's illness had deflated her, Charlie's accusations were quickly reviving her customary verve. "You know, you are such a—" She took a deep breath, searched for the appropriate word. "You are so...so—"

"Very eloquent." Charlie's lips twisted in mockery. "But I'm afraid this little oration of yours is going to have to wait until a later date." He turned back toward the sweeping stairwell.

This time, Flynn was determined not to let him walk away. She stepped into his path and set her small feet on the weathered hardwoods as solidly as a mule.

"Excuse me." He glared at her, waiting for her to step aside.

"No, excuse *me,*" Flynn said in a tone that bore no trace of real apology. "I hate to be blunt at a time like this, but *what,* exactly, is your problem?"

Charlie looked at Flynn as if she were a pesky mosquito he would like to swat." I think you know what, or who, my problem is. My grandmother has been taken in by a moneygrubbing, media-loving, cable television *celebrity* who cares only about what this property can get her. Never mind that my grandmother is a sick, elderly woman who shouldn't be making decisions like this at this point in her life. Never mind that this property has been in my family for generations. Never mind that it's all I—or my daughter, for that matter—will have left of our family once Grandmother is gone. Never mind that we may not *want* modern conveniences like Internet access and dishwashers and multiple stainless-steel ovens, and all those other absurd contraptions you are obsessed with adding to the historic homes you supposedly 'improve'!"

"I don't 'improve' them!" Flynn stamped her foot and instantly regretted the way it made her look and feel like a small child. "I *renovate* them. It's not the same thing at all. And if you hate me so much, what are you doing watching my show?"

"I don't *watch* your show." For a split second, Charlie was at a loss for words. A first, to the best of Flynn's knowledge. "I'll admit, I may have stumbled across it once or twice."

"Uh-huh."

A hard muscle twitched along Charlie's jaw line. "Enough to know that you're kept yourself busy manipulating people's dreams all over the country. You can have any house you want to work on. Why do you have to live here, with my daughter and me? Why don't you go 'play house' with someone else?"

"Whoa!" Flynn held up one hand in protest. "I can assure you, you're the last man on earth I have any desire to 'play house' with! Who said anything about me living here with you? "

"It's right here, in a note attached to the will, if you'll take a look." Charlie flipped through the pages. "It is Grandmother's desire that we both live on the property."

"Well, *that's* not about to happen! You couldn't pay me to live anywhere near you!"

"That's a relief!"

"We don't even live within five hundred miles of each other. And we're not about to start now, just because Virgie's had a whim to ask us to!"

"I should say not!" Charlie shook his head almost violently.

"Good."

"Good."

"Fine."

"Fine."

"Then it's settled."

"It certainly is." The two exchanged uncomfortable looks.

"So, I guess we can agree on one thing at least," Charlie said finally.

"That's something." Flynn stared at her shoes. What else, after all, was there to say?

"All right then." But Charlie didn't sound relieved. "So, what are we going to tell Grandmother?"

Flynn jerked her head up. "Oh, goodness. I hadn't thought of that."

"She sent us down here for a reason. She's looking for a reaction. She's going to want us to agree to her plan."

"But it doesn't make sense. Why would she want us to share the house in the first place?"

"Does it really matter why?" Charlie folded his arms across his broad chest. "Would it make a difference? Are you changing your story?" he asked, sounding suspicious.

"Of course not!" Flynn glared at him.

"Well, then, there's nothing to discuss. I propose that we simply go along with what Grandmother says. No matter what comes out of her mouth, just smile and nod."

"What? Are you crazy? We already agreed that we have no intention of sharing the property."

"And we won't. But saying so to Grandmother will only upset her at a time when she should be kept as calm as possible. Is that what you want, Flynn? To upset her?"

"You know it's not," Flynn said, indignant. He was trying to bait her, but it wouldn't work. "Or at least, you *should* know by now what kind of a person I am. I would never knowingly hurt Virgie."

"Then there's something else we can agree on." Charlie's lips twisted into something that Flynn barely recognized as a smile. "We won't question the will. As far as Grandmother is concerned, we're the best of buddies. Real chums. We assure her that we'll be happy to work out an arrangement that's agreeable to us both."

"Yeah, like she's going believe that," Flynn muttered.

"What was that?"

"I said, 'She'll be so relieved to see that.'" She flashed him a toothy smile.

"Right."

A movement down the hall caught Flynn's eye.

"Romy! There you are! How long have you been standing there? Charles, this is my friend and producer Romy Vandenberg. Romy,"—she bit back the urge to introduce Charlie as "Charlie the Horrible"—"this is Charles Kenilworth."

Romy nodded. "So I heard. Look, I hate to interrupt this little tête-à-tête, but the hospice nurse sent me down here. Virgie's asking for you both."

"Oh. Of course." Flynn ducked her head and turned away. How had she allowed herself to be distracted by a discussion about property, of all things, when Virgie was ill, perhaps dying?

She hurried back upstairs, Romy and Charlie at her heels.

When she reached the bedroom, she found Virgie lying quite still, her eyes closed. The teen Flynn had noticed earlier was standing near the headboard, close enough to touch Virgie, but her hands simply rested helplessly at her side. She looked up when Flynn came in, and her expression seemed to ask something of her, though Flynn could not guess what the request might be.

Flynn gave the girl what she hoped was a reassuring nod, then turned her attention to Virgie, who appeared to be sleeping quietly. She wanted to talk to her, comfort her, but was that the best thing to do, really? Perhaps what Virgie needed most was rest. Maybe if she got a good night's sleep she'd be better in the morning. Certainly not healed, but, God willing, possibly well enough to enjoy another week or month.

Virgie's eyes fluttered open, and she offered Flynn a wan smile.

"Well? What do you think of my surprise, my dear?"

Flynn felt Charlie's gaze rest on her. "I think you are a tricky old woman, Virgie, with a mind all your own."

"So, are you pleased?"

"Am I pleased? " Flynn bit her lip. She hated to lie. "I'm pleased that you've given yourself reassurance that Kenilworth House will be taken care of when you're gone someday."

"Ha! Baloney." Virgie clutched at Flynn's hand. "Where's that honesty I love?" she demanded.

"Now, Virgie—"

" 'Now, Virgie' nothing. You hate the will. You hate what I've done. For years, you and Charlie have mistrusted one another; don't pretend you haven't. My decision puts you both in a terrible spot."

"Well, now that you mention it," Flynn began.

"Flynn!" Charlie broke in, in a low, angry voice. He took a step toward her from where he had been standing near the girl.

"She wants honesty, Charles, for Pete's sake," Flynn hissed, turning in his direction. "What do you *want* me to say?"

She turned back to Virgie, a plastic smile pasted on her face. The girl looked from Flynn to Charlie, watching them both carefully.

Virgie, too, looked from one to the other. "The two of you are ridiculous, do you know that? Absolute children."

Flynn waited, her head bowed, while Virgie caught her breath.

A moment later Virgie went on as if she hadn't been forced to pause. "I don't know whom you think you're fooling, but even this dying woman isn't falling for your act." Virgie closed her eyes and sighed. "Make nice-nice all you want in front of me; I know you'll be tearing each other's hair out when I'm gone."

"Then why—?"

"Why put you through it? You'll see. One of these days it will all make sense." The old woman's voice dropped to little more than a whisper. "Hopefully, before the wedding."

"The *what?*" Flynn's soothing bedside manner was gone. She practically screeched the words.

"Now, Flynn." Charlie took another step of warning.

"What?" Flynn spun on him. "I'm sorry, Charles, but I will not smile and nod my way through a wedding, of all things! Virgie, what in the world can you be thinking?"

Virgie turned her head on the flattened pillow, so her tired eyes met Flynn's more directly.

"Just that you two will be very good for each other, Flynn, that's all. Charlie is too detached, too isolated." Virgie drew in a ragged breath. "Trudy is quite good for him." She struggled to lift her head, to include the girl in her gaze. "But he needs a partner. Your spunk and spirit and faith will be good for him too."

Flynn cringed inwardly. She'd shown a bit of spunk and spirit to Charlie, but no one could accuse her of being a stellar example of faith. Pushing back feelings of guilt, she resolved to be more polite to him in the days ahead, if for no other reason than because God would want her to be.

"You've always longed for a home and family of your own. And you need a good, loving man. Charlie is that. You just don't realize it yet, and I dare say neither does he." Virgie fell silent, the effort of speaking taking its toll. "But you will. Both of you. I have no doubt about that."

"You're asking the impossible. You know that."

Virgie ignored Flynn's firm protest. "In the meantime, you'll be business partners, at least. Agreed? Good. This house does need to be renovated, Charlie. Surely you realize that?"

Charlie maintained his stony silence, but, Flynn noted hopefully, at least he was not arguing.

"Whether you live here or sell the house, it really must be done," Virgie told him. "This place will be falling down around its occupants' ears otherwise. Besides, I've promised Flynn for years that she could renovate this place for me. Even when she was back in architecture school, before she started that television program of hers, we'd planned on it. I've also made an agreement with her production company." Virgie labored to get the words out. "The designs are nearly approved. Charlie, you have to let it happen. Consider it an old woman's dying wish."

Charlie nodded almost imperceptibly, but Virgie's still-sharp gaze must have caught it, because she appeared satisfied.

"And, Flynn, I don't believe I've ever asked anything of you. But I do ask this now." Flynn noted that Virgie's breathing had become more labored. "Keep an eye on my grandson after I'm gone. Be good to him."

"Of course," Flynn heard herself say through stiff lips.

"Good." Almost immediately, Virgie appeared to breathe more easily. "You two need one another. If only you could see it. But you will."

Flynn opened her mouth to make a retort, but stopped herself before Charlie could warn her again.

Virgie closed her eyes. "And now, if you will forgive an old woman, I am very tired. I need to rest."

Flynn looked at her suspiciously. Was this all a ruse? She wouldn't put it past Virgie. The woman did have a flair for the dramatic. A moment earlier she had been energetic enough to set her ridiculous plan in motion. Was she begging off just so they would be unable to argue with her?

She glanced at Charlie, and he gave a grim nod.

"All right, Virgie. You win, you crazy old dear," Flynn said fondly. She stood, then bent down and dropped a light kiss on the woman's temple. "I'll see you in the morning."

Virgie grabbed her hand and held on to it when Flynn would have pulled away. "I'm very proud of you, my dear."

Flynn felt a sudden longing to stop the clock, to preserve the moment always.

She leaned over so that her face was just inches from the old woman's. "You know I love you, Virgie. Don't you?"

Virgie's paper-thin lips trembled. "I've never doubted it for a moment, my dear. And my love will always be with you." Her eyes searched Flynn's. "Remember what I said about Charlie? Promise me you'll keep an eye on him? This is important to me."

Flynn nodded, and Virgie's scrawny hand squeezed her fingers so hard they hurt. Her eyes filled again as she stepped backward.

Charlie stepped forward, filling in the gap. "Good night, Grandmother," he said, stiffly bowing down and kissing Virgie on the cheek. "Don't you worry, even for a moment. We'll take care of everything. Isn't that right, Flynn?"

"Sure," Flynn said hesitantly, but Virgie didn't seem to be listening.

"I love you, my Charlie," Flynn heard the old woman whisper. "My baby boy."

Flynn turned away, unable to look at Charlie as Trudy joined her father at her great-grandmother's side.

"Come on," Flynn whispered to Romy, who was waiting in the doorway.

Romy followed her into the hall. There in the dim light, she turned wide eyes on Flynn.

"Unbelievable," Romy marveled. "Are you okay?"

Flynn leaned back against the paneled wall, suddenly feeling as though she might not be able to remain upright without its support.

"As okay as a woman can be, I guess, who is about to lose one of the most important people in her life."

An image of a distant, argumentative Charles Kenilworth came to mind.

She swallowed hard. "And who's just made a promise to a dying woman that's going to be virtually impossible to keep."

CHAPTER FIVE

"Give it to me straight." Charlie Kenilworth swiveled restlessly in his supple leather office chair, first staring out the wide window that gave him a sweeping view of crowded downtown Philadelphia, then spinning back to glare at the stocky man with the red hair and Perry Ellis suit seated across from him.

In the decade he'd worked as a real estate developer, Charlie had encountered his share of legal snags. Luckily, one of Pennsylvania's most successful, and expensive, law firms was on retainer, and so far none of the protracted battles had proven too difficult to win. During the past six or seven years, Charlie had found Art Gaines to be a particularly dogged lawyer and a not-half-bad racquetball player besides. As a result, Charlie had become as close to Arthur as to anyone.

"Well, Charlie," Art said, crossing his lanky legs, "I'm not going to pull any punches. Their side does have a case. Flynn Kelley has known your grandmother since childhood. We certainly can't argue that she came in at the last minute and insinuated herself into an old woman's life just to wangle an inheritance."

"Of course not," Charlie grumbled. "She insinuated herself into Grandmother's life decades ago. It's hardly a new development."

Art eased back in the paisley print wing chair positioned across from Charlie's desk. "Be that as it may, their friendship was a long-standing one. Now, the first thing to consider is the issue of competence. Was your grandmother crazy? In other words, was she in her right mind when she wrote that will?"

"'Right mind' is such a subjective phrase," Charlie observed dryly. "But if you're asking if she was insane, I can assure you she was not. A little nutty? Without a doubt. But certifiable? Hardly. And even if she had been, I wouldn't let you argue it in court. She *was* my grandmother, Arthur, after all."

"That's very noble of you, Charlie," Art sighed, "and, I've already decided, beside the point. You yourself have admitted to me that she was coherent up until the very end. And the will was written two years ago, before she was taken ill. There's no way we could realistically call her competency into question." He pulled a stack of notes from his bulging attaché case. "Consider it a blessing. If we'd gone that route, it would have been messy. A protracted battle, without a doubt; thoroughly unpleasant." He wrinkled his largish nose in distaste, though Charlie knew better. Arthur was at his best during prolonged legal skirmishes.

"Fine. So where does that leave us?"

"Well, we can't really question the girl's motives, either," Art said. "There's just no evidence that supports your belief that she was using your grandmother. Now, let me finish," Art said as Charlie moved to protest. He jabbed the yellow papers in Charlie's direction. "There are other options."

"It's about time," Charlie grumbled.

"I'm sorry, but I charge extra for rotten attitudes." Art made a notation in the leather-bound notepad pad on his knee.

"So sue me."

"Don't tempt me."

Charlie swiveled back toward the window and watched great puffs of cumulus clouds drift toward the east. It had been six weeks since his grandmother's death, and he still found it difficult—from his opulent Philadelphia office, far from the picturesque streets of Snow Hill—to believe she was truly gone. When he closed his eyes, he imagined her, still wandering the untamed gardens of her dilapidated estate on Maryland's Eastern Shore, her clipped gray hair like a cap of delicate feathers. He couldn't help but think that if he picked up the phone and dialed, he should still be able to reach her on her woefully outdated, ink-black rotary phone. Not that he had called her that often. Grandmother had lived her own life, and he'd lived his. Still, it had been comforting to know that he could reach her at almost any moment he chose.

He felt an uncomfortable burden in his chest and wished he could dismiss the unpleasant sensation as indigestion. But he suspected that it was, in fact, something much more serious: guilt.

There was no escaping the terrible truth that he'd spent much of his life avoiding his grandmother. Something he could do nothing to remedy now. When, as a teenager, he'd acted out his anger and grief over the loss of his parents through drug use and sexual exploits, she had faithfully prayed for him and urged him to redirect his life. But he'd continued to run wholeheartedly in the other direction. Then Vivian Polanski, a girl he'd been casually seeing, informed him that she was pregnant with his child and heading out to L.A. with her new boyfriend. The guy was the drummer in a local—and, Charlie was certain, quite terrible—punk-rock band.

Charlie hadn't challenged her decision to leave. He simply agreed to send Viv several hundred dollars each month. It seemed a small price to pay when he considered the alternatives: marriage to a woman he barely knew, full-time fatherhood—something he wasn't even remotely qualified for—or worse.

The first couple of months Charlie had struggled to come up with the money to send Viv; alcohol ate up nearly every spare dime he had. Vivian had responded with letters threatening legal action. Finally, Charlie had gone to his grandmother for help. After her initial shock, Virgie had moved swiftly, enrolling him in a local substance-abuse program and sending Vivian the required funds until he was released. Over the next year, Charlie had gotten himself clean and, at his grandmother's insistence, enrolled at Penn State.

He'd studied hard over the next four years, earning a degree in political science while working part-time to support his child. Upon graduation, somehow he had stumbled into the field of real estate development. But despite his grandmother's continued emotional support, he'd found himself pulling away from her. The shame of what he'd done was strong, and despite her kindness, he'd had difficulty facing her. His grandmother was a good, moral woman. She deserved to have the family she'd lost, he thought bitterly, not the one she'd been left. No doubt, his little cousins, Maya and Ricky, would have been star pupils, not to mention strong Christians as most of the Kenilworths had been. His parents, aunt, and uncle had been model citizens as well. Why had he been spared while they were lost?

It's a good thing they never saw the mess I made of my life. That's a blessing, at least, Charlie couldn't help thinking. *I'm just sorry Grandmother had to witness it.*

Art cleared his throat, then went on. "The note your grandmother left about you and Ms. Kelley both living on the property means nothing in and of itself," he said. "There's nothing binding about that. We can, however, use it to support our case."

"And what, exactly, is our case?" Charlie spun his chair back so that he was facing his friend.

Arthur leaned forward in his seat, his love of law displayed clearly in every feature. "We'll ask the judge for injunctive relief." He drew the legal term out slowly, lovingly. "What your grandmother proposed is inequitable. It's not reasonable to expect that you and Ms. Flynn would share the property. If one of you lives there and the other doesn't, the nonresident will still be responsible for half the property taxes, but won't enjoy any of the benefits. At the same time, it obviously isn't realistic to ask both of you to reside there, particularly as husband and wife, as your grandmother suggested."

"Obviously," Charlie agreed.

"You could, however, choose to use it as a vacation home and stay there on alternate weekends."

Charlie tried to envision this, but he kept coming back to the image of himself dealing with a strange woman's stockings drying in the bathroom or a house filled with heavily scented potpourri and cheap lace doilies.

"Absolutely not!" he barked, startled to find that he had, for a moment, seriously considered the possibility.

Although if he was perfectly honest, Charlie was forced to admit that Flynn Kelley's taste was exquisite. He'd watched her program more than once, and he knew that she was capable of making a breathtaking home out of one in shambles.

Art blinked at him. "Well then. Injunctive relief it is. We'll ask that the court order her to sell you her half. Either that or you could both sell the place and divide the proceeds."

"I am *not* going to sell my family's estate," Charlie said with finality. "And I'd appreciate it if you didn't suggest such a thing again."

"All right, all right." Arthur gathered up his papers and crammed them back into his briefcase. "I'm just giving you options. The choice is up to you. You should realize, however, that this is going to take some time. We're not going to be able to force her to give up her rights overnight."

"*Her* rights!" Charlie sputtered.

"You heard me," Arthur said in a calm, low voice. "Of course," he stopped and gave Charlie a thoughtful look, "there is one other option."

"Oh yeah?" Charlie drummed on the desk with his fingers, a nervous tic he'd developed years before. "Why don't I like the sound of that?"

"Don't be a child." Arthur stood and smoothed the wrinkles out of his suit jacket. "It's a perfectly reasonable solution." He waggled his shaggy eyebrows and gave Charlie a wicked grin. "If you can handle it."

"Handle what?" Charlie resolved not to rise to the bait.

"Go see this Ms. Kelley yourself and suggest that you settle out of court. If she dislikes you as much as you said—"

"Now, wait a minute. I didn't say she disliked me," Charlie broke in. He scowled. "I said she was *difficult*."

"You say to*may*to; I say to*mah*to," Arthur shrugged. "In any case, I should think she'd be happy to get rid of you. I know I would be."

"That can still be arranged," Charlie said through gritted teeth.

"Temper, temper." Arthur approached the desk and leaned against it with both hands. "Do you want my best advice? As your attorney. And as your friend?"

"You know I do." Charlie folded his arms across his chest.

"Call this girl up. Ask her to coffee. Be a gentleman. Have a friendly little visit. Then, once you've softened her up, suggest that in the interest of friendly cooperation, the two of you settle. Offer to buy her out. Get rid of her once and for all."

"Art, you can't be serious," Charlie fumed. "I'd just as soon invite an anaconda to breakfast." He could already picture the look of smug satisfaction on Flynn's face when he went to her, asking for her help.

"An anaconda can't help you get your grandmother's house back," Art pointed out. "Consider it an investment of your time."

"I consider it a *waste* of my time." There was no way this woman would agree to such a thing. She'd deliberately manipulated his grandmother into leaving her half the property, and she wasn't about to give it up now.

"You don't know until you try, do you?" Art said. "Go on. Call her up. Be charming. You *do* know how to be charming, don't you?"

Charlie threw him a withering look.

"Of course, I can always call her on your behalf," Art suggested. "I've seen her program, you know. She's a beautiful woman. Very wholesome with those great big dark blue eyes of hers and that slim little figure. And that mop of hair! Have you seen the way her dark curls fall across her forehead while she works? Could she be any sexier? Why I wouldn't mind—"

"All right, I'll do it, Art," Charlie snapped, pushing himself away from the desk. "Happy?"

A slow smile spread across Art's ruddy face as he followed Charlie to the door. "Oh, not quite," he said. "But I expect soon enough, one of is going to be!"

◆   ◆   ◆

"Call him, Flynn."

Romy leaned over her best friend's desk. "It's been two days since your designs for Kenilworth House were approved. I've called the demolition crew, the construction crew, the electricians, the plumbers, and the cabinetmakers. Everyone's ready to move."

"Romy, you're out of your ever-lovin' mind." Flynn peered over the top of her computer screen. "I'm not the owner of Kenilworth House yet, and I'm not going to be for some time. If I ever am. James says this is going to be very complicated."

"Your brother doesn't specialize in real estate law, does he?" A touch of impatience crept into Romy's voice. "Maybe you should get someone who does."

"Forget it. James knows what he's doing. Besides, he has plenty of associates who've handled cases of this sort. He'll take care of it."

"But by the time he does, it won't be news anymore!" Romy said. "Ever since *Entertainment Tonight* broke the story of the legal scandal, we've been getting calls from newspapers and programs all around the world. You were right, Flynn. The house is amazing. And the story's even better. We have to renovate it for the show. *Now,* while public interest is high. Think of the ratings!"

Flynn turned back to her computer screen. She despised the fact that the media had seized upon her peculiar inheritance. "Charles Kenilworth will never agree to that, Romy."

"Why not?" her friend argued. "He promised Virgie he'd let you remodel the house for the program. I was right there. I *heard* him with my own two ears."

"That's not especially binding," Flynn reminded her. "At least, not legally."

"Perhaps not," Romy said. "But morally—"

"Morally, you're barking up the wrong tree," Flynn said. "Men like Charles Kenilworth live by their own rules. You're not going to convince him to follow through on a promise like that. Especially one made under duress."

Her cheeks flushed as she remembered the promise she herself had made to Virgie. Keeping an eye on Charlie Kenilworth was the last thing she wanted to do. Although, at Virgie's funeral, Flynn had dutifully watched over him and his daughter throughout the service and the small gathering that followed.

She didn't see why she'd bothered. Charlie had appeared as stiff and emotionless as a mannequin. He'd responded civilly when Flynn had offered her condolences, nothing more. Flynn had seen no evidence that he'd offered any real sympathy or reassurance to his daughter. Flynn had found Trudy sitting alone in one corner of the church's meeting hall, but when she'd attempted to start a conversation, the girl had fled.

So much for promises.

"I agree," Romy said, pacing the room. She pulled from Flynn's shelf an oversize picture book filled with images of beachfront mansions and began flipping absently through it. "*I* won't convince him of a thing. Which is why you need to talk to him."

"Me!" Flynn blinked at her friend, hoping she'd misunderstood. "You're kidding, right?"

"Not in the least." Romy slapped the book shut. "He'll listen to you, Flynn."

"He will not!" she protested. "He thinks I'm evil incarnate."

"He thinks you're adorable," Romy said.

"Poor Romy." Flynn shook her head. "Haven't I told you to always wear a hard hat when you're on one of our construction sites?"

"I'm serious, Flynn." Romy jammed the book back onto the shelf. "There's serious chemistry between the two of you."

"The fact that sparks fly doesn't necessarily mean there's chemistry." Flynn gave Romy a reproving look.

"Maybe," Romy said. "But where there are sparks, there's fire."

"You mean, 'where there's smoke, there's fire,'" Flynn corrected her. "It's not the same thing."

"So, there's the *potential* for fire."

"Fire's dangerous," Flynn said.

"Not as dangerous as the lack of it."

Flynn sat back and sighed. "What is it you want from me, Romy?"

Her producer beamed. "I'm glad you asked," she said, dropping languidly into a swivel chair of gray cloth. "Call Charlie. Tell him you want to meet with him. Then retract your claws, and go make some sort of peace. Get him to agree to let us do the show while this media wave is still rolling."

"And how, exactly, do you propose I do that?" Flynn crossed her arms behind her head and locked her slender fingers together.

"Appeal to his better nature," Romy said.

"I'm pretty sure the guy doesn't have one."

Romy caught her breath, as if a thought had just struck her. "Well, I have an idea! It's a radical concept," Romy said. "But it just might work."

"Romy."

"All right, all right." Romy leaned forward and looked at Flynn intently. "I want you to try being charming."

"Ha-ha."

"I'm serious! I know it's a new concept for you, but try being nice to the guy. I'll bet it gets you further than you'd ever dream. You *do* know how to charm a guy, don't you?"

Flynn sat bolt upright. "I'll have you know, I can be very winning. Why, in college, men practically fell at my feet. I can be *quite* charming. Charming like a snake." She blinked. "Wait. That's not what I meant."

Romy brushed away her protest. "It works for me. Okay then. It's settled."

The intercom on Flynn's desk buzzed.

"Flynn?" the voice of her secretary, Stephanie, shrilled. "You have a call from a Mr. Charles Kenilworth. Are you available?"

"Is she ever!" Romy snickered.

"Romy!" Flynn hissed. She paused for the briefest of moments, then decided she might as well get this over with. "Ye-es. Put the call through."

Without asking permission, Romy promptly reached over and switched to speakerphone.

"Hello, Ms. Flynn?" The voice that came over the speaker was cheerful, friendly.

Completely unlike the voice of Charlie Kenilworth.

"Hello?" she said uncertainly. "Who's this?"

"Charles—er, Charlie Kenilworth."

"No, seriously."

There was a brief pause. "Seriously. This is Charlie. Is there a problem?"

Flynn stared at her telephone as if it were a snake.

"Uh, no problem. How are you, Charlie?"

"Fine, thanks. Just fine. Couldn't be better." To her ears, he could not have sounded more like a used-car salesman.

"Delighted to hear it." Flynn opened her eyes wide at Romy, who wasn't even attempting to conceal her delight. "What can I do for you, Charlie?"

"Well, the thing is, I—" Flynn heard what sounded like a muffled, choking sound coming from her speaker. "That is, I was just thinking of you," Charlie said, his voice sounding strained, "and I thought perhaps we could, er, get together for a cup of coffee?"

Flynn looked at Romy and stuck a finger in her mouth, pretending to be gagging. "How sweet," she lied, rolling her eyes. "I'd be delighted. You're in Philadelphia, though, so I don't see how we could manage it. What a pity. I—*ow!*" She glared at Romy, who had just pinched her in the forearm.

"I realize that," Charlie continued. "But I'm going down to Snow Hill next weekend, and I thought perhaps you might want to come down and, uh, pick up a few mementos. Grandmother showed me a number of gifts you'd given her over the years: the art, plants, and the knitted throws. I thought you might like to keep them."

Flynn was taken aback. "Why, that's very *decent* of you, Charlie," she said, wondering who had put him up to it. Romy bobbed her head in encouragement. "I'd like that very much," Flynn said.

"Great." Charlie didn't sound exactly happy about it, but he didn't retract the offer. "Why don't we meet at the new café in town on Saturday? We can have lunch around noon, then head up to the house."

"Fine, I'll be there." Flynn got off the phone as quickly as possible.

Romy smirked once Charlie had clicked off. "Told ya. He's been *thinking* about you."

"What do you think he's up to?" Flynn stared at the phone on the corner of her desk.

"Wooing? Courting?"

Flynn shook her head. "Try manipulating. Or maybe deceiving."

"You are so suspicious," Romy observed.

"Only when I have a reason to be." Flynn glanced at her watch, then jumped to her feet. "Uh-oh. I've got to get going. I'm late for the center." Once a week she helped out at a shelter for homeless women and children; this week she was scheduled to tutor several kids. She grabbed her suede jacket off the hat tree in the corner. "I'll see you at home later."

"Don't hurry," Romy said. "In fact, why don't you stop at Saks when you're done and get yourself something"—she gave a little sway of the hips—"alluring. You want to look gorgeous this weekend, don't you? A sundress, perhaps, with cute little spaghetti straps?"

"Forget it, Romy." Flynn let out a sharp, humorless laugh. "All I want is to get through this meeting without causing the guy any bodily harm. And as far as this matter of his 'liking' me is concerned," she said grimly, throwing the jacket over her slim shoulders, "Charlie Kenilworth can take me as I am…or suffer the consequences."

CHAPTER SIX

Raising one finger, Charlie flagged down the harried waitress servicing all ten tables in the Delmarva Café, named for the flat, verdant peninsula that stretched north to south through three states: Delaware, Maryland, and Virginia. Opened just six months earlier, the café was one of the town's handful of eateries, which included the Judge's Bench Restaurant, Evelyn's Village Inn, the Snow Hill Inn and Restaurant, and, to Charlie's horror, one ridiculously out-of-place international fast-food burger franchise.

He grabbed the sugar dispenser from the Formica tabletop and dumped its contents into a gleaming, unscratched spoon, measuring out two scoops into a cup of walnut-colored coffee. Flynn Kelley wasn't due to arrive for another fifteen minutes, but he had come early to have the advantage of making the booth his home "turf," a little trick he'd picked up in the real estate business.

Charlie sipped his coffee, strong and sweet, just the way he liked it, and watched the locals meander by: young mothers headed for the grocery, carrying doe-eyed, pouty-lipped babies or leading drunk-looking toddlers by the hand; old salts in fishing caps, taking their morning constitutional; teens in black, slogan-covered T-shirts, whirring by on Rollerblades or performing tricks on their skateboards or scooters, freely spending their summer freedom.

A moment later a petite woman with short, curly brown hair, blue eyes, and clear, alabaster skin appeared across the street. Her Georgetown sweatshirt was a loose fit, as were her Levi's, giving her a casual, unaffected appearance. Today her hair was tucked under a dark Yankees cap bearing the overlapping, white-stitched letters: NY. Charlie watched as she made her way down Snow Hill's singular sidewalk, laid with bricks once used as ballast in early English sailing ships, beaming at each person she passed.

As he observed the effect Flynn's smile had on those around her, he felt a tiny burst of pleasure that she was on her way to meet him. He immediately quashed the feeling. That she was beautiful was undeniable. But he was not here because of Flynn Kelley's looks. He was here to get her to relinquish what was not rightfully hers, and he would not let her admittedly comely appearance distract him.

Flynn flashed her brilliant smile at a city worker who greeted her on the street, and Charlie felt his stomach clench. Was she flirting? The possibility irritated him, though he could not put his finger on why.

When she finished socializing with the locals and entered the restaurant, he half stood and waved, offering the friendliest smile he could muster.

Flynn appeared to hesitate, then made her way deliberately toward him.

"Hello, Charles," she said, eyeing his coffee. "Have you been waiting long?"

"Not at all. Just came in a bit early to read the paper," he said, indicating the sheets of smudged newsprint beside his porcelain cup. "Please. Have a seat."

Flynn complied while he summoned their waitress.

"Can I get you anything to drink, deary?" the woman offered, snapping her gum.

"Just water." Flynn tucked her dark hair behind the curve of one ear, then leaned forward and whispered to Charlie earnestly, "I'm trying to break my diet pop addiction. I've heard aspartame may be a cancer risk, and I'm not going to take any chances."

"Good for you." He nodded as solemnly as if she'd announced she was running for the Senate, although he couldn't imagine how cutting diet cola from one's daily menu could be considered much of a hardship.

Over the next few minutes, they busied themselves with making their lunch selections: chunky chicken salad and a blueberry scone for Flynn; corned beef, French fries, and iced tea for Charlie. Then, with that formality over and the menus retrieved by their waitress, Charlie found himself searching for something to say to this attractive but dangerous thorn in his side. To his great relief, his cell phone providentially rang at just that moment, and he managed to kill several minutes talking to a client back in Philadelphia. He quickly mouthed "I'm sorry" to Flynn, but she appeared as relieved as he at the reprieve. All too soon, though, the call was over, and the awkward silence settled back over them.

Flynn was the first to break it. "I have to confess, it feels a little funny to be back in Snow Hill. I haven't been out here since—"

Charlie watched her with genuine curiosity. She appeared to be truly hurting.

"Since Grandmother died?" he supplied.

Flynn nodded, one dark curl escaping from behind her ear. "It seems strange. Like Snow Hill shouldn't exist without her. Or like, since it is still here, then she must be, too, somewhere." Charlie didn't admit that he'd experienced a similar feeling.

"Your brother still lives here, doesn't he?" He remembered James Kelley well. The younger boy had often played on his grandmother's grounds with Flynn before the summer things had changed.

"Yes. I'll be staying with him tonight." Flynn didn't say anything about James acting as her counsel in the matter of Kenilworth House, but Charlie knew this was the case. Arthur was keeping him well informed. But there was no point in talking about all that. Not now. Not if he was going to charm Flynn, as Arthur had advised. Better to steer the conversation to safer ground.

"Think you'll go canoeing tomorrow?" he asked, grasping at straws. "You always loved that as a kid. I could always get you to come with me when I went fishing, you loved being in the canoe so much."

Flynn opened her eyes wide. "I can't believe you remember that."

"Why not?"

"You don't seem very, uh, sentimental." Her hands fell palm-side up on the table.

"Perhaps not." Charlie averted his gaze. He knew what Flynn was really thinking: that he was a man with no feelings. He'd long been aware of her blatant disapproval of him. In fact, a year or so ago, he'd even commented on it to his grandmother.

"You have to try to understand Flynn," Virgie had told him. "She lost a lot the summer your parents died."

"And I didn't?" he'd lashed out.

His grandmother had explained then how Flynn had been banished from Snow Hill. Charlie didn't see how that had been his fault. The silly girl had come to Kenilworth House when she'd been specifically told not to, after all. And when she had stumbled across Chris Stafford and his other friends that day, Charlie had gotten her away from them before any real damage was done. The girl was shaken up, that's all. But was she grateful? Hardly. She still blamed him for what happened that summer.

Just as he blamed himself for her banishment from Snow Hill.

And for his own loss.

To Charlie's relief, their lunches arrived before he was forced to respond to Flynn's comment on his lack of sentimentality.

"You really should go canoeing again," he said, carefully shifting the subject. "Maybe I'll take you out myself," he continued, making an awkward overture of friendship. "I haven't gone in years. Too busy. It would be nice to get back out on the old Pocomoke."

Flynn raised one eyebrow but said nothing.

For several long minutes they ate in silence.

"How's Trudy doing?" Flynn tried after a while.

Charlie considered how to answer. Sharing the intimate details of his life with his legal adversary was the last thing he wanted to do. However, they had to talk about something, and the reality of his situation might actually help to break down the carefully guarded wall Flynn had thrown up between them.

"Trudy," he said at last, "is a handful."

"Well, she *is* a teenage girl," Flynn pointed out, stabbing her fork in his direction.

"True," Charlie said. "And I'm sure you know more about what that means than I do. But I confess, I really don't know what to do with her. She's moody, irritable—"

"She won't talk to you," Flynn supplied, "she sighs constantly, and her friends are more important to her than anything in the world, while you're chopped liver."

Charlie shot her a look. "How'd you know?"

"Been there. Done that," Flynn informed him, lifting a forkful of chicken to her full lips. "I was once a teenage girl myself, remember?"

He eyed her curiously. "I don't suppose you still know how to communicate with the species?" The prospect inexplicably caused him to brighten. Perhaps he had more to gain from a cordial relationship with Flynn Kelley than he'd initially realized.

"Are you kidding? I volunteer at a center for homeless women and children once a week. I work with kids like Trudy all the time. Boys *and* girls. Don't worry. Her behavior is perfectly normal."

Charlie felt himself begin to warm slightly to the woman seated across from him. The shift was small, almost imperceptible, but he recognized it as a definite change. He wondered if it was time to reconsider his position. If this woman could actually help his daughter, he was willing to swallow any amount of pride to make that happen.

"That's amazing," he said in earnest. "You know, I always wanted to help out kids myself," he admitted, leaning forward on his elbows. "When I was younger, I mean. I wanted to be a counselor for kids. Before the accident, that is. You probably find that hard to believe."

Flynn's expression betrayed that she was, in fact, surprised by his confession. But she was courteous enough not to say it.

"Don't worry, Charlie," she said politely. "I'm sure you're a very good dad to Trudy." She looked a bit amazed to hear the words coming out of her own mouth. "The two of you will work things out. You'll see."

"I hope so," he said, wrapping one large hand around his corned beef. "I want that more than anything in the world."

Flynn put her glass to her lips and sipped delicately. "Virgie said you were a good father. She understood how important that was to you, and she was really very proud."

"Proud?" Charlie looked away. He'd never given Grandmother a reason to be truly proud of him. Not really. "I'm afraid I was more of a disappointment to Grandmother than anything," he said. "I think you know this as well as anyone, Flynn. You were, after all, her closest confidante."

"I think you underestimate Virgie, Charles," she said. "Maybe Virgie was disappointed *for* you. But she wasn't ever disappointed *in* you." She leaned forward and met his eyes. "Virgie told me you had trouble accepting her forgiveness, but that doesn't mean it didn't exist."

"You sound exactly like Grandmother!" he said wryly.

For the first time since they'd become reacquainted, Flynn gave him what appeared to be a real grin. "That's the nicest compliment I've received in a long time."

Charlie felt a ridiculous thrill of pleasure. Flynn Kelley was an extraordinarily attractive, if difficult, woman. And a famous one at that. No doubt she got more than her share of affirming comments.

He tore his gaze away from Flynn's hypnotizing eyes. What was he thinking? He was here for one reason only, and that was to win Flynn's cooperation regarding Kenilworth House. He knew better than to be distracted by her charms. *He* was here to distract *her*. And by the open expression on her face, he guessed that there would be no better time for him to make his move.

"I'm glad to hear it, Flynn." He waved a crinkled, golden fry at her. "It's good to see that we can get past our differences. Since we're both named in Grandmother's crazy will, it's going to be important for us to work together to get things resolved."

Flynn appeared relieved. "I couldn't agree more." She let out a long breath.

"Obviously, we can't both live in the house," he said. "We've already agreed on that. Neither can one person live in it while the other is forced to share in the expenses. That will never work."

"No," Flynn said, swallowing a mouthful of chicken and celery. "It won't."

"So it makes the most sense to my attorney—and, well, to me— for one of us to sell his or her half of the property."

Flynn gaped at him. "Exactly what I was thinking!"

Charlie brightened. This was going to be much easier than he'd thought.

"Then I don't see any reason why we can't come to an agreement right away. There's no sense in engaging in a protracted legal battle. I'm perfectly willing to give you not only a fair, but also a *generous* offer for your half of the estate. With any luck, we'll be able to settle this by—"

Flynn's fork struck her plate with a clatter. "Me?" Her dark brows met at the bridge of her nose. "You want *me* to sell to *you?*"

"Well, of course." He looked at her, puzzled. "What else would I suggest?"

"Why…you…*man!*" Flynn cried out in frustration. "Of all the egotistical… Why on earth would you think I'd be willing to do such a thing?"

Her derision stung. Charlie scowled. "I don't know. Perhaps because it's my family home?"

"Yes, it is," Flynn said. "But Virgie didn't leave it just to you, did she? She left it to me as well. And she had her reasons."

Charlie pushed back his plate, his appetite quickly disappearing. "So. Just as I thought. You've wanted Kenilworth House all along, and you're not willing to do the right thing."

"The right thing? *The right thing?*" Flynn poked one delicate finger directly at his nose. "Don't you talk to me about 'the right thing,' Charlie Kenilworth! The right thing, as you call it, would be for you to let me restore Kenilworth House as Virgie and I had planned. You promised her on her deathbed that you would allow the renovations to proceed. Now you're taking legal action to stop it. Even worse," she threw down her napkin in disgust, "you've invited me out here in a pathetic attempt to charm me out of my legal rights! Well, I can assure you, Mr. Kenilworth, you won't succeed."

Charlie gaped at her. "How do you know that?" He didn't even try to deny it.

"Because I came here to charm you out of *your* rights!" She jumped to her feet, reached into her purse, and threw down several crumpled bills on the Formica. "And I'll have you know I am *quite* charming. Not that you noticed!" Then with her chin raised in cool dignity, she stalked out of the restaurant.

"It wasn't a *pathetic* attempt," Charlie muttered, ignoring the stares from the café's other patrons. Far from it. He'd almost won her over. If only he hadn't opened his big mouth. And what was all that prattle about *her* charming *him?*

Giving a heavy sigh, he threw down another ten, then followed Flynn out of the restaurant. By the time he'd caught up to her, she was nearly two blocks away.

"Flynn! *Flynn!* Come on, stop," he urged, panting his way down the cobbled sidewalk. "I'm not as young as I used to be."

She didn't stop, but did slow her pace a bit.

"No, you're not," she sniffed.

"Look, I'm sorry." He almost meant it. "I shouldn't have *assumed* that I would be the one to buy from you. Can't we discuss this like two reasonable adults?"

Flynn finally halted. "Do you think you can fake it?" She gave him a sideways glance.

"I'm willing to try if you are."

She folded her arms across her chest and regarded him with a wary eye. "Look, I won't beat around the bush. I've always wanted to renovate Kenilworth House. I never dreamed it would be mine, really, although I had suggested to Virgie that I buy it from her some-day and take care of her in her old age."

"Don't you think that was a bit presumptuous?" Charlie hated the feelings Flynn's revelation evoked. He should have been the one to make such an offer.

"At this point, I don't really care," she said. "Now, just listen for once, will you? I want a chance to restore the estate to what it was before time and life beat it down. Give me a chance to do that, okay? We can decide later what to do with the estate. Maybe by the time I'm done, you'll realize you don't want an old historic home anyway, because they take too much time and money to care for. Maybe I'll feel satisfied when the project is done, and I'll be ready to let it go.

Maybe we'll have to draw straws. But at least let me do what I planned to do. What Virgie promised I could do and what you agreed to. Please?"

In the face of her passionate plea, Charlie felt his carefully constructed resolve begin to disintegrate.

"We'll split the cost of the renovations," Flynn suggested, "then share any profit if the place is sold."

Charlie searched his mind, in vain, for an alternate solution. "I'll admit, I don't have a better idea. And my lawyer has informed me that it is in our best interests if you and I work together. I have to warn you, though, I have no intention of letting you take my grandmother's house when this is all over."

Flynn rolled her eyes.

Charlie considered his options. If Flynn renovated the home, it would save him the effort of doing so himself. And his grandmother had been right: The place was in desperate need of upgrading. Besides, if he gave Flynn what she wanted now, perhaps she'd be more willing to sell to him in the end.

Worst of all, she was right; he *had* made a promise.

"I suppose I could agree to let you proceed," he said reluctantly.

"Actually, you *already* agreed," he thought he heard Flynn mutter.

"What's that?"

"Oh, nothing." Flynn gave him a stiff smile. "I'll have James call your attorney to draw up a contract. We're ready to start work anytime. Will the week after next be acceptable?"

"I suppose so." Charlie reached in his pocket and drew out a charcoal-hued electronic day planner. "I'd planned on taking Trudy down to the house for the summer. I thought it might be good for her."

Flynn shook her head. "There's a fair amount of demolition to be done, so the main house won't be habitable. If you insist on staying at the estate, you should plan on staying in the guesthouse through the summer. The renovations will take at least three months to complete."

Charlie nodded. "Fair enough."

"There's one other thing." Flynn regarded him nervously. "It's imperative that I stay on site to oversee the project. Since you and Trudy are going to be in the guest house, I'd like to stay at the river cottage."

"Suit yourself." Charlie tried to sound noncommittal, but the prospect of living in such close proximity to Flynn somehow took his breath away.

"Great," Flynn said. "I'll have my assistant call you with the schedule in the next few days." Then she disappeared around the corner.

Feeling uncharacteristically helpless, Charlie stared for several moments at the spot where she'd just been. Then suddenly it struck him that his grandmother's wish for them to live together on the property was going to come true after all, even if it wasn't in the way that she'd hoped.

He walked back to where his Honda CRV was parked across the street from the café, considering how he and Flynn were constantly at each other's throats. As he climbed into the vehicle, it occurred to him that Grandmother's misguided but well-intentioned matchmaking plan probably would have been a lot more fun.

CHAPTER SEVEN

After a long morning of hard-core demolition, Flynn had just two things on her mind: a long, fragrant bath with soothing peppermint oils and a twenty-minute catnap.

With a sigh of relief, she slipped into her tiny cottage and let the door latch shut behind her. Thank goodness she'd managed to slip away. Romy had been driving her and the entire crew harder than Flynn could remember. Determined that the series' first episode air in early January, Romy had proposed a work schedule that Flynn had initially mocked but had ultimately taken as a personal challenge. After all, why not get things moving as quickly as possible before Charles Kenilworth changed his mind and retracted the offer to let her complete the renovations? The sooner she got things started, the sooner the two of them could get out of each other's hair for good.

She pulled off the Yankees baseball cap that she'd worn to keep the dust out of her hair and ran her fingers through her unruly curls. She'd need a shampoo too. She didn't mind looking slightly disheveled for the cameras, but Romy would throw a fit if she showed up looking *this* gritty for the afternoon shoot.

Flynn kicked off her sneakers and made her way through the cottage to the tiny bedroom and the antique iron bed with white chenille bedspread that practically called her name. She threw it a look of longing. *First bath, Flynn,* she told herself. *Then bed.*

She moved into the bathroom and turned the large knobs on the claw-foot tub, letting the rusty water flush through the pipes. While the water ran, she started to pull her gray T-shirt over her head, then, thinking better of it, crossed the small room to pull down the tiny shade. Her cottage was located far from the main house, on the bank of the Pocomoke, surrounded by the same wild undergrowth and towering cypress that framed the river. Her precautions were automatic, adopted after years of living in the city. It was unlikely that any human would pass by on the banks lining this particular stretch of water; she was far more likely to spy an osprey, a great blue heron, egret, or even a white-tailed deer. If she went to the water's edge, however, she'd have even more company: Sunbathing turtles, playful otters, and an occasional local or tourist might also paddle his or her way down the river's lazy current.

Flynn peered out the white-painted window frame and saw to her surprise that there was, in fact, a human figure lurking down by the riverbank. At first she was startled but then recognized a forlorn-looking Trudy Kenilworth.

Flynn hesitated. In the three weeks since beginning work on the project, she'd left the girl to herself. All initial attempts at friendship had been firmly rebuffed, and she'd wanted to respect Trudy's desire for space. For the first time, she found herself genuinely sympathizing with Charlie's position. Her own failure to connect with Trudy stung, and Flynn wasn't even related to the girl. She could only imagine how difficult it was for Charlie to be shut out by his only child, one with whom he'd been building a relationship for less than a year, and with whom he had just a few more years to connect before it was time for her to go out and make her own way in the world.

Yet, from the empty expression Trudy customarily wore, Flynn guessed that the girl was even less ready for the coming challenge than other teens her age. Flynn recognized the look; she'd seen it on the faces of the kids she worked with every week. Trudy Kenilworth was lost. If she was going to make it, someone was going to have to reach out to her.

Casting one last look of yearning at the tub, she wrestled the knobs back into the off position, then grabbed her cap and pulled it back down over her eyes before heading out the front door.

She moved stealthily, as if she were attempting to sneak up on one of the river turtles, which would slip shyly back into the water if a human came too near. She had little trouble remaining unnoticed. Lost in her thoughts, Trudy remained perched on a rock by the river's edge and appeared only mildly startled when Flynn addressed her.

"Hey there," Flynn said, keeping her tone light. She poked one dusty sneaker in the girl's direction. "Mind if I join you?"

Trudy shrugged. "It's a free country." She apparently was not too cool for clichés. Her fine, black hair hung limp around her shoulders, and her eyes were dull and red-rimmed.

"Thanks." Flynn lowered herself to the thick grass. She forced herself not to start asking questions, wanting to allow Trudy the opportunity to get used to her presence. Over the next ten minutes, she and the girl watched in fairly companionable silence as two couples drifted by in canoes rented from the local fishing shop. The first, Flynn guessed to be a young married couple on vacation, perhaps even on their honeymoon, based on the look of pure joy on their glowing faces. The second playful pair appeared to be high-school sweethearts from Snow Hill or a nearby town. She had a hard time picturing Trudy ever being that carefree.

"So, how's your summer going?" Flynn asked finally.

The girl gave her trademark shrug.

"You're probably spending a lot of time with your dad, huh?" When Trudy didn't answer, she decided to take her silence as permission to go on. "Did you know that your dad used to take me fishing when I was a kid?" The words ran out in a nervous prattle. "It's hard to believe I'm that old, huh?" Trudy stared at her. "Uh…or not." Flynn grinned sheepishly. "I never caught much, but he was a pro. Largemouth bass, shad, white perch, pickerel. Even the occasional eel."

"Well, he's never taken me," Trudy blurted out. "I hardly ever see my dad."

"You don't?" This puzzled Flynn. "I don't understand. I know he wants to spend time with you, Trudy. He told me so."

The girl turned away, her eyelids snapping shut like shades. She wouldn't even look at Flynn after that. She'd obviously shared as much as she was going to.

Flynn knew better than to push. "Grownups can be like that.

They don't do the things they really want to. We're all like that, Trudy. Even you, I expect."

The girl threw her a look that Flynn found impossible to interpret.

"Your dad loves you very much, whether you realize it or not," she said firmly, realizing as she spoke the words that she truly believed them. "Your great-grandmother loved you too, very much. And she was no fool, believe you me. Even your mother, I suspect, loves you in her own way."

"You don't know anything about my mother!" Trudy jumped to her feet.

"You're right," Flynn said, waving both hands in surrender. "I don't. I shouldn't have said anything about that. It's none of my business. I'm sorry."

Trudy looked at her, unable to hide her surprise. Flynn guessed that she wasn't used to hearing adults apologize.

"You're not asking my advice, and I respect that. I know your life hasn't been easy. But maybe you could try to be a little more understanding of your father," she suggested.

Trudy folded her bony, adolescent arms and regarded Flynn with a look of derision. "Oh, I see. Like you?" she said.

"Well…" Flynn felt her cheeks burn.

"I've seen the two of you argue." The girl tossed her hair back over one shoulder. "My great-grandmother thought the two of you would be good together. She was out of her mind." She stalked away in the manner perfected by teenage girls.

"Ouch," Flynn muttered, watching her retreat.

She was still sitting there several minutes later when a twig snapped behind her.

"Flynn." Charlie's rumbling voice cut into her reverie. "Have you seen Trudy?"

"You just missed her." Flynn turned to him, her new feelings still fresh. "Sit?"

Charlie eyed her suspiciously. Though the two of them had called a truce, it was still an uneasy one at best. "Is that poison ivy? Poison oak?"

"No, of course not. But I deserve that." Flynn patted a patch of grass to her right. "Please?"

Charlie considered her a moment, then lowered himself beside her. Flynn kept her eyes trained on the dark, swirling waters several dozen feet away, unwilling to meet his eyes.

"Charlie," she began uneasily, "I need to apologize. I just had a talk with Trudy. Well, 'talk' may be too strong a word. But she made me see something I should have seen a long time ago." She tucked her short legs and sneakered feet beneath her, Indian-style.

"All right," Charlie said warily.

Flynn cleared her throat. "Look. You and I have had our differences. The fact is, Virgie loved you very much. Despite a rocky start, you've been really great about the work we've been doing on the house. The first phase is always the hardest. So much has to be torn out before the upgrades can be put in. And you haven't complained at all. Even if that wasn't the case, even if you hadn't allowed me to move forward with the renovations, I've had no right to treat you the way I have." Flynn forced herself to meet his eyes. "I may not like choices you've made in the past, but that's no reason to treat you shabbily."

To Flynn's surprise, Charlie reached over and squeezed her hand.

"I appreciate that," he said simply. He gave her a sideways glance. "What did the two of you talk about, anyway?"

"Oh…girl stuff," Flynn hedged, wanting to respect Trudy's privacy.

He nodded in silent understanding, his gaze on an egret skimming the tops of the cypress on the opposite bank.

"You know, your daughter loves you. So did Virgie," she said gently. "She forgave you for everything that happened, you know."

Charlie's jaw tightened. "I know."

"And one of these days," she said, laying a hand lightly on his shoulder, "you're going to forgive yourself too."

"What about you, Flynn?" he asked at last, turning toward her. "Have you forgiven me?"

The question startled her, and she looked down at her small, work-callused hands.

"Me? Why should it matter what I think?"

"I don't know," he admitted, his voice heavy with emotion. "But somehow, it does. I know you blame me for what happened all those years ago. Grandmother said you lost a place that was home to you, at a time in your life when you needed it most. Can you honestly say that you forgive me for that, Flynn?"

Flynn turned to him then and studied his face: the tense muscles in his jaw and neck, the pain clearly visible in his stone gray eyes. For the first time since she could remember, Flynn found herself able to look at Charlie Kenilworth as if he were just a person. Incredibly, his was no longer the face of the enemy.

"Yes," she found herself able to say. "I forgive you. Really I do." Though the pain was still there, she no longer blamed Charlie for what had happened in her past. Besides, she'd made her own share of mistakes, as Trudy had so bluntly pointed out. "How about you? Can you forgive me for my behavior?"

Charlie looked genuinely startled by her request. "Of course," he said, sounding like nothing could be easier. He looked genuinely relieved.

Flynn smiled at him. "Wonderful," she said, kicking her legs out in front of her, like a child. "Virgie would be so pleased to see us making peace finally."

Charlie returned her grin and jerked his chin upward at the blue summer sky. "Funny. Something tells me she already is."

CHAPTER EIGHT

Flynn was hunched over a pile of specs, which she'd spread out on the kitchen counter, when she got the strangest feeling that she was being watched. Slowly she turned to find Trudy's accusing gaze aimed at her.

"Hey," said Trudy.

"Hey," said Flynn. She turned back to her papers and waited for the girl to make the next move. She imagined Trudy's eyes on the back of her neck.

"Don't you ever take a break?" the girl asked finally.

Flynn straightened and met Trudy's eyes. "Sure, if I've got a good enough reason."

"Like, what's a good reason?"

Flynn tried not to stare back at her. This was the most social Trudy had been since she'd met her. "Like…" Flynn scanned her memory banks for a possible diversion. "Frisbee and ice cream."

"What?" Trudy snorted. "You're kidding, right?"

Flynn took her by the arm and led her toward the front door. "Trust me, there are three things I *never* kid about, and ice cream and Frisbee are two of them."

Trudy took the bait. "What's the other thing?"

Flynn smiled gently. "I'll tell you one of these days, when you're ready." Trudy looked set to argue the point, but Flynn urged her toward the front door. "Come on. I've got two Frisbees in the trunk of my car. Pick the one you like best. Afterward, we'll go out for ice cream. We'll play to see who buys."

"I'm not going to buy," Trudy grumbled. "I don't have any money."

"A girl your age? You mean to tell me your dad doesn't give you any spending money?"

"Well," Trudy admitted, "he gives me some. I spent it all."

"Well then," Flynn said resolutely, "you'll just have to earn some more."

Trudy stared at her. "How am I supposed to do that?"

"You're not *supposed* to do anything, as far I'm concerned," Flynn said companionably. "But if you *want* to earn a few extra bucks, I'm sure I can put you to work around here. For now, we'll play for time. I'll teach you how to play Frisbee golf. The loser has to pay the winner an hour."

A light came into Trudy's eyes. "What if I win?"

"Then I'm at your disposal for an hour. We can do anything you want, as long as it's not illegal, immoral, or improper."

"You mean, as long as it's not fun."

Flynn laughed. "Oh, you'd be surprised!"

Five minutes later Flynn and Trudy were on Virgie's expansive front lawn, tossing a yellow disk at various "holes." To her delight, Trudy proved to be a good student. With the handicap Flynn had given herself, the score was even by the time they'd reached the fifth hole.

Flynn had retrieved one of Trudy's wilder throws when the girl called out, waving the Frisbee that Flynn had just tossed back to her.

"Hey!" Trudy hollered. "See if you can catch this one!"

"Trudy, no. We're playing Frisbee golf, not—" But the disc was already airborne.

Flynn sprang into action, pumping her legs as she chased the Frisbee. She stretched out her fingers to catch it…and ran smack-dab into a solid figure in her path.

"Oof!" the figure said as it wrapped its arms around Flynn to break her fall.

Breathless and embarrassed, Flynn looked up into the amused eyes of Trudy's father.

"I think she did that on purpose," Charlie observed, Flynn still resting in his embrace.

"Delinquent," Flynn murmured. Either the fall or the warmth of Charlie's arms still around her shoulders was making her head spin.

"Like grandmother, like granddaughter, do you think?" He raised an eyebrow.

Flynn shrugged at the suggestion, casting an eye in the direction of the teenager, now doubled over in laughter.

If Trudy was attempting to play matchmaker in her adolescent way, perhaps Virgie's thoughts about Flynn and Charlie weren't so ridiculous after all.

She squeezed Charlie's hand in thanks before letting it go.

"Come on," she said. "Such actions cannot go unpunished. It's time for a little parental discipline."

"What do you have in mind?"

Flynn gave him a sunny smile. "How do you feel about ice cream?"

◆　◆　◆

By the seventh week of renovations, Flynn had worked herself and her team into a frenzy of activity. Even the impossible-to-please Romy was impressed with the progress they'd made, and now, at the end of July, they were a full two days ahead of schedule.

Their breakneck pace made it difficult for Flynn to concentrate on anything other than the renovation. Still, she'd managed to squeeze in a Frisbee golf game with Trudy nearly every day, and the girl was thriving under her attention. She'd eagerly taken on every task Flynn had assigned to her, and Flynn had come up with a long list of projects for her, hoping that the feeling of involvement would boost Trudy's self-esteem.

The girl had responded even better than Flynn had hoped, and she often watched from the sidelines as Flynn's team worked. She was clearly drawn to Flynn. More important, Trudy and her father seemed to be warming to one another, a matter more gratifying than the attention Trudy was giving her.

Already completed were the demolition and the roughing-in of new services—natural gas, updated electrical boxes, new heating ducts—and the replacement of rusted, inferior pipes. The house was now wired for DSL Internet service, and there was a hookup for cable television in case the eventual owner should want it. The custom cabinets, moldings, windows, and doors had been completed off-site, right on schedule, and were ready for installation later that week.

Flynn was still inspecting the work late on Friday evening. The construction crew had gone home nearly an hour earlier, and even workaholic Romy had taken the afternoon off, insisting that she needed to get back to the city for a little "culture."

But Flynn could not bring herself to wind down for the day. The county inspector was due for a visit the following week, and she wanted to make sure everything was perfect. Two days' buffer or no, the schedule was alarmingly tight. They couldn't afford to have to redo any part of the renovation.

She was on the next-to-the-top rung of her aluminum ladder, head between two rafters, when she heard a call from below.

"Knock-knock?"

Flynn jerked around at the sound of Charlie's rich-timbred voice.

"Ow!" she cried as she cracked her head against a beam.

"Sorry!" She felt Charlie's hand give her ankle a friendly squeeze, just above the canvas tennis shoe. "You okay?" Flynn's heart began to race. He must have startled her more than she realized.

"Fine." She climbed back down into the dining room and found him regarding her with concern. She gave him a sheepish look. "My fault. I need to pay attention to what I'm doing."

"Yeah? Well, I shouldn't have startled you like that." He gave her a rigid little smile. "How's it going?"

Flynn looked at him more closely. Charlie seemed especially uncomfortable.

"All right. What's up?" she said, crossing to him.

"Who said anything was up?"

Flynn playfully kicked his shoe with her toe. "You're a terrible actor, Kenilworth. What's on your mind?"

"Nothing, really." He stepped aside to avoid her playful attack. "It's just that...well, Trudy wanted me to ask if you'd join us for dinner. We're going to head up to Ocean City to get a pizza. You're more than welcome to come along."

"Trudy did."

"Mm-hmm."

"That was very sweet of her," she said. "But how about you, Charlie? Do you want me to come?"

Charlie looked flushed. "Of course. That is, I mean…if you want." He shrugged helplessly.

"Well, I hate to disappoint you, since it's *obviously* so important to you that I go." Flynn started back toward her ladder. She didn't care about what Charlie Kenilworth thought of her. So why did it hurt so much that he was extending an empty gesture of friendship?

"Flynn." He reached out and took her by the arm, but much more gently than he had the night they'd both rushed to Virgie's bedside. "It's not that. You mustn't think I don't want you to join us."

"Well, what is it then?" Flynn pulled away and planted her hands on her hips.

"Look," he said nervously. "I didn't mean to extend a halfhearted invitation. It's just been a long time since I…well, since I asked a woman if she…" He ran one hand over his face, which had suddenly become damp with perspiration. "Let me try this again. My daughter and I would be honored if you would join us for dinner this evening. Truly. Please say you'll come."

Flynn wrinkled up her nose, considering the offer.

"We'll even let you choose the pizza. Pepperoni? Anchovy and sausage?"

Suddenly an evening with her head in the rafters didn't seem quite as appealing. "A girl's got to eat." She grinned.

"Wonderful. We'll pick you up in about ten minutes," he told her and moved away.

Flynn threw one hand to her tousled hair and glanced down at her dusty T-shirt and denim coveralls. "I'll have to get cleaned up. Give me at least twenty minutes so I can shower and wash my hair."

"Nonsense. You're perfect just the way you are." Charlie gave her an appreciative wink and headed out the door.

Flynn stared after him.

Charlie the Horrible did not seem quite so horrible anymore.

◆　◆　◆

"That," Flynn said, watching Trudy roll up her slice of pizza like a crescent roll, "is the most disgusting thing I've ever seen."

"'At's nudding," Trudy mumbled around a mouthful of crust. "'Ou shou shee wud I can do wid puddig."

Charlie nodded solemnly. "She's not kidding. Trudy can do *much* more disgusting things than this with her food."

"Well,"—Flynn shrugged—"everybody's got to have a talent."

Trudy swallowed hard, then let out a noisy chortle. "Don't make me laugh! You almost made pizza fly out of my nose!" When she brayed again, Flynn decided it was the loveliest sound she'd heard in years.

"Come on," Trudy said, "let's play a game. Rock, paper, scissors?"

"Hmm. I don't know." Flynn pretended to consider the request. "What are the stakes?"

"Your third thing."

"I beg your pardon?" Flynn took a long drink of soda pop.

"You know. You told me that there are three things you never kid about: Frisbee, ice cream, and one other thing. You said you'd tell me when I was ready. Well, I'm ready!"

Flynn gave her a gentle smile. "Yes, I believe you are." She pulled her small fingers into a fist, preparing for the child's game. As a little girl, she'd often agonized over which item—rock, paper, or scissors—to choose to win. How could she choose one so that Trudy would win?

She threw up a quick prayer, then pumped her fist in the air.

"Okay, then. Are you ready? One...two...THREE!" Flynn cast two fingers out in front of her.

"Yeeesss!" Trudy cried, her own fist still intact. "Rock beats scissors" She practically wiggled in her chair.

"So," Charlie commented to Flynn. "It sounds like you have to make a confession."

"Uh-huh," Trudy agreed. "So what's your third thing?"

"All right. You won fair and square," Flynn began, smoothing out the checkered tablecloth before her. "The one thing, besides Frisbee and ice cream, of course, that I don't ever kid about is the most important thing of all. And that's love."

Trudy looked at her blankly. "Love? Like, what does that mean?"

"It means," Flynn said gently, "that when I tell someone I love them, I really mean it. I mean that I will always love them, no matter what happens. I would never tell someone that I loved them if I didn't. I would never tell *you* that I loved you if I didn't, Trudy. But I do. Very much."

Trudy stared at her for several minutes, saying nothing. But Flynn could see the tears rise to her eyes.

"Cool," she said at last, then jumped up from the table and made a beeline for the pizza parlor's bank of video games.

Flynn turned to see Charlie looking at her in stunned silence. "What?" she said, feeling uncomfortable under his gaze.

Swiftly, and before anyone else could notice, Charlie reached over, placed one strong hand at the back of her neck, and drew her to him, pressing his warm lips against hers. As quickly as the kiss had begun, it was over.

"Just that," he said hoarsely. "And I wasn't kidding."

❖ ❖ ❖

"I don't believe this! You're in love with him!" Romy's teacup met the saucer with a clatter.

Startled by her friend's response to her news, Flynn tried to silence her. "Shh!" She looked at Romy in horror. "I am not in love with Charlie Kenilworth! I just went to dinner with him and his daughter, that's all." She looked around the porch of the river cottage where they were having afternoon tea, to make sure no one had over-heard Romy's comment.

"Yeah, like seven times in three weeks!" Romy observed. "It's become a regular date."

"It's not a date!" Flynn protested. "It's a, a—"

"The word you're looking for is 'date.'" Romy reached for the plastic bear full of honey. "Sweetie, I hate to be the one to tell you this, but you're hooked."

"I am not *hooked!*" Flynn sputtered. Romy was always jumping to conclusions. She knew better than to let it get to her.

"Hooked," Romy said evenly, "like a perch out of that beloved Pocomoke of yours. I just hope you don't wind up in the frying pan."

Flynn poured a second cupful of steaming water over her Earl

Grey tea bag. "And just what is that supposed to mean? I thought you liked Charlie. Not that I'm in love with him, because I'm *not*. But you're still the one who's yammered on about me 'charming' him since the very beginning."

"I do like Charlie," Romy assured her. "But I like *you* even more. And I'm a little worried about where this is all heading. He's a good guy, but you may be setting yourself up for a fall." She squeezed the plastic bear's belly until a thin stream of gooey, amber honey trailed into her china cup. "We're just a week and a half away from filming our last show. I've watched you nearly kill yourself getting this place fixed up over the last three months. You've turned it into the home of your dreams. It's ready to be occupied by the family of your dreams. In two weeks, you have to let it all go."

"You don't know that," Flynn said. "Charlie and I haven't decided what we're going to do with the house, exactly. We haven't even talked about it in months."

"No," Romy said. "But you agreed at the very beginning that you weren't going to share it. That means that, at the very least, you're going to lose him and Trudy. Quite possibly, you'll be losing a whole lot more."

"Besides, who said Charlie and Trudy are the family of my dreams?" Flynn ignored Romy's dire prediction. "What normal woman would choose a withdrawn, troubled teenager and an exasperating, maddening, emotionally wounded—"

"Gorgeous, kindhearted, growing-healthier-every-day man?" Romy finished for her. "Who said anything about a 'normal' woman? We're talking about you, missy. And your heart is plenty big enough to embrace this man and his child. You and I both know it already has."

Flynn gazed past her to the main house, a thousand feet away. Already, the painters had assembled their scaffolding and had begun scraping the wooden siding, to prepare for a fresh coat of white paint. As soon as their task was completed, the *Home for the Heart* crew would film the final episode on Kenilworth House. Then, just as Romy predicted, Flynn would have no excuse to remain on the property. She and Charlie had come a long way over the past three months, but even she could not pretend that he would allow her to stay on after the final renovations had been completed. Legally, he had much more right to the property than she, and he'd been gracious enough to let her use it as she'd requested. She couldn't reasonably ask for anything more.

"Do you know what this place needs?" she said.

"I'm afraid to ask," Romy said, stirring her tea.

"A dog," Flynn said with confidence. "Maybe a couple of them. Do you think it's possible to rent them?"

"Flynn." Romy leaned forward in her white wicker chair. "Have you been listening to a word I've said? This is exactly what I'm talking about. You're still trying to create your dream home. Now you're adding pets"

"Think of how great they'll look," Flynn cut her off. "Can't you just see it? Think how cozy and homey the place will seem. Our viewers will love it!"

Romy considered this for a moment. "Yes. But it's not just up to you. You're not the only one who lives here. In fact, you hardly 'live' here at all."

"You're right." Flynn jumped to her feet. "I shouldn't make a decision like this alone." She took one final drink of lukewarm tea. "I'll go get Trudy."

"Flynn!" There was warning in Romy's tone. "That's not what I meant, and you know it."

"Relax, Ro. Don't be so tense." Flynn took the cup and saucer from her friend's hand and carried it, along with her own, back toward the cottage. "Consider it part of the renovation. Every house needs a pet. Anyway, Charlie will adore having a dog."

"And if he doesn't?"

Flynn grinned wickedly. "There's always your room at the brownstone…"

CHAPTER NINE

The long drive from Philadelphia to Snow Hill took nearly four hours, but with the prospect of his daughter—and, Charlie had to confess, a certain lovely architect—awaiting him at Kenilworth House, it was worth every minute of effort.

As he wound down Route 12 south from Salisbury, he considered again how lucky he was to have Flynn around. Though his company had generously allowed him two months off, they had required that he come back to Philadelphia for several crucial meetings. In June, he'd been forced to drag a resentful teenager daughter back to the city with him for the first two. This time Flynn had suggested that Trudy stay with her for a sleepover.

He was not usually one to accept assistance from others, but Charlie had accepted her offer with eagerness and tremendous gratitude. Unfortunately, his team had been unable to complete their business on Friday, which meant that he would have to return the following week. His coworkers suggested that he stay in town for the weekend. Flynn would be willing to watch Trudy for a few more days. But he had no real desire to spend the weekend alone in the city. What he wanted, more than anything in the world, was simply to get back home to his family.

That is, to his daughter, Charlie corrected himself. Flynn was hardly a member of his family. She wasn't his wife, no matter what his grandmother had intended. Why, he'd actually accused her of using his grandmother to get her hands on his property! He was fortunate that Flynn was willing simply to speak to him, let alone befriend him. He was lucky that he hadn't completely blown their friendship with that crazy, impromptu kiss at the pizza parlor a few weeks ago. A romantic relationship was out of the question.

So why had he stopped in Salisbury to purchase an eight-dollar bouquet of daisies for a woman who would never, *could* never be more than his friend?

Charlie banged his head several times against the headrest. *Idiot,* he told himself. *You haven't got a chance with this woman.* Beautiful and intelligent; strong, spunky, and warm-hearted, Flynn Kelley was every man's dream, and he'd treated her horribly. There was no way she would be able to see past his mistakes and shortcomings. During the past month, they'd had more in-depth conversations than he could count, and he treasured each one. Day by day, week by week, Charlie felt as though he was getting tiny, precious glimpses into Flynn's beautiful soul. And she had reached out to his daughter, offering the gift of friendship to a moody, sullen, yet undeniably lovable girl who was, he realized with gratitude, blossoming under Flynn's glowing attention.

As was he.

He didn't kid himself. Flynn could not be interested in anything more than a casual friendship. It was absurd even to consider any other possibility. But she had brightened his life more than he'd ever thought possible. And after this incredible, momentous summer, neither he nor his daughter would ever be the same.

Charlie pulled into the driveway, and his heart beat faster at the sight of Flynn, standing in front of Kenilworth House with Trudy and several members of the *Home for the Heart* crew. Disappointment washed over him as he took in the crowd and camera. He'd hoped to have a few moments alone with Flynn. To give her the daisies. To tell her how much he appreciated her watching over Trudy. Perhaps even to invite her out for a twilight canoe ride on the mesmerizing waters of the Pocomoke.

He climbed out of the silver CRV and grabbed his briefcase from the passenger side of the vehicle. By the time he had almost reached Flynn, the state-of-the-art camera was rolling again.

"As we enter the final stage, crews are working overtime to complete the last stage of renovations," Flynn was saying. Her gaze met Charlie's over the cameraman's head, and her smile deepened. A single dimple appeared in the perfect rose of her right cheek.

Charlie grinned back idiotically.

"Hi, Dad," Trudy whispered, giving him a shy grin.

Charlie closed his eyes and breathed deeply, drinking in the scent of his grandmother's roses, enjoying the light of his daughter's smile, the musical timbre of Flynn's voice...

The grainy wetness of a large, slimy tongue tickling his fingers.

Charlie let out a sharp cry, dropping his briefcase and withdrawing his fingers from the offending animal.

Or rather, *animals.*

At his feet, Charlie saw in horrified shock, were not one, but *two* enormous black Labradors, their great, pink, slobbery tongues lolling at him.

"What...on...God's...green...earth...are these animals doing here?" he hollered.

Immediately the cameraman spun on him.

"Hello, Charlie!" Flynn said cheerfully. She turned to the cameramen. "Cut! Take a break, huh, guys?"

But Charlie's mind wasn't on the cameras.

"What? Who?"

Flynn blinked at the hefty canines, both of which had collapsed, contented, at Charlie's feet. "Look! Isn't that sweet? They already recognize you as the Alpha dog."

"The...?" Charlie stared at her. "I beg your pardon?"

"You know. The Alpha dog. The one in charge. The leader of the pack. They understand that you're their master!"

"Their *master.*" The larger of the two animals stood and dropped a mangled, saliva-soaked yellow tennis ball on Charlie's right foot.

"She wants you to throw it."

"She?"

"That's Martha," Flynn supplied. "The smaller one is Mary. You know, like Mary and Martha from the Bible? It fits their personalities exactly. Martha is the workaholic. She'll run around after the ball

all day if you'll keep tossing it for her. Mary's the lover. She likes to cuddle. See?" Flynn reached down and scratched the dog on her eye ridges, while the Lab's eyes rolled back in her substantial, squarish head.

"But…" Charlie set his mouth in a firm line. He adored Flynn, but this was absurd. "We never discussed getting a dog," he reminded her. "Much less two!" For a split second, he was distracted by the sound of the word "we." It felt even better than he would have imagined to use it to encompass himself and Flynn.

For the first time, Flynn's expression of delight wavered.

"Come on, Dad." Trudy tugged at his sleeve. "Lighten up!" She bent down and threw her arms around Mary, who obliged by giving the girl's face a generous, if smelly, soaking.

His daughter giggled as Martha stepped over to join the fun and nuzzle her ear.

Flynn laid one small hand on his arm. "I'm sorry. Please forgive me. I don't blame you for being mad. It was a silly impulse. I was hoping you'd like the dogs. But of course you don't have to keep them. Don't worry. In just a few weeks, it will be time for one of us to move on. I promise, when I go, the dogs will go with me."

Charlie could not help but notice that she was assuming she would be the one to vacate the premises. He hated to think that either one of them would go. But they'd agreed to part ways, and he had no choice but to keep his part of the bargain. He could no longer accuse Flynn of being disingenuous. She'd shown him time and time again that her heart was pure. She was continuing to show him so, even as she was preparing to withdraw from his life.

"Flynn." He fought the urge to reach out and take her in his arms. "There's no need to ask forgiveness."

"Why not? I acted selfishly and impulsively, didn't I?"

"Don't be silly." He reached out and stroked her smooth white cheek for just a moment. He could not help himself. "Are you kidding? I care about you too much to let a little thing like…er, make that, two *big* things, like these dogs, bother me."

Flynn reached up and caught his hand with her own. Charlie felt a warmth flowing from her fingers that seemed to stretch up his entire arm, across his chest, and reach deep into his heart. "You mean," she nearly whispered, "it's easy to forgive someone when you really care about them? Is that it?"

Charlie nodded wordlessly. He was way past being able to speak.

Flynn took one small step closer to him. She was near enough now for Charlie to lean down and cover her soft lips with his own. "That's what Virgie was trying to tell you all along, Charlie. That's how God feels about you. And it's why I—"

"Flynn," he interrupted, his voice ragged. What she was offering was too much, and at the same time, not enough. She'd given him her forgiveness. But he was sure that she would never give him her love. He didn't dare hope. What Flynn Kelley deserved was so much more than he could give.

He broke abruptly away, the loss of her touch instantly leaving him bereft. Thrusting the bouquet of daisies into his daughter's arms, he grabbed his briefcase, pushed past the open-mouthed camera crew, and headed for the guesthouse. A place where he would spend numerous long, sleepless nights, wishing for the one thing he had foolishly—and, by creating an embarrassing scene in front of Flynn's entire crew, quite publicly—thrown away for good.

CHAPTER TEN

Flynn hunkered down in her sterile editing booth, grateful for the rare solitude. It had been two full months since her team had finished filming at Kenilworth House, and she was tired of smiling stiff-lipped to the production crew: Romy, in particular. Tired of pretending everything was all right. Tired of acting as though her heart hadn't been horribly bruised, just as Romy had predicted it would be. Of course, her roommate suspected the truth, but Flynn refused to discuss it. Nothing could change the fact that Charlie Kenilworth had drop-kicked her, and the last thing she wanted to do was relive the experience. Why, she'd practically *thrown* herself at the man, and he'd run from her as though his shorts were on fire! Very complimentary.

Charming as a snake, indeed.

"Hey there." Romy peeked her head over the cubicle, her hands gripping the top of the wall, Kilroy-fashion. "Got a sec?"

"Huh," Flynn grunted. She kept her eyes trained on her editing screen. She'd figured out it was best not to leave an opening for conversation when Romy wanted to get deep and personal.

"Here. Take a look at this, would you?" Her producer stepped into the doorway and pulled a videotape out of her Italian leather bag.

"What is it?" Flynn's eyes flickered back to the glare of the screen. "I'm busy here, as you can see."

"Well, pardon me, Tom Brokaw!" Romy dropped the tape case on the desk with a bang. "But I think you'll want to see this."

"Romy, I—"

"Oh, for crying out loud. Just *do* it, Flynn."

Flynn looked up at Romy, startled. She was used to being gently bullied by her loudmouthed friend, but she wasn't accustomed to hearing her adopt such a severe tone.

"All right, all right," she grumbled. "How long will this take?"

"That depends on you," Romy said enigmatically. Then she was gone.

"Of all the—" Exasperated, Flynn ejected the tape she'd been viewing. "Does it look like I don't have anything better to do with my time?" She flipped open the cheap brown case Romy had left and examined its contents, but there was no label, no editorial notation.

"Lovely. Just what I need. A mystery job." Flynn shoved the tape into the machine, half hoping the viewer would jam. Having to call a repairman would, of course, throw her off schedule but also might teach her dictator of a producer a thing or two.

Flynn was still grumbling to herself when the first image appeared on screen. It took several seconds for her to fully grasp what she was viewing: the messy scene between herself and Charlie that had taken place two months earlier.

"No," she whispered, as if by will alone she could make the image go away.

"Flynn," she heard and saw Charlie say. "There's no need to ask forgiveness." The sound of his tremulous voice hypnotized her, and she could not bring herself to eject the tape. Flynn shook her head. She distinctly remembered telling the cameramen "Cut." Apparently, they had continued filming without her knowledge, something she would personally make certain they regretted before the workday was done.

Flynn folded her arms over one another, trembling within her camel-colored silk shirt, as she watched Charlie gently caress her. Then, half thrilled, half horrified, she saw herself snatch up his hand with her own. Tears burned her eyes. Why had Romy brought this? Wouldn't she have known how it would torture her? Still, she could not tear her eyes away.

"You mean," she heard herself murmur, "it's easy to forgive someone when you really care about them?"

She watched, horrified, as Charlie nodded, listened to her feeble attempt to explain grace, then pulled away. After a moment, the image on the screen shuddered and faded, and another blipped into its place.

This picture, too, was of Charlie. But Flynn herself, the camera crew, and Trudy all were gone. No longer were the stately lines of Kenilworth House in the background. Instead, inexplicably, Charlie stood on what appeared to be a typical East Coast city street, not unlike the one on which her own studio was located. His thick, wavy hair had been cropped closer to his head, so that his ears popped out like a small boy's, and the thinness of his face indicated that he had lost weight: ten, twelve pounds at least. He was dressed casually, in faded jeans and a heavy fisherman's sweater. Winter had struck not just her life, but the entire Atlantic Coast.

"Hello," he was saying. He was staring bug-eyed at the camera, as though a death ray might, at any moment, fire out of it and disintegrate him.

Flynn's lips shaped themselves into a quavery smile. One of her cameramen must have taken it upon himself to get some extra interview footage.

"I'm Charlie Kenilworth, co-owner of Kenilworth House." He licked his dry lips. "And what you have seen over the last few months is an incredible renovation. Not just of a house. But of a life."

Flynn leaned forward, one hand finding its way to her open mouth. *What in the world?*

"I…uh." Charlie blinked at the camera for a moment, then stepped forward in his eagerness, getting too close, so the cameraman had to back up to bring him back into focus. "Look, I'm not great with words. I could never host a show like you do, Flynn. In fact, I'm so much in awe of you I can hardly see straight." Flynn's pulse quickened; her palms grew damp. "But I can tell the truth, and that's what I'm going to do. Even though putting my feelings on the line like this feels like it might kill me." Charlie looked so pained, Flynn considered for a moment that it actually might.

"And the truth," he said, "is this: Flynn, you've changed my life. You've changed my daughter's life, and I owe you more than I could ever repay. But this isn't about repaying anything. It's about telling you how I feel. And what I feel is…"

Flynn held her breath.

"I feel empty. Miserable. Lost," Charlie said, looking all those things and more. "Nothing's been the same since you've been gone. Trudy misses you. Mary and Martha—thanks for letting Trudy keep them, by the way—miss you." He took a long, shaky breath. "But most of all, *I* miss you. I know I've been a clod, but, well, someone very important to me once said that it's easy to forgive people if you really care about them. And so, I'm hoping that somehow, someway, you can find it in your heart to forgive a fool who is wise in only one way: in loving you."

"Yes! YES!" Flynn reached out and gripped the video viewer in both hands. "I forgive you, Charlie!"

"Do you really mean that?"

Flynn spun crazily in her rickety office chair, swiveling toward the sound of her beloved's voice.

"Charlie!" Before she could step into his outstretched arms, he was holding her, as she had so often imagined in her dreams over the past two months.

"Hello, you." Charlie spoke in a low voice thick with emotion, making the pronoun sound like a private endearment. Flynn felt his strong arms encircle her shoulders and draw her to him, then her cheek was pressed to his heart, and she marveled at how familiar and right it felt to be in his embrace.

"But what *is* all this?" she murmured against the rough threads of his sweater.

"Haven't you guessed?" Charlie pulled back and held her by the shoulders, at arm's length. "I made the tape with the help of your crew. Romy helped me set it up. It's an apology. And, you'll see if you finish watching it, an announcement of my intentions."

"Your *what?*" A tiny laugh rolled forth from deep in her throat.

"It may be an antiquated custom," Charlie admitted, pulling her to him once more. "But what could be more appropriate, considering the historic nature of our hometown?"

"'Our' hometown?" Flynn snuggled in deeper. "Mmm. I love the way that sounds."

"You do?" He sounded as if he still found it hard to believe but was determined to try. "Because, you know, I'm talking about much more than sharing a piece of property. God willing, I'm talking about sharing a life."

"Well, I would certainly hope so," Flynn said, all mock seriousness. "After all, it's what Virgie wanted all along!"

Charlie tenderly tucked one unruly curl behind the delicate curve of her ear. "Despite what we thought at the time, Grandmother did know what she was talking about. But this isn't about what she wants," he said, his voice thick with meaning. Flynn closed her eyes, feeling his lips brush against her hair. "You need to know that this is what *I* want."

"It's what I want too," Flynn murmured. She leaned back, his strong hands at her waist, and wrapped her arms around his muscled neck. "How could I want anything else?"

"I love you, Flynn Kelley," Charlie said, cradling her chin in one powerful hand. "No kidding."

"And I love you." Flynn leaned forward to meet the first honest-to-goodness kiss from her beloved, secure in the knowledge that, after years of hoping and searching, her heart had finally, and miraculously, found its home.

BESIDE THE STILL WATERS

Barbara Curtis

*Thanks be to God—and to all those
who helped with this story.*

*"O magnify the LORD with me,
and let us exalt his name together."*

PSALM 34:3

*"He leadeth me beside the still waters.
He restoreth my soul."*

PSALM 23:2-3

CHAPTER ONE

K. C. McKenzie walked to the picture window of her ninth floor furnished apartment. Her few possessions were packed, ready. She just had one final farewell to say. Pressing her hand against the cold glass, she looked out beyond Lake Shore Drive to Lake Michigan.

"Good-bye," she whispered to the waves pounding below. She'd once loved these waters that had been part of her life, all twenty-seven years of it, here in Chicago. The waves were an old-time companion, sometimes nipping at her feet as she'd run along the beach, other times drenching her clothes in their awesome show of power. But no longer could she laugh at or delight in the waters below. Especially on a day like today, when the waves displayed their pounding, brutal ability to heave, to crush...to snatch. Just as they had the day they left her a widow.

She shuddered and stepped back from the window, her gaze going to her leather briefcase, the last item to be placed in the BMW. Inside was her lifeline, a rose-scented letter containing the one thing she needed to start a new life. *Hope.*

Brian's Great-aunt Lidia probably had no idea what the oft-read letter in an arthritic scrawl meant to her. But a few memorized snatches clung to K. C.'s heart.

Dear Kathryn,

I'm sure you've found that two years do not erase your grieving.... I thought you'd want to know

Mother's old farm is up for sale.... Such fond memories I have of you and Brian playing there as children....

From my front door I can see that the old house
could use a touch of repair. Perhaps now is the time
for it to belong to the McKenzie family once again.

Should this be the Lord's leading for you, please
stop and see me when you get here....

Buying Brian's Great-grandmother McKenzie's old house, a place
of childhood memories, a place she could call home, seemed the perfect balm for her restless heart. Using her interior designer skills to
remodel the place that also held a part of Brian would bring healing,
a sense of comfort. Of course she'd miss the city, the familiarity, the
pace, but maybe the waters over on the Michigan side of the lake
would be kinder, the way she remembered them.

Turning to an end table, K. C. touched the heart-framed photograph of a laughing couple, arms linked at the wheel of a sailboat.
They belonged together, complemented each other. He with blond
hair, hers dark and caught up in a ponytail as it was now, both with
brown eyes sparkling with love, both so full of promise.

She picked up the white frame and clasped it close. This couple
no longer existed. Brian was gone, and she, too, had been robbed of
the spark of life, even while living. She wondered if she would ever
laugh like that again.

K. C. placed the photograph inside her briefcase next to the letter
and two long-ago snapshots of the farmhouse Aunt Lidia had enclosed. With one last glance around the apartment that had served as
a temporary home for two years, she locked up for good.

Though she didn't need a map for the drive around the lake and into
the southwestern corner of Michigan, K. C. did need some directions
once she pulled off I-94 at the Hartley exit. She hadn't been back to
the fruit farm since she was twelve and was uncertain of the exact location, but she hoped the locals downtown could direct her.

If only… If only Aunt Lidia hadn't waited weeks from dating the letter to mail it. If only she'd remembered to put postage on it so it wouldn't have been returned to sender. If only she'd had K. C.'s current address instead of where she and Brian had once lived.

If only Brian hadn't died, none of this would matter.

K. C. shook her head, stopping such wasted thoughts. In spite of the delays and the irrationality of the venture, she knew this was what she should do and therefore had to accept the timing as well.

At the single stoplight in town, modern-day Hartley took her by surprise. The farming community had shriveled through the years. Several of the shops in the two-block business district had boards across their windows and signs hanging on their doors: *Closed.* For good, it appeared.

Finding a nice hotel where she could spend a couple of weeks until her inherited lake cottage was readied might be more difficult than she had anticipated. But she'd worry about that later. She wanted to see the old farmhouse first.

Locating my farm shouldn't be hard—everyone must know where it is. Well, she amended to herself, *it isn't actually mine yet, but it will be.* She had enough money set aside that no one could refuse her offer.

Pulling into the only gas station in sight, K. C. stopped at the full-service pump, waiting for an attendant. She lowered the automatic window midway as a man around thirty, shrugging into a jacket over his green-and-navy plaid shirt, strode out from the small building. Each step he took declared confidence. His attire stated otherwise, though, with his wrists protruding inches below the sleeves of the jacket that bore a worn Bob's Auto Service logo stitched above the pocket.

Catching herself staring at the attractive face and thick, wavy hair almost as black as her own, K. C. guiltily looked away. How could she be aware of such things? Better to focus on his knowledge of cars and local farms.

When she looked back to get his attention, he readjusted his course and headed toward her. She managed a smile.

"Hello. Fill it with premium, please." She shivered a bit in the cold spring air. "And could you also check the oil?"

Surprise flickered across the man's gold-flecked eyes, making it apparent that he wasn't used to providing such service. But before she could rescind her request, he was pumping gas and had grabbed a squeegee out of a bucket.

"Sure. Just pop the hood." He started on her windows.

And again, K. C. caught herself watching him, noticing how his eyelids crinkled at the outer edges. Laughing at her, no doubt. There was no hiding the fact that she was an outsider, flagged by her out-of-state license plates and gray BMW. It even lacked the farm dust of other passing cars.

"The oil is fine." The man wiped his hands on a paper towel he pulled from the outdoor dispenser.

"Thank you." The pump clicked off, and she handed him the exact change.

"No problem. You're quite welcome." He half smiled, and his eyes took on a warm, charmingly boyish look that made K. C. feel—what? She wasn't sure, nor was she comfortable with it. It was as if she were attracted to him, which, of course, was ridiculous.

"Sir," K. C. called after him as he turned to head back inside. How could she have gotten sidetracked so quickly?

"Yes?"

"Could you please give me directions to Sixty-sixth?"

His eyes lit up with amusement. "Sure. Are you looking for Sixty-sixth Street or Sixty-sixth Avenue?"

"Street, avenue—" She shrugged. "Does it make a difference?"

"Well, yes, here in Hartley it does. There's one of each." His compelling gaze, highlighted with that teasing glimmer, held hers. "And the two intersect."

"Oh." K. C. scrunched her face. "I don't know. I'm looking for the old Walter McKenzie farm. I don't remember exactly how to get there. Are you familiar with it?"

"Yes." His eyes narrowed, and his tone turned cautious. "Why?"

"I'm interested in seeing it."

"Why?" he asked again.

K. C. wasn't sure how to answer. Was he just a busybody or suspicious of strangers, or was this the small-town way of looking out for each other?

"Personal reasons," she said simply, deciding against being specific.

"I see." He looked at her strangely, and in that moment, all charm was replaced with a cold stare.

"Well," K. C. persisted after a prolonged silence on his part, "do you know where it is?"

"Yes."

"May I get directions?" She tried to keep the building exasperation out of her voice.

He stared at her a moment longer, seeming to debate whether or not to provide the information.

"Turn left at the light," he finally said, "heading toward the interstate. Go two miles to Sixty-sixth Avenue and turn right." His tone matched the precision of his directions. "The farm is on the left, nine-tenths of a mile. The next right is Sixty-sixth *Street*. If you come to the green-shingled house on the corner there, you've gone too far." He crossed his arms, signaling the finality of the conversation.

"Thank you," K. C. said. The directions sounded familiar now, and simple. Good thing, too, as his stance made it clear he was not going to repeat them. The only sound competing with his silence was the whir of her window as she pressed the button to raise it. At least he knew his way around here. Hastily she put the car into gear and took off. A quick peek back in the mirror showed him staring after her, arms still crossed, his scowl even deeper.

The sun was inching toward the horizon as K. C. made the turn onto Sixty-sixth Avenue. She knew exactly where she was now. This was the stretch of gravel road where summers ago she'd ridden her bicycle countless miles, back and forth between the farm and this corner. Her heart accelerated along with the car as second by second she drew nearer to the hill not quite a mile down the road.

Then, just before the crest, there it was—her farm! Acres and acres of fruit trees stood like watchmen among the last remains of a late-season snow. And the sun's final glow presented her with a welcome mat as it bounced off the packing shed, reflecting a warm, pinkish image into the small pond.

K. C. pulled to the side of the road a moment and gazed at the wondrous scene before her. The duck pond was peaceful and still, unchanged from the long-ago days when she and Brian and his brother, Colton, rowed across it. The sight kindled a tiny longing. These waters were safe. Maybe someday she could venture onto a boat again…something small, like the old, unwieldy rowboat they'd used.

Plans and memories tumbled together. She couldn't wait to find the lilac bush that bloomed outside Great-grandmother McKenzie's bedroom window. Even the lilac soaps and candles Brian once bought her didn't begin to compare with the fragrance of that old tree. When she moved into the house, she'd make the front bedroom hers, where she could wake up to the scent of purple lilacs in the spring.

I'm home. The peace settling in her heart confirmed the rightness of this wild move she'd made.

She pulled back onto the road, anticipating the moment she'd glimpse the farmhouse. She'd never even wondered before, but might not the single-level wing have been an afterthought decades ago? The framework of the small living room, bathroom, and music room resembled an odd appendage growing from the side of a two-story farmhouse. She made a mental note to research it.

K. C. spotted the red barn, dulled through the years but standing ramrod straight. And then, as she crested the hill, the house came into view. She hit the brake so hard she had to brace herself against the steering wheel.

A touch of repair? Aunt Lidia's sight must be poor, very poor. The building was *dilapidated*.

Pulling into the long, sloping driveway, K. C. brought the car to a halt and sat without moving, staring at the house. Behind the yellow police tape that stretched across the front porch, the windows were broken out and boarded up. Paint splatters on the once-pristine white siding matched the bright, greenish blue trim around the window frames. And the privet hedge, once growing sedately beneath the music room window, now looked like a jungle attacking the side of the house and creeping around the front. Known to thrive with neglect, this shrub was flourishing.

K. C. got out of her car and walked through the front yard, weeds catching at her knees. Standing carefully on the broken glass beneath the front bedroom window, K. C. peered inside. Empty— except for shotgun shells scattered across the floor.

The tattered, dingy pillowcase hanging out an upstairs window seemed to be a limp, silent plea of the house for help.

K. C. followed the ugly siding around the house to the back. Here the colors faded to dull lime on the two-story portion with graying wood showing beneath rotted shingles on the rest. The rear entrance was ajar, though not welcoming. Anyone pushing against the thick cardboard door could enter. K. C. shivered, wondering if indeed she was alone on the property.

The old kitchen was gone, but the wide concrete porch around which Great-grandmother McKenzie had planted hollyhocks partially remained. K. C. bent down, pushing away weeds from the edge of the porch to reveal three small handprints pressed into the cement almost twenty years ago.

Brian, Colton, K. C. The names and ages were barely readable now. Brian, the leader of the trio, had been ten, and she and Colton seven. Gently she placed her hand over Brian's small imprint, her throat tightening at this nearly forgotten memory of him. Brian, always so sure of himself, so strong and steady.

I'm so sorry.

She stood, pushing aside the emptiness as she had done so many times before. Repairing this house would occupy her time and thoughts, she realized as she surveyed the ruin around her. It'd take months and no telling how much money to restore this place, but it could be done, of that she was certain. Even with the disrepair and the condemning police tape, the house had escaped being torn down. It was a survivor.

Somewhere upstairs a door banged. K. C. shuddered, glancing up at another paneless window. She hoped it was just the wind. This place would make a pretty good home for a vagrant.

As the sun dropped behind the apple trees for the night, K. C. knew she couldn't go inside. She'd be foolish to do so, especially with no electricity to offset the approaching darkness. The thought of going inside triggered another long-ago memory. The pact. After Great-grandmother McKenzie's funeral, K. C., Colton, and Brian had promised that the next time they ever entered this house, it would be together. Now that wasn't possible. Only she and Colton remained.

Debating whether to stop by Great-aunt Lidia's house tonight, K. C. glanced at the green-shingled house down on the corner. She saw no lights on, and she didn't want to barge in on her this late in the day.

As dusk settled around the farm and K. C. knew it was time to leave, the sound of an approaching engine broke the silence. Not one vehicle had come down the road since she'd arrived. But a green Jeep Wrangler slowed as it crested the hill and neared the driveway, as if someone was looking for something. She caught her breath, suddenly aware of the isolation of this place…of her vulnerability. Her car was left wide open with her cell phone thrown on the seat. And she was too far away to get to it now without being seen.

K. C. stepped into the shadows behind the privet just as the Jeep stopped opposite the bottom of the driveway. K. C. held her breath, her heart thudding in terror, as she realized she was about to be blocked in. Then the driver accelerated and sped away—but not before K. C. recognized his green-and-navy plaid shirt and almost black, wavy hair.

CHAPTER TWO

Her heart still pounding, K. C. ran to her car, got in, and slammed the door. The wheels spun in the gravel as she turned toward town, to safety.

It's nothing to worry about. He probably lives down this road and is just going home and wondered who was in the driveway. He recognized my car. That's all. But she still checked the mirror to be sure he hadn't turned around. Someone with such compelling eyes couldn't be dangerous. Could he?

Now would be a good time to start looking for a motel for the night. After things were settled with the farm, she'd take care of readying her own grandmother's cottage in South Haven on Lake Michigan. She'd prefer living inland, but she'd cope near the lake. She'd be relieved when the farmhouse was habitable, though, and especially glad for the additional miles it would put between Lake Michigan and her. But for tonight, she'd be grateful just to find a comfortable bed in a safe place.

Her hands had finally stopped shaking, and she concentrated on checking along the main road for a motel. None. Taking a right at the light in town, she drove east. Still nothing. And as the farms grew larger and more spread apart, the less likely the prospects looked.

Retracing her route back to the traffic light, she tried the opposite direction. On the edge of town across the railroad tracks she spotted an old, red-brick building identifying itself as the Hartley Hotel. But as she got closer, the disrepair of the three-story structure glared at her from dimly lit windows. She kept going. She found nothing farther on, and now the gloom of a moonless night was settling around the town. Taking a deep breath, she knew she'd have to go back to the Hartley.

It's only for a night. It'll be all right. I hope.

After checking in and climbing the deserted, narrow stairs to her room, K. C. bolted the door. Not hungry enough to dare leave the safety she felt behind the locked door, she was staying put for the night.

She fluffed two lumpy pillows and leaned against them, pondering the turn her life was taking. She had cut ties with everyone who knew her as Brian's wife. She didn't fit in anymore, and people seemed not to know what to say. Her parents lived in Hawaii, eagerly accepting her assurances that all was well here. Brian's family lived relatively close, though, and were still kind and supportive. *Especially Colton.*

She pulled out her brother-in-law's business card: Pot-Shots in downtown South Haven. Just a couple of miles up the lakeshore from her cottage. Now that she was so close, she expected to see a lot of him.

She stared at the card a moment, feeling secure in God's leading on this venture.

Thank you, Lord, she whispered. *I want to follow.*

She dialed the number, hoping Colton was still working in the back even after closing hours.

"Pot-Shots."

K. C. smiled at how easily Colton spoke the name, remembering how he'd cringed when his partner had insisted their combination florist-photography business needed a touristy name in a touristy town.

"Colton—"

"Kace! How are you? And where are you?"

"I'm fine, and I'm in Hartley."

"What are you doing *there?* There's nothing there except—"

"—your great-grandmother's house. I heard it's for sale."

"Does this mean what I think it does?"

K. C. laughed. "Probably. I plan to buy it and restore it. So I had to call to keep the pact."

"Ah, the pact." There was a moment of silence. He, too, probably was recalling the day the official pledge was made to enter the house together—originally as a threesome. "So, how about if I come over tomorrow morning and meet you there at nine?"

She chuckled softly. "I guess I can wait that long. See you tomorrow, then."

Digging into her briefcase, K. C. pulled out the two old photos Aunt Lidia had sent. This was how the house would look again—stately against meticulous landscaping on the outside with the ornate, hand-carved woodwork uncovered inside. After today's visit, her vision of a complete restoration was looking pretty remote, but she'd cling to her hope, no matter how threadbare.

Of course she still needed to purchase the house. Although obstacles immediately filled her thoughts, she pushed them aside. No use looking for trouble. After all, how many people were standing in line to buy a dilapidated old house?

K. C. settled under the thin hotel blanket, glad for the street lamp shining through the window like a night-light. She would have slept peacefully, looking forward to seeing her house again, if it hadn't been for the recurring memory of a green Jeep on a lonely gravel road, and a man with dark wavy hair.

The next morning K. C. pulled on work clothes, ready for the dust and dirt of the farmhouse. In the crispness of the bright, clear day, things looked much better as she approached the farm. The apple trees bordering the road appeared healthy, and the pond sparkled in the sunlight with the weathered barn towering behind it.

But as she pulled into the driveway, one glance at the house reconfirmed K. C.'s initial appraisal. Even in broad daylight, with the sun aiming its best light on it, the house was dilapidated. She looked around, a sense of despair threatening, then turned as a black Integra pulled up beside her car.

"Colton!" K. C. called and ran over to greet him, glad that he was so different from Brian. Colton was dark-haired, serious, like her. But as she looked into his eyes, so filled with caring and compassion, she was again reminded of her loss.

"Kace!" Colton swung out of the car and pulled her into a hug. "It's been months, maybe a year since I saw you."

"Way too long. Can you believe this?" K. C. gestured toward the house.

"Man, it's a wreck. It's gone downhill since I last saw it." He shook his head. "Have you looked around much?"

"It was already getting dark when I arrived yesterday." She laughed self-consciously, embarrassed now at her fright. "I panicked when a man from the gas station stopped." She shrugged. "It's kind of isolated out here at night. That's probably why—"

"What man?" Colton frowned.

"An attendant who gave me directions. But it's okay," she reassured him. "He just acted strange when I asked about the farm. I was almost ready to leave here, and he stopped down by the foot of the driveway. He probably lives out this way and was just wondering who was here, then recognized my car. He knew I was coming here. Anyway"—she shrugged—"he didn't bother me, and he's probably harmless." She would have been convinced of that if she didn't now keep picturing the coldness in his eyes when he had finally given her the directions.

"Just be careful." Colton wrapped a protective arm around K. C.'s shoulders in a brotherly hug.

"I will. But, Colton," she lamented, pointing to the yard and house, "isn't this such a shame?"

Colton nodded. "My great-grandmother would be horrified."

"But someone did take care of the barn." She looked at it through an artist's eyes. "It's beautifully rustic and weather-beaten and doesn't look like it's missing a single board."

"That's simply business," Colton said. "The barn is needed for the farming operation, the house isn't. No one lives here—who's supposed to, anyway. I know migrant workers used it years ago, but obviously no one saw any need to sink money into it to keep it livable."

Together they walked around the yard. "Colton, look!" K. C. laughed with delight as they reached the side of the house at the corner bedroom "The lilac bush! It's still here."

He grinned. "How about that."

"It needs some pruning," K. C. said, running her hands over the cracked bark of the oldest branches and trunk, "but we'll get to see it bloom this year. Remember how your great-grandmother tended it?"

"Sure." Colton chuckled. "No one cared about that tree like you two. Remember when we'd come sometimes in May and play hide-and-seek, and we could almost always find you here?"

K. C. nodded. "This was the best spot, even if you and Brian always did know where to look. So," she said, heading to the back of the house, "let's go in. By the way, do you have any idea who the owner is?"

Colton stopped midstep and threw his hands up like a traffic officer. "Whoa, wait just a minute. Are you telling me that *you* don't know?"

"No, that's why I'm asking you."

"Then, correct me if I'm wrong, but I would take that to mean that you don't have permission to be here." He lifted an eyebrow as if waiting for her response.

"Well, no," K. C. admitted, "but the door's open." She gave the piece of cardboard a push with her foot.

"So that's an invitation for you to walk right in?"

"Well…"

"No, K. C. Absolutely not." He spread his feet wider and crossed his arms.

She shrugged one shoulder and took a step forward. "If you're not coming with me, fine."

Colton gently grabbed her arm. "Really, Kace. We can't go in."

"Why not? It's empty."

"We don't know that. Besides, we're trespassing. What if someone calls the police? Who's going to bail you out of jail?"

"Not you, I take it." She rolled her eyes at him.

"You wouldn't just walk into a place in Chicago because there wasn't a door or it happened to be open, would you?"

"Of course not!"

"Well then…?" He raised his chin as though it was obvious there was no further argument.

"Oh, all right," she said, letting out a sigh. "Then let's go into town and get permission." She took a step toward her car before Colton stopped her with a hand around her wrist.

"From whom, since neither of us apparently has any idea who owns it?"

"I don't know. In your Aunt Lidia's letter, she said she thought some big fruit company owned it, but she wasn't sure." She'd known she'd have to figure this all out eventually—maybe she should have gotten the information before coming. She bit her lip. It was too late for that now. "We'll start by asking at Bob's Auto."

"Bob's Auto? Why would they know?"

"They seem to be a center of information. The attendant knew this place as the Walter McKenzie farm."

"So?"

"So…the McKenzies haven't owned this property for years. I bet the man knows a lot of what goes on around this town—like, for instance, who does own this house." She shot him a triumphant look.

Colton shrugged. "Okay, let's go then."

Information. That was all she wanted from Bob's Auto, nothing else. Not to see that dark-haired man again, not to look into those deep eyes. Just some information, that's all she was after.

After making the short trip into town, she hopped from the car and walked toward the service station. A middle-aged man rolled out on a creeper from under a car, tossed aside a rusted muffler, and stood, dusting himself off.

"Help you, ma'am?"

"I'm looking for Bob."

"I'm Bob." He again swiped a hand on his work pants before extending it to her. "What can I do for you?"

"Oh, excuse me." She politely shook his hand. "I'm looking for your other man. The one who was working last evening."

"That'd be Billy, but he's off today."

Billy. Somehow she'd never have guessed the man with those twinkling, gold-flecked eyes was a Billy.

Squelching her unexpected disappointment at his absence, K. C. reminded herself why she was here. This was strictly a fact-finding mission.

"Maybe you could help me. This, uh, Billy, gave me directions to the old Walter McKenzie place, and later I saw him driving by the farm. I was wondering if he's a neighbor."

Bob scratched his head. "Nah, that couldn't have been Billy. He sure knows cars, but he doesn't even own one that would go that far."

"He was driving a green Jeep," K. C. said. "I'm sure he was the same man from your station. I didn't get a good look at his face, but it was the same dark hair and—"

Bob threw his head back and laughed. "That definitely wasn't Billy, ma'am. He's pushing sixty and is 'bout as bald as an oil can."

"Then it'd be one of your younger employees, around thirty."

"I don't have any other employees. Just me and Billy, and he was on duty yesterday from seven until seven. I'll have to ask him about this. He lives right above there"—Bob pointed across the street to a forsaken furniture store—"if you want to ask him yourself before I see him."

K. C. looked at the dirty-windowed apartment where Bob was pointing. "No, that's all right." Who was the man who helped her? And of greater concern, why had he followed her?

"Anything else, miss?" Bob asked, eyeing his watch, then the discarded muffler.

"Yes, just one more thing. I understand the McKenzie farm is for sale, and I need to find out who the owner or real estate agent is."

"Was."

The word came like a blow. "Excuse me?"

"Was for sale. Some hotshot from Chicago bought it. It's a done deal, signed over and everything."

Sold? It couldn't be!

Reeling with panic, she tried to think.

The purchase price would be public record, so she could easily find out the amount and hopefully offer substantially more than whatever this person had paid. What businessperson wouldn't be interested in making such a quick profit on an investment? She *had* to have the farm!

"Would you by any chance know how to contact the new owner?" She opened her purse to pull out a notepad and pen.

"Funny thing is, actually I do. He's been in a couple of times and we got to talking. Hold on." Bob walked over to the desk in the office area, rummaged around, then scribbled on the back of a blank invoice form. "Here you go." He handed K. C. the paper.

"Thank you so much." She shook his hand and walked outside to read the scrawl. *Raleigh Kincaid, Kincaid Architects, North Michigan Avenue, Chicago. What,* she wondered, *would an architect want with a fruit farm?*

K. C. motioned for Colton to come over, and within minutes, using the pay phone outside the station, she had made an appointment for the next day.

"Don't worry," Colton reassured her. "No one can refuse your charm. And after he says you can look around first, just promise me you won't go in alone if I'm not available, and you're released from the pact."

"Deal," K. C. agreed, shaking hands on it.

Chicago seemed alien somehow, even though she'd only been gone two days. Now that she had cut all ties here, she felt like a guest. This just reinforced what she already knew: Hartley was her new home.

K. C. took a seat in the immaculate reception area of Kincaid Architects and smoothed her black, calf-length dress. She looked up from the open issue of *Restorations Today* on her lap, just about ready to read a contest announcement, as the receptionist approached.

"Ms. McKenzie, Mr. Kincaid will see you now. Follow me, please."

K. C. stood, absently replaced the magazine on the chair, and followed her escort down a plush hallway to an open door.

The dark-haired man behind the desk stood, his navy suit tailored to fit him perfectly.

"Ms. McKenzie." He extended his hand as a surprised, familiar half smile formed and lit amused, gold-flecked eyes. "Don't tell me I missed a spot on your windshield?"

Shock at unexpectedly finding the mystery man momentarily dissolved her composure. Finally remembering her manners, she offered him her hand. "My apologies. I discovered you're not an attendant there." She frowned, studying the man who now owned *her* farm.

Raleigh Kincaid folded his arms. "No, I'm not. I never said I was. You're the one who made assumptions and asked me for service."

That was true. K. C.'s cheeks burned at her audacity.

"I was merely a customer myself," he calmly stated, "who happened to borrow a jacket while my Jeep was being serviced. It was my pleasure, though, to assist you." His eyes twinkled again before his expression changed, revealing open curiosity mixed with skepticism. He pointed to a visitor's chair, indicating that she should sit across the massive mahogany desk from him.

"So, Ms. McKenzie, what brings you all the way here to my office?"

K. C. weighed his set mouth, crossed arms, and unwavering look, already sensing the outcome of this meeting.

He's not going to sell.

Chapter Three

Raleigh sat straight-backed while he considered the question he'd been pondering for two days: What interest did his farm hold for her? He'd contemplated numerous possibilities, none of which seemed likely. But now things were starting to make sense. He'd assumed this appointment with a McKenzie had something to do with his property, and now it turned out to be Ms. BMW herself. He was about to get his answer.

Ms. McKenzie's clear, brown eyes seemed to lock with his gaze while he waited for an answer. He hadn't even dared hope to see those warm, expressive eyes again. Quickly he dismissed such a thought. He certainly didn't have time, nor did he want to get involved with anyone. The unexpected pleasure at the warmth of her hand in his didn't matter. Nor did the seemingly perfect fit.

"Mr. Kincaid—"

"Call me Raleigh."

"Raleigh."

"And may I call you—?" He glanced at his appointment book. "I just have the initials K. C. here…" He looked up, waiting for her to give a name.

"Kathryn Claire."

He nodded. "Kathryn Claire." The name fit her, just as did her classic dress and simple but expensive-looking jewelry—a diamond solitaire on a thin, white-gold chain and diamond stud earrings. While at the gas station her dark hair had been in a ponytail, it now lay in gentle curls against her shoulders. His eyes moved to her hands. No rings. He chided himself for having let his gaze drop to her left hand. He didn't need to know anything personal about her. So what that she was lovely and poised, charming and purposeful?

"Now, what brings you here today?" He wondered what she was thinking as she glanced past him to the view of Lake Michigan from his office window, then back with a slight frown.

"I understand you're the one who bought the McKenzie farm in Hartley."

He stiffened, ready to defend his actions should she accuse him of trailing her to the house on Sixty-sixth Avenue. He had, of course, but with good reason.

He felt a momentary tinge of relief when the accusation didn't come. "Yes, I did."

"That house belonged to my relatives years ago. I was hoping to buy it and restore it."

He caught himself before his mouth dropped open. That would never have occurred to him as even the remotest possibility. "Restore it?"

She nodded.

He didn't understand. She'd seen the house, knew its condition. Didn't she realize the almost impossible effort involved? Why would she even consider it?

"That would be quite an undertaking." He reached for a trade magazine lying open on his desk and meticulously aligned it against the edge, pondering how to point out the absurdity of her dream without making her feel foolish. "Do you understand what's involved in a project like that?"

"Yes, I do. I'm a freelance interior designer, specializing in restoring old homes." She nodded toward *Restorations Today,* still beneath his fingertips.

An interior designer. Her vision certainly was noble but totally unrealistic. He glanced down at the magazine, still turned to the article announcing an old-house restoration contest. He'd even briefly considered doing something like that himself. But he was fully cognizant of the time, money, and headaches involved. Obviously she wasn't.

"And I hope to live there," she added. Her smile was wistful. Endearing. Beautiful.

He cleared his throat, forcing his attention away from her face.

"Your goals are admirable, Ms. McKenzie, but I'm sorry I can't help you. It's not for sale." He watched for her reaction, while considering the irony. He designed houses; she designed homes.

She gave a single nod, as if she'd already anticipated that answer. "May I ask why?"

"I have my own plans for it." He held her gaze, but didn't like the way this was going. As far as he was concerned, the subject was closed.

"I was hoping we could negotiate something." She paused a moment as if preparing for her final appeal. "What you paid for the farm is public record. I'm willing to offer you an additional $10,000."

"It's simply not for sale. At any price." He stood, cutting off further discussion and ending the meeting. How could that place mean so much to her? If she knew this business, she had to realize it'd cost more to renovate than to tear the whole place down. Start from scratch. Which was exactly what he planned to do.

As she gracefully rose and extended her hand, the simple beauty of her movements caused him to stare, captivated. What was it about her that radiated such a gentle spirit? Quite the contrast, he knew, to his cultivated detachment. He shrugged off the comparison; business, hard knocks in life—things like that had changed him years ago.

"Thank you for your time, Mr. Kincaid." A trace of disappointment in her eyes accompanied her words. "I'm sorry this didn't work out."

Raleigh was hesitant to shake her proffered hand again, because he had liked the feel of it in his before, the touch of her soft skin, the firm grip, the way it molded into his. Figuring this would be the last time he'd see her, he reluctantly took her hand then withdrew it quickly, uncertain how to end the meeting. *Thank you for coming?* He rather wished now she hadn't. *I'm sorry?* Apparently not enough to do something about it. He said nothing, just moved his head once in what could be perceived as a cordial nod.

She walked toward the door, then turned back when she reached it. "Good-bye, Mr. Kincaid. And, Raleigh—"

He lifted his brow.

"Thank you again for meeting with me." She gently closed the door behind her.

She's beautiful, gracious, composed, intelligent... And he was a heel. He was also a businessman. He'd searched diligently for the perfect, remote, country setting on a hill to build a getaway house. Why should he forfeit that just on the whim of a beautiful, winsome woman who showed up, claiming to have family roots to that old farm?

He needed the already-designed dream house just to get away from the relentless race of the city. The two- to three-hour commute every few days would be worth it to give him a retreat in an isolated country setting. That was where his heart was leading him, to the top of the hill beneath that dilapidated old farmhouse.

When he'd stood in the front yard this winter, his hiking boots the only mark in a fresh, powdery snow, he'd known that was the place to build. Only a few miles from town, the low hill offered a scene of acres and acres of apple and peach orchards and farmhouses spread as far as he could see. Each tree seemed to be vying for its due share of dancing sunbeams on snow-wrapped branches. He'd never thought of himself as poetic, but that afternoon he had pictured himself sitting in the front sunroom his plans called for, growing old there. Strangely enough, there had also been an elegant, loving woman sitting beside him.

Raleigh opened the door and headed down the hall, unconsciously taking the same route K. C. McKenzie had taken moments before. When he reached the reception area, he compulsively picked up a magazine lying on a chair, ready to return it to the coffee table where it belonged. *Why can't people put things back where they found them?* And this reader hadn't even bothered to close the cover, leaving the pages turned to—

He stared at the magazine, then frowned. In his hand was the waiting-room copy of *Restorations Today,* opened to the "Reliving the Past" restoration contest—the same article lying open on his desk.

He'd casually read the promotion for the contest that was open to anyone restoring a house at least a hundred years old. The top three winners would be featured in the magazine, and first prize was $150,000 and a trip to Paris for two.

"Who was sitting here?" he asked the receptionist.

"The woman who just walked out, sir."

Raleigh thumped the magazine against his other hand. *Coincidence? Or providence?*

He walked back to his office. Should he try for the contest, to restore the house? It was an eyesore, aside from all the hidden hazards bound to be in the structure itself. As an architect, he'd already considered the remote possibility, but there really was no point in trying to salvage it. The cost would be prohibitive. Poking around the place had convinced him of that. He planned to tear it down, then build his manor on the hill, the perfect respite for his loneliness.

But, again, maybe there was something to this. Raleigh read the contest rules carefully, weighing the pros and cons. He was sure no one would have any worse structure to work with than he did—the "before" pictures would be great, definitely show the challenge. It would take more money than he'd intended, but it might end up being a good investment. There would be plenty of PR for the winner along with a feature article.

He grinned. Who knew how many new clients winning something like this would generate?

He hadn't been to Paris in years, not that he wanted to go back, but he supposed he should visit his parents if he got that close. And the $150,000, well, that would go a long way toward the cost of the renovations. If he didn't like the restored house, he could always sell it and go back to his original plan—build his dream manor.

So why not?

His smile faded as he considered the *cons*. His interior designer was out on maternity leave and not taking any new projects until fall.

CHAPTER FOUR

Now what? K. C. wondered as she drove back to Michigan. It was too late to get her apartment back even if she had wanted it, which she didn't. Just this small taste of Hartley made her want to stay. Here the memories were sweet and the pace was quiet. But with the farm no longer within her reach, she was back to her original dilemma. *Now what?*

She'd stop by today to tell Brian's Great-aunt Lidia that she'd tried, but this wouldn't be the time the house came back into the family.

Oh no! A horrible possibility occurred to her. *What if Raleigh Kincaid demolishes the house?*

She'd fight him. Somehow she'd get more money; he must have a selling point. She didn't need the farmland, just the house. Maybe she could negotiate with him, show him how he might benefit too.

As she turned off I-94, she headed out to Sixty-sixth Avenue, feeling the sting of tears in her throat as she drove past the old farmhouse. At the right-hand corner just past the end of the apple orchard and across the road, she pulled into Aunt Lidia's driveway. K. C. waved to the petite elderly woman shaking a rug on the back porch. With her white hair combed back into a perfect bun and her trim form, she hadn't changed since K. C. last saw her at Brian's funeral.

"Kathryn, dear." Aunt Lidia's smile was welcoming. "I've been expecting you. Come in, come in." Her pale blue eyes lit up as she

pulled K. C. into the parlor. "I hope this means you got my letter."
She paused, looking hopeful. "Is the farm in the family once more?"

"I did receive your letter." K. C. patted her purse containing the
rose-scented envelope. "But—"

"Good. I knew you were interested in family history, the way you
tagged after my mother around the farm—when you weren't following Brian and Colton, that is—asking all kinds of questions about
the house and flowers and all."

K. C. smiled. "I loved the hollyhocks all around the porch. And
the lilac bush."

"Yes, the lilac bush." Aunt Lidia nodded. "My father planted that
for me the day I was born, right outside the room where I was deliv-
ered." She pointed up the road to the farmhouse.

"About your letter, though, Aunt Lidia—"

"I'm so glad you received it. I didn't know where to send it, so I
used the address I had for you and Brian."

"It did reach me, but I'd moved to an apartment in Chicago. By the
time I got it, someone else bought the place. I tried to buy it from him,
but he won't sell. I'm sorry." She lowered her eyes in disappointment.

Aunt Lidia patted K. C.'s hand. "Not to worry. Thank you for
trying. If it's not to be, then that's that."

"When I got your letter," K. C. said, "I was so sure that God was
leading me here." She held up both palms. "Now I don't know quite
what to do."

"Well, he brought you to me, and I'm glad for that." Aunt Lidia
gathered K. C. into her embrace. "Sometimes he's just not in as
much of a rush as we are. Now, will you stay here with an old lady for
a while until you decide what to do?"

K. C. laughed. "You're not old in spirit. But, yes, thank you, I'd
like that. I'm hoping to get Grandma's summer cottage opened up by
mid-April, but until then I'm staying at the Hartley Hotel."

"You shouldn't be in that rickety old place one more night." Aunt
Lidia shook a bony finger at K. C. "You go right back there, get your
things, and bring them here."

"Yes ma'am." K. C. grinned and obediently headed to her car,
feeling hope again.

Thank you for your leading, Lord. Step by step.

When K. C. returned with her belongings, Aunt Lidia showed her to a room upstairs.

"What's this?" K. C. asked, picking up a brown-jacketed book from the nightstand.

Aunt Lidia beamed. "That is *The McKenzie's Family History.* It tells all about us right there." She reached for the book and opened it. "Here's a picture of the family as I remember us—my parents, brother, and me on the front porch of our old house. Of course," she said, pointing to the little girl in the picture, "this was taken years ago. But that house has quite a history. Shortly after my parents married and had saved up some money, they wanted to buy a house with some land for farming. When they heard the house on the hill— that's what folks around here called it—was for sale, they bought it. A bargain, I might add, as it was in pretty bad condition."

"It was?"

"Yes. People told them it was beyond repair. But bit by bit, they renovated it. They added on a kitchen and porch out back. Mother planted hollyhocks all around it, like a fence. She could step right out of the house and be in the middle of her flowers."

She paused and seemed to be looking back in time. "I watched as the kitchen was torn down a few years ago after some fire damage, though. Now I stand out in my garden and look up at the hill and want to weep for what's happened to our old home."

K. C. nodded. "It's so tragic the way it's been neglected."

Lidia closed the book, her shoulders sagging. "It is. But if nothing else, let this house teach you what just a little bit of care can do where there's neglect. Don't ever give up hope, dear. God is always in the business of restoring."

"I'll try to remember that," K. C. said solemnly. "May I borrow your book?"

"Please, keep it. Your enjoyment would mean more to me than if I kept it."

K. C. hugged the older woman. "Thank you so much. It's a treasure to me."

"I'd like to show you something else while we're up here."

K. C. followed her to the closed door at the end of the hall. Aunt Lidia unlocked the door, then stood aside as she opened it.

"Go in," she directed.

K. C. looked around the room. "All this furniture!" She rubbed her hand across a dresser holding a ceramic water pitcher and basin. "These pieces are beautiful."

"They were Mother's."

"Great-grandmother McKenzie's, from her house? I was afraid everything was gone." K. C. walked from one piece to another through the narrow spaces between them. "They're lovely. Is this the plant stand in the picture you sent?" She ran her hand across the hand-carved design.

"Yes, it is. Why don't we set it up in your room?"

"I'd like that. But why aren't you using any of these pieces yourself?"

"It's already too cluttered downstairs. But I couldn't part with them, either. I was hoping someday to pass them on to the boys, Colton and Brian. Now…" She hesitated. "I'd like you and Colton to have them."

"I'd be honored."

She patted K. C.'s arm. "Dear, don't give up."

Often during the next few days, after helping Aunt Lidia around her house and yard, K. C. walked up the hill to the farmhouse. Since Raleigh Kincaid wouldn't sell, this was her only chance to enjoy the peacefulness of the farm before he showed up one day. Even though technically she still didn't have permission to be on the property, she was willing to take her chances. Working in the yard was the least she could do in memory of Great-grandmother McKenzie. And no one ever stopped to question what she was doing.

The afternoon sun daily caressed her back, urging her to shed her jacket and work in fleece shirts. She spent hours running bare hands through knee-high grass, picking up debris, and donned gardening gloves to painstakingly pick up broken glass from underneath the windows. And always, the daily work found her beside the lilac bush when the shadows lengthened and it was time to return to the corner house to fix Aunt Lidia's supper.

At the end of the week, confident the yard was clear enough to safely mow, K. C. walked Aunt Lidia's push mower up the road in the morning and started on the front. With each lap, the overgrowth slowly transformed into a well-groomed lawn. On the sloping hillside, she carefully kept her footing, clearing off as much as safety allowed.

When Hartley's noon whistle blew, K. C. stopped for a last peek from the front porch before going back to Aunt Lidia's to prepare lunch. How she wished she could see more than darkness between the cracks of the boarded-up windows. Even the side window off the porch offered only a view into the barren bedroom.

She sighed. So far she'd kept her promise to Colton not to go inside. Getting permission, she knew, was never going to happen, but somehow she just *had* to get in. If only she could work something out with Raleigh Kincaid.

That afternoon K. C. hurriedly returned to the house after fixing lunch and making sure Aunt Lidia was resting. She stooped to pull more knee-high weeds near the back porch, then walked around to the far side of the house.

"Oh no! No!" She stopped abruptly at the sight of the freshly dug hole underneath the bedroom window. All that was left of the lilac bush was a tangle of broken branches. Sinking to the ground, she ran her hands through the mounds of soil, letting small clumps sift through her fingers.

Who did this? And when? She'd only been gone a couple of hours.

Someone was trespassing—besides her—except this person was destroying property.

A vehicle pulled into the driveway, but K. C. didn't look up, didn't try to hide. If it was the trespasser, she intended to have words with him.

CHAPTER FIVE

Raleigh parked his Jeep, came around the corner of the house, then stopped. There she was, K. C.—Kathryn Claire—McKenzie.

Without an address or even a phone number, he hadn't known how to locate her. There was a K. C. McKenzie in the Chicago phone book, but the number had been disconnected. He remembered she had Illinois license plates, but if not from Chicago, she could be from anywhere within the state. Driving to this property had been his last hope. He had counted on her love for this old place to draw her back. But as he stood there watching her, he didn't care that she was trespassing or had taken liberties with his property. He was just happy to see her again.

Kathryn Claire McKenzie. He tested the name again silently. Simple and elegant. It suited her. Even in work clothes she was lovely and intent as she knelt, sifting the soil through her fingers.

When he'd stopped by shortly after noon, he had been sure the mowed lawn was her doing. Deciding to help her with the heavier yard work while he waited—and hoped—for her return, he'd cut down the overgrown bush on the side of the house. She probably didn't have the proper equipment to do that, anyway, and she didn't look strong enough to haul away all those branches herself. The pleasure of surprising her with his work had spurred him on. And now, after he'd run into town for a late lunch—he smiled in satisfaction—here she was.

He was eager to tell her of his plans for the house, to ask her to work with him as a consultant or even a designer if her portfolio proved her capable. He could imagine her thrill at being asked to work on the project. Not only would the house be restored, but it would be done under her guidance. What more, other than actual ownership, could she want? And it made sense, as, after all, she was the one familiar with its former state.

Raleigh nodded his head and started forward again. The gentle-natured woman he'd been studying turned her head toward him.

"*You!*" she sputtered, still kneeling by the discarded heap of branches. "You did it! How could you cut down my lilac bush?" Her tone left no room for doubt that he was already convicted of a terrible deed.

"Bush?" he demanded, her biting accusation catching him by surprise. "It was a half-dead tree. An overgrown eyesore that was taking over the place." His eyes narrowed. He'd only been trying to help. It was his property, his tree or bush or whatever it was. He could do with it what he wanted. Besides, she was trespassing.

K. C. stood then, tall and straight, looking prepared for battle. "Of course that's all *you* would see, just what was on the surface."

What was she talking about? Raleigh contemplated the look on her dirt-smudged face and was certain he was better off not asking.

"It's not even your property." He sounded like a spoiled child. He didn't care. His intentions of charming her into helping him quickly faded.

"I offered to buy it." She crossed her arms.

"And I refused." He sounded petty, but the words kept coming. "And, since you *are* trespassing, I could ask you to leave."

"You don't have to." She brushed her hands on her jeans. "I'm going. But," she flung at him as she headed toward the driveway, "it's not like this place means anything to you. You probably can't wait to demolish the house. What *do* you want it for anyway?"

"I'm going to remodel it and live here."

K. C.'s mouth dropped open, and she gaped at him.

"You're going to live here?" She enunciated each word carefully, as if the combined thought didn't make sense.

And she was probably right. He didn't fit in here. Yet, even with her designer shirt and BMW, she somehow looked right at home.

"That's the plan," he said. "Though I don't know why you find it so incomprehensible. Even I need to get away to somewhere peaceful. Quiet. I've found the perfect place." In the lull while they glared at each other, the only sound he heard was from a few birds overhead, also bickering. He folded his arms. "Is there anything wrong with that?"

She glowered at him a moment longer, then shook her head, her features softening. "No. Of course not."

But her sorrowful expression as she turned away put a dent in his defenses. Maybe she had hoped for one last chance to buy the house.

"Wait. I'm"—he lowered his hands and tried not to choke on the unaccustomed words—"sorry. I appreciate the effort you've put into cleaning up the yard. You mentioned that you're an interior designer…" He paused, meeting her eyes.

She nodded.

"And do restorations of old houses. Would you be interested in helping me restore this one? You know its history. Your knowledge would be helpful."

"You want me to help you so you can live in it?" Disbelief seemed to radiate from her eyes, to the set of her mouth, then all the way to her feet as she widened her stance. "Do you realize how many thousands of dollars it'll take to make this house livable? Let alone restore it to its true state?"

"I thought that's what *you* wanted to do with it."

"This place is part of my family's heritage. But aside from sentimental value or a major restoration project, I can't imagine why anyone would want the house. The land is worth something. If you considered selling just the little piece of property it's on, you could make a nice profit."

So she didn't really think he was going to live in it. "Theoretically I agree. But I've entered it in a contest," Raleigh stated quietly.

"It appears to have already been condemned, and—you did *what?*" K. C. stared at him.

"I entered a contest for restoring a house that's at least a hundred years old." He innocently lifted one brow in question. "I assume this one qualifies?"

"Well…" She shook her head, apparently trying to switch gears along with him. "Yes, definitely."

Raleigh smiled, pleased he'd derailed her line of reasoning. "I'll be honest," he said. "I'm under time constraints with this contest. If I don't feel I have a good chance at winning, I'll withdraw and revert back to my original plan—to tear this thing down and rebuild. On this spot." He crossed his arms again, having laid down the gauntlet. She probably hated the thought of working with him, but maybe the house had a strong enough pull for her to overlook that. Should she turn him down, he'd be disappointed—not just for the contest's sake, he realized, but because he wanted to work with her.

She seemed to weigh the options for a moment. "So you want my help?"

"Yes. For input into the original state of the house, for one thing. And since my interior designer is on maternity leave, if you can show me your work is of the level I require, I'll consider you for that position too." Too late he realized that his offer had a patronizing sound to it.

"Well, thank you," she said sweetly. Then with a lift of her chin, she added, "And you won't mind if I check *your* credentials also, seeing my professional reputation is at stake as well?"

Raleigh closed his eyes and took a deep breath. He deserved that. Of course he had to be careful whom he chose to represent his company, but he supposed he could have worded it better.

"If I win," he continued, choosing to ignore her retort, "you can have the trip for two to Paris. And house visitation rights." He tacked that on with a slow grin, hoping to seal her decision with the added enticement. Working with her meant his patience would be taxed to its limit, but he certainly wouldn't mind seeing that brown-eyed gaze around for a while.

Slowly her stance relaxed. "I'll consider it."

Raleigh breathed a sigh of relief. He was still in the running.

◆ ◆ ◆

K. C. counted this a victory of sorts. If she couldn't buy the house, at least she'd have the pleasure of helping to restore it. It wouldn't be torn down. She'd finally get to go inside, and no matter what Raleigh Kincaid had done to the lilac bush beneath Great-grandmother McKenzie's bedroom window, another would be in its place.

While she stood frowning at him, the charming gleam she'd first seen at the gas station crept into his eyes. How could this man be so exasperating and so boyishly charming? Working with him all summer certainly would be…interesting.

"Well, then," he said as if the outcome was decided, "shall we go in and look around? Or have you already done that?" He raised a brow.

"No, I haven't." She glared at his suspicious expression and silently thanked Colton for his advice to stay out.

"Good. This is probably a haven for vagrants. You stay here, and I'll check."

K. C. impatiently waited on the concrete porch for his return, aware of her quickened heartbeat. Never had she suspected that today would be the day she would finally stand inside.

Raleigh finally poked his head around the side of the makeshift door. "All clear. Allow me." He held open the corrugated flap, allowing K. C. to step past him into the living room.

Her first footsteps inside the entrance were little skips of elation. She paused inside the living room, letting her eyes adjust to the dim afternoon sun struggling through cracks in the crudely boarded-up windows. A dank, musty odor filled her nostrils.

"I hope you don't have allergies," Raleigh said from a few steps behind her.

He flicked on a flashlight, but K. C. could see well enough without it to know they were standing in the midst of ruin. This was worse than what she'd glimpsed when peeking in from the front porch. She kicked aside a heap of ceiling tiles lying on the floor.

"Be careful where you step," Raleigh cautioned. Then he, too, lapsed into silence.

K. C. was grateful for these few moments to quietly absorb the extent of decay without feeling the need to verbalize it. She couldn't bear to sound the death knell of her dreams just yet. She closed her eyes, trying to recapture her vision for this house. Even so, the image was still one of peeling paint, bare rafters, and holes punched into walls.

Raleigh stood silently, reassessing the house in a different light. He had to see beyond the visible to the possibilities.

He glanced at K. C., caught in the flashlight's shadowed edges. What must she think of the house now? What did she think, period? Figuring her out was becoming a complicated puzzle. What made her so intriguing? It certainly wasn't her interest in him, for he sensed none. She didn't respond to him the way women usually did, nor was she intimidated. She was feminine and cultured and unaffected. And yet, for all her beauty, he sensed an underlying sadness about her. With her head slightly bowed, she seemed bent with sorrow from surveying the damage surrounding them. Her expression made him wonder if this house contained a piece of her heart she was trying to reclaim.

Raleigh momentarily forgot his own ambitions. *We can do it, K. C. Even if we don't win, we can bring this house back to life.*

K. C. sighed and opened her eyes. Then she coughed as she drew in a breath. "This is a lot worse than I imagined."

"Cosmetically, it is pretty bad," Raleigh said. "But don't rule it out yet. Once I have an engineer come in and check the structure, we'll know exactly what we're working with. If he agrees that it's doable, we'll go from there. If it'll end up taking longer than the contest allows, then I'll see. Do you want to look around some more?"

K. C. smiled. "Of course."

"The flooring down here seems to be in fairly decent shape, considering—but please walk carefully. There's no telling what kind of internal damage it's got. With so many windows out, it's had years of exposure to snow and rain."

"I wish I had my camera with me. I'll come back tomorrow and take pictures," K. C. said.

"Until I have a real door installed and the windows replaced, please don't come in by yourself. What if you fell through the floor? Who'd ever find you?" Seeing K. C. was about to protest, he softened his voice. "It's for your own safety. Agreed?"

The slight nod of her head assured him that she'd abide by the rules.

He pointed his flashlight's beam into a small room off the living room. "The bathroom." He stepped closer and squinted into the darkness. "I've got a problem with it. According to the contest rules, the house's interior can be changed to make the place comfortable. Enlarging rooms, even adding on with certain guidelines, is okay. We can use modern fixtures, but they should have some similarity to the original era."

K. C. crowded behind him into the tiny square. "Are you saying you'd like to enlarge this room?"

Even with K. C. standing in the shadows, he could tell by the crack in her voice that she was laughing at him.

"Yes."

"I agree," she said, again sounding as if she was teasing him.

"I get the feeling there's a catch." He scowled in the dark.

"Not really. See the other little room?" She backed out into the miniscule hall and pointed to another room barely larger than a walk-in closet. "This was the music room."

"And just how did anything other than a harmonica fit in there?"

"That's the point—it didn't. The music room used to extend into here." She pointed to the bathroom. "What I'm saying is, maybe you'd want to put the music room back the way *it* was, because technically the bathroom was never part of the original house."

"I can believe that."

"It's true. The music room was cut in two when indoor plumbing became available."

"So," he raised one hand, palm up, "do you want the bathroom redesigned, or"—he lifted the other hand and moved them as if weighing the balances—"do you want to keep the integrity of the house? Your call."

"Redesigned," she said with a soft chuckle. "And don't forget we need a kitchen, too."

"Whoa. What do you mean, 'we need a kitchen'?" He turned her around and pointed back through the other side of the living room. "We have one."

"No, that's the dining room." They walked into the room.

"It looks like a kitchen to me. It has shelves, a linoleum floor, and a refrigerator, but, okay, I'll bite. Where's the real kitchen?"

"Torn down. It was on the other side of this back wall and extended out to a large concrete porch. Most of the porch is gone too. Great-grandmother McKenzie displayed her dishes on some beautiful built-in shelves in this room. So *that,*" K. C. said, pointing across the room to a crude plywood cupboard, "has to go."

Raleigh grinned at the intensity in her voice. "Okay, we'll just build a kitchen, new shelves, rebuild the back porch, and enlarge the bathroom." So far he agreed. "Are we finished down here then?"

"No. I haven't seen the front bedroom."

"Be my guest." Raleigh stepped back. "It's by far the best-preserved room in the house." He followed K. C. into the room. "See? Someone even put up new plasterboard on this wall, so that's a start. Of course, the room needs paint, windows, and some cosmetic work, but it's fairly decent, considering."

"No." K. C. shook her head. "The dry wall has to go."

"It's fine." He pounded along the wall with his fist, proving his point.

K. C. shook her head. "According to Aunt Lidia's picture, there should be a hand-carved chair railing behind it. If it's still there, we have to uncover it." Her tone was soft yet determined, as if she was issuing a plea on behalf of the house. She smiled wistfully. "You should see the way it used to be."

All Raleigh could see were dollar signs multiplying even faster than he'd imagined. He might as well mention the reason he wanted this location in the first place.

"There is one room that will have to be added on…" He paused, grimacing as K. C.'s smile vanished. Just what he was afraid of. This stubborn woman was about to put on the brakes rather than spoil her precious memories. "A sun room," he finished. "Across the entire front of the house."

"A sun room?" Her eyes widened and she appeared to consider it. "That would be lovely—except it will spoil the integrity of the original design. Utterly. Please, no."

Just as he expected.

For a moment, neither one spoke. Finally he broke the silence. "Do you want to see the upstairs?" The question was pointless, though. Her willingness to help was fading minute by minute.

The only answer he received was a curt nod.

They started up the staircase, Raleigh in the lead. "Be careful on the landing. You can see right into the cellar through the boards. Some are loose." He reached the midway point and paused for a moment before continuing. "Just take it slow."

He maneuvered past a few creaking, wobbly steps and turned to check on K. C. She glanced up at him, a mixture of purpose and adventure in her expression. In that moment, she stumbled, letting out a gasp.

Reflexively he reached his hand out to her. Alarm flickered in her eyes before she accepted his steadying grip.

Once again, Raleigh was amazed at how at-home her hand felt in his. And the moment she withdrew it, the emptiness seemed to radiate throughout more than just his hand.

"Just be careful," he mumbled, not sure whether the warning was meant for her, or himself.

CHAPTER SIX

The next morning K. C. arrived at the farmhouse early. She had just settled onto the dewy concrete surface of the back porch when Raleigh pulled up.

She stood, brushed herself off, and handed him a black leather binder as he neared.

He looked puzzled. "What's this?"

"My portfolio."

"You're applying for the job?"

K. C. ignored the amused look in his eyes. "I'd like to interview for the position—sir." She shot him what she hoped was a disarming smile. It hadn't taken all that long last night to make her decision. The offer on the table wasn't her first choice, nor was she happy with his suggested plans, but it made sense to accept it. If Raleigh Kincaid was serious about the restoration, even if it was only to win a contest, she'd put aside her own desires for the sake of the house. At least she could provide details, accuracy, and, whether or not anyone cared, love. Without her input, who knew what he might do to it?

"Fine, Ms. McKenzie," Raleigh said formally. He sat down on the concrete and motioned to her. "Please be seated."

After discussing the designs and photos in her portfolio and answering Raleigh's extensive questions, K. C. sat up straighter as he closed her book. She folded her hands primly as she awaited the verdict.

"Your work is quite impressive," he finally said. "You have to realize that this is quite a step, taking on a new designer for a project like this. My current designer and I entwine our work seamlessly, which makes us a good team. I must ask that you prove yourself."

Prove herself? What more did he want? Did she have to take this man to each site to inspect her work? Or maybe he'd like to poke around in her box jammed with awards? Is that what would prove her skills to him?

K. C. bit her lip, trying to resist opening her mouth before Raleigh Kincaid heard exactly what she was thinking.

Raleigh gazed at her with a challenge in his eyes. "K. C. McKenzie, if you can design a sunroom that meets my approval without making it an addition, you're hired."

She broke into a smile. She all but had the job.

Thank you, Lord! She needed this job—not for the money, which they hadn't even discussed. But for something inside her, something unseen, that she knew would be long-lasting. Any number of people could do a wonderful remodeling job here. But this house required more. It was like Psalm 127:1, the verse Grandma had instilled in her years ago. *Except the LORD build the house, they labour in vain that build it.* This house, more than any she'd ever worked on, cried out for that essential element. It needed a special kind of love.

Raleigh stood and pulled a measuring tape from his jeans pocket. "Ready to get started?"

The two spent the morning scribbling notes on a pad of paper. K. C. played photographer, taking roll after roll of film for the "before" pictures.

"K. C., where are you staying?" Raleigh asked as if it had just occurred to him.

"Just down the road on the corner—the green-shingled house." She pointed out the front room window. "I'm staying with Aunt Lidia, but once it warms up, I'll move into my summer house in Pine Hills in the South Haven area on Lake Michigan."

"Did you grow up around here, or how did you ever find this one-light town?"

"I'm from Chicago. As a girl I spent summers with my grand-mother at her lake home. That's the one I inherited. We used to drive over and visit Aunt Lidia and her mother on this farm a lot. That's one of the reasons why it's special to me."

"So you're a country girl at heart?" Raleigh smiled and squinted as though trying to see beyond her khakis to a little girl in overalls.

"I suppose so." K. C. smiled. "And speaking of Aunt Lidia, after lunch she wants to come over to meet you. She's the one who really can help you. She's looking through her attic to find old pictures of the place."

"Good. I'd like to see them."

After lunch, K. C. returned with Aunt Lidia.

"Raleigh, I'd like you to meet your neighbor, Lidia Gregor. Aunt Lidia, Raleigh Kincaid."

"It's nice to meet you, Mrs. Gregor." Raleigh held out his hand.

"Lidia, please." She shook his hand. "I brought some photos I thought you might enjoy."

"Thank you, *Miss* Lidia. I'd like to see them." He smiled kindly at the woman.

Aunt Lidia hooked her arm through his and led him to the kitchen.

K. C. watched the two of them huddled in front of a broken-out window, their source of light, as they studied old snapshots. Never would she have pictured Raleigh enjoying the company of an older generation. Yet, with his head down, he appeared immersed in Aunt Lidia's reminiscing, not just tolerating it for the sake of research.

She finally turned away from the touching scene.

"I have something to show you too, Raleigh," K. C. said after Aunt Lidia had left. She handed him a drawing she'd done while he and Aunt Lidia were talking. "It's a rough sketch of the floor plan, including the sunroom." She hoped his dropped jaw was not an indication of disapproval.

He trailed his index finger across the extension she'd drawn that stretched across the back width of the house. "I thought you didn't want to add on."

"That's not exactly what I said. I didn't want to change the front or sides. Since we need to rebuild the kitchen and back porch anyway, why not expand the entire rear? The new extension will house the kitchen, lengthen the living room, and include a master bedroom. The old bathroom/music room will become the master bath. And the front bedroom will become the sunroom."

K. C. awaited Raleigh's response, suddenly apprehensive from his unreadable expression. Her dreams hung on his answer. Several seconds ticked by. "So, about the interior designer job…?"

He pushed her drawing aside. "I've already found the person I want."

Her heart dropped. He hadn't even given her a chance! Only yesterday had he made the offer and then this morning tacked on his ridiculous stipulation that she prove herself. And now he'd already decided, without even waiting to consider her ideas? If this was how he conducted business, then maybe she was better off not being involved with him in any fashion.

She forced herself to remain calm. She swallowed hard, battling to regain some composure before she answered. "I see."

"When can you start?" A mischievous grin made the gold in his eyes dance even more.

At the end of the day, Raleigh found K. C. in the living room writing more notes. His footsteps seemed to echo in the quietness of the darkening room.

"K. C., it's time to close up for the night."

She stood from her seat on the floor. "All right, but I'd like to discuss one more thing. We need to come to some agreement on the colors, furniture style, curtains, appliances, and everything, so I can start ordering. Will you trust my judgment, or"—she held his gaze as if daring him—"are you going to have to approve every little thing before I proceed?"

"I don't know," he said skeptically, shrugging his shoulders. "I have no idea what your intentions are."

"Ruffles and lace and pink walls."

For a moment, Raleigh couldn't even form a single, silent cohesive word at the appalling thought.

"Absolutely not!" he finally sputtered. "I don't care what it looked like before. I'm going to be living in this place and I am *not* about to—"

"Okay, okay. I see we've reached an understanding." The satisfied nod of her head made her ponytail swing, and a slow smile of victory formed on her lips.

"We've reached no such thing. If you think—" He stopped when he recognized the merriment on her face and the twinkling in her eyes.

"So will I have access to the premises while you're gone?" She grinned, obviously pleased with his reaction.

"As long as you're with someone and watch your step. This place is a mess." He still didn't like the idea of her being alone in the place, unprotected. He pointed to the sheet of cardboard behind them. "I can't very well give you a key to the place."

"An 'open-door' policy. I like that." She continued to smile up at him.

He led her to the door and held it open for her. "Good night, K. C."

She took a few steps then stopped and turned when he called out to her. "You will be careful?"

She grinned and nodded, not looking the least bit worried. "I promise."

Raleigh returned to Chicago, leaving K. C. to finalize the interior plans and send them to him, while he submitted his blueprints to obtain a building permit. Now he had to wait for the town's approval.

Leaning back in his chair, Raleigh put his feet up on the desk and stared out over Lake Michigan. He had his best contractor lined up to give his undivided attention to this project and to order new doors and windows. Lumber. Dry wall. Trim. Cement. Siding. Paint. The list went on. Not only was this a contest, it was a race. Six months from start to finish, that's all the time allowed before the winner was declared mid-October. The unheard-of time frame for such an undertaking alone might keep some would-be contestants from entering. But he had confidence in his contractor and suppliers.

This should be some summer. He couldn't remember the last time he'd been this excited about a project. It wasn't just the thrill of a contest that lured him. He could get in some sailing on Lake Michigan, watch the view from the hill change from spring to summer to fall…and work with a fascinating interior designer.

He pictured K. C.'s soft features, the light in her eyes when she was in that old house, the patience and gentleness she showed Miss Lidia. Stretching to work out some of the tightness in his neck and shoulder muscles, Raleigh sat upright as a new thought invaded his mind: *What would it feel like to have K. C.'s hands kneading away the tension?*

He pushed away from his desk with a sigh. He had to stop thinking like that. He had work to do, a contest to win. Once the building permit was approved, he'd talk with her again. Until then—if she needed to contact him—she could go through his secretary. As much as she intrigued him, he couldn't risk any emotional ties. He'd learned years ago in boarding school not to get too close to anyone. He was a loner and intended to stay one. It was the safest way.

◆   ◆   ◆

Once the water was turned on for the season at the Pine Hills area along Lake Michigan, K. C. moved out to her cottage. Though Grandma had always called it a cottage, it was a good-sized two-story house. If she winterized it, it'd be a perfect year-round home. The steep hill running down to the beach provided a safety zone between her and her memories on days the waves turned wild and threatening.

Promising to visit Aunt Lidia often, K. C. settled in, taking *The McKenzie's Family History* with her. While waiting for Raleigh's go-ahead, she intended to use the time to study the family stories and photographs. She carefully tagged every page offering glimpses into the original interior of the house.

Along with catalogs and fabric swatches and vendor information, the book was added to her backpack. Her bag was her companion, from the stone patio outside her kitchen to the wide expanse of sandy beach at the bottom of the hill. After studying and combing antique centers during the day, her evenings were spent walking the hilly, winding roads and wooden footbridges. The private neighborhood offered solitude and peaceful sunsets, but she used even the walks as planning time.

This evening she sat at her favorite spot, the old halfway house. Two worn benches sharing a roof and half walls formed a shelter midway along the steep, wooden stairs leading to the beach. It offered rest to winded swimmers on their trek back up the hill. It invited neighborly camaraderie to retirees and vacationers out getting their daily exercise. Young and old alike met at the benches, looking back down to the beach for a final evening farewell before continuing on to cozy cottages.

K. C. watched preschoolers dig in the sand and older kids play catch-me-if-you-can as gentle, lapping waters tickled their bare toes. She listened as mothers called to reluctant children that it was time to go home.

She stared out over the lake, lost in long-ago memories. How many times had Colton, Brian, and she played in the water just as these children were doing?

But, Grandma, we didn't hear you, she had so often claimed. And of course they hadn't. How could they hear anything over their giggling shrieks as the waves tumbled and rolled, then took them under as they fought to right themselves?

Back then the waves had been fun...

K. C. stood. Dwelling on too many memories wasn't good. Tonight she needed more than longing for the old times of fun. She climbed the stairs and headed back to her own patio. In the quiet evening, she pulled out the book she needed to read. Not *The McKenzie's Family History.* No, tonight the book on her lap was Grandma Matthews's worn, black leather Bible. Nightly during those long-ago summers, Grandma had read to her after the supper dishes were washed. That's what she longed for now.

"'The LORD is my shepherd,'" Grandma had read. "'He leadeth

me beside the still waters.' When you look out over the lake, don't ever forget that, honey. He'll lead you whether the waters are already still, or whether he has to still them for you."

K. C. looked out over the peaceful lake. "Beside the still waters..." If only she could find that for her soul.

Feeling restless, she laid the book aside and stood, heading toward the beach. This time she bypassed the planked stairs, instead scrambling down the aged footpath worn into the steep hill. The lake was friendly, inviting, practically motionless, trying to lull her into forgetting its fickleness. She could forgive the lake—she knew storms came up, accidents happened, waves could turn treacherous. Still, it shouldn't have taken Brian.

K. C. aimlessly wandered down the partially deserted beach, vaguely hearing sounds of the living—children still squealing, a dog barking, a boat horn blaring in the distance.

Lord, sometimes it's hard to follow, because I just don't understand. I thought you led me here to buy the farm. Why can't I do that? But I'll do my best—for you and for the sake of the house and for Brian's family. Why can't Raleigh Kincaid simply sell? The house doesn't mean anything to him, other than winning the contest.

And that brought up another matter for prayer—Raleigh Kincaid. She sighed as she turned and headed back up the beach. He was a human contradiction—stubborn and agreeable, rigid and gentle, unfeeling and kind. Plus just plain funny, handsome, and charming. All in all, very dangerous.

I promised Brian "till death do us part." What do I do now?

She'd never pictured herself caring for anyone else. Yet when Raleigh had clasped her hand in the simple gesture of steadying her on the stairs, she'd also felt his potential to touch her heart. And it scared her.

God, please guard my heart. K. C. looked once more at the waters barely lapping against the shoreline. After a moment she turned away and headed up the stairs. She paused only long enough to stomp sand from her feet and plead one more time. *Please, Father, still the waters.*

Back on the patio she picked up Grandma's Bible and headed

inside to the glow of the kitchen light as dusk settled around the hills. She had just opened the old travel trunk and pulled out the faded lavender-colored candy box filled with loose pictures when the phone rang.

She had barely lifted the receiver and said hello when she heard Raleigh Kincaid's voice.

"K. C.? We got it! I have the permit in hand. Can you be at the house Monday morning to begin work?"

◆　◆　◆

Man, what a sight! Raleigh grinned as he pulled into the farm early on Monday. The rising sun made the countryside glow. Even that eyesore of a house couldn't discourage him today. By October it would stand like a sentry on the hill, a beacon among the orchards. And it was all his!

He groaned, realizing he certainly wasn't the first to arrive. He counted four pickup trucks and K. C.'s BMW. The entire crew—including his designer—was already here, witnessing him dragging in behind them.

"Good morning." K. C. stepped outside and greeted him with a smile.

Cheerful. He hated *cheerful* in the morning. He was an early riser, yet somehow she—along with everyone else—had beat him here. *Must have something to do with being cheerful this early in the day.*

"Where's the coffee?" he muttered after a quick nod.

Her smile broadened. "There might be some inside—if the crew left any."

They apparently had been here some time, as the generator and portable facilities were already set up. And, he discovered a moment later, long enough to have consumed most of the coffee too.

"I've already met your contractor and his men and gotten them started," K. C. said, again with that smile. "I hope you don't mind."

Raleigh grunted. "I'll go say hello to them."

The workmen stopped their hammering and sawing as he stepped into the living room. He greeted each one, appreciating their good start on the job. The floor had been swept, resulting in one large pile of debris in a corner. And where splintered boards were pulled from the living room windows, light and freshness surged in, transforming the ugly room into something tolerable. As though they'd caught the vision, the crew seemed more high-spirited today than when he had spoken to them over the weekend. Raleigh inhaled deeply, loving the aroma of morning-crisp air mixed with the scent of fresh sawdust.

He headed through the kitchen doorway to the worktable. K. C. already had the blueprints spread out across a cracked piece of plywood balanced over two sawhorses. As they leaned over the plans together, she bent her head near his. She was too close. She smelled like spring and flowers.

"What's that?" Raleigh straightened as he lost his concentration and looked at her.

"Where?" Looking alarmed, K. C. brushed her fingers across her arm, then through her hair.

"No," he said. "That's not what I meant." He cleared his throat. "I meant, what are you wearing?"

She glanced down at her jeans and work shirt, then into his eyes, obviously puzzled.

"You know, the smell." He felt his face grow warm and forced his gaze back on the blueprints, away from her inviting brown eyes.

"The *smell?*" She took a step away from him, looking horrified.

"No, I mean, the flavor, scent. What is it?"

Her features relaxed and a twinkle replaced the look of alarm in her eyes. "The *fragrance?* It's lilac."

"Lilac. I should have guessed. That's not too common, is it?" He'd never known anyone with that scent. So soft, so entrancing.

"No. Actually, this brand has been discontinued." Her cheek color deepened, as if she was embarrassed at the intimate turn of the conversation. "And I'm almost out." Her voice softened, and he wasn't sure that last comment was even directed to him.

"Sorry. I can't help you there." He shrugged a shoulder. "I don't know anything about women's fragrances."

"Well, there's honeysuckle, wildflower, jasmine, spring meadow…" She gave him a soft smile, a look both sad and shy.

"Too flowery." He didn't know why a woman would want to smell like a field.

"Okay, then there's apricot, apple, raspberry—"

"That sounds like a fruit farm. We could grow them out back." He pictured bottles of perfume hanging from branches throughout the orchards.

"Then what would you suggest?"

"Let me see." He pondered her question. His thinking was more along the lines of food, especially since they were standing in the kitchen. Unexpectedly he thought of his mother baking cookies when he was a boy. He gave his half smile. "Vanilla."

"Vanilla?" She sounded surprised.

"Yeah. I'm just a plain, simple guy."

"Right," she said barely under her breath.

By late afternoon K. C. headed up the stairs to the second-story bedrooms. She knew the men were finishing up, most of them gone already. From a front window she saw the last of the pickups head toward the road, spinning gravel in its hurry.

She sighed. *Alone with Raleigh.* As long as she kept her distance, she was safe. And that didn't appear to present too much of a problem. All day, while he'd freely spoken with the contractor and crew, he'd mostly just watched her, no doubt contemplating her ability. That didn't bother her; she was confident in her skills. And so competent, she chided herself, that she'd left her notes downstairs. She rounded the corner to the stairs—only to run head-on into Raleigh.

"Hey!" He grabbed for the wall, bracing himself. "What are you doing?"

"Trying to go downstairs." She felt foolish colliding with him.

"We're going to need traffic lights around here with all the congestion. I was just coming up to check on the upstairs crew."

"That's a good idea—except they've all left."

"Oh."

K. C. struggled to contain a nervous laugh. No doubt it was rare that Raleigh Kincaid looked so flustered.

"I think we should call it a day too," he said, recovering. "How about dinner, since we're the only ones left?"

"Dinner?" she managed, already off kilter from their close proximity.

"Yes. I'll cook. What's your favorite meal?"

"My favorite?" She thought a moment. "Filet mignon, tiny red potatoes, and corn on the cob."

"You're a hearty eater."

K. C. felt her cheeks warm as he eyed her with a skeptical look. She hadn't realized how hungry she was. She hadn't felt like eating like this since…the evening of her last sail with Brian. The night he planned to take her for a steak dinner onshore.

She swallowed around the sudden lump in her throat. "Actually, just a nice tossed salad would be fine."

"No, you get your first choice. I could go for something like that myself." He rubbed his hands together as if it was set. "I'll drive into town and buy groceries. Meet me back here in an hour."

He paused as if taking into account K. C.'s startled expression. "Is that all right?"

"Yes." The word slipped out before she'd meant it to.

CHAPTER SEVEN

Getting ready for dinner presented more decision making than a day at work, K. C. discovered as she rifled through her clothes. What to wear—a dress, skirt, jeans? Chinos? Hair up or down?

Why in the world did I agree to this? She'd managed fine throughout the day, acting strictly professional. Except for when he had sent her emotions ricocheting by noticing her lilac fragrance and then that collision on the stairs… If she hadn't forgotten her notes, she'd be safely chopping up a salad right now.

Whatever was she doing? She grabbed the chinos and a denim shirt and scooped her hair up. This certainly wasn't a date. It was simply dinner, and they both had to eat.

But exactly how, she wondered, *does he plan on preparing such a meal with no facilities?* Takeout from the interstate truck stop was her guess.

When she returned to the farm, she smelled meat grilling before she got out of her car. Somewhere Raleigh had come up with an old kettle grill. It now stood on the concrete porch with thick cuts of filet mignon sizzling atop aluminum foil. A nearby generator had a hot plate plugged into it, and red potatoes and corn on the cob were gently boiling together in a small pan.

But it was the table setting that made her stop in wonder. The worktable had been moved outdoors and was set with red plastic cups, plates, and eating utensils. Only the legs of the sawhorses stuck out beneath a red-and-white checkered cloth. And in the middle sat a bottle of sparkling cider. Surely Raleigh didn't mean anything other than an after-work dinner. So why had he gone all out?

Raleigh stepped outside and gave her a deep smile. "I'm glad you came."

So was she.

Raleigh nodded for her to take a seat, then he drained the water from the corn and potatoes and placed the pan on the plank. "This isn't five-star dining, but dinner is served."

"With genuine country ambiance." K. C. gracefully settled onto an upended apple crate across from him.

She started to bow her head, then stopped, lifting her eyes to Raleigh.

He knew he shouldn't have been staring. "You were about to say a prayer—grace—weren't you?" His crate creaked as he shifted.

"Yes, I was," she said, obviously ignoring his discomfort. "Raleigh—"

"Yes?" He was becoming mesmerized by the shimmer in her eyes.

"Are you a praying man?"

That brought him back to his senses. "Uh, not generally. Of course, I'm not against it. I just don't, uh, do it too often myself anymore."

"Are you a Christian?"

"Huh?" The probing question caught him off guard. No one had asked him that in years, and now her direct gaze demanded the truth. "Yeah. I am. Sure." He squirmed under her look, but it was the truth.

I am, he reiterated in silent emphasis. He knew exactly what she meant, and the answer was, yes, twenty-three summers ago when he was seven, he'd given his heart to Christ during a children's Bible club. But he had no intention of sharing that with her nor dwelling on the recollections it brought.

If he said another word, she'd see straight to the bitterness he'd buried, and she'd be lecturing him. Yes, he knew exactly what she meant, and he didn't want to encourage that line of conversation. This was what made her so different from other women he knew.

And, sadly, that was another reason for him to make sure he kept his distance.

K. C. just smiled. "You don't mind if I give thanks, do you?"

"No, please do. You can even say it out loud if you want to."

"Okay." She bowed her head again and offered a brief prayer of thanksgiving.

Raleigh opened one eye to peer at her while she prayed. Even in those few words she sounded so—how could he explain it?—so at home with God. When was the last time he'd felt like that? Had he ever?

When she looked up she met his gaze and smiled again. There was a mischievous look in her eyes as if she knew his thoughts.

"This is good," K. C. said after she'd tried a bite of filet mignon. "You're quite the chef."

"Thanks. It came out pretty well considering the limited resources. So," he said, hunting for a neutral topic, "you're a McKenzie. Are you a granddaughter of the old homesteaders?"

"No, only by marriage, if that counts. My husband, Brian, was a great-grandson." She fingered the diamond on the white-gold chain she wore.

"Oh." Raleigh knew his face was red. Maybe she'd chalk it up to the heat of the charcoal still burning. He felt so foolish to think he'd worried about being attracted to her. His gaze traveled to her bare left hand. "I wrongly assumed you were single."

"No. A widow." Her tone warned him not to probe.

A widow! That took him by surprise. *How, when—?* But he heeded the warning in her voice and let the subject drop. They weren't close enough to exchange confidences, that was for sure. But this new fact puzzled him. When she had prayed, she sounded so close with God, not the least disappointed in him. Raleigh shook his head. He didn't understand this at all.

"Do you always go by K. C.?" he asked, fishing for a safer subject.

"Occasionally I use Kathryn." She sipped her sparkling cider, watching above the rim of the cup, appearing relaxed again.

"Kathryn is a nice, elegant name." He passed her more corn. "But," he grinned, waiting to see how she'd interpret this, "K. C. suits the real you."

Her response was laughter. The lilting, joyful sound captivated Raleigh. It was even more beautiful, more musical than he'd imagined. How ironic that now that he'd found a woman who interested him, he needed to keep her at a distance.

"I've been K. C. since I was little." She held her hand above the concrete floor like a measuring rod. "Brian and his brother used to call me that growing up, and it stuck."

"Then I'll save *Kathryn* for special occasions, such as when I'm trying to win an argument with you," Raleigh added quickly, in case she might think he had anything else in mind.

After a few minutes of eating in silence, Raleigh glanced at K. C.'s completely empty plate. "I think it'd be safer eating around a hound than trying to compete with you for food. There's not a scrap left!" He tried to sound aghast even as he winked at her.

Again her musical laugh spilled into the evening air. "Right. So you'd better keep your fingers out of my way when we eat. At least you won't have to wash my plate now. I've practically licked it clean."

Raleigh threw his head back and laughed out loud.

After they cleared the table and bagged the plastic plates and utensils, they sat on the porch on their crates, leaning against the house, talking as dusk settled around them. Their silences stretched, joining the quietness of the farmland settling down for the night, interrupted sporadically by a twittering bird or lone car passing by.

"This," Raleigh sighed, almost wishing he had a piece of straw to hold between his teeth, "beats the view from the one-person-at-a-time terrace at my condo. Can't see anything but another high-rise."

"It is beautiful here at night," K. C. said. "Where are you staying, by the way? Obviously this house is uninhabitable."

"So you don't think I could rough it here, huh?" He laughed. "Actually, I'm staying in South Haven too."

"I'm not surprised. You seem more like a bed-and-breakfast person than the Hartley Hotel type. Am I right?"

"For now." Raleigh reached into his pants pocket. "This is for you." He tossed her an untarnished brass key, sidestepping any more questions.

K. C. stared at it as it landed on the plywood table in front of her.

"It's to the house," he said. "Now that we have a real back door as of today, we should lock up at night, with the generator and tools and all. I'll be commuting to and from Chicago. You can still get in." Her face lit up as if filled with some ideas of her own. "To supervise the workmen," he hurriedly tacked on.

She fingered the key. "To supervise, of course."

He leaned back against the house, catching her fleeting, wistful look. He didn't doubt that she wished the *house* was hers as well.

◆　◆　◆

On Thursday, visitors pulled into the driveway.

K. C. ran out to greet Colton and Aunt Lidia, giving them each a hug. "Come on in." She led them toward the house. "Everything is a mess right now. We're in the middle of repairing walls, but I think you'll be amazed at what the men have done already. Just look!" She pushed open the heavy wooden door to the back entrance.

"That in itself is an improvement." Colton rubbed his hand over the solid wood. "It'll help keep out trespassers." He grinned and poked her arm.

K. C. made a face at him and pushed his hand aside. "Some temporary windows have already been installed to give us additional light. They'll help protect the house from weather damage." She walked past a couple of workers, nodding her approval. "The electricity will be turned on as soon as the rewiring is finished. Until then, we deal with the generator." She escorted them through the rooms, pointing out the progress and the planned alterations.

"Right now you have to use your imagination," K. C. told them, "but we'll get there."

"Dear," Aunt Lidia said, "simply mowing the lawn and trimming the bushes has made this house look welcoming once again." She pulled out an embroidered handkerchief and dabbed at her eyes.

"It's a good start," Colton said. "Now, if you could do something about the paint job, too—unless you're sold on greenish blue trim in front and lime out back?" His eyes glinted with humor.

"Going to one color is already on the to-do list," K. C. said with a laugh. She then noticed Raleigh watching them from the doorway. "Raleigh, come on over. You already know Aunt Lidia—"

"Yes, it's nice to see my neighbor again."

"And this is my brother-in-law, Colton McKenzie." K. C. studied the two men as they eyed each other warily. Both dark-haired and serious, Raleigh barely half an inch taller than Colton. Both taking a furtive glance back toward her. K. C. wasn't sure what was going on between them.

Colton's usually quick smile was missing as he formally shook hands with Raleigh. "Nice to meet you."

"You, too," Raleigh echoed, but the pleasantry wasn't reflected in his eyes.

Colton turned back to K. C. "I have to go. I just stopped by to make sure Aunt Lidia wasn't getting into any trouble. Thought I'd bring her by to see what you're up to."

"I'm glad you did." She followed them out to his car.

Colton pulled K. C. into a hug. "That guy mistrusts me."

"What do you mean?" She pulled away, but he gathered her close again.

"He views me as competition," he said, chuckling in her ear.

She stepped backward, feeling her cheeks brighten. "You're crazy." She looked at Aunt Lidia for help, but the elderly woman just grinned, saying nothing.

"So is he your boyfriend?" Raleigh asked from behind K. C. as Colton and Aunt Lidia drove away.

She jumped, unaware that he had come outside. "Colton? No, he's not!" This was getting ridiculous.

"He cares for you."

"Of course he does. We grew up together, I married his brother, he's family." She turned to walk away.

"It's more than that," he called after her.

K. C. stopped and turned back. "You don't know anything about our relationship," she said, feeling defensive. "Why would you even say such a thing?"

"It's obvious from the way he looks at you and watches you…" He raised a brow. "Shall I go on?"

"No." She crossed her arms. How dare Raleigh make such presumptions, especially having just met him? He had no idea what she and Colton had been through. "We're best friends. What you see is the result of years of caring, of watching out for each other."

"People marry their best friends, K. C." He looked away, out toward the farmland spread below the hill.

"And who is your best friend, Raleigh?"

The question seemed to catch him off guard. He turned back and held her gaze for a moment. "I don't have one." He lowered his eyes, as if the admission saddened him.

Before she could contemplate this gentler side he'd revealed, he spread his feet wider. "I'm telling you, that guy loves you." His gaze met hers almost as if challenging her to deny it.

K. C. glared at him. He was wrong. So wrong. What did he know about her and Colton? About the bond of sorrow they shared? Obviously he'd never had a close friend. Did he really know so little about love and loyalty and trust? And, anyway, what was it to him?

"Hey," Raleigh said in a softer tone, "I'm sorry." Then as if to reassure her that he was dropping the issue, he added, "Look, I appreciate all the work you're putting into this place. You work as hard as any of the guys on the crew."

"Well, I should," K. C. said, glad for the change of subject. "I mean, after all, you *are* paying me to do it."

"You'd do it anyway."

So true. It hurt her to think of the restoration as a job, receiving money for what love called her to do. "Yes, but I have to eat too, you know." She shrugged.

"Exactly. That's my point."

"Your point being…?"

"That you have to eat. I was wondering if I could persuade you to go out to dinner with me in South Haven Saturday night. There's a great place there called Sandpipers."

His hopeful expression touched K. C.'s heart. "What I meant was—"

"I know what you meant. But I'm asking if you will allow me to take you out to dinner to say thanks?"

"I…" A whirl of confusing emotions filled her mind.

"I don't mean as a date," he said, as if reading her mind, "if that's what you're worried about. Just a simple thank-you."

"That would be nice," she said, meeting his gaze.

"I'll pick you up at your place, okay?"

"I'll give you directions." K. C. hurried back inside to look for a slip of paper, but mostly to get away from those watchful, gold-flecked eyes.

CHAPTER EIGHT

As usual on Saturday evenings, the tables at Sandpipers were noisy with animated conversations, except for one corner window table overlooking the marina. Raleigh might as well have eaten alone for all the impact he seemed to have on his companion. She had been unnaturally quiet since he'd picked her up at her cottage an hour before. Cottage nothing—once he'd found it towering on a hill among the steep, winding lanes of the Pine Hills section, he discovered a two-story house overlooking lakefront property.

"You never did tell me where you're staying in South Haven," K. C. said during dessert. "Near the lake?"

Raleigh looked up in surprise at the first personal topic of the evening. The entire conversation so far, what there'd been of it, had focused on the work at the McKenzie house. Even he thought of it as that. He'd have to remember to start referring to it as the Kincaid home.

"You're right, I didn't. I've moved since then anyway." He felt a grin spreading across his face. "I'm living near the lake, not far from here. I'll show you after a walk out to the lighthouse, okay?" Maybe his surprise would spark some interest from her.

"I'd like that. I love the old lighthouse."

As Raleigh pulled out his wallet, K. C. reached for her purse.

"No, I've got it," Raleigh said. At her look of protest, he added, "It was a business dinner, remember?" *That's all,* he reminded himself.

Minutes later they walked in silence out to the long concrete pier, listening to the waves slosh against the high sides.

"If you haven't ever been here in the winter," K. C. said, "you should come. Waves crash over the pier and freeze midair just as they're about to slam into the lighthouse."

Raleigh looked at her askance.

"It's true. I'll bring you back in January and show you."

"It's a date." He could have kicked himself. He hadn't meant it like that, simply that he'd like to see it then. K. C.'s narrowed eyes made it clear that a date was not what she intended, either.

As Raleigh led the way back to the beach, he again lapsed into silence. That seemed to work better with her.

"Do you skip rocks?" he asked, picking up a few flat stones from the shoreline.

In answer, she took a couple of the smooth stones he offered and sent them skimming across the water.

He laughed. "You're a lake person!"

"Right." Again, that warning was in her voice, signaling another topic to be avoided.

Raleigh eyed her. He was both curious and puzzled. Did she like the water or not? And he still didn't understand why, with that gorgeous lake house, she wouldn't want to sink her money into winterizing it, why she'd been so set on renovating a farm some twenty miles away. She hardly needed both, did she?

"Want to walk along the channel?" He doubted he'd have gotten answers to his probing questions, anyway. "I'll show you where I'm staying."

Raleigh lengthened his stride, aware of how easily K. C. matched the pace. Some men showed off their trophies or kids; he couldn't wait to show her his boat. Sleek, fast, spacious, with bags of custom sails stored below deck. If she knew anything about sailing at all, she'd be impressed.

As they approached the municipal marina, Raleigh led the way to the red gate by the harbor master's office.

"Raleigh…" K. C. slowed her steps, coming to an almost complete stop. "Isn't this private beyond here, just for the boat owners? I think I've learned my lesson about trespassing."

"No, it's okay. The gate's open."

"Raleigh! That doesn't mean we can just walk on through."

But he was doing exactly that, pulling her with him. "K. C.,"— he turned toward her—"isn't this great?" He swept the expanse of the docked boats with his arm. In his excitement he barely noticed how the color had drained from her face.

He didn't wait for a response. "And this one"—he stopped beside a forty-two-foot Hunter—"is mine. *Under the Stars.* This is where I'm staying." He ran his hand proudly along the polished fiberglass hull. "A friend just sailed it over this week. There's still time to take her out and watch the sunset on the lake, if you'd like."

Her gaze darted from the boat to his face, then back again to *Under the Stars.* "So what do you think?" he asked with a proud grin.

K. C. didn't answer. She seemed to be absorbed with the couple at the next slip, though he could see nothing special about them. They were holding hands, laughing together. Obviously in love, they kissed. At the same moment K. C. turned away to stare at the wave-driven waters around the mouth of the channel.

"K. C." Raleigh tried to get her attention. "Would you like to—"

She shook her head.

"Hey, I'm sorry. I got so wrapped up showing off my boat, I never even asked if you like sailing. I guess I sort of assumed everyone does. Do you? Sail, I mean?" His voice trailed off at her raw expression of fear.

He barely heard her response.

"Not anymore."

K. C. couldn't meet Raleigh's confused eyes and shuddered as the cold memories assaulted her. Tears stung her eyes, and her throat burned. She would not cry in front of Raleigh Kincaid. She would not let him see her vulnerability.

Oh, Brian. She covered her mouth and swallowed hard, as the tears continued to build and sting. *Please help me, Lord!* She turned away from Raleigh, from the boats, from the water, rubbing her hands over the escaping tears now streaming down her face.

Vaguely she was aware of Raleigh taking her arm and guiding her away from the marina, heading in the direction of his Jeep.

"I'm sorry," he repeated several times, still gently leading her.

"So am I," she whispered, though she knew he had no idea what she was sorry for.

Minutes later they climbed into the Jeep where she huddled against the passenger door.

"K. C." Raleigh's voice dimly sounded above the roar of her memories. "K. C." She felt gentle strokes on her clenched hands, much the same as she might comfort a hurting child. But she couldn't respond; all she could do was stay pressed against the door, feeling crushed inside.

"I'll take you home."

K. C. nodded. That was all she could manage.

After a silent ride to her cottage, she finally spoke. "I guess I owe you an explanation." She smiled self-consciously as they pulled into the driveway.

"Not at all."

"Could I entice you to stay a few minutes? I'll put on some coffee."

"If you're up to it." He seemed hesitant.

This endearing side of him was what made him dangerous. The gentle caresses he'd planted on the back of her hands, the soothing voice in her ear...the fact that he'd offered no useless words...no demand that she be reasonable. He deserved an explanation. "Please, come in."

She filled their coffee mugs a few minutes later. "Shall we sit on the patio? That's where I sit to contemplate things or talk."

"Who do you talk to?" he asked when seated. "I mean, I hope you have a neighbor or somebody to, uh, discuss things with."

"You mean to confide in?" She smiled, trying to ease his awkwardness.

"Yes, that's the word."

"The Lord."

He almost sloshed his coffee at her answer. "I see."

He's hurting somehow too, Lord, isn't he? Please help both of us.

"Well, Raleigh…" K. C. sipped her steaming coffee, then set the mug on the table between them. "To give you a better answer to your question, yes, I know how to sail. Used to love it, as a matter of fact."

"Used to…"

"Yes. It's odd how all of a sudden a trivial word or sight can trigger a memory, even after two years." She fell silent for a moment, liking how Raleigh simply listened and waited.

"My husband, Brian, and I had looked at a boat so much like yours, a Hunter. He wanted to upgrade from what we had, which was very nice. Our boat was special, though, because it had so many memories for us. I agreed, since he was so excited, and we already had a buyer for ours. Brian, Colton, and I were going to take one last overnight sail, just as we did when we first bought it." She blew on her coffee, deciding how much to confide in Raleigh. "It was my idea." Again, guilt surged through her.

Raleigh watched her above the rim of his mug, his expression full of compassion.

"Brian kept the boat in top shape, always checking it before we ever took it out." She paused again.

"The sign of a good sailor—very careful, cautious."

"That's why the whole thing never should have happened." Never would she forget the utter terror, surging as high as the rising swells, or the screech of the gulls as if in warning…

"K. C., I don't need to know." Raleigh's voice was soft. He pushed his cup aside.

She nodded, but strangely his gentleness gave her courage to continue. "By late afternoon, the lake started getting choppy. We put the sails down and started motoring toward a marina. We planned to have an early steak dinner and walk around town before nightfall. After a while Brian realized there was a fire in the engine compartment, probably from a hidden wire already burning behind one of the walls. But with the engine noise and exhaust smoke, it'd already grown to the point where it was difficult to control before he saw the signs. After using the fire extinguishers, there was nothing else we could do to save the boat. Colton got the dinghy in the water and helped me into it. By this time the lake had gotten really rough and was tossing the dinghy around while we tried to keep it close enough to the boat for Brian to jump in."

She stopped and swallowed hard. "When he did jump, a wave pushed us away from the boat, and Brian fell into the water. Just as he surfaced, another wave slammed the dinghy up against the boat." Her eyes filled, and she looked away. When she began speaking again, her voice was barely a whisper. "Brian was in between. The Coast Guard arrived, and they were able to get him out of the water, but his head was bleeding, and he was unconscious. They took us all to the marina."

Raleigh gripped her hand and silently held it.

"We finally got to a hospital, but it was too late. He woke up just once." She wiped her eyes with her other hand. "He said he loved me and…asked Colton to take care of me for him. " She looked up at Raleigh. "That's what you see between me and Colton."

"K. C.," he said with a gentle stroke across her cheek. "Kathryn." He put his arm around her and held her close.

◆ ◆ ◆

As the work progressed week by week, Raleigh knew he wasn't actually needed on site any longer, and his clients in Chicago needed his attention. He'd miss watching K. C. at work. He certainly didn't need to worry about whether she could handle the construction workers. Had he not known these guys, he wouldn't have believed what wonders she'd done with them. And it certainly wasn't because they liked working with a woman. That he knew.

She worked alongside them, teased them, fixed them lemonade and coffee as if she were the hostess at a family picnic, bragged on their progress, and just talked with them, asking about their families, their goals. She softly sang old hymns as she worked, and hours later he'd hear whistled snatches of the songs from the men.

K. C. seemed more relaxed around him since that dinner out a few weeks ago, and they'd eaten lunch together often at the house, talking and laughing. But he hadn't dared broach the subject he was considering. Until now.

He waited for the right moment. It came one Thursday afternoon as K. C. passed by the kitchen with a hammer in hand.

"May I take you out to dinner again?" Raleigh called out to her.

Her eyes sparkled as her gaze met his in a questioning look.

He cleared his throat. "This time I mean as a date."

He swallowed as her lips curved into a lovely, inviting smile. He knew he was crossing the line from friendship to something more with this captivating woman. But it was already too late to turn back. "Tonight?"

"I'll need some time off to get ready."

Her words surprised him. "You mean you'll go?"

She grinned and nodded, twirling the hammer in her hand like a majorette's baton. She walked through the back door humming.

Raleigh stood there, staring at her back. A real date with K. C. McKenzie—what was he getting himself into? He shook his head and headed back into the living room, absently humming a little tune himself.

◆ ◆ ◆

That evening K. C. stepped into the shower and pulled out the last tube of lilac gel from the carton Brian had given her. She needed to start carefully rationing now. Once it was gone, so was another memory of Brian. Ever so slowly through these two years his lingering presence was fading.

So what was she doing, going on a date? Never would she have imagined being remotely interested in anyone again. Yet Raleigh Kincaid was beginning to stir her heart as no one but Brian had ever done.

Lord, please don't let me be making a mistake here.

When the doorbell rang, K. C. was ready. She opened the door to Raleigh, who held a picnic basket in one hand and a large blanket in the other.

"Dinner is ready, ma'am. I thought maybe some fine dining on the beach?"

"Perfect." K. C. laughed in delight, her worries disappearing. She'd been fretting over sitting in an elegant restaurant, feeling awkward, trying to find something to talk about. A picnic on the beach! Raleigh had thoughtfully made their first real date so nonthreatening. And so enchanting. And festive. She grinned up at him and accepted his proffered arm, linking hers in his.

The evening was wonderful—a simple dinner of cold chicken and potato salad, a companionable walk on the beach, and then they sat back down on the blanket, talking comfortably as they watched the crimson sunset.

"Raleigh?"

He looked up, seeming to realize that K. C. had been waiting for an answer.

She laughed softly. "Hey, dreamer. I was just asking if you'd like to go with me to church on Sunday. I found a delightful congregation in town, and—"

He stared at her for a moment. "Sorry, K. C. I go back to Chicago this weekend. I need to start taking care of my clients there."

"Of course." She tried to hide her disappointment.

"I'll be gone most of every week now, just returning on Fridays to check the progress. Unfortunately I can't run the firm by fax, phone, and e-mail, even in this day and age. I need to be there."

"I understand." She hoped that was the real reason, not just an excuse. "Maybe some other time…"

He shrugged noncommittally. "How about if I take you out to dinner Saturday night before I leave? Maybe a nice French restaurant?"

"French?" She managed a small smile. "I'd like that—spending time with you before you leave, I mean."

"I know just the place. Very special. It's charming, old-country."

Lord, K. C. prayed as she and Raleigh climbed the steps back to her house, *please help him. His eyes said he was telling the truth when I asked if he was a Christian, yet he acts so indifferent. Please, whatever the problem is, restore his relationship with you.*

◆   ◆   ◆

Saturday night as Raleigh knotted his tie, he found himself whistling a song K. C. had been humming earlier in the week. But he immediately stopped when he realized what the tune was—*What a Friend We Have in Jesus.* Another reminder of how far apart they were. This evening was designed to make up for not going to church with her on Sunday. Leaving for Chicago happened to be a convenient excuse. This time.

Why did the one woman who truly seemed to draw his heart have to be a reminder of what he didn't want to think about? It was a mistake to date her. He gave his tie a hard, final yank. He threw on his suit jacket and headed for the door, determined to enjoy one last evening with her. Le Château, farther up the shore, was the perfect place for dinner with K. C.—even if it was their last.

A half-hour later he escorted her into the restaurant. They followed the maître d' to a window table overlooking blooming gardens below.

"This is beautiful," K. C. whispered, as if the flowering colors deserved hushed tones of reverence.

Raleigh loved the way her eyes glowed in the soft candlelight and her face lit up when she smiled. Yes, this was the right place to bring her.

"What are you staring at?" she asked after they were seated and handed menus.

"You." He grinned as her cheeks reddened. "Have you decided what you'd like?"

"Why don't you surprise me? Anything but *escargot.*"

Raleigh studied the menu again. When he did order, it was in fluent French.

"I'm impressed," K. C. said.

"It's nothing," Raleigh mumbled, reaching for his water glass.

"What do you mean, 'nothing'? You sound like a Frenchman."

"I just picked it up."

"Picked it up? I took four years of French and never spoke like that."

He shrugged. "Do you have brothers or sisters?" He didn't know why he'd never asked that before, but it was a good topic now. Anything to get this conversation away from himself.

"No, I'm an only child. The closest I had to brothers were Brian and Colton. Colton and I were almost like twins, and we were always tagging after Brian. How about you? Tell me about your family."

Immediately Raleigh regretted, in his haste to change subjects, that he hadn't considered where this would naturally lead.

I might as well tell her and get it over with. Then he wouldn't have to worry about how to withdraw from her; she'd drop him before they could even get out of the restaurant.

"No brothers or sisters." He was deliberately vague.

"Well, what about your parents? You've never mentioned them."

"Neither have you." He loosened his tie, dreading the question he knew would come momentarily.

"Mine are—what should I say—semiretired at fifty? Adult beachcombers?" She shook her head with a slight smile. "They live in Hawaii and seldom come to the mainland," she added with a shrug, as if that explained them.

"Right," he said with a wry smile. "They live in Hawaii, and you live in the middle of nowhere. And you wonder why they don't come this way much?"

"I like it here." She tilted her chin in a charmingly defensive gesture. "So what about yours? Where do they live?"

"Let's see. They were in France for a while, then Germany. They're back in France now." He braced himself for the next obvious question.

"Are they military or ambassadors or something?" She leaned forward, eyes shining with interest.

Raleigh laughed out loud, though it sounded like a snort to him. The short sound contained absolutely no humor.

"They'd say they're ambassadors. Ambassadors for Christ. They're missionaries." He leaned back to let that statement sink in.

"Missionaries," K. C. sputtered. "Your parents are missionaries?"

"Yeah, you got it. I'm an MK. A missionary kid. Does that surprise you?" He'd known it would. He waited for the look of shock to evaporate from her face. "While they were out serving the Lord, winning souls, caring for refuges, I was sent off to boarding school. I speak fluent French and German, and pretty good Italian, too.

"Oh sure," he continued, holding up his hand to ward off any objection, "I understand they wanted the best for me, my safety, my education, all that. Plus, at the time, the mission board they were under required all the kids to be in a missions school. Out of harm's way, I suppose, while their parents devoted their attention to their calling. And it did work out well, actually. I became interested in architecture over there. I got a good education, all right, studying famous architectural designs firsthand." He crossed his arms with a smug expression, daring her to challenge him, to begin a lecture.

"Oh, Raleigh." And instead of any words of reprimand for his feelings, his behavior, his obvious bitterness, K. C. laid her hand on his and tightly held it, imparting a comfort that he'd never imagined possible. And that simple gesture went straight to his heart. Her eyes held no pity or condemnation. Just compassion.

He clung to her hand, hungry for its warmth. Here was a woman who herself had had love torn away, who understood loss and pain. Yet he saw no trace of bitterness in her.

He looked into her eyes again, reveling in the understanding and acceptance he saw there. How could he detach himself from this remarkable woman when he was beginning to need her?

CHAPTER NINE

Raleigh was glad to be back in Chicago for the week, to have some distance between himself and Kathryn Claire McKenzie. What should he do now? He'd made a huge mistake in letting his guard down. He'd thought that getting to know her better couldn't hurt. But the better he knew her, the more he was drawn to her.

He sank his aching head, cushioned by his arms, to his desk. Maybe banging his head on the desk would be more useful. He simply wasn't the kind of man K. C. needed. Sure, he measured up pretty well in many respects—success, wealth, even personality, perhaps. But in what mattered to her, the spiritual department, he was a failure.

K. C. had never questioned him again about his relationship with God, but she must wonder. His lack of interest in prayer or church or anything spiritual likely made him even less appealing in her eyes. And, he admitted, he probably hadn't started off with much of a chance, anyway.

Raleigh stood and walked to the window overlooking the lake. Normally this spot relaxed him when he felt stressed, but it didn't work today. No point in driving out to Hartley for the weekend to see her. He'd skip this week's progress check—his contractor knew how to reach him if there were any problems. He'd stay here and bury himself in his work, just as he should have been doing all along.

He glanced over toward Navy Pier and the boats skimming along out on the open waters. Another difference between himself and

K. C. Sailing was his life; she would always be moored. Her life was inland, on a farm.

He turned away from the window, back to his desk. There was one decent thing he could do. When the project was complete, regardless of winning or losing the contest, he'd sell the house to K. C. He'd build his manor elsewhere, though he'd retain ownership of the rest of the farm. Maybe he could even go out and see her once in a while. They'd drift apart, and, thankfully, she would never know what she was beginning to mean to him. Or what he foolishly wished might have been.

All he had to do now was stick with it.

◆　◆　◆

Sunday afternoon K. C. pulled into Aunt Lidia's driveway. She'd missed Raleigh's presence in the house this week. Even with the men hammering and banging and working to create miracles, the place was missing something. Someone. It was the contractor who told her Raleigh didn't plan on being back for yet another week.

If it wasn't for church and taking Aunt Lidia to the nursing home, the whole weekend would have been unbearably dreary.

As soon as Aunt Lidia had settled into the car, she looked across at K. C. "If Clara isn't up to my visiting today, I think I'll sit in on the church group's singing and Bible lesson."

K. C. turned the car onto Sixty-sixth Avenue. "We'd love that."

Aunt Lidia patted K. C.'s hand. "I'm glad you come with me each week, but I want you to find time to be with some young people, too. You like old things too much. Even old people."

K. C. laughed. "Old things and old people, as you put it, all have stories to tell. I think God wants us to learn from each other."

"I do too, dear. Now," she said, gazing at the old farmhouse as they passed, "I want to hear more about the new neighbor who has put that spark in your eye."

"Aunt Lidia!" But K. C. couldn't help a peek of her own through the window, hoping to spot Raleigh's Jeep.

"I see life coming back into your eyes, dear. And that's good." Lidia covered K. C.'s hand. "Brian would be pleased."

"Do you think so? I feel like I'm betraying him because I enjoy being around Raleigh."

"Let God lead you, of course, but he gave you four good years with Brian, then took him, for whatever reason. Now perhaps he's giving you someone else. He's a God of love, dear. Don't try to hamper his ways. Regardless, Raleigh needs our prayers. He's a hurting man."

K. C. looked at Aunt Lidia in surprise. "How did you know that?"

"Don't forget I spent some time talking with him. It's more from the topics he avoids than from anything he says."

"He comes from a Christian background, but he's bitter toward God." K. C. bit her lip, wondering how she could help him.

"Just let him see God's love in you, dear."

K. C. smiled her thanks. Aunt Lidia's words somehow gave her permission to think of Raleigh. Already he'd become an important part of her life, and she missed him. She'd gotten used to loneliness without Brian for two years, but this was different. This was missing someone living. She still honored Brian's memory. But he was gone, having taken a piece of her heart with him. What was left, she silently acknowledged, indeed had growing feelings for Raleigh Kincaid.

K. C. drove up the hill to the farmhouse Friday morning after another week of missing Raleigh. From the outside the place was already transformed into something lovely. The back addition was up and sided, the entire house was painted a gleaming white, the yard was immaculately trimmed, and Raleigh's sunroom windows were hung. She hoped the house would truly mean something to him by the time it was done, for it looked like a home to her. *A dream home,* she added sadly.

As she crested the top of the driveway, she gave a little shriek—Raleigh's Jeep sat in the driveway.

"Raleigh!" She ran inside the house. "Raleigh!"

A painter working on the staircase looked up midstroke. "Out back."

She hurried out onto the porch now bordered with blooming pink hollyhocks. Jumping off the step, she ran toward Raleigh as he jogged into sight from behind the barn, pulling one hand behind him when he saw her.

"I'm so glad you're here!" She drew up short before she embraced him. "What are you hiding from me?" K. C. clasped her hands as she tore her gaze from his face to the arm behind his back.

Raleigh solemnly held out his hand, presenting her with two fuzzy pieces of fruit.

"The peaches are ready!" She took them and wiped them on her pants.

Raleigh smiled slightly. "Yeah, and you get the first ones I picked."

K. C. bit into one. "This is a Jim Dandee. That one's a Redhaven, which is the first out, usually around the beginning of August."

He looked surprised. "How'd you know?"

"Remember, I was practically a farm girl during the summers. Here." She tossed him the Redhaven. "Try it."

Raleigh took a bite.

"Now you're officially a fruit farmer," K. C. teased him. "Don't forget to add that to your credentials."

"Even if I hire out all the work?" He looked away, sounding defeated, as if he were anything but a farmer.

"Well, sure." What was wrong with him? He was standing in the sunlight, and she took a good look at him. His face seemed drawn, and the circles under his eyes made her worry that he'd been spending too many long hours at the office. "I'm glad you're back," she said softly. "I missed you."

He didn't answer right away, then mumbled something, not quite meeting her eyes.

K. C. again studied him. Something wasn't right. His guarded expression confirmed it.

Sitting next to Raleigh on the South Haven beach that evening, K. C. stared out toward the lake. Though she was glad to be here with him, she was surprised he'd suggested it. All day at the house he'd been authoritative, getting involved where he wasn't needed. He spent precious minutes remeasuring cabinets when the carpenter's work was faultless. He told the painters they hadn't put on enough coats of paint when the walls were beautifully rich and smooth, practically glowing in the afternoon sun. And the unfortunate electrician who installed a lone outlet the barest fraction off-center…it was a wonder he finally agreed not to quit—yet.

It couldn't simply be stress from *Restorations Today* magazine sending out a staff writer and photographer for an interview. They were in the *middle* of a restoration, and the contest didn't call for everything to be perfect now.

"The water is so still," K. C. said, hoping to break through to Raleigh.

"Uh-huh."

"There's not a ripple on the lake, let alone in the channel."

"Nope."

"Raleigh…?"

He finally looked at her.

"I've been considering something, praying about it, and I think it's time. Do you think we could go out on your boat?"

He sat up straight, eyes wide in surprise. "Now? There's no wind."

"I know, but we could motor out to just past the lighthouse, watch the sun set, and come back. I need to do this when the water's calm."

"K. C., you don't need to do this for me, if that's what you think. I understand what you've been through. I'd never ask you to go sailing."

"I want to. I need to. Just this once. Maybe I won't ever enjoy sailing again, but I need to know that I can do it. It'll help me to"— she swallowed, keeping her resolve—"put the past behind me…and go on."

Raleigh nodded mutely, took her hand to pull her up, and led her toward the marina.

Raleigh almost wished he hadn't given up on praying. He could use someone to talk to right about now, other than himself. If K. C., of all people, could put the past behind her and go on, why couldn't he?

He knew the answer to that—the reason she *could* go on was the same reason he *couldn't*. It all came back to faith. To God.

And, he concluded, *doesn't it figure that she'd choose me to help her face her fears.*

Unwilling as he felt, he'd help.

"I'll start getting things ready to cast off," K. C. said as they stepped onboard. "Can we stop just past the end of the pier?"

"We'll stay as close as we can without blocking the channel entrance. There aren't many boats out tonight, so that shouldn't be a problem."

K. C. smiled shakily and nodded. "Okay, then, let's get ready."

Raleigh watched from the cabin steps as she went to work. She knew exactly what to do without being told and moved like a seasoned sailor. He joined her on deck after taking care of things below.

"Everything looks good. I'm ready to start the engine. Okay?" He almost hoped she'd change her mind.

"Ready, Captain." She closed her eyes as if dreading the instant the key was turned.

He sighed. "Okay then." He turned the ignition. When she flinched at the sound of the engine turning over, he ran his hands through his black hair. How could he do this? Watching her tore at his heart. She no longer took the initiative, acting without being told. She sat motionless, white-knuckled, as if she needed to be prompted toward any move.

"Can you get the fenders and cast off," Raleigh asked, "while I steer us away from the dock?" He looked over his shoulder at her to see if she really wanted to go through with this.

She nodded and did as directed.

"Are you all right?" he checked again as they headed slowly down the channel.

He waited as she bit her lip, then nodded.

"Just let me know if you change your mind."

Again she nodded but said nothing.

"You're at home on a boat. You must have sailed a lot." He wasn't up to small talk, but he figured if he kept her talking, she wouldn't have so much time to worry.

"Since I was a little girl. Brian's parents owned a boat, and I went with them a lot. During the summers in Michigan, Brian, Colton, and I sailed a small Sunfish down at the cottage. After we were married, Brian bought our beautiful boat…" She turned her head as her voice trailed off, and Raleigh remained silent. He didn't press her to go on.

As they passed the lighthouse and left the safety of the channel, reaching the entrance to the open waters of Lake Michigan, K. C. sat down.

"Not much farther, okay, Raleigh?"

"Just enough to get out of the way, and then we'll let her drift. Do you want to take the wheel for a bit?"

Wordlessly she stepped behind the wheel to steer.

"I'm all right," she said in answer to his questioning gaze.

Raleigh laid his hand over hers. He didn't dare let it linger, or he'd be taking her in his arms and kissing her, assuring her that everything would be all right. He quickly removed his hand before it was too late, before he ended up telling her things he knew couldn't be true.

In silence they watched the red sun dip quietly into the water.

"I did it, Raleigh," K. C. whispered, wiping the tears that had slipped along her cheeks.

Raleigh watched in awe as she lifted her face to the sky. "Thank you, Lord," she breathed.

He looked away, feeling like an intruder.

"Are you ready to go back?" he asked after a moment.

She nodded, tears still glistening on her cheeks, her eyes clear and wonder-filled.

Silently they motored back through the channel, and Raleigh maneuvered into his slip.

They stepped onto the wooden dock. "Thank you, Raleigh." Her shining eyes spoke of something he couldn't begin to comprehend, and her expression left him breathless. How he longed to take her into his arms, to ask her to help him find the same peace he'd seen on her face.

She tilted her head, and Raleigh took a step toward her.

"Anytime." He clasped her arm a moment, picked up her sailing bag, and walked her to her car.

◆ ◆ ◆

Over the next couple of weeks, K. C. continued to wonder about Raleigh. He still came out to the farm on Fridays to confer with his workers and check on their progress, but something was troubling him, and she was pretty sure she was involved.

Lord, be near to him, was her daily prayer.

One Friday evening as she was out on her patio reading her grandmother's Bible, she looked up at the sound of footsteps.

"Raleigh!" She stood, placing the Bible on a small table.

He frowned at the book. "Did I interrupt something?"

She followed his gaze. "It's my grandmother's Bible. I like to sit here, looking out at the water, when I read it. She marked so many verses, sometimes I just thumb through to see what was important to her. And it always speaks to me, too."

His glance took in the open pages. "I learned Psalm 23 when I was a kid," he mumbled, looking away from her.

"Those are the verses that helped me the most when Brian died," K. C. said softly. "They were my comfort." *Please let them be Raleigh's comfort too.*

Raleigh shifted, looking uncomfortable. "I came to tell you I'm leaving for Wisconsin tonight. I have a couple of on-site jobs that will keep me away for a few weeks."

Deep disappointment bore down on her. "Well," she sighed, trying to be lighthearted, "that's what you get for being so good at your job." She took a step closer to Raleigh, longing for him to stretch his arms around her in a good-bye hug.

"Yeah." He turned and walked away, leaving K. C. baffled. Had she been so wrong? Never had she imagined that the man she wanted to open her heart to would be unable to open his.

Three weeks. This was the longest Raleigh had been away, and now the calendar had flipped over, with the days edging along well into September. If he didn't come soon, he'd miss standing in his sunroom with beautiful fall colors filling the windows.

K. C. and the crew worked long, hard hours, drawing the restoration to a close ahead of schedule. She knew the contractor had assured him all was on track, but why didn't he want to see for himself? This was the house they'd dreamed of, had drawn all the plans for. Didn't it mean anything more to him than just a contest?

When she pulled up for work on Friday morning, the green Jeep was back in the driveway. Raleigh stepped off the back porch and strode toward her with a cordial nod.

"Raleigh." She was guarded, surprised.

For a moment neither one spoke.

"Have you been inside yet?" She tried to fill the awkwardness between them.

"No, I just got here a few minutes ago. Went straight to the orchards to talk with my contract farmer." He rubbed a peach against his pants then tossed the fruit to her. "It's a Redskin, one of the last varieties of the season."

"I see you're learning your crops." She took a bite, glad that Raleigh was at least aware of what he had growing.

"Yeah, well," he shrugged, "that's what Mr. Harley told me."

"You'll be surprised at the work the men accomplished while you were gone." They stepped up onto the porch. "Other than a few minor details, the restoration is finished. The furniture just arrived this week, along with a few antique pieces you might be interested in." She grinned. "It's ready for you to move in."

"Finished?" He stared at her. How could it be? His contractor had given no indication they were this close when he'd asked for a status report.

"Your men are great. We worked day and night to finish ahead of schedule." She looked at him curiously. "Aren't you surprised?"

"I'm surprised, all right." He knew he sounded exactly as he felt—downright shocked and, yes, disappointed. "How'd you get them to work overtime?"

"Out of love, basically."

"Love!" He threw his hands up at the answer. "What do you mean by that?"

She took a step back, looking bewildered. "Well, love for their work, of course, and for the vision they caught and for you as their boss. Isn't this what you wanted?"

No! he wanted to shout. How could they do this to him? He'd planned on a few more weeks to work with her before the contest ended, before he offered her the house, before he said good-bye to K. C. He wanted to dream a little longer about holding her in his arms, feeling her closeness, looking into her eyes.

"I'm sorry." K. C. broke the strained silence between them. She looked close to tears. "We were only trying to please you, to help you win your contest." She started to back away.

"The contest?" Raleigh reached for her hand, attempting to stop her.

K. C. jerked her fingers free from his, her face red. "I'll admit it, Raleigh Kincaid. I care for you. But since caring means so little to you, then..." Her voice trailed off as she took a step off the porch. She moved past the hollyhocks, then turned again to face him. "My prayer was that you'd see God's faithfulness, whether you ever cared for me or not." She brushed a hand across her eyes. "There's just one more thing..."

He stood speechless, waiting.

"Since I won't be here in the spring to remind you, don't forget to order lilac bushes to plant beneath the sunroom windows. Purple lilacs."

She turned and strode down the driveway, a crunch of gravel sounding with each step. She didn't even turn around to see if he still stood there.

CHAPTER TEN

Stunned, that's what Raleigh was.

She cares for me? He fought the urge to run after her, to stop her, to pull her into his arms just as he had wanted to do in the first place.

Let her go. Of course that was the best course of action. It was better to let her go now than to break her heart later. But watching her struggle to maintain composure as she got into her car, he knew he was far too late for that. He'd already crushed it with his feigned indifference.

In the long run, though, this had to be best—even if his heart didn't agree.

Dejected, he wandered through the house, noticing the changes that K. C. had wanted to surprise him with. The interior was finished, clean, ready to live in. He roamed from room to room. The tiny bathroom and music room he'd made fun of now comprised a luxurious bath off the added master bedroom. New fixtures gleamed around a claw-foot bathtub, high windows let in sunlight, let out steam. Who'd have imagined something so grimy and distasteful could be made new, restored so completely?

Even with the beautiful inner shell, the house was empty. Not because it lacked furniture. It was all in place. It was empty because it lacked K. C.'s sweetness, her laughter, her singing, her love filling the rooms just as she'd begun to fill his life.

"Hey, Raleigh, man." A carpenter came in humming. "How do you like what we did while you were gone? Miss K. C.'s something else, isn't she?" He grinned. "Where is she? I have a couple of finishing touches to ask her about. I thought I heard her pull up."

"She left."

"When's she coming back? I need her approval."

"I don't know when she's coming back," he snapped. *Or if she is.* "You can show me the problem. It's my house. I give the approval."

The smile faded from the man's face. "Sure, whatever you say—Boss. If you don't mind coming with me, I'll show you."

Raleigh took care of that problem, then sat down on a stepladder, head in his hands, desperate to ignore his bigger problem. It was a good thing the project was at a close. The end couldn't have come at a better time. Already he couldn't bear this ache of missing K. C. Had there still been work to do, he knew she'd have fulfilled her obligation to him—probably in silence.

The contest, that was all he had left. He raised his head, a new idea hitting him. Of course. Just what he needed to shake himself out of this despair. He would contact *Restorations Today* and set up an appointment for their review team to come out. Maybe that'd keep his mind off K. C.

But even that didn't help as day after day slipped by with no word from her. A number of times he started to dial her number but hung up. He'd get over her in time. He was just missing her because he was used to having her around working, singing, humming, laughing. The pain would go away. Someday.

◆ ◆ ◆

K. C. was not going to waste time pitying herself, moping about, even though that's exactly what she longed to do. She had other business to tend to. She pulled out a phone book and called several places to inquire about winterizing her summer cottage. She should have done this months ago, but she'd gotten too involved with Great-grandmother McKenzie's—rather, she corrected herself, Raleigh Kincaid's—house. Just because he took away her dream of living on the hill did not mean she was leaving the vicinity. But she had to have her house winterized to make that happen. Even with this new project occupying her days though, the week passed slowly.

Sunday morning as K. C. showered, she reached for her tube of lilac gel. She gave it a gentle squeeze, but nothing came out except air. She tapped the bottom, then shook it.

Come on. Just a little more.

Nothing.

She panicked. It couldn't be gone. Not yet. She needed just a little more time. Needed to—

She shook and squeezed the tube again, and the last remnant squirted out, missing her hand, sliding down the side of the tub. Trying to salvage even a dab, K. C. bent to catch it before it reached the drain. The pulsating water won, though, as it swept the treasure from her grasp. Getting on one knee, she desperately covered the drain with her hands even as the gel was sucked away.

Her lilac soap was gone…Brian was gone…the house was gone from her reach…Raleigh was gone…everything, even hope, was gone.

Doubling over, she sank to both knees and sobbed.

Why, God, why? Her tears followed the path of the lilac gel down the drain.

◆　◆　◆

After a cold, sparse Sunday lunch, Raleigh wandered around the yard. Though the gardener was coming tomorrow, Raleigh found the lawn mower and started on the yard. After the front was finished, he stood wiping his forehead.

A shaky, soft feminine voice broke into his thoughts. "Hello, there!"

He looked around and saw his little white-haired neighbor climbing up the bank from the driveway into the yard.

"Miss Lidia! Hello." He stepped over to give her a hand up the incline. "Won't you come in? I'll give you a tour of the finished house—and a glass of lemonade."

"I don't see how I can refuse either," she chuckled. "You haven't heard from Kathryn, have you?"

The question took Raleigh by surprise. Had K. C. told her about her last visit here?

"No, I haven't. Why?"

"No particular reason. I'm just a bit worried about her, that's all."

"Is she all right?" That he had to ask made it obvious he hadn't spoken with her recently.

"I'm not sure. She usually takes me on Sunday afternoons to the nursing home to visit, but she said she couldn't make it today. She insisted she was fine, though she didn't sound it. I was just wondering if you knew anything." She said it innocently enough, but Raleigh wondered if he was being set up, baited.

He shrugged. "I haven't talked to her in a few days," he said cautiously.

"I see." And he was afraid that perhaps she did see more than she let on. "About that tour?" she asked.

"Of course. Come on in." He led her around back to the newly added kitchen, master bedroom, and extended living room. "I hope you approve of the final restoration."

"Raleigh, any restoration has to be for the good."

"Yes ma'am." He was getting the idea it was safer to keep his responses to a bare minimum, as he had no idea where she was headed in most of her conversations.

They walked through the rest of the house with Miss Lidia occasionally nodding or making a comment.

"I don't remember if I told you the history of this house," she said as they completed the tour.

They'd been over the facts a couple of times, but he decided it was best to just let her ramble.

"This is the second time this house has been restored," she said, taking his arm as they descended the stairs. "When my parents bought the place, it was in shambles." She pointed a thin finger at him, as if he, being the current owner, were responsible for its past condition. "They made it into a beautiful house and a loving *home*. It took *hard work*." She narrowed her eyes, making him inwardly squirm under her gaze.

He nodded. He already knew all this.

"When they died, it was sold and resold. When you found the place, its condition was due to *neglect*. But by the grace of the good

Lord, you cared enough to salvage it, to restore it back to what it could be. That's the way things work, Raleigh. Some people neglect, some people care. You've seen what's happened to this house in both instances."

Raleigh stared at the small woman. "Yes ma'am." Again, it seemed the safest response.

"Thank you for the tour. I'll just mosey on back home now—unless you feel like driving a senile old woman over to the nursing home for the afternoon?"

Raleigh blushed as she pinpointed his exact thoughts of her repeated stories. "Of course—I mean, I'll drive you—not that I meant that I think—"

"Pshaw—" Miss Lidia waved a hand at him, thankfully cutting off his faltering explanation. "Let's go. And bring a book or something. I don't want to bore you with our stories of the good old days."

On the ride over, Miss Lidia was quiet, giving him time to think. So this was what K. C. did on Sundays. He knew she went to church, which he'd declined attending with her. But other than that, he had no idea what she did. He'd supposed she spent time with her pal Colton.

Now was Colton's chance to make a move, and no doubt he would, as Raleigh couldn't imagine any man wanting simply to remain a friend with K. C. McKenzie. Well, he'd better just get used to it. As much as he hated to admit it, K. C. deserved someone like Colton. Someone who wasn't lacking in his commitment to God or to her.

At the nursing home, Lidia met her friend in the lounge off the cafeteria. Raleigh found a seat on a sofa in a corner and pulled out the magazine he'd brought. From here he hoped to tune out the hymns the church group had started singing. The leader played the piano, adding his gravelly baritone to those of a myriad of raspy-voiced patients. The noise grew louder and louder until Raleigh could hardly think.

The singing stopped, and it was quiet for all of a moment. Before Raleigh could start the last paragraph again, the energetic leader invited a white-haired patient to sing in her native German. The words sung in a scratchy, off-tune voice reached Raleigh with a jolt.

Ich hinterlasse mein Land
Ich hinterlasse meine Liebe
Aber Ich werde Dich im Jenseits sehen.
Wir verabschieden uns jetzt schweren Herzens,
Aber wir werden uns im Jenseits wieder begrüssen.
Gott sei mit Dir,
Gott gehe mit Dir.
Gott sei unser Tröster.

Raleigh looked around to see the impact the song made on the others. Incredibly, all seemed oblivious, not understanding the German words. But the tune, the meaning of those words, the memories, all tore into his heart.

I am leaving my land,
I am leaving my love,
But I will see you in the land over there.
We say good-bye now, with a sad farewell,
But we'll say hello over there.
God be with you,
God go with you.
God be our comfort still.

"We sang this song," the woman explained, "to our children as kind families smuggled them out of the country during the war. Our hope was they would someday board a ship bound for America. I said good-bye to my own daughter, not knowing if I'd ever see her again, but giving her a chance to escape, a chance to be safe. It was our longing to see them again, and if that was not to be, then knowing they were in God's care. This was our good-bye to them."

Yes, Raleigh knew it was a farewell song. He could still hear his mother singing it into the ear of her eight-year old son as she held him tightly outside the door of the mission boarding school. He could still feel the tears trickling down his face as she turned and left, and he forlornly waved good-bye. It was a song of finality.

> *Gott sei mit Dir,*
> *Gott gehe mit Dir.*
> *Gott sei unser Tröster.*
> God be with you,
> God go with you.
> God be our comfort still.

How many times had his mother sung or written or said those words to him? If he could cover his ears with both hands to keep them out of his thoughts, he would. Raleigh glanced at his watch, then over to Miss Lidia, wishing she'd hurry up. He wanted to get out of here. Now.

Miss Lidia didn't seem anywhere near ready to leave, especially as the group leader stepped up to the microphone.

"Maybe sometime in your life," the wiry man said, "you drifted away from God. But do you know that he always loved you? Never once did he leave you through the years." He paused, his voice intent. "Maybe you even feel abandoned by your families here. But you're not alone. Know that God loves you." The man continued, offering words of hope to these people confined to these walls. But Raleigh quit listening.

His throat burned, and his eyes felt scratchy. He must be coming down with a cold or something, that's all. It sure wasn't from what that lady had sung or anything the leader said—because he didn't care.

> *Gott sei mit Dir,*
> *Gott gehe mit Dir.*

He slammed the magazine closed and looked over at Miss Lidia. Why couldn't she meet her friend up in her room like other visitors did?

"Are you ready to go?" Lidia caught his glance.

"Yes," he answered, clutching his magazine as he stood. "I'm ready." Raleigh escorted Miss Lidia home, feeling more despondent than ever.

◆　◆　◆

The days slowly passed into yet another week. Raleigh didn't know why he bothered coming out to the farm on weekends anymore, let alone staying over a Sunday again, but here he was. The house was finished, beautifully restored beyond what he'd even imagined possible. The built-in shelves K. C. had insisted on in the formal dining room were the focus of the room. Set with antique dishes, that was the sidebar shot she wanted for the magazine article should they win. The wooden farm table already spread with a muted tablecloth was long enough to hold ten guests for a Thanksgiving dinner, while the cozy kitchen table seated four. The living room didn't need lights turned on until dusk on days that the sun was out, as it filled itself with the sun's glow. The sunroom, well, it was just plain perfect—three sides of windows overlooking a variegated carpet of farms across the countryside.

Even the furnishings throughout the house were perfect—muted, earthy plaids in the master bedroom and living room, soft garden colors in the kitchen—not one ruffle, piece of lace, or pink wall anywhere. K. C.'s taste was artful, understated, elegant. And that was the problem. The house was beautiful, wonderfully restored—but so empty.

He paced around the rooms again. He needed some overlooked detail to busy himself with, but there was nothing left to do. He glanced at the mantel clock. About this time last week Miss Lidia was climbing the bank into his yard. He hoped she didn't need a ride to the nursing home today; he just wasn't up to hearing that church group again.

Raleigh walked out the front door into the perfectly manicured yard and looked down the road at the green-shingled house on the corner. K. C.'s car was there. So close and yet so far.

He wanted to run over and bring her back to enjoy the final result of her work. But he couldn't face her. He stared at her car a moment longer before heading toward his Jeep. At least he didn't have to worry about whether Miss Lidia needed a ride to the nursing home.

◆ ◆ ◆

One October morning K. C. was waiting outside Pot-Shots, just blocks from the South Haven marina, as Colton unlocked the door.

"Kace!"

"Here," she said, handing Colton a cup of coffee. "Can we talk?"

"Sure." He led her to a small table by the window.

"Brace yourself." She knew of no way to prepare him for this. "I'm in love."

"I know."

She looked at him, stunned. "Do you think I'm betraying Brian?"

"Of course not! It's been over two years. He'd want you to be happy. I'm just concerned about it being Raleigh. He seems to have problems."

"He's been hurt. But you don't have to worry. Raleigh doesn't care for me, anyway."

"There you're wrong. There was caring in his eyes the first time I saw him with you."

"I don't think he's ever allowed himself to be close to anyone." She looked down. "I let him know I cared, and now he's withdrawn from me, too."

"Raleigh obviously has your heart, whether he cares or not. If he doesn't want it, then personally I think he's a fool. But if he's really who you want, Kace, talk to him."

As she stepped out of Pot-Shots, K. C. headed the few short blocks to the beach. She needed to walk and pray before she sought out Raleigh, to be sure of God's leading. As she passed the marina, she thought of the day Raleigh had first brought her here and showed her his boat. He'd been so sweet, wanting to surprise her, and so touchingly awkward in trying to comfort her. Yet he had helped her more than he knew.

Raleigh, I miss you.

Before the accident, this had been her favorite type of beach day, nearly empty in the off-season cold with the waves high, crashing, pounding. Pulling her jacket sleeves down over her hands to warm them, she walked along the shore, then almost as if pulled from someplace deep inside, turned toward the lighthouse at the channel's entrance.

Waves crested and exploded as she stepped onto the pier leading to it. She scrambled onto the concrete anchors of the catwalk as waves rolled across. Leaning into the wind, she kept her head down and continued on.

Few people ventured onto the pier when the waves swept so dangerously across, and those making their way back now shouted warnings that the waters were too rough to continue. But K. C. forged ahead. Finally, she reached the lighthouse and sought a handhold on its wet, slick sides. It would be easy for the wind or the crashing waves to sweep her into the angry waters.

But as she clung there, chilled by the wind and water, she paused, transfixed by the power, the majesty, the awe of the lake, of God.

If he's really who you want, Kace, talk to him. Colton's advice was good, but was that what she wanted? Was it worth more pain and rejection to pursue Raleigh?

As yet another wave receded, water pooled in slight impressions in the concrete at the lighthouse's base. *Handprints.* Like hers and Colton's and Brian's on the old porch at the farmhouse. These handprints had weathered storm after storm out here. Battered and pounded, pooled with floodwaters, they were just as solid as the lighthouse, sitting on the same concrete foundation. They had survived. Like the handprints, like Great-grandmother McKenzie's old house, she, too, would survive.

Dear God, thank you for showing me. But, please, please help me. Be the strength we both need.

She didn't know whether she was wiping tears or spray as she swiped moisture off her face, but K. C. made her way back slowly and carefully.

Once off the pier, she continued walking, back up to the marina, looking for *Under the Stars.* But even before she reached Raleigh's slip, she could see the boat was gone. Sometimes, she knew, he was assigned a different slip when he returned from his sailing trips. Even so, with many boats pulled out of the water for the season, *Under the Stars* should be easy to spot.

She'd check at the marina, but in her heart she already knew. Raleigh was gone.

When she returned to her cottage, an overnight delivery package was on her doorstep. She opened it apprehensively when she saw it was from Kincaid Architects.

She looked through the stack of papers then let them fall on the steps as the tears came. The contents were self-explanatory—a hand-written note from Raleigh, "Congratulations, we won," two tickets to Paris, and a drafted sales contract for the house and two acres of land. On top was a typed letter requesting her to contact his lawyer if the price didn't seem fair to her.

He really was gone from her life for good.

CHAPTER ELEVEN

In his Chicago office, Raleigh sat staring at the winner's letter sitting on his desk. *Empty,* that's how winning felt—empty, just like the remodeled Kincaid house. He shoved the letter aside, not caring when the magazine sent their photographers and writers and promo crew. He had to wonder whether the intangible emptiness would be reflected in the pictures.

He pulled out his notes for his next project. He had plenty of time to devote to it. So much for his dream of working days on end from the top of the hill, being inspired by the vast farmlands outside his sunroom. Maybe the noise of the city would heal his heart, be a balm to his weary mind, or at least numb it. Sailing back across Lake Michigan certainly hadn't.

He stood and walked to the window, staring bleakly out at the lake with its high, cresting waves. The breakers commanded awe and respect, but they were brutal, pounding, with no destination, simply being tossed about, hitting the shore over and over again.

Just like my soul. He ran his hands through his hair. What was wrong with him?

This really is for the best, for both of us, he argued, trying to convince himself of that truth. *She deserves real love—and what do I know about love?*

God is love. He remembered those words from a summer long ago—*God is love*—and a little boy praying. He could still remember almost word for word his prayer that day as he'd given his heart to God.

His head was throbbing. What had happened to that little boy who knew how to love? Through the years, anger and resentment had chipped away at his heart. What had he become? A successful businessman, a renowned architect, a wise financial investor—and a man afraid to love. A man afraid to accept love—from God, from K. C.

> *Gott sei mit Dir,*
> *Gott gehe mit Dir.*
> *Gott sei unser Tröster.*

Raleigh bowed his head first, then his knees, then his heart.
God, he said as he knelt in front of his office window. *O, Lord.*
He couldn't formulate the words for what he wanted to say, but his heart cried out for forgiveness, for cleansing, for a closeness once again with the God he had loved as a boy. And now, for the first time, he truly understood the song his mother had sung.

> God be with you,
> God go with you.
> God be our comfort still.

It had been her prayer for him.
Raleigh raised his head. The raging in his soul was gone. He felt a sense of joy at the stillness and an unexplainable peace.

◆ ◆ ◆

Day after day K. C. wanted to jump in her car and drive to Chicago, to see Raleigh, to talk to him. But something held her back. She waited and listened for God's gentle urgings, but days passed without a clear indication of his leading.

This evening she sat on her patio, her lap full of new projects that had been referred to her. She tried to give them her full attention but couldn't. She pushed them all aside. Right now she had too many things to decide. She needed to find roots again.

She stared out at the lake, smooth and motionless. She'd already talked with contractors about winterizing her cottage, yet this place didn't feel permanent. It wasn't home.

He leadeth me beside the still waters. The waters were still, but there seemed to be no leading.

The phone rang, startling her from her reverie. K. C. walked into the kitchen from the patio to answer it.

"K. C., it's me," said a voice she would recognize anywhere.

"Raleigh!" She had longed to hear from him, yet now that he was on the phone, what was she to say?

"I know it's late notice." He sounded apologetic. "But could I persuade you to join me for dinner? I have steaks on the grill, and I'm boiling up small red potatoes and corn on the cob. We can eat and then talk. Please?" There was an endearing plea in his voice.

"You're in Hartley?"

"Yes, I'm back."

Home? Her heartbeat quickened. She was afraid to hope what this might mean. For a moment she couldn't speak. Besides, she wasn't sure dinner with him was a good idea right now.

"I've done some gardening," he said as if sensing her reluctance. "And I'd like your opinion."

Raleigh gardening? And this late in the season? She supposed he meant in the sunroom. The only "gardening" she'd known him to do was digging up her beloved lilac bush. But to see him working his hands in the dark soil, carefully following the directions on a package, planting seeds that would one day bring forth life and beauty…

"All right," she agreed, curious. Plus there was something different about his tone, a hopeful sound. "When should I come?"

"As soon as you can get here."

When she pulled into the driveway half an hour later, she sat a moment, recalling her first sight of the house months ago. Not even her initial vision had been grand enough for the potential this place held. She sat transfixed as she gazed at the stately house atop the hill. It was restored.

Raleigh waved from the back porch where he tended a bright-red kettle grill. Another improvement through the months.

"Hi, K. C." He seemed ill at ease, but the light in his eyes was undeniable.

"Raleigh." Her heart urged her to run to him, but her head said no.

"It's good to see you." Raleigh gave K. C. a light hug when she reached the porch. She didn't stiffen at his touch, but neither did she seem very enthusiastic. She responded about as he'd expect a guest to act.

"Congratulations on winning the contest." She gestured toward the house.

Raleigh mentally kicked himself. Would she ever again laugh easily with him or turn those brown eyes on him with a look of joy? "I just got back from Chicago today."

She nodded. "I was at the marina a few days ago and didn't see your boat."

The gentle fall wind tossed her hair, lifting it playfully off her shoulders. How he'd love to catch the flying dark strands and wrap his fingers in them, drawing her head close to his...but she scooped them all up with a quick twist and tucked her hair inside her jacket collar.

"Yeah, well." He scuffed at the concrete, embarrassed at his quick departure and lack of a good-bye. "I took it back to Chicago to dry-dock it for the winter."

"I see."

No, you don't. I couldn't stand it without you. I love you. But the words wouldn't form. "I had some things to take care of there." *Not much of which got done.* "I rented a car to get back. Needed to pick up my Jeep." *I couldn't wait to get back to you.*

K. C. nodded, a thin smile on her pale lips. He longed to hold her and tell her how much he loved her, yet he feared her rejection. Undoubtedly he was the cause for the dullness in her once-sparkling brown eyes. Maybe during dinner the right moment would come.

Raleigh led her into the new kitchen, grateful to see a genuine smile form at the sight of the inviting table set for two in the cheerful room. Once seated, he reached across the table for her hand. "I'll ask the blessing tonight."

K. C. blinked in surprise but said nothing as she bowed her head.

"Dear Lord," Raleigh began hesitantly, "thank you for providing for us. And for leading us. Uh, especially for leading us. Because your way is better. Amen." He looked up, relieved to see that K. C. wasn't laughing at his attempt to pray.

"Amen," she quietly echoed. She met his gaze for a moment before reaching for her fork.

Dinner was accompanied by sporadic attempts at conversation. K. C. was probably afraid he'd stomp on her feelings again.

He realized her floral scent was missing. "Are you using a new fragrance?"

Almost imperceptibly she blanched before she answered. "Yes."

What was wrong? She always used lilac. "It smells like…" He had no idea what it smelled like, other than clean and fresh, no frills.

"Vanilla," she finished for him.

Hope flickered. So this was what vanilla smelled like. In a way, it *was* like his mother's cookies baking. Warm, lingering, invoking a feeling of being loved. "What happened to your lilacs?"

She laid her fork down and fumbled with her napkin. Her eyes held such sorrow that Raleigh was sorry he'd asked. "I used it all," she said simply, then let her gaze drift from his.

After finishing dinner in silence, he stood. He'd really made a mess of things. Now he'd just have to plunge in and take the risk of being rejected. "K. C., are you ready to see my gardening?"

She nodded.

Raleigh reached for her hand. When she didn't resist, he tightened his hold to a firm grip. He led her outdoors to the side of the house and pointed to a short, scrawny bush beneath the sunroom window.

"This is your gardening?" K. C. sounded as if she didn't have the energy to laugh had she wanted to.

"Yes. So what do you think?"

"What is it?" She stooped beside it.

"A lilac bush."

She looked up in surprise.

"A purple one." He reached down and helped her stand. "I dug it from around Miss Lidia's bush. She said hers was originally a shoot from the one that used to be here. So this is the closest I could come to replanting Great-grandmother McKenzie's bush for you."

Astonishment, highlighted by the setting sun's glow, reflected on her face. Two robins twittered back and forth then fell silent as if they, too, awaited K. C.'s reaction.

"Oh, Raleigh…" She looked again at the scraggly bush, then back to him.

"K. C., I'm so sorry. I was a fool to walk away from you." He took a step closer to her. "Please, will you forgive me? Give me a chance?"

K. C. wiped her eyes with her fingertips. She took a step toward him, and Raleigh pulled her into his arms.

"I've discovered something while I was in Chicago," he said against her ear. "I love you."

K. C. leaned back and smiled up at him. "I discovered the same thing," she said as if in awe at his admission.

Raleigh placed his hands gently behind her head and again pulled her into his arms for the kiss he'd been longing to share. It was gentle, sweet, tender—everything he'd imagined it would be.

Holding her gaze, he stepped back and then reached for a silk lilac blossom he'd hidden in a pail of gardening tools. He untied the white ribbon and held up a ring. The last rays of the sun caught the diamond and made its facets dance and sparkle.

"Raleigh…" K. C. smiled through tears. Her gaze moved from the ring back to his eyes.

Raleigh pressed a finger softly against her lips. "I want you in my life, to be there to wake up beside me, to smell lilacs through our window." He swallowed hard. These were the words he'd too long been afraid to say. "Kathryn Claire McKenzie, will you consider marrying me?"

Raleigh's heart thudded. He'd done it. The love and warmth radiating from K. C.'s eyes left him breathless.

K. C. pulled him into an embrace and kissed him. "That's my answer." She held out her left hand.

He slipped the ring on her finger.

◆ ◆ ◆

K. C. took Raleigh's hand and led him to the front yard. She stopped and pointed back to the house. "Fully restored," she said softly. "Remember how hopeless it looked when we first saw it?"

"Ruined by neglect," Raleigh said.

K. C. looked at him in surprise.

Raleigh laughed. "That's from the speech Miss Lidia gave me. She was right about what love and care can do."

K. C. ran a finger along Raleigh's cheek. "Now it's reinforced, stronger, solid, totally beautiful both inside and out. That's what love and care can do. 'He leadeth me beside the still waters,'" she quoted.

"'He restoreth my soul,'" Raleigh said softly.

The two stood together viewing the results of their restoration project.

"Oh, by the way," K. C. said with a wide smile, breaking the silence of the evening, "I'll take care of the honeymoon plans if you'd like. I just happen to have tickets for a trip to Paris."

EPILOGUE

Two years later

Aunt Lidia carefully slit the envelope she'd just received in the mail. She would have known it was from Kathryn and Raleigh, even without the return address of the old McKenzie—or rather, Kincaid— place, simply by the handwriting. Her arthritic fingers trembled slightly as she pulled out the engraved announcement:

From God's loving arms to ours

Alexander Raleigh Kincaid

Born October 5 at 6:03 A.M.

6 pounds, 12 ounces

We are truly blessed!

Kathryn and Raleigh Kincaid

DON'T LOOK BACK

Jane Orcutt

To Lisa and Diane

CHAPTER ONE

"*What* a dump!"

"Mama, it's not that bad," Laurie said, though her heart sank in agreement with the cinematic words her mother affected to describe their new home.

Agnes Joy Bertram Cartwright just looked at her daughter, her eyes glowing like Bette Davis's. Laurie's kids stood off to the side, not saying a word. Slouching, Gaby had her arms crossed, her Walkman turned up loud, scuffing a shoe in the dirt with teenage disinterest. Face scrunched, Garrett studied the house with his ten-year-old analytical mind, probably remodeling it into Camelot, board by weather-beaten board.

If the house hadn't faced the road, it would have been difficult to tell the actual front. Each side had a door with a covered porch supported by matching columns. Varying-sized hip-roof dormers hung above.

At one time it had probably been one of the finer farmhouses in Honor—now the only polite description was that it was in the beginning stages of disrepair. Tattered curtains and shades hung uselessly at dirty windows. Paint flaked and peeled from the weathered boards. Set up off the ground with three-foot-high stacks of bricks at strategic spots, the house listed at one corner like an old man with an arthritic spine.

"It's not so bad," Laurie repeated. "Doesn't it sort of remind you of Tara in *Gone With the Wind*?"

Agnes snorted, but she moved closer to the house, as though she wanted a better look.

Gaby flicked off her Walkman. "Right now it looks more like the Bates Motel. Why'd you buy this place, Mom? Why didn't we just stay in Dallas?"

"What? And miss the opportunity to live the country life?" Laurie said breezily, then smiled. "It's going to be fun here, Gaby."

She felt a hand slip into hers. "It's pretty interesting, actually, Mom," Garrett said. He stared up at her, looking earnest as only he could. He pushed his wire-rimmed glasses back up on his nose and offered a smile.

She smiled back and, still holding his hand, turned again to the house.

Laurie's mother—Agnes—had been born here, just before what was commonly called the Roaring Twenties, but Laurie doubted if anything in the small North Texas town of Honor had ever made much more noise than a polite whimper. Most of the original settlers farmed cotton, Agnes's family included. She hadn't left this home until Abner Cartwright swept her away to the big city of Dallas, where she'd been living ever since, even the last few years since his death.

Built in the late 1800s, the house had originally belonged to her grandparents, then passed on to her parents. Agnes had been born in the largest of the upstairs dormer rooms—the one with eight identical windows—that stuck out over the wide back porch.

With one hand on a paint-peeled column that flanked the front steps, Agnes turned. Bette Davis had slipped from her eyes, and she smiled at her daughter. "It's a dump now, but a little paint, a little elbow grease…"

"So you like my surprise?" Laurie relaxed. "I probably should have consulted you before I bought the house, Mama. But it seemed like a good place for all of us. Dallas is just too big anymore."

"Dallas is *better*," Gaby said, leaping beside them on the steps. "Who wants to live out here in the sticks?"

Laurie shot her a look that quieted her long enough for them to head inside.

She'd been here two weeks ago, outside and in, with real estate agents, an inspector, and a contractor. The real estate agent seemed keen on her buying Mama's old house, and the others had given their approval, while hesitant, as well. "Well, Miz Golden, it's a fine old structure, solid as they come. But it'll require some remodeling, some upkeep. If you've got the time and the money..."

The truth was, she did. Gary had been generous in the settlement, and nearly a year after the divorce, his largesse had enabled them to eventually move to Honor. It'd taken a good deal of money to buy Agnes's old homestead. "Strangest thing," the Realtor said. "That property's been on the market for nearly four years. Now all of a sudden I've got two buyers."

Laurie had bid back and forth from her portable phone, even as she packed the crystal and china in Dallas. The final word had come when she'd been supervising the draining of the pool, but she'd immediately hung up with the Realtor and called Agnes. "Mama, pack up. We're going home."

Inside, the house smelled vaguely of mildew, but at least it was cool and dark. It was only June, but temperatures were already up in the high eighties, pushing ninety. Laurie knew it wouldn't get any better before late September, and she hoped the central air conditioning someone had installed several years back would hold out.

Laurie wondered if the house had really looked like this when she'd been here by herself. Large cracks punctuated the walls. Small, aged brown stains dripped from the ceiling. Dust caked the baseboards.

Gaby ran a finger across the handrail of the stairs, then sneezed. "Look at this place. Who's going to clean up?"

Laurie closed a closet door that housed an old fishing net and an ancient, rusty rifle. "We are. Starting tomorrow, after a good night's sleep."

Gaby paused, then the corners of her mouth twitched up. "I thought people moved to the country to rest."

Laurie laughed. So far, the truce she and her teenage daughter had formed in the past year seemed to be holding.

"Mom, Mom!" Garrett bounded up the front steps, his face lit up like a jack-o'-lantern. "There's a cemetery beyond the far side of the house, did you know?"

"Yes. I didn't have a chance to look at it when I was here before, but—"

"A cemetery?" Gaby squealed with fear, as though she were six instead of sixteen.

"It's just a family plot. I remember it from when I came here as a little girl. But the adults wouldn't let any of us kids go in there."

"Cool! Can I go look?" Garrett loved adventure and wasn't afraid of anything.

"Sure." There wasn't much any of them could do here for the rest of the day. The sun was already starting to sink.

Shivering, Gaby rubbed her arms. "We're going to be living next to a cemetery?"

"Oh, come on, Gaby. This is cool!" Garrett was already racing down the steps.

Gaby followed, then stopped at the bottom and called back into the house. "Coming, Grandma?"

Agnes looked around the house as though for lost friends. She waved her hand at them, her gaze fixed on a cheap print somebody had hung over the fireplace. Laurie paused, then followed the kids across the yard. It seemed disrespectful to intrude on Mama and her memories right now.

Laurie hadn't done more than glance at the iron-fence-enclosed plot when she'd done her real estate scouting. It hadn't changed at all since the times she'd visited her mother's family as a girl. Mama's father died before Laurie was born, and she had vague memories of her grandmother—a sad-faced, God-fearing woman. Laurie remembered how she and Mama had put their heads together, relegating Laurie outdoors to play. Grandma Bertram had hollered from the front porch at her and one neighbor boy in particular when they'd lifted the latch of the cemetery gate. "You kids stay out of that boneyard, you hear?"

The Bertrams took family very seriously, and it occurred to Laurie as she unhitched the rusty latch, standing beside her own kids, that for the first time in her life, she felt as if she was doing the same.

Why would anyone else want to buy this land, especially with its family plot?

Garrett's eyes were as big as clay pigeons, taking in everything as he moved slowly among the chipped, crumbled headstones. "'Isaiah Bertram. Jerusha Bertram. May 24, 1894. Together they entered heaven.' Mom, they died the same day!"

Laurie squinted at the headstone, trying to recall her family history. What a shame that she'd made light of it all these years and only now wished she'd paid better attention. "Maybe they both got sick. A little thing like the flu could wipe out an entire family back then."

"Maybe they were both killed in their sleep by an ax murderer," Gaby said, still standing at the fence, one hand on the gate.

"That only happens in Dallas," Laurie said dryly, following Garrett to another set of closely aligned tombstones.

"Yeah, well, this place gives me the creeps," Gaby muttered. "Garrett's young enough to be goofy about a bunch of dead people underground, and you certainly don't mind. You're always digging into family histories for your job."

Laurie smiled to herself. Gaby didn't fool her. She'd heard her daughter bragging over the phone to her friends that her mother was a professional genealogist, the tone in her young voice indicating she put that career on the same plane as Indiana Jones's archeological pursuits.

"This place is great." Garrett's eyes shone as he stooped next to a small grave. "You can tell so much about people from what their tombstones say. Or who they're buried next to. A lady over there had four babies that never lived past two or three days each." He touched the head of a chipped lamb nestling atop a tiny marker. "These people are all your relatives, Mom."

"Yours too." She resisted the urge to ruffle his hair. He was getting older now, and she had to learn to let go, as much as she hated it.

Garrett stood and moved toward her, then slipped his hand into hers. "I'm going to miss my friends in Dallas, but I think this place will be okay."

Laurie swallowed hard. Neither he nor Gaby had been too excited when she'd first told them about their move. It was good to see that he was willing to adjust so quickly. Gaby might take a little more time. "I think this place will be okay too, Garrett. That's why I bought it."

For months after the divorce, she'd wanted to run far away from everything that reminded her of Gary, which meant every place in Dallas. As the city's highest-paid and best-known TV news anchor, he seemed to be everywhere, even smiling down at her from billboards on the expressways.

But instead of giving in to her initial cowardice, she'd stuck it out, even holding her head high, facing her worst fears that everyone in their social circle thought her a fool for not knowing that Gary was having an affair with a coworker. She hadn't even realized their marriage was sailing in troubled waters, let alone washed up on the rocks.

Now, though, she'd had time to sort through the flotsam from the wreckage and save only what was valuable. And leaving a city that had grown too crowded, polluted, and downright dangerous was tops on her list. Here in small-town Honor, they would rebuild—not only the house, but their lives, as well.

Laurie turned and walked toward the gate, and her children—even Gaby, for once—followed silently.

Agnes had already set out a small dinner for them, provisions that they'd purchased at the last convenience store on the highway before they'd reached Honor. It was an eclectic dinner, for they had each picked their favorite. They had an assortment of standard overpriced, dusty shelf fare—canned potato chips, beef sticks, shrink-wrapped cheese and crackers, bean dip.

Agnes stood up, waving a half-eaten pickle in a dramatic circle. "Repeat after me: 'There's no place like home. There's no place like home.'"

Gaby and Garrett exchanged a glance. Laurie could see them suppress their laughter, but they chimed along. "There's no place like home. There's no place like home."

Agnes beamed. She sat down and popped the rest of the pickle into her mouth.

"Well." Elbows on the table, Laurie rested her chin on her steepled fingers. "After we clean up from this feast, what shall we do? I have a deck of cards in my purse. Anybody up for some gin rummy?"

Gaby made a bored face. "I'd rather listen to music."

"I brought my Game Boy," Garrett said, then wistfully added, "But I guess I could play cards."

"No TV?" Agnes said, her face crumpling. "No VCR for movies?"

"Not tonight, Mama. The movers will be here with the furniture tomorrow, and we'll set up your entertainment area first thing."

"Good." She sat back in her chair, smiling.

"Grandma, don't you think maybe you watch too much of those old movies?" Gaby said. "I mean, I think it's great that you've seen so many and you know so many lines, but it's always kind of embarrassing when you say them in front of my friends."

Laurie resisted rolling her eyes. Gaby's friends probably hadn't seen a movie made before the 1990s, much less the classics of her grandmother's time. Another reason that Laurie could acknowledge for their move here. She wanted Gaby to have friends that were less concerned about what kind of clothes they wore and whether or not they drove the latest model sports car. Kids in Honor, small-town Texas, would surely be different. Kids in Honor wouldn't have names like Tiffany and Amber, or worse yet, Skye and Pacifica. They'd have good, solid, down-to-earth country names like Mary or Susan.

Agnes scooped a fresh pickle into the bean dip. "Art imitates life, Gabrielle. Movies reflect our lives."

"I don't know, Mama," Laurie said, cutting in before Gaby could come up with one of her smart-mouth answers. "I've always thought that life imitates art."

Agnes took a sip from her Big Red soda, then closed her mouth and burped silently. She wiped her mouth daintily with a paper napkin. "Then we're set either way, now aren't we?"

Garrett yawned, and his head drooped. "Where are we sleeping tonight, Mom? I only saw one bed upstairs."

"That's for Grandma. The rest of us will sleep downstairs in the sleeping bags."

"Oh great." Gaby groaned.

"I could sleep anywhere," Garrett said. "I'm exhausted."

Laurie rose. "Me, too. You guys clean up this stuff. I'll get our gear, then move the Cherokee into that old shed out back. I don't think anybody around here would mess with the things we brought, but we'd better not take any chances."

"A body can't be too careful," Agnes said, nodding wisely. "I think I'll just make up my own bed upstairs and be off to sleep."

"You need some help?"

Laurie must have sounded overly solicitous because Agnes frowned and waved her away. "Laurie, I've been living alone and taking care of myself since your father died. Do you think I'm a candidate for the home? I agreed to move in with you, but I don't need a keeper."

Laurie grinned. "Okay, Mama. Sorry. Good night."

Agnes leaned over and kissed her on the top of her head, as she had when Laurie was a little girl. "Good night, dear. See you in the morning."

Gaby was still listening to her CDs when Laurie dozed off with her head resting against the warm, worn planks of the front room. She couldn't have been asleep more than a hour or two when she felt an insistent hand on her shoulder. "Mom. Mom, wake up!"

Laurie sat up slowly, brushing her eyes. "What's the matter, Gaby? What time is it?"

"I don't know. But I saw headlights outside the house, and I think I heard a car door slam."

"Go back to sleep," she said, yawning, lying back down. "You were just dreaming."

"I'm not dreaming. I haven't even been asleep," Gaby insisted. "Mom, I'm telling you, *somebody's on this property!*"

Laurie opened her eyes. Gaby's face was only inches from hers, and she could read the fear.

Through the broken window, they heard the distinctive creak of the cemetery's iron gate. Gaby trembled, and her voice dropped to a whisper. "Now do you believe me?"

"What's going on?" Garrett rustled upright in his sleeping bag.

Laurie's heart thumped like a jackrabbit's. "Let's go to the window and have a look." She tried to keep the fear from her voice.

"What if he sees us?"

"Don't be silly, " Garrett said. "The light's not on in the house. We can at least peek around the curtain."

Rising to her feet, Laurie felt two pairs of hands gripping her arms, two children cowering behind her. They edged their way to the window, then peeped around the curtain. A hazy beam from a flashlight sliced through the darkness, scanning the tombstones. She couldn't quite make out the figure holding the light, but it looked like a man. Sure enough, when he turned the light toward a piece of paper in his hands, she could tell it was so.

"A graverobber!" Gaby whispered behind her. "He's probably come under the cover of darkness to dig up one of the graves so that he can use the bodies for some evil experiment."

Laurie resisted the urge to laugh. "Now who's been watching too many old movies, Gaby? People don't dig up graves. Sometimes people vandalize them, but he doesn't seem particularly intent on mischief. He probably wouldn't have come alone."

"He's looking at graves again," Garrett reported from his station at the farthest window. "Why don't we go ask him what he's doing?"

Moving from grave to grave, the stranger flashed the light across the tombstones then occasionally down at the paper he held. Laurie had the absurd impression that he was hunting for a street address.

"What's all the ruckus?"

Agnes stood behind them, hands on her blue-flannel-pajama hips. Her gray hair, usually pinned up in a fastidious bun, had spilled down her back. Laurie waited for another comment, but Agnes just stared at her silently, demanding an explanation. "There's someone tramping around the graveyard," Laurie said.

"No fooling! This time of night?" Agnes's face looked downright gleeful as she came toward the window, taking up her place next to Garrett. She watched the stranger for a moment, then turned away disappointed. "Bah! He's just looking for a grave. I'd rather see folks coming up out of them, not poking around the top."

"Oh, for Pete's sake. If that's all he's doing, then I'll go ask him if we can help." Feigning a bravery she didn't feel, Laurie retrieved the rusted rifle from the closet. "It's not like we're defenseless settlers waiting for the Indians to attack."

"The cavalry!" Agnes grinned at the sight of the gun.

Gaby stared, wide-eyed. "Where did you get *that?*" Garrett's voice glowed with admiration.

"Someone must have left it here," Laurie said, moving toward the door. She grabbed a heavy-duty flashlight and switched it on, wishing her hands wouldn't tremble quite so much. "Now you guys stay in the house, and I'll go see what our visitor's up to."

"Are you crazy!" Gaby's high-pitched voice rang after her as she headed down the steps and across the yard.

Laurie tromped through the tall grass, fearing not so much insanity as pure foolishness for confronting a strange man in her family's cemetery. She didn't know anything about rifles, let alone this decrepit, possibly Revolutionary-vintage model. What if he called her bluff? She'd not only wind up on the front page of the *Honor Tribune,* but in some "Oddities Around the State" column in the *Dallas Morning News,* as well.

She squared her shoulders. So what if her friends back home found out? This was her property now, and she'd defend it in true historical Texan fashion, if need be.

"Hey!" She slammed open the gate, leveling the powerful flashlight at the stranger. He turned and instinctively ducked, like a skunk caught in the headlights of an oncoming semi. Laurie hefted the rifle a little, to show him she meant business. "What are you doing on my property?"

"I'm sorry." He held up his hands, obviously having glimpsed the firearm. "I didn't know you were living here yet. I was just looking for a grave."

"At this time of night?" She aimed the light straight at his eyes.

The stranger ducked his head. "Ow! Lady, would you mind turning that thing away? It's hard to talk when I'm being blinded."

Laurie aimed the light downward, but still kept him in full beam. Now that she'd had a chance to study him, he didn't look too frightening. He wore a light-colored, short-sleeved plaid shirt, creased blue jeans, and work boots. He had short, wavy brown hair. She couldn't tell the color of his eyes, but from the tiny lines around them, she'd guess he was probably close to her own age.

The man relaxed but kept his hands raised. "You know, you can't fire that thing and hold the flashlight too. Besides, the safety's still on. Probably even stuck, from the looks of it." He paused. "Would it make you feel any safer if I tell you I live just beyond that rise over there? I'm your neighbor."

Laurie lowered the useless rifle to her side. "Not very neighborly to go stalking around other people's property. Especially when it's dark."

With a sigh of relief, he slowly lowered his hands. "You're right. I should have waited till you moved in, then introduced myself proper. But when I heard that one of the Bertram clan had bought this place, I figured you wouldn't want me on your property."

"I'm not so sure I want you on it now." Laurie paused, curiosity grabbing hold. "What grave are you looking for, and why wouldn't I want you looking for it? In the daylight, that is."

"I'm looking for my ancestors' graves. I have reason to believe they're buried here, and the obvious place seemed the cemetery."

A thrill raced up her spine. "Are you kin to my family, the Bertrams, Mr., uh…?"

"MacGruder. Jack MacGruder. And no, we're not related at all. The people I'm looking for are my great-great-great-grandparents—Howells. I haven't quite pieced the story together, but apparently they knew the Bertrams and may have lived on their land. But they weren't related."

Laurie felt vaguely disappointed that they had no familial connection. She had moved to Honor to investigate her own family tree, and it would have been a pleasant surprise to find an unknown relative right here in the cemetery. And alive, at that.

"Laurie!" Gaby and Garrett clinging to her bathrobe, Agnes yanked open the gate and thrust an iron skillet in Jack MacGruder's direction. "Is he bothering you?"

"No, Mama, he's just looking for some of his family's graves. He's a neighbor."

"Oh." As if that settled the entire matter, Agnes lowered the skillet. She smiled sweetly. "I'm Aggie Bertram. So glad you could come."

Jack never missed a beat. "Jack MacGruder, Mrs. Bertram. As I was explaining to your daughter, I didn't realize you were living in the house yet. I'm sorry if I frightened you."

"Frightened us?" Agnes's grin broadened. "This is the most fun we've had in ages!"

Laurie cleared her throat. "Those two hanging on to my mother are my children, Gaby and Garrett. And I'm Laurie Golden. We just moved here from Dallas, Mr. MacGruder."

"Call me Jack," he said, nodding at the kids, then he smiled wider. "Laurie. That's a pretty, old-fashioned name you don't hear much anymore."

The kids suppressed their laughter, and she shot them each a look. "My mother named me after the heroine in *Oklahoma!*"

"Grandma has a thing about old movies," Gaby said. "Tonight, while eating dinner, the rest of us were hungry, and she—"

"Hungry?" Agnes backed up a step, then raised her fist. " 'As God is my witness, as God is my witness, they're not going to lick me! I'm going to live through this, and when it's all over, I'll never be hungry again—no, nor any of my folks! If I have to lie, steal, cheat, or kill! As God is my witness, I'll never be hungry again.' "

Laurie wanted to hide. "We should set down some rules about this movie-quoting business, Mama," she said, making a halfhearted attempt at laughter.

Jack took Agnes's hand and stared gravely at her. " 'I wouldn't give you two cents for all your fancy rules if, behind them, they didn't have a little bit of plain, ordinary, everyday kindness and a—a little looking out for the other fella, too…' "

Agnes clapped her free hand over her mouth. "*Mr. Smith Goes to Washington*! Oh, Laurie, you've found yourself a movie lover!"

"I didn't exactly find him; he found us," Laurie mumbled. Forty-five years old and she was blushing, for crying out loud, because Mama'd used the word "lover" to describe Jack MacGruder. Thank goodness for the cover of darkness. She didn't know whether she was glad he couldn't see her or that she couldn't see what were probably twinkles in his eyes—whatever color they were.

Jack stepped back, releasing Agnes's hand. "It's late, and I'm sure you're tired. May I take you all to breakfast tomorrow morning to make up for scaring you?"

"Well…," Laurie paused, considering.

"If you're researching your family history, Laurie here is the perfect person to consult," Agnes said. "She's a professional genealogist."

"Really?" Jack turned, his eyes shining in the wavering light.

Laurie's resolve weakened. She should probably help this poor man. Genealogy was serious business, and maybe research for him would actually help her own family hunt as well. "All right. Breakfast it is."

Jack MacGruder smiled, nodding at a pickup parked just down the gravel road. "I'm afraid I don't have room for you all in my truck, but I'd be delighted to meet you at Lainie's Café. It's on Main Street. You can't miss it. Shall we say six o'clock?"

Gaby groaned. *"Six?"*

Laurie felt her own insides clench at such an early hour, even though she knew they'd eventually all have to readjust their Big City night owlishness to the more early-bird schedule of country living. "Shall we say *seven* o'clock?"

"I look forward to it." Jack smiled, dropping his gaze to the gun in Laurie's hand. His smile broadened, and he gave them all a quick two-fingered salute. "See you tomorrow."

They watched as he hauled himself into his pickup. The engine turned over smoothly, the headlights flickered on, and the truck wound its way up the gravel road. Laurie silently led the way back to the house.

"Guess I'll head upstairs and get back to sleep," Agnes said, sounding disappointed.

"Grandma…" Gaby tugged Agnes's flannel sleeve tentatively. "Do you mind if I come up there with you? Sleeping on the hard floor hurts."

Laurie turned to lock the front door, hiding a smile. The floor here wasn't any harder than their parquet game-room floor back in Dallas. Gaby had slept on it countless times at slumber parties.

Agnes didn't look fooled either. She smiled at Gaby, playfully nipping her cheek with a knuckle. "I remember how my little sisters, Birdy and Eula, would snuggle in with me. There's room for you, all right."

Laurie watched them stroll arm in arm up the wide, creaking stairs, and she settled down in her sleeping bag.

"Mom?" Beside her in his own sleeping bag, Garrett propped up on a elbow.

"Hmm?" she said sleepily.

"What would you have done if Mr. MacGruder had been mean and tried to mess with us?"

She caught the anxiety in his voice and opened her eyes. Garrett squinted at her through his glasses, looking so childlike, yet so much like the preteen he was becoming. She swallowed hard, thinking about how quickly time could slip away, and she reminded herself that that was why they were here.

"Why, Pilgrim, I reckon I'd a-shot him," she said, tweaking Garrett's nose.

"Huh! I don't think that gun would have fired, Mom. Was that gun even loaded? Would it have actually fired, Mom?"

"Well…maybe I would have just whacked him on the noggin. Even if I couldn't have shot him right between the eyes."

Garrett giggled, then lay back down, glasses and all. As Laurie drifted off to sleep, she wondered just exactly what color Jack MacGruder's eyes really were.

CHAPTER TWO

Laurie stood at the bottom of the stairs, jingling her keys. "Come on, everybody. Let's go. We'll be late."

Yawning, Gaby slouched down the stairs, looking fashionable in jeans and a tie-dyed crop top. "Do we really have to go?" She slumped against the parlor doorjamb in the teenage posture she'd affected over the last year. "Do we really have to start cleaning up this place when we get back?"

"Yes and yes. Maybe we can even buy some paint after breakfast."

"Do you think there's enough buckets in town to take care of this house?"

"I imagine so." Laurie actually looked forward to the outing. Besides finding out more about the mysterious Jack MacGruder, she wanted to get a better feel for the area. Filling up on some local food seemed like a good way to get started. "Mama? Garrett?" she called.

Garrett pounded down the stairs, brandishing an ancient mop. "This place is so cool! All kinds of history. Grandma and I were chasing cobwebs, and she found a broken key and a bottle—lots of old stuff."

Gaby edged away from the mop, sneezing. "Old stuff is right," she said.

"That's great, Garrett. We'll probably find more things as we clean up. Now get Grandma and let's go. We're going to be late for breakfast."

Garrett raced back upstairs, then back down again, alone. "She doesn't want to go."

Sighing, Laurie thudded up the staircase, each foot eliciting a groan from the steps. She wondered if they, too, needed repair or if it was just the emptiness of the house that made them sound so desolate. "Mama?"

The head of the stairs opened onto a small landing that fed into four bedrooms, each one facing a different direction. Agnes sat on the bed in the west-facing room, where she'd slept last night. Still as stone, she stared out at the graveyard, where their midnight visitor had prowled. The wind ruffled the tattered curtain at the open window and wisps of gray hair at Agnes's temples, as well.

Laurie moved forward slowly, floorboards creaking with every step. "Mama, we're going to breakfast now."

Agnes waved her away. "I'll just stay here. If I get hungry, I'll snack on some of the feast from last night."

The floorboards creaked again as Laurie shifted her weight from one foot to the other. "Wouldn't you like to get out and see what's become of your old town?"

Mama cracked a smile. "I guess I know what's become of it, dear."

Laurie sat beside her mother on the bed and followed her gaze out over the cemetery. Why would Jack be nosing around the graveyard at midnight? "Who all's buried there, Mama?"

"Who knows?" Agnes shrugged. "Does it matter? I never have understood why people make such a fuss about buryin's and cemeteries and such. When you're dead, you've left the earth. People bury folks in the ground like they think they can hold them there. Silliest thing I ever heard of."

Laurie sighed. She wanted to question, but there was time for that later. Lots of time, now that they'd moved here. Life would be slower. Instead, she said, "Why don't you come with us, Mama? When's the last time you were in Honor? It might be fun to see the changes."

Agnes rose and turned her back to the window. Smiling, she shook her head. "No, I'll stay here. I want to get a feel for the old place here by myself. Besides, I can get a jump on the cleaning. I can use a rag and mop as good as Garrett and Gaby." She winked. "Probably better, even."

"Come downstairs, anyway." Laurie touched her arm. "That way I won't have to worry about your falling."

"I'm not that old, Laurie," Agnes said, but she let her lead her as they made their way back down to the first floor.

Garrett and Gaby were both waiting impatiently. Gaby, Laurie noticed, had even abandoned her Walkman and spruced up her hair. After all, who knew? She might meet a good-looking farm boy in town. Laurie was willing to encourage a wholesome relationship—anything beside the pseudotough rich boys Gaby used to hang out with, the ones with expensive clothes and postures that emulated gang members and rappers.

They left Agnes standing on the porch, waving enthusiastically after them as though they'd only come for a Sunday visit. "Tell that nice Mr. MacGruder he's welcome here anytime," she hollered after them. "We should all get acquainted."

Laurie felt her ears burn. She knew what that last sentence really meant. Mama'd made no secret of the fact since the divorce that she thought her daughter should hook up with "a decent fella."

Laurie studied the landscape as she drove. It was certainly prettier than the hustle-bustle of concrete in the city. Gentle rises undulated across the plains, dotted with mesquites and live oaks. Where Gary had once pronounced it plug ugly—flat and boring—Laurie had always appreciated the spaciousness and inherent freedom of seeing every point where the sky kissed the earth. What some might see as desolation had always felt like home, even though she'd never lived here before.

Now she did.

"Where's the town?" Garrett said, squinting out his window at a herd of cows that stared back at him over a barbed-wire fence.

"It's right up ahead." Laurie paused at a stop sign, then took a right turn on a dirt road.

A weathered green sign welcomed them to Honor, Texas just before they hit Main Street, a collection of four red brick buildings with faded signs painted on their sides. One announced a feed store, another, a forty-year-old logo for Dr Pepper.

A modern sign hanging above another doorway said *Lainie's*

Café. Laurie parked the Cherokee in front, marveling that she didn't have to fight for a good parking spot.

The place looked like everything she'd imagined about a small-town eatery: Formica tables, metal napkin dispensers, a jukebox blaring George Strait in the corner. At a window table, an elderly man read a newspaper while shoveling down bacon and eggs.

Jack MacGruder stood up from a table near the Formica counter with chrome barstools. "Hi." He looked them over as he pulled out a stool for Laurie, next to himself. "Where's your mother?"

"She decided to stay home." Realizing how rude that sounded, Laurie started to explain, but a cheerful-looking young man appeared from behind the counter.

"Hey, Mr. MacGruder. How ya doing?"

"Just fine, Russell. These are the Goldens. They're new in town."

Laurie nodded to the young man. He couldn't have been more than seventeen, but he had a strong, clear face, deep blue eyes, and curly hair—a sandy color, not dyed black or orange, like most of Gaby's Dallas male friends. Also unlike them, this boy sported no earrings, nose rings, or any other visible piercings.

She glanced at his arms. No tattoos, either.

He nodded a greeting. "Hello, ma'am."

Laurie nearly swooned. This young Russell was too polite to be true. "Uh, can we see some menus?" She hoped her voice didn't sound as squeaky as she thought.

"Don't have any," he said. He glanced at Gaby, and his smile broadened.

"Do you have any *food?*" Gaby smirked.

Russell's smile didn't fade.

"They don't need menus here at Lainie's," Jack said. "You name it, and they've probably got it."

Russell winked at Gaby, who turned her face, shaking her head. "Hicks," she muttered under her breath.

Laurie wanted to kick her daughter under the table. "I'm sorry," she said to the boy. "We're all a bit cranky, since we just pulled into town last night. We bought what used to be the old Bertram property, and we're moving in."

Russell lowered his order pad. "No kidding? That's a cool old place. I live right up the road." He looked pointedly at Gaby. "I'd be glad to show you around town. My family runs this place, and I've lived here all my life."

"I don't think I need anybody to show me around." Gaby crossed her arms. "There's not much to this place that I can't see just standing on the street."

Laurie shot Gaby a sideways look and held out her hand. "I'm Laurie Golden, and these are my kids, Garrett and Gaby."

"Russell Pratt, ma'am. Good to meet you." He pumped her hand enthusiastically, and he nodded at the kids. "Garrett...Gaby." His glance lingered a bit longer on Gaby, then he cleared his throat. "What'll y'all have to eat? I can vouch for the country breakfast—ham, eggs, and pancakes. My mom does all the cooking here. In fact, she's the Lainie of the café's name."

"How wonderful!" Laurie was entranced that the family worked together. "We'll have three country breakfasts then, since you recommend them."

"Good choice," Jack said. "I'll have the same, Russ."

"Right away." Russell nodded, then disappeared into the back.

"Mom!" Gaby hissed. "I'd rather have had a bagel. You know I don't eat meat."

"You didn't have any problem with those Slim Jims last night," Laurie said. "Although I suppose one couldn't rightly call them meat."

Gaby lowered her gaze and picked at a scratch in the Formica.

Jack cleared his throat, turning to Laurie. "So your mother didn't want to come?" He sounded hurt.

"It's not that she didn't want to see you." Laurie paused, unwilling to sound as if she was fishing for male company. "She, uh, said you should stop by anytime to get acquainted."

"She grew up in that house?"

"Yes. I thought it would be nice for us all to live there. To buy back the property for the family. Mama's getting on up in years, and it's difficult for her to live alone."

"I don't mean to pry, but is there a Mr. Golden?"

Laurie smiled wryly. "We left Mr. Golden back in Dallas," she said. "At his request. The divorce was final over a year ago, but I finally decided we'd all be better off out of the city."

"I'm sorry," Jack said. "About your divorce, I mean. A lot of that going around these days, unfortunately. On the bright side, I think you'll find Honor to be a great small town."

Laurie warmed to this turn in the conversation. "We're looking forward to getting to know people here. Have you and your family lived here long?"

"I don't have any family here. But to answer your question, I've lived here for the past ten years, since my own divorce."

"Oh. Now *I'm* sorry. Divorce isn't pretty."

"Not at all." His expression brightened. "But the people in the town have been great about it. Then there's my land. It always acts as a balm on my soul. Maybe sometime you and your family would like to come over and see my farm. I grow what crops I can and raise a few head of cattle. Some dairy cows, too."

"It sounds lovely," Laurie said, enchanted, leaning forward on her elbows. Here was a man living an idyllic life, not driven by cold ambition.

And she could finally see that the color of his eyes was clear blue, like a cloudless day over the plains.

Laurie, Laurie, get a grip! You don't have time for romance. Didn't twenty-two years wasted on Gary Golden teach you anything?

Laurie leaned back and crossed her arms. "You still haven't explained a few things, Mr. MacGruder."

"Jack."

"Jack," she said. "You never did explain why you were poking around our cemetery at night."

"From the information I got from the Realtor, I thought you were moving in today. I was sitting around my house, dejected that I haven't found those graves, and I thought I'd just have one last look. I've been over the cemetery with a fine-tooth comb, but I still can't help feeling that I missed something."

"Why not just wait until we were moved in, then come over and ask to take a look? I certainly wouldn't mind." Laurie paused. "What did you mean last night about me, being from the Bertram clan, not wanting you on my property?"

"Here you go. Four orders of ham, eggs, and pancakes." Russell set down the plates and beamed that ever-present smile. "Anything else?" As he poured coffee into cups for Jack and Laurie, he looked pointedly at Gaby, who stared down at her plate, frowning.

Jack smiled at the exchange between the two teenagers. "I think we're set. The breakfast looks good as always."

"I'll pass the word along to Mom… Say, it's real convenient, you and Mrs. Golden meeting up like this. Considering what you have in common and all."

"You know about his ancestors being buried on my property?" Laurie said.

"Is *that* why you wanted to buy that place?" Russell said to Jack. "I thought you just wanted to expand your land."

Laurie set down her fork. "*You're* the one who bid against me."

Jack smiled. "No hard feelings, I hope. As Russell says, I was hoping to expand my land, but I have to admit that the possibility of taking my time at finding those graves was extra incentive." His smiled broadened. "I can see why you'd want it back in the family. It passed from the Bertrams to Benjamin Tremble about thirty-five years ago. But I do remember when your family still owned the place. I bet you don't recall the time your grandmother yelled at us about going into the cemetery."

"That was you? The neighbor kid?"

Jack nodded. "I lived here when I was growing up, and my folks still lived here until their deaths, just about the time of my divorce. Old man Tremble was as mean as they come. He didn't want me to set foot on his property, even just to research family history. But it's only been the past year that I've gotten interested in genealogy. Dad never talked much about family, and there aren't any family records to help out, either."

"Genealogy can be tough work. Maybe if we put our heads together and share our research, we can help each other. My mother might remember some mention of the family you're looking for, the Howells."

"Are you sure you want me out there?"

"Why wouldn't I? I can forgive you for scaring us last night."

Jack looked surprised. "You don't know about the feud then."

"What feud?"

"The one between your family and mine."

"I never heard of it."

Jack smiled, buttering a piece of toast. "It seems we have a lot of genealogical information to share."

Laurie set up her computer in the cleanest, least cluttered corner of the living room. It wasn't hard to find a spot because their furniture had yet to arrive from Dallas. But duty called, and she needed to start on her weekly quota of genealogy research. She'd studied journalism at the University of Texas in preparation for a career as an investigative newspaper reporter. When her editor assigned her to interview Gary Golden for a personality features article, she'd been disappointed, but dutifully agreed.

With his blond good looks and year-round tan—not to mention the on-air savvy of professionals twice his age—Gary had landed a job at a local television station as their weekend news anchor. Even though he was still a student in UT's radio-television-film department, Gary was a star on the rise. He'd charmed her during the interview and right out of the next twenty-two years of marriage as he worked his way up to becoming the highest paid news anchor in Dallas.

Even his name was Golden.

She'd never thought of herself as the trophy wife Gary apparently did, but when the marriage began to fall apart—when he began to favor younger trophies—she realized how little she'd done to nurture her own interests. Oh, she'd raised her children, gardened, decorated her house so that it was comfortable and cheerful, but she'd ignored the tiny spark of the secret ambition that had been smoldering for years. The Saturday night Gary left, she'd cried aloud to the Lord, begging for direction. The next morning, an elderly friend from church mentioned that she'd like to attend a workshop on genealogy research, but her eyesight was failing. Desperate to keep busy during school hours, Laurie volunteered to attend the workshop, and the next thing she knew, she, too, was hooked on researching family trees.

The friend was so pleased with Laurie's enthusiasm that she hired her to do the research. Word of mouth soon had Laurie with her own small business on her hands, and she took community ed courses and bought the necessary equipment—computer with Internet access, software, and even a secondhand microfiche machine—to build her business.

But it was fascination, not any monetary reward, that held her captive to researching family histories. She found the enthusiasm she'd once harbored for investigating hard-hitting news articles replaced with the patient investigating process of tracing a family tree. When the kids were home, she spent every minute with them, picking up the broken pieces their father's departure had created, forging a new bond that would see them all through the worst times. But when Garrett and Gaby were in school, she occupied her time surfing the Internet and flipping through borrowed microfiche pages to uncover the missing pieces of others' lineage.

In the last few months, she'd turned her attention to her own family. It surprised her that she didn't know much about them, beyond a few names and years. A chance inquiry into her mother's childhood home seemed like an ideal way to combine her new business and her maternal desire to move her children and aging mother to a better environment.

They'd been here three days now, but it seemed that they'd accomplished little work on the old house. Laurie had been under deadline to e-mail some research to one of her more cranky clients. Without her supervision, Gaby and Garrett had found numerous ways to get out of their chores. Agnes did what she could with a bucket and mop, but Laurie tried to limit her to the lightest work possible.

Laurie moved to the screen door, left open to catch a breeze. Her mother sat on the front steps, shelling green beans. Laurie squinted, picturing the house the way it must have looked sixty, seventy, eighty years ago, and she could see her mother as a young girl, laughing with her sisters as she snapped the beans into a bowl. Laurie thought suddenly that it was unfair, parents knowing their children from the very moment of birth, while children could only guess at the lives their parents had previously led. She wondered what she would have thought of Agnes if she'd known her as a girl—and more important, what Agnes would have thought of her.

Laurie sat beside her. "So you don't know anything about this supposed feud between the Bertrams and the Howells?"

Agnes shook her head. "I always heard some silly talk about it, but nothing substantial. Even Papa didn't seem to know what it was all about."

Tires rumbled along the gravel road, and a red Ford pickup made its way toward the house. When Jack pulled his truck up beside Laurie's Cherokee, Agnes set aside her bowl and waved wildly. "Yoo-hoo! Mr. MacGruder!"

"Hello, Laurie. Mrs. Bertram." Grinning, Jack started up the steps.

Agnes took him by the elbow. "Come on inside, Mr. MacGruder, and set a spell. Laurie told me you were planning to drop by some-day. I was wondering when you'd come."

"Mama, there isn't any place inside to 'set,'" Laurie said in a low voice, then turned to Jack. "I'm hoping our furniture will arrive today. But you're welcome to come in and look around."

Jack walked inside and took a turn around the room. "A little fix-ing up, and this place will be nice. When are the workers coming out?"

"They're not."

"You haven't hired anybody yet?"

"I don't plan to hire anybody at all. We're going to do it ourselves."

Jack let out a low, long whistle. "You've got a lot of work ahead of you."

"You think it's too much for us?"

"It depends on how much experience you have remodeling old homes."

"Well…none, really." Her self-confidence deflated like a leaky balloon. "But I bought a book on remodeling. And I'm good at in-terior decorating. How difficult can remodeling be? It'll be a solid family project."

Agnes stood by the front door, studying them. "Why don't you show him the cemetery, Laurie? That's what he came for."

"Sure." Laurie led the way down the steps, and Jack's heavy work boots thudded slowly behind her on the creaking planks. Laurie winced at the sound. The steps obviously needed some repairs too.

He followed her silently through the tall grass—Johnson grass, Mama used to call it, Laurie remembered suddenly. A blue jay squawked overhead, then a scissortail, bringing back another memory. As she opened the iron gate, Jack said, "What are you smiling about?"

"I was thinking about when Mama brought me here as a young girl, I heard that bird call. The sound always made me think of someone opening a screen door, yet when I'd turn around, no one would be at the house. It was years before I learned it was just a bird."

Jack squinted at the large oaks shading the cemetery. "Lots of birds have nested and gone from this area, that's for sure. How long has this place been in your family?"

"Since my great-grandparents built it in the late 1800s. It's been passed from each generation to the next. At least until Mama and her sisters sold it off to old Benjamin Tremble after their mother died. Now it's back in the family again." She paused. "Mama says she doesn't know anything about a feud between our families."

"I didn't think so. My father didn't either. It's probably just one of those misunderstandings between families that gets everybody huffy for a few generations, then they forget what started it."

Jack pulled out a piece of paper from his jeans pocket. "I've copied this information from various sources—just bits and pieces I've picked up from the Internet. But according to what little I know, my great-great-great-grandparents, Luther and Enid Howell, may be buried here. Here're their dates of birth and deaths. They're not necessarily accurate, but at least I'm in the ballpark."

Laurie studied the paper. "These people died in the 1880s, Jack. Like I said, this house wasn't built until the 1890s."

Jack shrugged, stuffing the paper back in his pocket. "I don't know, Maybe the dates are off."

Laurie thought he probably had the wrong information but kept silent. It wouldn't hurt to look. Maybe she'd spot something he overlooked. They took separate rows and studied tombstones. Some had crumbled with time, and she wondered how anyone would remember the dead people's lives if the markers disintegrated. She made a note to come out one day soon and write down all the names and dates, to save for future generations.

Jack dropped down on a crumbling rock bench under a live oak. "The information I got must have been wrong. Then again, I suppose it makes sense that Howells wouldn't be buried in the Bertram cemetery, since they were feuding."

Laurie sat beside him, at a respectable distance. "Where did you find out they were buried on this land?"

"I've been swapping information online with a man in Tennessee. He's researching another offshoot of the Howells, but a few months ago he ran across an 1880s obituary for Luther and Enid. They died at the same time, and the obit lists their being buried in the Howell family cemetery, located on their property. Through other research, I've discovered that Luther and Enid owned part of this Bertram property at one time. According to a deed I tracked down, the Bertrams bought it from the Howells in the 1880s."

"After Luther and Enid died." Laurie grinned. "So the feuding families lived next door to each other?"

He nodded, returning her smile. "Maybe they had gun battles across that rise, like the old Hatfield-and-McCoy stories." He glanced at his watch. "I'd better get going. You have work to do."

"Not that much," she lied. "Listen, uh, if you'd like some work on that research…I'd be glad to help. I've got all kinds of resources at my disposal."

Jack rested his chin on his steepled fingers, considering.

"I can give you references for my work," she said, then paused. Maybe he couldn't afford what she normally charged. Did he think she'd charge a neighbor? "And I'd do the work for free, Jack," she said, hoping she hadn't offended him.

He turned, all smiles. "I'd hate to take up time that could be spent on other clients. But I tell you what. Let's swap services. You research for me, and I'll help you fix up your house."

Now it was her turn to look skeptical. "Do you know anything about old houses?"

He grinned, as if with the slow progress she'd made, it didn't matter. "I restored my own family's home. If you're curious, why don't you come over this Saturday and I'll barbecue? Bring your family, and I'll invite a few friends to get you acquainted."

"Well…"

"Come on, Laurie. The barbecue will be a lot of fun. And as far as the work, why, it's neighborly to help each other. You share your expertise, and I'll share mine. We'll both benefit."

It was just a business agreement, after all. Not like we're planning a wedding. No sense worrying about getting involved with somebody when it just isn't going to happen.

"Okay," she heard herself say, then wondered where that voice had come from.

CHAPTER THREE

Whenever Laurie walked through the house, the ghosts of her ancestors seemed to walk with her. Not in a supernatural way, of course. She was too wise and too old to believe in ghosts. But it was almost as if each former occupant had left a little physical evidence of himself embedded in the walls, the ceiling, the floorboards. Clues to their lives.

Crayon marks low on a corner wall indicated a child's favorite play place. Grooves in the lackluster dining room floor indicated the scraping of mealtime chairs. The wooden stair handrail showed the wear of many hands.

The house stood as a silent witness to all the daily dramas played out within its walls.

Every morning Laurie rose from her sleeping bag, nearly too excited to sleep. She'd stand at the window and stare out over the property, imagining she saw Agnes and her sisters playing in the old oak with its sagging branch that must have been perfect as a natural swing. Sometimes she'd touch the walls or kneel to caress a badly scarred wooden floor plank, as if she could touch the hearts of all who'd ever lived here before. The house felt alive. It moved and breathed, pulsated with the rhythm of the past, vibrated to a cadence of its own.

The house she and Gary had occupied in Dallas had its own life too, but only that which she'd given it. In the end, the house had been emptied to a moving van and a new life. Saying good-bye, she'd knelt in the front hallway on the expensive Saltillo tile, washing it with her tears. The whole house had felt so cold, she had to rub her arms against the chill. Her love and attention had been in vain, and the house had betrayed her.

She was more certain with each passing day that her mother's house was different. It expected nothing of her, and so she couldn't fail it, as she had the home in Dallas. This one needed her help and love, yet it stood patiently and asked for nothing but to exist. Which made her love it all the more and want to prove her love in a thousand ways.

Yes, she wanted to say, *yes, I will care for you. As those who lived here before, who dwelled within and allowed you to surround them and their lives. I will make you grand again. You will be a testament to their past and a marker for my family's future.*

At last the furniture arrived, but instead of making things more homey, it just seemed out of place. Laurie and the kids covered everything downstairs with bedsheets to prevent the destruction of her sofa and love seat, favorite antique chaise longue, and dining room set during the renovations. Gaby had continued to sleep upstairs with her grandmother, and that night Garrett and Laurie moved their sleeping bags to the sheet-covered couches.

As she tried to fall asleep the night before the barbecue, Laurie studied the moon through the blinds, thinking about Jack. She hadn't had time yet to work on his genealogy, but he'd told her to take her time. Perhaps they could start researching Monday, while they walked through the house and discussed repairs.

Jack was certainly an enigma. Why had he divorced? He'd certainly given away nothing about his ex-wife, but maybe he wasn't the kind of man who liked to talk much about himself. That would certainly be a switch from living with Gary.

No, Jack had talked about his family history search, but little else.

The next morning Laurie rolled up her sleeping bag, grumbling to herself about the kinks in her back from sleeping on the sheet-draped sofa. She wanted to sleep in her own bed, but the large four-poster leaned sadly against a paint-peeled wall upstairs, yet to be reassembled here in her new home.

Sighing, she tucked the bedroll under the drop cloth, then glanced upstairs. They'd all already eaten breakfast, and Garrett and Gaby had headed outside. Agnes had disappeared to her room and hadn't come down during the past hour. It wasn't her nature to be quiet for so long.

"Mama?" Laurie called, as she ascended the stairs.

Agnes sat on the old iron bed, staring out at the cemetery. Laurie stood in the doorway and watched her, concerned at her silence. "What was this room like when you were growing up?" she said, trying to encourage her mother to talk.

"Rosebud."

Laurie laughed. Good. Everything was all right. "Mama, I don't mean *Citizen Kane*. I'm talking about this bedroom."

Agnes turned, nodding. "Rosebud. This room had wallpaper the lightest shade of green with little pink roses all over it. My mother said that it was just like her girls, all young and pretty, waiting to unfold. I don't know about my sisters, but I used to think on that a lot, lying here in bed at night."

Laurie looked at the current wallpaper, a torn, dizzying lavender-and-cream stripe that had peeled from the ceiling. "Would you like rosebud wallpaper again?"

Agnes studied the walls for a moment, then glanced out at the cemetery. "I don't believe so, thank you."

Laurie followed her gaze. Down below, Garrett and Gaby moved into view, tossing a baseball between them. That was one thing Laurie could be thankful to Gary for—he'd taught them both the simple beauty of America's game.

The kids moved farther away from each other, laughing with delight as they threw the ball. Laurie smiled. "I think they're glad to be here. How about you?"

Garrett threw a high fastball. Gaby stretched out her arm, and the ball smacked into her glove. She crowed with delight.

Agnes rose, smiling, looking more like her normally cheerful self. "Oh, it'll do for a house, I 'spect. A building's just a building. It's who lives inside the walls that makes the difference."

Laurie moved closer and put her arm around her mother. "The kids helped me clean up the graveyard. We pulled some weeds."

"I saw," Agnes said. "I'm glad you left the wildflowers. Most people consider them weeds too."

Pleased that she'd noticed their extra effort, Laurie just nodded.

Agnes peered into her face. "You excited about the shindig this afternoon at Jack's?"

"I suppose so. It'll be nice to meet some of the other people from town."

"And maybe get to know a certain neighbor a little better?'

"Now, Mama, don't go playing matchmaker on us. After getting over that heartache with Gary, I'm ready to swear off men."

Agnes put her hand on her hip and affected her best Mae West accent. " 'Well, it's not the men in your life that counts, it's the life in your men.' "

Laurie laughed, trying not to blush. Sometimes she wondered who was the mother and who was the daughter. "Oh, Mama."

"You just watch, Laurie Golden," Agnes said, waggling her finger. "I have a feeling about you and that Jack MacGruder. You're two kindred souls all right. Love is definitely in the air."

Laurie thought maybe it was potential allergies, not love, that permeated the air around Jack's house. Their pungent odor tickling her nose, the cedars flanking the road to his home signaled a potential sneezing attack. Fortunately, her allergic susceptibility to cedar fever didn't kick in, and she seemed free to enjoy the day without clutching a wad of Kleenex.

Several citizens of Honor awaited them as they drove up. Some greeted Agnes as a long-lost town daughter, some ruffled Garrett's hair, and some of the teenagers—including Russell—fussed over a bored-looking Gaby until she uncrossed her arms and chattered about the last big concert she'd seen in Dallas.

Laurie hung back, bemused by the spectacle.

"Feeling lonely?"

Startled, she turned. Jack MacGruder stood behind her, smiling, holding a plate filled with a large, aluminum foil-wrapped package. Laurie nodded at the platter. "Is that the barbecue?"

"Yep. Brisket. This is a great way to cook it. Why don't you come with me while I throw it on the grill?"

"Sure." She followed a few paces behind him, feeling unusually shy. Probably because he'd shown up in her cemetery at midnight. Or maybe because he'd been her competitor for the purchase of the Bertram land.

Or maybe it was because he looked entirely too handsome today, in blue jeans and a plain white cotton T-shirt. Men in their forties shouldn't be that good looking. Well, maybe men like Gary, whose whole career revolved around their looks. Unless he'd chosen to tell his latest girlfriend, Laurie alone was privy to Gary's plastic surgery secrets.

Men like Jack MacGruder came by their good looks naturally.

"Well, what do you think?"

"Huh?" Laurie snapped back to reality. "About what?"

Jack set the brisket on the grill and closed the lid. "About my house."

"Oh. That." Laurie breathed an inward sigh of relief and turned her attention to the home he'd restored.

Pristine white with green shutters, the farmhouse looked like it could be featured in *House and Garden*. He'd retained the original style—tall columns and a wraparound porch—but complemented it with large tropical plants in terra-cotta pots, iron side tables, and modern rockers painted bright, cheerful colors.

It was the perfect combination of past meeting present, and it was the house of her dreams.

"I think…" She glanced up and saw him looking straight at her, his blue eyes holding hers. Her heart skipped a beat. "I think it's wonderful," she whispered.

"Mr. MacGruder!!" Agnes swept between them. "How wonderful to see you again. Thank you for inviting us."

"Hello, Mrs. Bertram. How's life treating you?"

"Ah, 'life is a banquet and most poor suckers are starving to death,'" she said, then winked. *"Auntie Mame."*

Jack grinned. Laurie resisted the urge to cringe. She didn't think

Agnes had cracked more than a half-dozen movie lines since the last time they'd seen him, but she imagined they'd be hearing more now. If only Jack hadn't encouraged her mother the first time they'd met, maybe the family could have cured her of this silliness.

"I hear you're going to help us with our remodeling project," Agnes said. "You like working on old houses, do you, Mr. MacGruder?"

"It's Jack, Mrs. Bertram. And yes. I helped my father restore many houses in Honor. Twelve in all, when I was growing up, and a couple since I moved out years ago."

"I remember what this one used to look like, and you've done a fine job," Agnes said, studying his home. She cocked her head. "You don't have a secret family somewhere? Kids? A wife?"

Jack smiled. "I'm not Mr. Rochester with a mad wife locked in the attic."

Agnes beamed. *Jane Eyre* was not only one of her favorite movies, but one of her favorite books as well. She patted Jack's arm. "You just call me Aggie then, dear. I'm glad you'll be working for us. Laurie could use a little male company."

"Mama…," Laurie said in a low, warning voice.

"Oh, look! There's Ned Weathers from the hardware store. I used to baby-sit for him when I was about Gaby's age." Moving away, Agnes waved. "Yoo-hoo! Neddie!"

When she was out of hearing distance, Laurie laughed, trying to cover her embarrassment. "My mama. She's quite a character, isn't she? You can't take anything she says seriously."

"I hope she wasn't being completely dishonest." Jack grinned.

"Hey, Jack!" Russell Pratt's voice rang out. "I brought gloves and bats. Let's play some ball."

Jack set down the empty platter and smiled apologetically at Laurie. "Do you mind? It's a barbecue tradition around here to have a game before we eat."

"No. Go right ahead." Inwardly, Laurie breathed a sigh of relief—or was it disappointment? Jack MacGruder had been standing entirely too close. "My kids like to play too. It'd be a good way for them to break the ice."

"Great. I'll make sure they join in. How about you?"

She shook head. "No, thanks. I'll just watch."

"Hey, Jack! Come on!"

Jack flashed her a smile, then jogged to the open field where the game was setting up. Laurie found a seat on the front steps and watched as a game got under way. Jack quickly became the captain of one team and Russell of the other. Laurie was pleased that Russell picked Gaby and Garrett, even designating Garrett as the leadoff hitter.

With his team in place, Jack took the mound. He threw a few warmup pitches to his catcher, then Garrett stepped up to the plate. Despite his owlish appearance and small size, he'd been playing well in Dallas's Little League, and Jack didn't take it easy on him now. He tossed a slow curve ball that Garrett missed badly.

Laurie was proud that her son didn't get upset as some boys his age might. He simply dug his sneakers into the dirt, took his stance, and gritted his teeth. Jack went into his windup and sailed one straight down the strike zone. Garrett connected with a *crack!* The ball flew into the tall weeds at the edge of the property, and the spectators cheered, Laurie loudest of all.

While the game proceeded, several women sat beside Laurie and introduced themselves. A few kept a close eye on toddlers as they tumbled in the manicured lawn around the house, while others chattered to Laurie with enthusiasm about Honor's schools. One invited Laurie to a weekday quilting group, another to a monthly scrapbooking party. Agnes held court from the largest rocker on the porch around a circle of other elderly women.

Laurie felt as if she'd landed in the middle of a Norman Rockwell painting.

When the game finally broke up, everyone fell into line for brisket, potato salad, beans, and a table groaning under the weight of homemade desserts. Laurie found herself in line beside Jack, and he followed her back to the steps. Others moved away to join their families at long tables set up on the lawn, leaving Laurie and Jack by themselves.

As she proceeded to eat, Laurie couldn't help but notice the cheerful, curious glances thrown their way. "Do you think they left us alone on purpose?" she said.

Her mother whispered to Ned Weathers, sitting next to her at one of the tables, then waved. Jack grinned. "Could be. I've had a lot of matchmakers over the years, but everyone my age in this town is already married. But don't worry. They're not the pushy kind."

"You don't know Mama," Laurie said.

"That bad?" Jack grinned.

"And then some." She chewed thoughtfully on a roll, then swallowed. "Where'd you play ball?"

Jack turned and shaded his eyes against the sun. "I spent a couple of years in the Blue Jays minor league system, then gave it up after I tore my rotator cuff. Surgery didn't improve things like I'd hoped."

"Pitcher?"

He nodded. "Actually got to pitch in the bigs for a couple of games. A lot of people had high hopes for me."

"The surgery must have been a huge disappointment then. For you, I mean."

"Maybe for a few days." He shrugged. "I came back here for a while, then finished my college degree in Austin. Met my wife, got married, and when that didn't work out either, I came back here again. The Bible says not to look back, so I don't."

"Most people I know would. They'd be pretty disappointed at missing out on a chance to play professional sports." She picked at her potato salad. "Not to mention a failed marriage."

"Most people spend their whole lives looking back or looking too far forward. I just try to enjoy the present and plan for the immediate future."

"What about the research into your family's past? Isn't that looking back?"

"Yes, but I'll be satisfied with whatever I find. Or don't find. I'd like to know more about my family, and I'd certainly like to find those missing graves. But if I don't, then there's a divine reason why I shouldn't."

Laurie wondered if he also believed in a reason for the failure of his marriage, but she didn't ask. It'd probably be best to stick with a safe topic like family research. "Maybe while we're working on my house, we can take breaks and search the property for any sign of graves... I'd be glad to help you look."

"Thanks, Laurie. I'd appreciate your help. Just don't let me keep you from your real work."

"Not at all. Besides," she said, suddenly feeling bashful. "Mama was right. We could all use a little company. I think you've hit it off with us."

Jack nodded in the direction of the tables. "I'm not the only one. Look at your kids over there."

Garrett was surrounded by several boys around his age, and they chucked pieces of corn bread at each other, laughing.

At a separate table, Gaby sat close to Russell Pratt, gesturing some story with animation, smiling. She stopped in midsentence and beamed, moony-eyed, at Russell, who returned her smile with a broad one of his own.

"Well, I'll be," Laurie whispered.

"It doesn't take kids long to find friends," Jack said. "And there's a good group of kids in this town. Garrett and Gaby'll fit right in."

"What about me?" Laurie said, teasing. "Can a Dallas gal find friends here too?"

Jack smiled, his blue eyes solemn. Laurie felt a tingle run up her spine. "I'd bet the farm on it, Laurie," he said softly. "You've already got at least one."

"I *knew* you'd finagle a way to get him over." Agnes winked at her daughter. "You've definitely got some flirt left in you, all right."

Laurie sighed with exasperation. "Mama, he's just coming to look over the house and give it his best assessment. He'll help me figure out what needs to be done first—the major stuff, you know."

"Mm-hmm."

"Mama, *please* don't say anything embarrassing."

Gaby looped an arm around Agnes. "Yeah, Grandma. You don't want to embarrass your daughter. Like back in Dallas when Mom turned on the porch light when David Buell was telling me good night."

"That's not the same, young lady," Laurie said. "That was a real date, and he was a real, hormonal teenage boy."

"And Jack MacGruder's—"

A knock sounded and Jack peered through the screen door. "Am I bothering you, ladies?"

"No, not at all," Laurie said, glaring at Agnes and Gaby, who suppressed giggles. "Come on in."

"Thanks." Jack wiped his boots on the grass mat. The hinges squeaked when he opened the door, and he drew notepad and pen out of his back jeans pocket. "Oil screen door," he said, writing on the pad. When he glanced up and saw her staring, he shrugged. "I figured we might as well catalog everything."

"How very efficient!" Agnes clapped her hands, as though Jack had just said he was taking them all to the Bahamas for a week.

"Come on, Grandma." Gaby tugged her elbow, winking at Laurie as if to say *I'll help you out this time.* "Let's go find Garrett. I think he's around back, pulling weeds."

"But I want to stay and help Jack and Laurie!"

Gaby silenced her grandmother with a look, then propelled her out the door. "Have a good time!" Agnes called over her shoulder.

Laurie cleared her throat as the screen door slammed. "Why don't we have a look around and see what we can add to that list?"

"Uh, sure." Jack looked a little embarrassed himself, but he covered by studying the ceiling and walls. "Here are a few things…"

For the next few hours, they studied every nook and cranny of first the living room, then the formal dining room, the kitchen, then the rest of the house. Jack made a separate page for each room, adding every detail, small or large, that needed attention. He assessed the house with a critical eye and suggested new Sheetrock here, plaster for wall holes there, a fresh coat of paint in every room, new flooring and some cabinet repair in the kitchen, some upgrading of appliances…

"The best news is that the wiring looks sound," he said. "Whoever updated it knew what they were doing."

Laurie nodded numbly, trying to squelch the sinking feeling that the repairs were more than she—with or without Jack's help—could handle. "If you're finished, maybe this would be a good time to head outside to look for your family graves."

"Great idea." Jack stuffed the now-filled notebook into his back pocket and eagerly followed her outside.

Garrett and Gaby were heading down the gravel road on their bicycles, with Agnes trailing behind on an old ten-speed. She'd tucked her skirt up into her waistband, and the material flapped around her knees like an errant nun's habit. Agnes threw back her head and laughed, pedaling hard to catch up with her grandchildren.

Laurie quickly turned Jack's attention to the far edges of her property, hoping that he hadn't seen or heard her mother. "I own everything from here to that fence, that fence, and that rise over there."

"I know, Laurie." Jack grinned. "I own the adjoining property, remember?"

"Oh." At least he hadn't commented on her mother's behavior. "I was just trying to show you our boundaries for searching. If the Howells once owned part of this property, we should logically start at the border between yours and mine. Why don't we begin at the far edge and gradually work our way inward?"

"All today? You've got quite a few acres here."

"Over time, I mean. We can put a marker where we stop searching, then start there the next time."

They moved to the farthest edge of the property, the top of the rise overlooking his land. Jack drew a deep breath. "It's beautiful here. Green grass, sturdy trees, blue sky—"

"Heat, humidity."

Jack laughed. "Are you sure you're a native Texan? Usually only outsiders point out the climate."

"I'm a realistic native." Laurie poked through the brush.

Jack worked alongside her, then finally stopped. "What exactly are we looking for? What kind of signs that there are graves?"

Laurie shrugged. "There's usually something telltale. A broken headstone hidden by grass, remnants of an iron fence that might have enclosed the graves… Just look for old things."

"Old things," Jack mumbled, resuming his search. "Seems like that's what genealogy is all about. Old names, old dates…"

"True. But this is the physical detective work. It's a great break in the routine from researching online or going through musty records at the courthouse all day."

"Do you search for grave sites often?" he said.

Laurie stopped. "This is actually the first time I've been asked to do this. Always before, it's just been following paper trails."

She upended a long-dead tree branch with the toe of her boot. Satisfied that nothing lay underneath except for a colony of bugs, she eased it down again with a sigh. "It's a shame that graves are the only legacy to our lives. Along with the ubiquitous papers—birth and death certificates, divorce papers…"

"There's more to mark a life than those things. Kids, for example. A life that's lived in the way we influence others for the better. That's what endures."

Laurie nodded, then, embarrassed that they'd fallen into so serious a subject, cleared her throat. "I wonder why the Howells sold off part of their property to a family they were feuding with."

"One of the family history's mysteries, that's for sure. Do you think we can find out why?"

"I doubt it. Unless you can find an old journal, paper trails don't usually reveal motives." She paused. "If your information is from an old obituary that says Luther and Enid are buried on their property, why do you think it's here and not on your land?"

"The obituary also says that the family cemetery is situated at the top of the rise overlooking the rest of their land."

"That would be on my property then." Laurie tramped through the grass to get a better view of the Bertram cemetery, just around the house. "Some of the graves in the Bertram yard are older than what we're looking for. So that part of the property must have always belonged to the Bertrams. Somewhere between the beginning of the rise here and the cemetery, we should find the Howell graves."

"That makes sense."

Laurie thought for a moment. "Are you sure you don't have another family cemetery on your land?"

"Luther and Enid were the first Howell settlers in this area. Their descendants are buried in the town cemetery."

"Interesting. I wonder why only Luther and Enid are buried around here. Did they have children who died before they did? Most families did back then."

"Yes, the records show a couple of newborn babies, and an older child who died of measles. Their graves are missing too."

Thinking hard, Laurie glanced at the top story of the house, then seeing a small window, groaned. Jack stopped tramping down tall grass. "Something wrong?"

"We forgot to check that upstairs bathroom. The plumbing doesn't work, so we don't use it. We might as well add all its faults to the list."

"Come on, let's take care of it now."

"It can wait," she said. "We can look here some more."

"I'd rather make the house repair list complete before we start looking for old graves."

"Okay." Laurie stabbed a broken bottle upside down in the ground to mark where they'd stopped. Jack was already heading toward the house, and she hurried to catch him.

Inside, it took only a few minutes to assess the old bathroom, for it'd never been sufficiently modernized. While Jack added details to the list in the notebook, Laurie sighed. "All this seems like an awful lot of work just to fix up a family home," she said.

"It's really not that bad." Jack scribbled a note to the list. "Nothing that a little sweat equity and a few years' time can't handle."

"*A few years?*" Laurie sat down on the edge of the tub, then remembered Jack had discovered its aging claw feet were threatening to buckle. She hastily stood. "That long?"

Jack nodded. "Restoring old homes is a lot like working on relationships. It takes patience and attention. Time. The more carefully you invest, the more you get back."

Laurie turned her head, ostensibly to think. Instead, she studied Jack's reflection in the peeling silver of the ancient mirror. Did she know any more about him than she did about this old house? They'd worked closely together for the last few hours, sharing small laughs, especially at the aging condition of the home. He'd also offered a few observations about the town, about the people she'd met at the barbecue, but he hadn't revealed anything personal about himself. He'd said nothing about his divorce, nothing about his ex-wife.

As she watched him add a note with careful precision to the pad, the thought struck her that perhaps instead of reluctance to divulge more information, he was patiently waiting for her to open up first.

She wondered if she did, if he then would open up as well.

Laurie crossed her arms. Maybe directness was needed here. "Why are you suddenly talking about relationships? Are you talking about us?"

He looked up from the notebook, not startled in the least. "Yes. Does that bother you?"

"Maybe you're just giving in to the town's efforts to find you a date. Or maybe my mother's to find *me* one. Maybe you just want to get everybody off your back once and for all."

Jack grinned. "Maybe so. I have to admit I get tired of all the pushing and prodding. And since everybody in town is eventually going to push and prod you, too, maybe we should just save them all a lot of trouble."

Laurie paused. Couldn't he just come out and say it? "Are you asking me out on a date?"

Jack laughed. "I'm forty-six years old, Laurie. I'm too old for dating."

"Well, *what* then?"

"Dinner at my house next Saturday night?"

Her heart thumped. This was all so new, she didn't know what to do. She hadn't had a single date since the divorce. Where was Gaby when she needed her? She'd know just the proper amount of skepticism a girl should add to her voice so that she didn't give away her eagerness. "I had dinner at your house Saturday."

"That was a party. This'll be just a casual dinner for two friends… Business associates," he added. "Do you like liver and onions?"

"Uh, no," she said.

"Good. Because we're having chicken." His eyes twinkled. "Is that all right?"

Vastly relieved, she nodded. "It sounds great."

Jack stuffed the notebook back in his pocket. "I may be pretty busy this week, so if I don't see you beforehand, let's make it seven o'clock next Saturday night."

"Sure. Can I bring anything?"

"Just yourself. And conversation. We have lots to talk about."

As he left the bathroom and headed down the stairs, Laurie wondered just exactly what subjects he had in mind.

CHAPTER FOUR

"Now dear, you *will* remember the difference between the salad and the dessert forks, won't you?" Agnes said.

Staring into the hall mirror, Laurie pursed her mouth and applied pale pink lipstick. "Mama, it's not a multicourse dinner at The Mansion on Turtle Creek, you know. It's just a bite to eat at Jack's place."

"Yes dear, but I wouldn't want you to embarrass yourself and ruin any chance you might have with that nice young man."

Laurie turned from the mirror. "Mama, Jack MacGruder and I are in our forties. You act like this is my first formal date, and it's neither."

"Neither what?" Agnes said, cocking her head.

Laurie sighed with exasperation. Sometimes Mama just pretended to be difficult, and sometimes she truly was. "It's neither formal nor a date."

"Well, in my day, when a gentleman asked a young lady to dine on chicken, we called it such." Agnes studied her nails. "Of course, in *my* day, a young lady wouldn't be allowed to dine with a young man alone at his house."

Laurie threw up her hands in mock horror. "Mama, it's probably only fried chicken from a striped bucket." She kissed her mother on the cheek, leaving a light pink imprint. "But thanks for the compliment. I can't remember the last time anybody called me a young lady."

"Well…" Agnes allowed herself to smile, exaggerating the kiss's mollifying effects. "You do look like a sweet young thing in that getup."

"You like it?" Laurie turned slowly, allowing her knee-length full blue silk patchwork skirt to flare slightly.

Agnes's eyes misted. "You look lovely," she said softly, then needlessly adjusted the white silk peasant blouse at Laurie's shoulders. "Just like your first date, when you were sixteen years old."

"Thanks, Mama," Laurie whispered, covering her mother's hand. Mama had seen her through some rough times during the past year, yet they'd seldom shared such tender moments.

Garrett waltzed into the room, imitating a violinist in full performance. "It is getting pretty mushy in here," Gaby said, trailing behind. "Mom, can I borrow your turquoise earrings? Russell's going to pick me up. Some of the kids are going to the movies tonight."

"What are you going to see?" Laurie said, dreading the title of the latest slasher flick.

"Oh, Mom." Gaby rolled her eyes. "They don't even show R-rated movies in this town. We're just going to see the original version of *The Parent Trap*. They're showing it at the old Bijou."

"Isn't that the theater that doesn't have air conditioning?"

"Yeah. They never bothered to fix it. Russell says it isn't so bad, even in the summer. They put out a bunch of fans and give you water bottles with misters to keep yourself cool. Now *please* can I borrow your earrings?"

Laurie smiled inwardly. She never would have thought that Gaby would get dressed up for such a low-key date. "Go right ahead. Just be home by midnight, all right?"

"No problem. Russell says his mom skins him alive if he misses his own midnight curfew."

Agnes prodded Laurie in the arm. "Go on with yourself, girl. You'll be late, and then that nice Jack MacGruder will think you don't like him."

"Okay, Mama. Don't wait up. Bye, kids!"

Amid a chorus of farewells and background smooching sounds from Garrett, Laurie hiked toward Jack's home. The sun wouldn't set until around nine o'clock, and Jack promised to walk her back home again, even though to her it seemed unlikely she'd be in any danger.

As he'd predicted, she hadn't seen him all week. She'd done some preliminary planning on the repairs—picking out paint color, wallpaper swatches, eyeing some crown molding—but she'd mostly been busy herself, working on genealogy. She wished she had even a scrap of information to report to Jack, but she hadn't had time to do anything beyond sending an e-mail to his contact in Tennessee, pumping for more information.

Halfway to his house, she saw a warm glow from the front porch. By the time she'd passed through the stand of cedars, she could see that he'd lined the ground outside the porch with wicker tiki candleholders. A white cloth-covered table was set at one end with china plates and crystal glasses. Soft jazz drifted from speakers hanging at the eaves.

Just as she reached the bottom steps, Jack stepped through the front door. He stopped when he saw her, then smiled slowly, his eyes crinkling with pleasure. Laurie caught her breath, feeling like the sixteen-year-old girl her mother remembered.

"You look beautiful," he said.

Laurie blinked. When was the last time a man had spoken that word in reference to her? Gary'd said it derogatorily when she'd accidentally shattered his glass Anchorman of the Year award, but she couldn't remember him using the word to describe her physical appearance.

"Thanks," she said. "You look very nice too." Wearing tan chinos and a light plaid shirt, he looked every inch like a confident, self-made man. Not only handsome, but caring.

"I thought you might like to eat out here on the porch. The citronella candles should keep the bugs away, but if it's—"

"No, it's perfect." And it was.

He smiled, then gestured her to a chair.

During this night she knew she would never forget, Laurie wanted to pinch herself several times. The sun set in a glorious display of orange, red, and purple, giving way slowly to a rising full, white moon. Jack arranged dripless wax candles on the table and served perfectly cooked chicken cordon bleu, fresh asparagus, and crème brûlée for dessert. Throughout the evening, low, relaxing sounds of oboes and saxophones came from the speakers above.

Gary had treated her to many fancy dinners, but mostly so that he could be seen in public. Never anything this romantic, not even when they were just dating.

"Was everything good?" Jack asked, after he'd cleared away the dishes. "You didn't say two words during dinner."

Laurie grinned. "I was too busy stuffing my face." She couldn't hide her curiosity any longer, and she blurted out, "Where did you get food like that catered in Honor?"

Jack laughed. "I made it myself, Laurie."

"You're kidding! And you mean to say that no woman within one hundred miles of here has rushed you to the altar?"

Jack feigned a hurt expression. "Is that all you women think about? Food?"

"I didn't mean it that way," Laurie said, wishing she could sink through the wooden porch planks. "Gary always said I had a habit of saying the wrong thing at the wrong time."

"Tell me about your ex-husband," Jack said, leaning forward.

"What's to tell? He was a high-profile TV anchorman in a big city, and he finally decided to have a lifestyle that he thought matched. He left me for a much younger woman." She was amazed at how she spoke the words—factually, without a trace of bitterness. Maybe Jack had put a sedative in the crème brûlée.

"I know something about what you've gone through," he said. "My wife left me too. For another man."

"Oh," Laurie said. "I'm sorry."

He shrugged. "I didn't choose the divorce, but I couldn't stop it, either."

"I wanted Gary to change too, but he didn't. Or wouldn't. Still, there are days where I wonder, what if I'd hung in there? What if I'd—"

Jack took her hand. "Laurie, sometimes you just have to let go of the past and look forward. It sounds like you didn't choose your divorce any more than I chose mine. When I want to look back, I remember the Bible's advice: Run the race that's set before you.

Racers don't look over their shoulders—they keep their eyes focused straight ahead."

Tears welled in Laurie's eyes. "That's why I moved my family here, Jack. I wanted us to have a fresh start, a simpler life. New friends, good, solid friends. I…I'm sorry." She dabbed at her eyes. "You must think I'm foolish, blubbering like this."

The music melted from live and jazzy to slow and bluesy. Smiling, Jack rose. He held out his hand. "Come on, Laurie," he said softly. "Dance with me. Tonight we're just two runners taking a rest from the race."

Laurie hesitated. She did *not* want her heart broken again. She didn't want to be doomed to repeat past failures because she'd refused to learn from her mistakes.

"Laurie," he whispered so softly that it sounded like a caress. "Just dance with me."

Slowly she rose. She slipped her shoes under the table, then placed her hand in his. He drew her gently into his embrace, then swayed with her on the smooth planks of the wraparound porch, under the brightness of the full Texas moon.

Later she scarcely remembered going home. They walked silently from his property to hers, and at her doorway, he kissed her good night. It was sweet and tender, full of promise—all the gentleness of a teenager's first kiss, tempered by adult experience. Jack must have said something about coming to work on the house the next day, for she nodded, then somehow found herself inside the house.

Thankfully Agnes wasn't waiting up. Laurie never would have been able to explain the expression she was certain lingered in her eyes, if not full on her face.

When he showed up at the screen door the next morning, she nearly tripped over her own feet, embarrassed and eager at the same time. He ruffled Garrett's hair as the boy let him in and ignored Gaby's giggles, even though Laurie was sure he must have heard.

"Hi, Laurie," he said. "Ready to work on that house?"

Her heart fell. He was going to pretend that last night had never happened. That he'd never held her in his arms or kissed her...

Jack turned so that Gaby and Garrett couldn't see his face and winked.

Laurie smiled. "Uh, yeah. How about we get started on these cracks down here?"

Gaby sighed loudly. "Come on, Garrett, or they'll get us involved in this repair. Let's find something else to do."

They moved to the dining room. Jack and Laurie heard the sound of cartoons coming from the black-and-white portable television set.

Jack grinned, then turned to examine the cracked wall in earnest. He probed a pinkie into the fissure.

Laurie hung back, still trying to get accustomed to his presence. Like a schoolgirl with her first beau, she was almost afraid to stand too close. "The, uh, the book I've been consulting said to use joint compound for cracks. I got some at Ned's hardware store the other day."

"We need plaster. The joint compound's good for small cracks, but not large ones. Otherwise, it'd just shrink."

Agnes swept into the room. "There you are, Jack. Good to see you." She grinned like a Cheshire cat. "I'll just leave you two experts to your work and take the kids down to the Tastee-King for a cone. It'll do the three of us good to get out of this dusty old house. Mind if I take the car, Laurie?"

"No, Mama." She shot her mother a look that clearly said she was onto her mother's matchmaking schemes. "You need some money?"

"Not at all." Agnes smiled innocently, then reached down the front of her dress and pulled out a wad of bills.

Jack turned his head and suppressed a laugh. Laurie wanted to throttle her mother right then and there. Agnes quickly moved outside, calling for Garrett and Gaby.

Composing himself, Jack smiled. Laurie smiled back, then cleared her throat. "If it's plaster you think we need, instead of joint compound, do you have any? I don't."

"I'm fresh out, but I'll head down to the hardware store and pick some up. Want to come along for the ride?"

The question made her heart pound. Being alone with Jack here at the house, with the express purpose of restoration was one thing. A car ride with time to talk was another. "Well…"

"I just thought you might have other things you need. Or that you might just want to get out of the house, like your mother and your kids."

She relaxed. "I suppose I ought to go along and pay for things. And I've only been to the hardware store once."

"I've talked to Ned Weathers there." Jack led the way out to his truck. "He's been in business here ever since he took over from his father. Might even know something about the architecture of the area. Or even about your house in particular, if you have questions. He knows a lot about the region's family history."

"If Ned Weathers knows a lot about Honor's history, I guess you've already asked him for information about your family."

Jack nodded. "As a matter of fact, he said that he thought he remembered something about the Howells, but he couldn't quite put his finger on it. He's going to ask his mother. She's in a nursing home over in Waxahachie."

"Why, Ned Weathers must be seventy-five, if he's a day! How old is his mother?"

"Ninety-nine this year."

Jack eased the truck to the side of the road. He set the brake, then draped an arm over the steering wheel and smiled. The light caught a few strands of gray in his hair. Laurie was utterly charmed and completely forgot what they'd been talking about.

"Laurie, are you comfortable with what happened between us last night?"

Her heart thumped. "Yes," she whispered, then paused. "Are you?"

"More than comfortable. I'll admit that I've dated several women from around here—mostly due to proddings from friends—but you, you're…"

He leaned forward slightly, then shook his head and sat back.

"I just wanted you to know that I'm sincere when I say I want to see you again. And not just for home repairs or genealogy research."

"Me, too, Jack." She grinned. "Won't it be fun for Mama and your friends?"

"I hope it won't be so bad for us, either." Jack grinned and started the engine, heading them once again toward town.

The hardware store wasn't even on Main Street, and she wondered how it could stay in business. It was everything she'd imagined about a small-town mercantile: pegboards lined with saws, hammers, and screwdrivers; plastic bins filled with nuts, bolts, and hooks; plumbing and electrical supplies braced against one wall; rows of small kitchen appliances and knickknacks down the center aisles. She found the small selection of paints and light fixtures liberating, rather than limiting. Having too many choices was often burdensome.

Ned was playing checkers behind the counter by himself. Laurie caught his eye, and he smiled, but when he caught sight of Jack, he rose quickly. "Hi-dee, Jack. Good to see you!"

"Hi, Ned. How's the arthritis?"

"Oh, can't complain." Ned kneaded his knuckles, as if he suddenly remembered they hurt. "As long as it don't rain, I'm in pretty good shape." He smiled shyly at Laurie. "And how are you doin', Miz Golden? Right nice kids you got there. I enjoyed chatting with them at Jack's shindig."

"Thank you, Mr. Weathers."

Ned leaned forward on the counter. "So what can I do for you two? You hard at work on that old Bertram place?"

Laurie was pleased that the locals still referred to it by her family's name, even after nearly thirty-five years. "Jack tells me that the cracks in my walls need plaster."

"Big cracks?"

"Large enough for roaches to crawl through sideways," Jack said cheerfully.

Ned whistled, chuckling. "I always like to see the old Honor homes restored, but they usually mean lots of work, don't they?"

"So it seems." Laurie laughed along with him.

Ned fiddled with an open box of penny nails. "And how's Aggie, er, your mother? I saw her tool down the street a little while ago in one of them fancy soo-burban-type vehicles."

Laurie winked covertly at Jack. "Mama's just fine, Mr. Weathers. You should come out to the house someday."

Ned glanced up, blushing. "Oh, I couldn't do that, Miz Golden."

"Why, to see the house, I mean," Laurie said, smiling. "*And* Mama. She said she used to baby-sit for you sometimes, Mr. Weathers. Is that right?"

"Yep. Her and her younger sisters, too—Eula and Birdy."

"They've both passed on. I only met them a time or two myself. They married and moved out of Texas altogether, Mama said, and didn't care to return to visit."

Ned shook his head, tsking. "Bless their souls. Can't blame them much for getting far away."

"Why do you say that?"

"On account of your grandpa, that's why." He looked puzzled.

"I'm afraid you'll have to explain," Laurie said, with an apologetic smile. "My grandfather died long before I was born."

Shifting his eyes nervously toward Jack, Ned bit his bottom lip. "I'd better be getting after that plaster." He scurried to a back room.

Laurie started around the counter, but Jack touched her arm. "Don't follow him," he said softly.

"Why? I just want to know what he meant about my grandfather."

Jack drew his hand away from her arm. "Laurie," he said in a low voice. "This is something you need to talk over with your mother. Don't put Ned on the spot like that. I'm sure he wouldn't have spoken up if he thought you didn't know."

"Know *what?* That's what I want to find out." Her cheeks flushed. There was obviously something about her grandpa that other folks knew and she didn't. And it wasn't pleasant.

"You probably don't understand small towns. People know everything about each other, but they can also be pretty loyal. Even about the past. Especially about bad things in the past."

The way he said *bad things* made her skin crawl.

"Let it be until you can talk to your mother," Jack said quietly.

"Don't you think she'd rather tell you than have you find out from a stranger?"

"Then why *didn't* she?" Laurie dashed a hand at her eyes, furious when she brushed away tears. "I'm forty-five years old, Jack. Whatever it is, she's had plenty of time to talk."

Jack's laugh was gentle. "I never knew a woman to tell her age outright. Laurie Golden, you're one of a kind."

She glanced up at him, finding solace in his eyes, clear blue like a summer sky just after a storm. Jack pulled a handkerchief from his pocket and wiped a last tear from her cheek, a gesture more intimate than any words.

Laurie swallowed hard.

"Here you go." Ned slapped an eighty-pound bag of plaster on the counter. "I'm sure you know this stuff sets fast, so only mix up what you need."

"Will do." Jack laid some money on the counter and, before Laurie could protest, hefted the bag onto his shoulder. "Thanks, Ned. We'll be seeing you, I'm sure."

"Anytime, Jack. You, too, Miz Golden. Say, you two ought to go see Mama at that rest home in Waxahachie. She'd love the company, and you two might get some of that Howell family history you're looking for."

"Thanks, Ned. Maybe we will."

Out at the truck Jack effortlessly tossed the bag into the back. "I...I'll pay you back for the plaster," Laurie said, easing open her door. She scrunched down in the seat, still feeling embarrassed about crying in front of him.

Jack climbed behind the wheel. "Don't worry about it, Laurie. I'm more concerned about getting you home. I have a feeling you want to talk to your mother right away."

She nodded, unable to speak past the lump in her throat.

Jack touched her hand in sympathy, then started the engine. When they pulled into her driveway, they saw the Cherokee still gone.

Jack helped Laurie out of the truck. "I'll come back tomorrow and help you with the plaster, okay? That'll give you and your mother some time to talk."

"Sure."

He studied her closely. "I'd be glad to stay awhile—in case you need a friend for support, that is."

Laurie smiled at his thoughtfulness. "Thanks, but I'd probably better go this alone."

"Call me if you need anything, hear?" Jack kissed her on the cheek.

She nodded. He touched her hand in a silent farewell, then drove his truck down the gravel road toward his place.

Tire wheels spun gravel on the road, and car doors slammed. Garrett raced inside, madly licking the largest chocolate cone the Tastee-King had to offer. Drops spattered to the floor, the ice cream melting fast in the summer heat.

Waving with her free hand, Gaby slurped from a straw planted firmly in a sixty-four-ounce cup. "Hi, Mom!" she paused long enough to say, then went back to her slurping. She paused again, giggled, then turned to Garrett. "Come on, let's go back outside!"

Laughing, they raced past Agnes, who entered the house, one hand holding her black vinyl handbag, the other, a small drink cup. She smiled large and wide. "Hello, Laurie." She looked around the room. "Where's that nice Jack MacGruder?"

"He went home for the day. He'll be back out tomorrow."

"Oh." Sounding disappointed, Agnes plopped down on the sheet-covered couch.

Laurie sat beside her mother, hesitating. "I had an interesting talk with Ned Weathers at the hardware store, Mama."

Agnes noisily sucked up the last of her drink. "Now what could Ned Weathers have to say that could possibly be important to you and me?"

Laurie picked at a loose thread on the sheet. "He made a remark about understanding why your sisters would have moved out of state. Something having to do with your father. I started to ask him what he meant, but Jack convinced me I should ask you instead."

Setting her paper cup on the floor, Agnes sighed. "That was a long time ago, Laurie. Can't you just let things alone? I have."

"I want to know what he meant." Laurie drew a deep breath. "What haven't you told me about your father all these years?"

Mama angled closer. "You're fixing up this place so nicely."

Laurie took her mother's hands. "What happened, Mama? Is it painful to be here?"

Agnes clasped Laurie's hands tighter, smiling gently. "My papa... Laurie, he drank on occasion."

Laurie sagged with relief. "Oh, Mama, that was looked on as terrible back then, but now it's not so—"

"You don't understand, Laurie," Agnes said. "When he was sober, he was fine. But when he was drunk, he'd raise a real ruckus. Usually he got drunk in town on Saturday night, and someone had to bring him home. Sometimes he'd spend the week's grocery money. Once it was even the money for our school shoes. We had to go barefoot until Christmas, and we were so ashamed. He was always sorry the next day, so dreadfully sorry, but he was never sorry enough to stop." Agnes paused. "He was known as the town drunk."

"Oh, Mama," Laurie whispered. "Did he hurt you or your sisters? Your mother?"

"No, not once."

"Why didn't your mother say something? Or tell somebody?"

Agnes laughed. "You didn't talk about things like that back then, even though they were obvious. There wasn't even the word *alcoholism*. You might speak quietly about a man not being able to hold his liquor, but that was it. Certainly nothing was ever done. And no one would ever come between a man and his wife, to intervene for Mama."

"But the town knew? Even Ned Weathers, who was younger than you?"

Agnes nodded, smiling gently at her naiveté. "I'm sure they did. Honor's always been a small town."

Laurie wanted to cry but felt silly that she was taking this so hard when her mother obviously wasn't. "You never told me all this before, Mama. I always thought your childhood was wonderful."

"Just because I don't speak about the past doesn't mean it was perfect," Agnes said. "I've put the past behind me, Laurie. Now you need to let the Lord show you how to do the same."

Laurie couldn't speak. Why was it easier for everyone else? She swallowed hard until the words cleared her throat. "After growing up with that, how did you make it after you left this house? How are we all going to make it here now?"

"You know how?" Agnes made a sweeping motion across the room. "'Just head for that big star straight on. The highway's under it, and it'll take us right home.'"

Laurie laughed, a tiny spark of joy burning off the tears still lingering at the back of her eyes. "Oh, Mama, you've got a movie line for everything, don't you?"

"Yes, I do." She patted Laurie's hands. "Listen, honey, I know you've worked hard this past year through your own pain, so you know it doesn't happen quickly. When it does, you smile, thank the Lord, and move on. Even when it doesn't, you smile, thank the Lord, and move on. But whenever that joy comes, you grab it with both hands and hold tight." She winked. "Like that relationship you've got going with Jack."

Laurie leaned over and kissed her mother on the cheek. When she pulled back, Agnes looked surprised. Laurie smiled. "'Pop, do you want a shock? I think you're a great guy.'"

Agnes chuckled, then let it expand to a full laugh. "Close, Laurie. You've got the right idea, but you need to work on fitting the line to the gender. You're lucky I recognize *It's a Wonderful Life.*"

"Everybody recognizes that movie, Mama."

"Not obscure lines like that. Good thing you used it on me. I'm an expert." She squeezed Laurie's arm, smiling.

Laurie smiled back. Her mother's compliments didn't come easily, and even at her age, Laurie basked in the glow. Still, as she glanced around the work-in-progress of their house, she wondered if it would ever be a true home, especially given its history.

Chapter Five

Early the next morning, Laurie was up, ready in her grubbiest work clothes. She didn't feel like working on the house, but maybe if she dove into the repairs, she'd feel better about her mother's revelation.

They were still eating breakfast in the kitchen when they saw Jack's truck up the road. Winking, Agnes nudged Laurie, who headed for the front porch to wait for him.

She smiled as he ambled toward the front steps. "You're just in time for breakfast. Have you eaten?"

"Well…no."

"Great." She led him to the kitchen, where he was met by a chorus of greetings.

"Pull up a chair," Laurie said, munching on a piece of toast with jam. "Just watch that flooring over by the sink. Remember, you said it had a bad case of dry rot."

"How could I forget?" Jack grinned. "I nearly fell through when we were doing our inspection."

He drew up a chair beside Laurie. Agnes set a plate in front of him and poured a cup of dark coffee. He bowed his head for a moment, then lifted his fork. "Still want to start on the living room walls this morning, Laurie?"

She was too overwhelmed at the sight of him praying to answer at first, then she nodded. "You and I can work down here. Mama and the kids volunteered to take on the upstairs. They can use the joint compound there—the cracks aren't as big."

After breakfast, she followed Jack out to his truck. He'd brought an old wheelbarrow for mixing the plaster. "Everything go okay yesterday with your mom?" He opened the gate of the truck.

"Pretty much." Laurie crossed her arms, suddenly shy now that she was alone with him. "It turns out my grandfather was an alcoholic. The town drunk, as Mama put it." She paused. "Did you know already?"

Jack set the wheelbarrow on the ground with a thud. He leaned up against the truck and studied her. "I'd heard the rumors. Nobody likes hearing things like that about their family, even if it's in the past."

"No." She wrapped her arms around herself, sighing.

"Come on." He took her arm. "Let's go for a walk."

"But the house…"

"It'll keep. If it'll make you feel better to be working, we can look for the Howell graves." He started down the road. "What's the point of living in the country if you don't get outdoors every day?"

They took the direction toward the Bertram cemetery and beyond. Laurie winced when they passed the iron gate, knowing that her grandfather and grandmother were buried there.

Silently they walked toward his property, passing neatly planted rows of corn. She remembered riding as a kid through land like this, her nose pressed against the car window as she stared in awe. Rows of corn and cotton would race by, like the long legs of a runner across the land. No matter where they went in the country, the runner always raced beside their car, and the magic and history of such agriculture filled her heart even into adulthood.

She'd always imagined her ancestors who settled this land as hardy; now she wondered what secrets had fueled their work.

"You okay?" Jack said.

"Yeah," she said, drawing a deep breath.

Jack took her arm and steered her into the cemetery, leading her to sit on a stone bench by her grandfather's grave. She bowed her head.

After a moment, she raised her head, only to be drawn to the carvings on her grandparents' tombstones. Her grandfather's had flying birds; her grandmother's, a weeping willow. "I wonder if they chose what they wanted before they died or if someone else decided after they were gone," she said.

"A stone doesn't leave much room to summarize a life, does it?" Jack said.

"Carvings are generally made for a reason. Flying birds signify flight of the soul. A willow symbolizes earthly sorrow." She smiled bitterly. "I wish Mama had told me about her family a long time ago. Maybe I shouldn't have brought her here."

"You didn't know, Laurie. You wanted a nice, ready-made past to step into, and you chose this place because it was your family's," Jack said. "Until they learn otherwise, everybody wants to believe their ancestors came over on the Mayflower, helped settle the West, or fought for a noble cause. It's difficult to learn about the skeletons in the family closet."

"It sure doesn't seem like most people learn bad things about their families. Otherwise, why all the genealogy buffs?"

"People learn a lot of bad things about their families when they're searching their trees. But it's better to know about your family— warts and all—even if they're not what you've hoped. What's in the past doesn't reflect the present." Jack put his arm around her. "Now that you know about your grandparents, just let them rest in peace."

"I know I can't change their lives, but I wanted to change mine— and my family's—by moving here. I thought we could fix up this place and make it new—start over, so to speak. I sank all my money in this place, Jack. I want it to be something special. And yet…"

She glanced at the house, shuddering. Maybe Agnes didn't see the ghost of her father in that place, but that didn't mean his memory wasn't there.

Laurie rose. "Let's look for the Howells' graves again, Jack. We can cover the rest of the ground we haven't searched. Surely we can find them."

"Do you really want to spend that much time? It'll take us a few hours, at least."

"I'd rather do that than work on the house. I want something good to happen today. I *need* something good to happen."

◆ ◆ ◆

Four hours later they'd found nothing.

Laurie plopped down on the front steps, brushing a strand of hair from her face. "I don't understand. There's not a trace of a grave."

"Maybe they didn't mark them to begin with." Jack sat beside her. "Maybe they didn't want the Bertrams to know where they were buried."

"But they'd have to know. They lived right next door."

Jack shrugged. "Maybe the family buried Luther and Enid under cover of darkness."

"That seems pretty sinister."

Jack studied the countryside. "Maybe we're going about this all wrong, Laurie. Instead of looking for graves, maybe we should be talking to the living."

"Like who?"

"Ned's mother. Do you feel up to a visit to a Waxahachie nursing home?"

Laurie glanced at the house. "If it's that or mix up plaster, the nursing home wins."

Nettie Weathers laughed. "I haven't thought about that old Howell-Bertram feud in years."

Laurie and Jack exchanged glances. "Do you remember how it got started, Mrs. Weathers?" Jack said.

"Gracious me, no. It started before my time…though I do remember my daddy saying something about it being over a land sale."

"When the Howells sold some land to the Bertrams?" Laurie said. Her fingers tingled, something that always happened when she was close to a genealogical revelation, even if it was for a client.

Nettie wrinkled her brow. "That might be it. Back before I was born, times were tough, and a lot of local folk had to sell off all or part of their land just to pay the taxes."

Jack turned to Laurie, his eyes glowing with excitement. "Luther and Enid's oldest child was only eighteen when they died. He apparently took care of the rest of the kids until they were married off. He was still fairly young when the land was sold to the Bertrams. Maybe he needed the money for taxes."

"Was that enough to start a feud?" Laurie bent down to Nettie's level, where the old woman sat in a wheelchair. "Mrs. Weathers, are you *sure* you don't remember anything else?"

Nettie shook her head, smiling apologetically, then she slowly raised a hand. "Wait. I do remember Daddy saying something else. Something about the Bertram homestead."

"The house that's still standing?" Laurie said.

"Yes, though what he meant, I don't know. " Blinking, she tilted her head against her shoulder.

"But do you—"

"Laurie," Jack said softly. "She's asleep. I think we've gotten all the information we can."

They rode back to Honor in disappointed silence. Outside the kids were playing ball, and Agnes sat on the front steps. She rose quickly when they got out of Jack's truck. "What did you find out?"

"Not much," Laurie said, sighing. "Just that the Howells may have sold land for tax money. And Nettie Weathers remembered her father saying something about the feud having to do with our house."

"Maybe the Howells were just jealous," Agnes said, lifting her head a notch.

"Oh, Mama. Jack's family home is just as nice."

She sat down on the steps and put her chin in her hands. Agnes sat beside her and adopted the same posture.

"Hey, Jack! How about throwing the ball with us?" Garrett called across the field.

"Sure." He jogged toward the cemetery and Garrett took up a spot close to the side of the house.

"Don't break any of my windows, okay?" Laurie yelled. "Jack, don't throw too hard to him."

"Okay."

Gaby sat beside her mother and grandmother. "I'm out of that game. It's too hard to throw the ball with them. You know, Garrett's getting pretty good, Mom."

Laurie beamed at the compliment Gaby paid her brother. She'd noticed a closeness in them that had developed ever since they'd moved to Honor. Maybe it was the country air. Maybe it was Russell Pratt's steadying influence. Maybe it was…

Wham!

Laurie jumped. "What on earth was that? Jack MacGruder, if you damaged the siding on my house…"

"Relax, Mom," Garrett said. "The ball just hit the brick pier here and rolled under the house. I'll get it." He got down on his hands and knees and crawled underneath.

"Gross," Gaby said. "There's probably bugs and things under there."

Jack jogged up. "Sorry, Laurie. Didn't mean to scare you."

"Garrett said it just hit the bricks. Lucky for you," she said, smiling. "This house doesn't need any more damage."

"I don't think—"

"Mommmmm!"

"Garrett?" Laurie dropped to her knees and peered under the house. *"Garrett?"*

Jack crawled under the house, his legs and feet quickly disappearing. "Garrett, what's the matter?"

"Mom! There's…there's…"

"What, Garrett?" Laurie's heart pounded with fear.

"Laurie, get a flashlight from the back of my truck. Quick!" Jack said, his voice muffled.

Laurie rapidly complied, getting down on her stomach to pass Jack the light. "What's going on? Is Garrett okay? Garrett, are you—"

A long, hazy beam emanated from the light, swooping and swirling. Jack seemed to be looking for something. "Well, I'll be," she heard him say.

Frantic with fear, Laurie crawled on her elbows and knees. "Jack! *What's going on?"*

Her eyes followed the track of the light to where it landed on a tombstone. She gasped.

"Enid Howell," Jack said, then adjusted the light. "And there's Luther. And those little tombstones beside them must be the children who died before them."

Laurie swallowed back her shock, maternal fear kicking in. "Garrett, are you okay?"

"Yeah, Mom. This is cool."

Cool? "Garrett Golden, get out from under this house immediately."

"Aw, Mom."

"Actually, Laurie," Jack said, "I think we're right under your kitchen. If we want to investigate, we can go through that flooring that has dry rot, anyway."

Laurie sneezed, then coughed, brushing dirt and cobwebs from her face. "Sounds like a good idea to me." She backed out as quickly as she could.

Gaby and Agnes followed them into the kitchen, talking a mile a minute. "Under the *house?*"

"Who would have thought of such a thing?"

"Creepy, Grandma! Kind of like *Amityville Horror* or something."

Agnes crossed her arms. "I've never seen that movie, Miss Gaby. Horror movies don't count as real cinema."

In the kitchen Jack looked at Laurie for approval to break through the floor. She nodded, and in no time, he had pulled back several planks and lowered himself into the hole.

"Be careful," she said, edging close to watch. The others took up spots beside her.

When he came out, he coughed, headed to the sink, and poured himself a glass a water. "It's Luther and Enid's children all right. The dates match the ones I have in my records."

Laurie sat down hard on a chair. "But Jack…it doesn't make sense! Didn't the builders of the house know those graves were there? How could they miss them?"

"They couldn't, Laurie," Agnes said. "This is probably why the feud started. The Howells sold the land to the Bertrams, who built their house on top of the graves."

"But why?"

Jack shrugged. "We'll probably never know."

Laurie felt sick to her stomach. "Jack...oh, Jack." She looked away, unable to meet his gaze. "I can't restore this house. Why should I work to hide my family's sins?"

"Not to mention the fact that we'd be living on top of old graves," Agnes whispered loudly to Garrett.

Jack grinned. "You're right, Mrs. Bertram. It's a creepy thought."

"This isn't funny, Jack," Laurie said, shaking her head. A cobweb stuck in her hair fell over her eyes, and she brushed it away with exasperation.

Garrett and Gaby giggled, and even Agnes and Jack suppressed laughter. When Jack saw that Laurie was unmoved by the humor in the situation, he rose. "I'll head out and let you have a family council."

"I think you should stay," Agnes said, glancing from him to Laurie with a smile. "Why, after all, it's your family under there."

"Maybe so, but it's your house."

"Of course, dear, but—"

"Jack's right, Mama," Laurie said. "The four of us need to talk. Then we'll let him know what we decide."

"Call me whenever you're ready," he said, then smiled at each of them in turn.

When they heard the front door shut, Agnes turned to Laurie. "You've driven him off."

"Mama, this isn't about Jack and me. This is about how this family is going to hold its head up in this small town once word gets out about what's under our house. About what our ancestors did to Jack's."

"What are you saying, dear?"

Laurie drew a deep breath. "Maybe we should move back to Dallas."

"No! No way!" Gaby got to her feet.

"I don't want to go either, Mom," Garrett said quietly. "Is it really that big a deal? I mean, it's not like *we* built this house."

"Yes, but we'd be restoring it. How is that any different from our ancestor Bertrams' building it over the graves in the first place?"

They sat, dejected, staring down at the table.

"Mom, we can't leave," Gaby said softly. "I like it here."

Her words stabbed Laurie to the quick. She'd wanted to build a new, better life for her family here, but it seemed impossible. "I'm going for a drive," she said.

"Can I come too?"

Laurie smiled at her son, ruffling his hair. "I need some time alone, Garrett. Maybe I'll figure out the answer while I'm driving."

Agnes touched her daughter's shoulder. "You'll do the right thing, Laurie. I know you will."

The right thing.

Laurie headed out in the Cherokee. She didn't have a destination in mind, but she knew she needed to get away.

It crossed her mind to head for Jack's and attempt to apologize for what her family had done. But she knew she wouldn't find the words any easier now than several hours ago.

She drove aimlessly around Honor, hoping the friendly sights would cheer her, but she found herself only more depressed by what she would be forced to abandon. Main Street looked cozier than ever, the elementary and high schools—where the kids would attend this fall—seemed bright and wholesome down to their solid brick corners, and yard after yard of smiling children peeked out around crisp laundry hanging on their lines.

She'd moved here expecting Norman Rockwell. She'd landed her family in history, all right, but their own house was more like something from one of Picasso's blue-period paintings than cheerful innocence.

Sweeping the sidewalk in front of his hardware store, Ned Weathers stopped long enough to wave at her. She waved back. She knew she should probably stop and chat, but she had a feeling they'd only wind up talking about the history of Honor in the hushed tones the living employ to speak of the dead. Ned would cheerfully remember the town the way it was, and she'd remember it the way that for her family it could never be.

Laurie steeled herself to drive back home. As she got out of the Cherokee, Agnes scuttled down the steps like an angry fiddler crab. "Where've you been, Laurie? Jack's here."

"Jack? Oh, Mama. I need to talk to him, but I didn't really want to do it right now."

"But, Laurie, he—"

"Mama, I love it here in Honor, but how can we stay here with our family history? Your father…and now his ancestors before him who built this house over the Howell graves."

Agnes's mouth turned up at the corners. Laurie frowned. "What's the matter? Do you think this is funny? Don't you care?"

Agnes's slow giggle built, but she squelched it and put her arm around her daughter. "Of course I do, dear. But I was thinking that now I knew where Papa got his mean streak. It must have run in the family." She nodded wisely at Laurie. "But it stops with you and me, doesn't it?"

"Well…"

"We could leave this place, but our family history is still the same. Just because we're descended from a pack of old fools doesn't mean people will judge us as such. It's *our* character that counts, Laurie dear, and I'd say we both have plenty to spare. When the wind hits, you just lean into it and fly into the clouds like a kite on a string. "

Laurie took her mother's hand and squeezed it. "That's pretty, Mama. What movie is it from?"

"It's not. I just made it up." Agnes winked. "Now come inside. Jack's got a plan that I think might just solve our problems." She pulled her daughter to her feet and toward the door.

Inside, Jack sat on the sofa with the kids. They talked animatedly, gesturing. They stopped when they saw Laurie, and Jack rose. "Laurie, I've got a—"

"No, listen to me first." Laurie drew a deep breath. "I need to say this before I lose my nerve. The only decent solution I can see is that I sell you my property, if you're still interested."

"But, Mom!" Garrett scrambled to his feet.

"You don't want to sell your property," Jack said, his expression serious. "That land's your dream."

"*Was* my dream. Everything's changed now."

"Has it?" He walked her toward the open door and gestured outside. "Has your love for the land changed, despite how you feel about your ancestors? Does what they did—or may have done—change this land? It seems to me that it keeps existing in its own quiet way, no matter who lives on it."

Laurie looked out over the gentle hills; the mesquites in the distance that grew alongside; a stand of live oaks at the edge of Jack's property; the single, rolling hill that looked down from her own. She blinked back a tear. "Jack, it's the right thing to do. For you. For the memory of the Howells."

"Laurie, Laurie…" He gently turned her around and took her into his arms. "I don't want you to leave. Especially because you're trying to right the wrongs of the past. I want you to—"

He broke off and leaned down, kissing her flush on the lips. Laurie ignored the collective sigh from her family and tentatively wrapped her arms around him. "Please don't make this harder. It's what needs to be done. This house shouldn't even be standing where it is."

Jack pulled back. Taking her hands, he smiled. "I agree, Laurie. And I know what we can do to solve everything. We can move the house."

"Yeah, Mom," Gaby said. "That's what we've been trying to tell you." She stared at her mother and Jack. "Whew. That was some kiss."

Laurie was still in shock, though from the kiss or the suggestion, she couldn't be sure. "Move the—"

"It's a perfect solution, Laurie," Agnes said. "We move this old place, then fix it up."

"Don't you want this land, Jack?" Laurie frowned. "After all, your family's here."

"All I wanted was to find where they were buried. I didn't want to do anything with their graves, Laurie." He smiled. "Besides, I trust you to take care of them. I've seen you with that rifle before, remember?"

Laurie glanced around the room. "Moving the house would just mean extra work."

"Then extra work it will be. It's worth looking into, isn't it? If it's the race set before us, God will make the course straight."

Laurie smiled. Mama and Jack were right. She was tired of looking back. It was time to look forward, as far into the future as the unbroken horizon of her land where the sun sank every evening only to rise anew each morning.

One Year Later

Laurie and Jack stood at the top of the rise overlooking his property. The sun dipped just behind his farmhouse, orange and red spreading out across the horizon in a panorama of natural beauty.

"The view's wonderful from here," she said, smiling at him.

Jack eased her against him and put his arms around her. "I never thought I'd like having a woman look down on me," he said, chuckling. "Maybe we can change that in the future. Maybe you'll propose, and I can move up here with the rest of your family."

Laurie laughed, glad that he couldn't see her blush.

Directly behind them stood the house, painstakingly moved over several months' time, then carefully, lovingly restored by them all, including Jack. "I have a vested interest in this place, after all," he'd said.

Farther beyond the house stood the cemeteries—the iron-fence-enclosed Bertram plot and the freshly tended, open Howell one. To the sound of country music emanating from a boom box, Russell Pratt, Gaby, Garrett, and Agnes worked there now around the graves, planting bulbs that would bloom in profusion come spring. Russell crowned Gaby with a daisy chain, and she giggled like a twelve-year-old.

"You sure your mom's okay?" Jack said, moving his gaze back to Laurie's family.

"She likes country western. Or whatever they call it these days."

"I meant about the house. She seems to be studying it. I wonder what's going through her head."

Laurie turned toward her mother, who waved. "It's not the house she's studying, Jack. It's us. And I can tell you exactly what she's thinking." She slipped into her best Bogey accent. "'Louis, I think this is the beginning of a beautiful friendship.'"

Jack smiled and she leaned her back against him. Together they turned to face the final, glorious rays of the setting sun, knowing many more would follow on the road that lay ahead.